# The Graysons

## A Story of Illinois

**Edward Eggleston**

**The Graysons: A Story of Illinois**

ISBN: 978-1-63637-386-7

# CONTENTS

# PREFACE

I had thought to close up the cycle of my stories of life in the Mississippi Valley with "Roxy" which was published in 1878. But when I undertook by request of the editor to write a short story for "The Century Magazine," and to found it on a legendary account of one of President Lincoln's trials, the theme grew on my hands until the present novel was the result. It was written mostly at Nervi, near Genoa, where I could not by any possibility have verified the story I had received about 1867 from one of Lincoln's old neighbors. To have investigated the accuracy of my version of the anecdote would have been, indeed, to fly in the face and eyes of providence, for popular tradition is itself an artist rough-hewing a story to the novelist's hands. During the appearance of this novel in serial form I have received many letters from persons acquainted in one way or another with the actors and sufferers in the events, of which these here related are the ideal counterparts. Some of these letters contain information or relate incidents of so much interest that I have it in mind to insert them in an appendix to some later edition of this book.

EDWARD EGGLESTON
Joshua's Rock, Lake George, 1888

This Book is respectfully inscribed to the Hon. Jonathan Chace, United States Senator from Rhode Island; the Hon. Joseph Hawley, United States Senator from Connecticut; the Hon. W. C. P. Breckenridge, Representative from Kentucky; and the Hon. Patrick A. Collins, Representative from Massachusetts, who have recently introduced or had charge of International Copyright Bills, and to those Members of both Houses of Congress who have coöperated with them in the effort to put down literary buccaneering.
E. E.

> To my friend, Mabel Cooke,
> I Dedicate the Ideals of
> which these Illustrations
> are the Faint and Awkward
> Shadows.
>
> The Illustrator

# I

## TURNING THE BIBLE

The place of the beginning of this story was a country neighborhood on a shore, if one may call it so, that divided a forest and prairie in Central Illinois. The date was nearly a lifetime ago. An orange-colored sun going down behind the thrifty orchard of young apple-trees on John Albaugh's farm, put into shadow the front of a dwelling which had stood in wind and weather long enough to have lost the raw look of newness, and to have its tints so softened that it had become a part of the circumjacent landscape. The phebe-bird, locally known as the pewee, had just finished calling from the top of the large barn, and a belated harvest-fly, or singing locust, as the people call him, was yet filling the warm air with the most summery of all summery notes—notes that seem to be felt as well as heard, pushing one another faster and yet faster through the quivering atmosphere, and then dying away by degrees into languishing, long-drawn, and at last barely audible vibrations.

Rachel, the daughter of the prosperous owner of the farm, was tying some jasmine vines to the upright posts that supported the roof of a porch, or veranda, which stretched along the entire front of the house. She wore a fresh calico gown, and she had something the air of one expecting the arrival of guests. She almost always expected company in the evening of a fine day. For the young person whose fortune it is to be by long odds the finest-looking woman in a new country where young men abound, and where women are appreciated at a rate proportioned to their scarcity, knows what it is to be a "reigning belle" indeed. In the vigorous phrase of the country, Rachel was described as "real knock-down handsome"; and, tried by severer standards than those of Illinois, her beauty would have been beyond question. She had the three essentials: eyes that were large and lustrous, a complexion rich and fresh, yet delicately tinted, and features well-balanced and harmonious. Her blonde hair was abundant, and, like everything about her, vital. Her hands and feet were not over-large, and, fortunately, they were not disproportionately small; but just the hands and feet of a well-developed country girl used to activity and the open air. Without being more than ordinarily clever, she had a certain passive intelligence. Her voice was not a fine one, nor had her manners any particular charm except that which comes from the repose of one who understands that she is at her best when

1

silent, and who feels herself easily ahead of rivals without making any exertion. Hers was one of those faces the sight of which quickens the pulses even of an old man, and attracts young men with a fascination as irresistible as it is beyond analysis or description. Many young men were visitors at John Albaugh's hospitable house, and where the young men came the young women were prone to come, and thus Albaugh's became a place of frequent and spontaneous resort for the young people from all the country round.

But it had happened with this much-courted girl, as it has happened to many another like her, that with all the world to choose from, she had tarried single longer than her companions. Rachel was now past twenty-three, in a land where a woman was accounted something of an old maid if unmarried at twenty. Beauties such as she find a certain pleasure in playing with their destiny, as pussy loves the excitement of trifling with the mouse that can hardly escape her in any way. Prey that comes too easily in reach is not highly valued. Every bid for such a woman's hand leads her to raise her estimation of her own value. Rachel's lovers came and went, and married themselves to young women without beauty. Lately, however, Rachel Albaugh's neighbors began to think that she had at length fallen in love "for keeps," as the country phrase expressed it.

"I say, Rache," called her brother Ike, a youth of fifteen, who was just then half-hidden in the boughs of the summer apple-tree by the garden gate, "they's somebody coming."

"Who is it, Ike?"

"Henry Miller and the two Miller girls."

"Oh! is that all?" said Rachel, in a teasing tone.

"Is that all?" said Ike. "You don't care for anybody but Tom Grayson these days. I'll bet you Tom'll be here to-night."

"What makes you think so?" asked Rachel, trying not to evince any interest in the information.

"Don't you wish you knew?" he answered, glad to repay her teasing in kind.

"Did you see him to-day?"

"Say, Sis," said Ike, affecting to dismiss the subject, "here's an awful nice apple. Can you ketch?"

Rachel held up her hands to catch the apple, baring her pretty arms by the falling back of her loose sleeves. The mischievous Ike threw a swift ball, and Rachel, holding her hands for it, could not help shrinking as the apple came flying at her. She shut her eyes and ducked her head, and of course the apple went past her, bowling away along the porch and off the other end of it into the grass.

"That's just like a girl," said Ike. "Here's a better apple. I won't

2

throw so hard this time." And Rachel caught the large striped apple in her two hands.

"I say, Ike," she said, coaxingly, "where did you see Tom?"

"Oh! I met him over on the big road as I went to mill this morning; he was going home to his mother's, an' he said he was coming over to see you to-night. An' I told him to fetch Barbara, so 's I'd have somebody to talk to, 'cause you wouldn't let me get a word in ageways with him. An' Tom laughed an' looked tickled."

"I guess you won't talk much to Barbara while Ginnie Miller's here," Rachel said; and by this time Henry Miller and his two sisters were nearing the white gate which stood forty feet away from the cool front porch of the house.

"Howdy, Rachel!" said Henry Miller, as he reached the gate, and "Howdy! Howdy!" came from the two sisters, to which Rachel answered with a cordial "Howdy! Come in!" meant for the three. When they reached the porch, she led the way through the open front door to the "settin' room" of the house, as the living-room was always called in that day. The fire-place looked like an extinct crater; curtains of narrow green slats hung at the windows, and the floor was covered by a new rag-carpet in which was imbedded a whole history of family costume; a patient geologist might have discovered in it traces of each separate garment worn in the past five years by the several members of the Albaugh family. The mantel-piece was commonplace enough, of "poplar" wood—that is, tulip-tree—painted brown. The paint while fresh had been scratched in rhythmical waves with a common coarse comb. This graining resembled that of some wood yet undiscovered. The table at the side of the room farthest from the door had a cover of thin oil-cloth decorated with flowers; most of them done in yellow. A tall wooden clock stood against the wall at the right of the door as you entered, and its slow ticking seemed to make the room cooler. For the rest, there was a black rocking-chair with a curved wooden seat and uncomfortable round slats in the back; there were some rank-and-file chairs besides,—these were black, with yellow stripes; and there was a green settee with three rockers beneath and an arm at each end.

Henry Miller was a square-set young fellow, without a spark of romance in him. He had plowed corn all day, and he would have danced all night had the chance offered, and then followed the plow the next day. His sisters were like him, plain and of a square type that bespoke a certain sort of "Pennsylvania Dutch" ancestry, though the Millers had migrated to Illinois, not from Pennsylvania, but from one of the old German settlements in the valley of Virginia. Ike jumped out of the apple-tree to follow Virginia, the youngest of the Millers, into the house; there was between him and "Ginnie," as she was called, that sort of adolescent attachment, or effervescent reaction, which always appears to the parties involved in it the most serious interest in the universe, and to everybody else something deliciously ridiculous; a sort of burlesque of the follies of people more mature.

This was destined to be one of Rachel's "company evenings"; she had not more than seated the Millers and taken the girls' bonnets to a place of security, when there was a knock on the door-jamb. It was Mely McCord, who had once been a hired help in the Albaugh family. There were even in that day wide differences in wealth and education in Illinois, but class demarcations there were not. Nothing was more natural than that Mely, who had come over from Hubbard township to visit some cousin in the neighborhood, should visit the Albaughs. Mely McCord was a girl—she was always called a girl, though now a little in the past tense—with a stoop in the shoulders, and hair that would have been better if it had been positively and decoratively red. As it was, her head seemed always striving to be red without ever attaining to any purity of color.

Half an hour later, Magill, an Irish bachelor of thirty-five, who, being county clerk, was prudently riding through the country in order to keep up his acquaintance with the voters, hitched his horse at the fence outside of the Albaugh gate, and came in just as Rachel was bringing a candle. Though he had no notion of cumbering himself with a family or with anything else likely to interfere with the freedom or pleasure of "an Irish gentleman," Magill was very fond of playing at gallantry, and he affected a great liking for what he called "faymale beauty," and plumed himself on the impression his own sprucely dressed person and plump face—a little overruddy, especially toward the end of the nose—might make on the sex. He could never pass Albaugh's without stopping to enjoy a platonic flirtation with Rachel. George Lockwood arrived at the same time; he was a clerk in Wooden's store, at the county-seat village of Moscow, and he could manage, on his busiest days even, to spend half an hour in selling a spool of cotton thread to Rachel Albaugh. He had now come five miles in the vain hope of finding her alone. The country beauty appreciated the flattery of his long ride, and received his attention with a pleasure undisguised.

George Lockwood's was no platonic sentiment. He watched intently every motion of Rachel's arms only half-hidden in her open-sleeved dress; even the rustling of the calico of her gown made his pulses flutter. He made a shame-faced effort to conceal his agitation; he even tried to devote himself to Mely McCord and the "Miller girls" now and then; but his eyes followed Rachel's tranquil

4

movements, as she amused herself with Magill's bald flatteries, and Lockwood could not help turning himself from side to side in order to keep the ravishing vision in view when he was talking to some one else.

"You had better make the most of your chance, Mr. Lockwood," said pert little Virginia Miller, piqued by his absent-minded pretense of talking with her.

"What do you mean?" he asked.

"Oh, talk to Rachel while you can, for maybe after a while you can't!"

"Why can't I?"

"She's glad enough to talk to you now, but just you wait till Tom Grayson comes. If he should happen in to-night, what do you think would become of you?"

"Maybe I'm not so dead in love as you think," he answered.

"You? You're past hope. Your eyes go round the room after her like a sunflower twistin' its neck off to see the sun."

"Pshaw!" said George. "You know better than that."

But Virginia noted with amusement that his smile of affected indifference was rather a forced one, and that he was "swallowing his feelings," as she put it. He took her advice as soon as he dared and crossed to where Rachel was sitting with the back of her chair against the jamb of the mantel-piece. Rachel was smiling a little foolishly at the shameless palaver of Magill, who told her that there was a ravishing perfiction about her faychers that he'd niver sane surpassed, though he'd had the exquisite playsure of dancing with many of the most beautiful faymales in Europe. Rachel, a little sick of unwatered sweetness, was glad to have George Lockwood interrupt the frank criticisms of an appreciative connoisseur of loveliness.

"I hear Tom Grayson outside now," said Mely McCord, in a half-whisper to Henry Miller. "George Lockwood won't be nowhere when he gits here"; and Mely's freckled face broke into ripples of delight at the evident annoyance which Lockwood began to show at hearing Grayson's voice on the porch. Tom Grayson was preceded by his sister Barbara, a rather petite figure, brunette in complexion, with a face that was interesting and intelligent, and that had an odd look hard to analyze, but which came perhaps, from a slight lack of symmetry. As a child, she had been called "cunning," in the popular American use of the word when applied to children; that is to say, piquantly interesting; and this characteristic of quaint piquancy of appearance she retained, now that she was a young woman of eighteen. Her brother Tom was a middle-sized, well-proportioned man, about two years older than she, of a fresh, vivacious

5

countenance, and with a be-gone-dull-care look. He had a knack of imparting into any company something of his own cheerful heedlessness, and for this his society was prized. He spoke to everybody right cordially, and shook hands with all the company as though they had been his first cousins, looking in every face without reserve or suspicion, and he was greeted on all hands with a corresponding heartiness. But while Tom saluted everybody, his eye turned toward Rachel, and he made his way as quickly as possible to the farther corner of the room where she was standing in conversation with George Lockwood. He extended his hand to her with a hearty,

"Well, Rache, how are you? It would cure fever and ague to see you"; and then turning to Lockwood he said: "Hello, George! you out here! I wouldn't 'ave thought there was any other fellow fool enough to ride five miles and back to get a look at Rachel but me." And at that he laughed, not a laugh that had any derision in it, or any defiance, only the outbreaking of animal spirits that were unchecked by foreboding or care.

"I say, George," he went on, "let's go out and fight a duel and have it over. There's no chance for any of us here till Rachel's beaux are thinned out a little. If I should get you killed off and out of the way, I suppose I should have to take Mr. Magill next."

"No, Tom, it's not with me you'd foight, me boy. I've sane too many handsome girls to fight over them, though I have never sane such transcindent——"

"Ah, hush now, Mr. Magill," entreated Rachel.

"Faymale beauty's always adorned by modesty, Miss Albaugh. I'll only add, that whoever Miss Rachel stoops to marry"—and Magill laughed a slow, complacent laugh as he put an emphasis on stoops—"I'll be a thorn in his soide, d'yeh mark that; fer to the day of me death, I'll be her most devoted admoirer"; and he made a half-bow at the close of his speech, with a quick recovery, which expressed his sense of the formidable character of his own personal charms.

But if Magill was a connoisseur of beauty he was also a politician too prudent to slight any one. He was soon after this paying the closest heed to Mely McCord's very spontaneous talk. He had selected Mely in order that he might not get a reputation for being "stuck up."

"Tom Grayson a'n't the leas' bit afeerd uh George Lockwood nur nobody else," said Mely rather confidentially to Magill, who stood with hands crossed under the tail of his blue-gray coat. "He all-ays wuz that away; a kind'v a high-headed, don't-keer sort uv a feller. He'd better luck out, though. Rache's one uh them skittish

6

kind uh critters that don't stan' 'thout hitchin', an' weth a halter knot at that. Tom Grayson's not the fust feller that's felt shore she wuz his'n an' then found out kind uh suddently't 'e wuzn't so almighty shore arter all. But, lawsee gracious! Tom Grayson a'n't afeerd uv nothin', nohow. When the master wuz a-lickin' him wunst, at school, an' gin 'im three cuts, an' then says, says he, 'You may go now,' Tom, he jes lucks at 'im an' says uz peart 's ever you see, says he, 'Gimme another to make it even numbers.'"

"An' how did the master fale about that?" asked Magill, who had been a schoolmaster himself.

"W'y he jes let him have it good an' tight right around his legs. Tom walked off an' never wunst said thank yeh, sir. He did n' wear uz good close in them days 's 'e does now, by a long shot. His mother's farm 's in the timber, an' slow to open; so many stumps and the like; an' 'f 'is uncle down 't Moscow had n't a' tuck him up, he 'd 'a' been a-plowin' in that air stickey yaller clay 'v Hubbard township yit. But you know ole Tom Grayson, his father's brother, seein' 's Tom wuz named arter him, an' wuz promisin' like, an' had the gift of the gab, he thought 's how Tom mought make 'n all-fired smart lawyer ur doctor, ur the like; an' seein' 's he had n' got no boy to do choores about, he takes Tom an' sends him to school three winters, an' now I believe he's put him to readin' law."

"Yis, I know he went into Blackman's office last May," said Magill.

"Ole Tom Grayson 's never done nothin' fer the old woman nur little Barb'ry, there, an' little Barb'ry 's the very flower of the flock, accordin' to my tell," Mely went on. "Mrs. Grayson sticks to the ole farm, yeh know, an' rents one field to pap on the sheers, an' works the rest uv it by hirin'. She sets a mighty sight uv store by Tom. Talks about 'im by the hour. She 'lows he'll be a-gittin' to Congress nex' thing. But I d' know"—and here Mely shook her head. "High nose stumped his toes," says I. "Jes look how he's a-carryin' on with Rache, now."

"She's older 'n he is," said the clerk, knowing that even this half unfavorable comment would be a comfort to one so far removed from rivalry with her as Mely.

"Three years ef she's a day," responded Mely promptly. "Jest look at that Lockwood. He's like a colt on the outside of a paster fence, now,"—and Mely giggled heartily at Lockwood's evident discomfiture.

In gossip and banter the time went by, until some one proposed to "turn the Bible." I do not know where this form of sortilege originated; it is probably as old as Luther's Bible. One can find it practiced in Germany to-day as it is in various parts of the United States.

"Come, Sophronia, you and me will hold the key," said Lockwood, who was always quick to seize an advantage.

These two, therefore, set themselves to tell the fortunes of the company. The large iron key to the front door and a short, fat little pocket-Bible were the magic implements. The ward end of the key was inserted between the leaves of the Bible at the first chapter of Ruth; the book was closed and a string bound so tightly about it as to hold it firmly to the key. The ring end of the key protruded. This was carefully balanced on the tips of the forefingers of Lockwood and Sophronia Miller, so that the Bible hung between and below their hands. A very slight motion, unconscious and invisible, of either of the supporting fingers would be sufficient to precipitate the Bible and key to the floor.

"Who can say the verse?" asked Lockwood.

"I know it like a book," said Virginia Miller.

"You say it, Ginnie," said her sister; "but whose turn first?"

The two amateur sorcerers, with fingers under the key-ring, sat face to face in the dim light of the candle, their right elbows resting on their knees as they bent forward to hold the Bible between them. The others stood about with countenances expressing curiosity and amusement.

"Rachel first," said Henry Miller; "everybody wants to know who in thunderation Rache will marry, ef she ever marries anybody. I don't believe even the Bible can tell that. Turn fer Rachel Albaugh, and let's see how it comes out. Say the verse, Ginnie."

"Letter A," said Virginia Miller, solemnly; and then she repeated the words like a witch saying a charm:

"'Intreat me not to leave thee, or to return from following after thee: for whither thou goest, I will go; and where thou lodgest, I will lodge: thy people shall be my people, and thy God my God: where thou diest will I die, and there will I be buried.'"

The key did not turn. It was manifest, therefore, that Rachel would never marry any man whose name began with the first letter of the alphabet. The letter B was called, and again the solemn charm was repeated; the company resting breathless to the end. The Bible and key refused to respond for B, or C, or D, or E, or F. But when Ginnie Miller announced "Letter G," it was with a voice that betrayed a consciousness of having reached a critical point in her descent of the alphabet; there was a rustle of expectation in the room, and even McGill, standing meditatively with his hands behind his back, shifted his weight from his left foot to his right so as to have a better view of any antics the Bible might take a notion to perform. Just as Virginia Miller reached the words "and where thou diest will I die," the key slipped off Sophronia's fingers first, and the book fell to the floor.

"G stands for Grayson," said Magill gravely, but he pronounced his "G" so nearly like "J" that a titter went around the room.

"Don't you know better than to spell Grayson with a J, Mr. Magill?" asked Rachel.

Magill did not see the drift of the question, and before he could reply, Lockwood, without looking up, broke in with: "What are you talking about, all of you? It's not the last name, it's the given name you go by."

"Oh!" cried Mely McCord, in mild derision, "George begins with G. I didn't think of that."

"Yis," said Magill, reflectively, "that's a fact; George does begin with jay too."

"I tell you it's the last name," said Tom, laughing.

"I tell you it isn't," said Lockwood, doggedly; but Henry Miller, seeing a chance for disagreeable words, made haste to say: "Come, boys, it's the good-natured one that'll win. Hang up the Bible once more and let's see if it 'll drop for Lockwood when it gets to L, or for Tom when we come to T. I don't more than half believe in the thing. It never will turn for me on anything but Q, and they a'n't no girl with Q to her name this side of Jericho except Queen Brooks, an' she lives thirteen miles away an' 's engaged to another feller, and I would n't look at her twiste if she wuz n't, nur she 't me like 's not. Come, Ginnie, gee-up your oxen. Let's have H."

The Bible refused to turn at H.

"Rachel won't marry you, Henry Miller," said the county clerk.

"No," said Henry, "Rache an' me 's always been first-rate friends, but she knows me too well to fall in love with me, an' I'm the only feller in this end of the county that's never made a fool of myself over Rachel."

Neither would the Bible turn at I, J, or K. But at L it turned.

"Of course it'll turn at L, when Lockwood 's got hold of the key," said Tom with another laugh. "That 's what he took hold for."

"That's the same as saying I don't play fair," said Lockwood, with irritation.

"Fair and square a'n't just your way, George. But there's no use being cross about it."

"Come, boys, if you 're going to quarrel over the Bible you can't have it," said Rachel, who loved tranquillity. "As for me, I'm going to marry whoever I please, and I won't get married till I please, Bible or no Bible"; and she untied the string, put the rusty

9

key in the door, and laid the plump little book in its old place on the mantel-piece, until it should be wanted again for religious disputation or fortune-telling.

Grayson went rattling on with cheerful and good-natured nonsense, but George Lockwood, pushed into the shade by Tom's ready talk and by Rachel's apparent preference for him, was not in a very good humor, and departed early in company with Magill. After all the rest had gone, Barbara Grayson had to remind Tom more than once of the lateness of the hour, for nine o'clock was late in that day.

"Send him home, Rachel," she said, "at half-past nine; he'll never go while you look good-natured." Then, taking her brother by the arm, Barbara led him to the gate. Rachel followed, almost as reluctant to close the evening as Tom himself.

# II

# WINNING AND LOSING

The next Friday evening Grayson and Lockwood were again brought together; this time in the miscellaneous store of Wooden & Snyder, in which George Lockwood was the only clerk. Here after closing-time the young men of the village were accustomed to gratify their gregarious propensities; this was a club-room, where, amid characteristic odors of brown sugar, plug tobacco, new calico, vinegar, whisky, molasses, and the dressed leather of boots and shoes, social intercourse was carried on by a group seated on the top of nail-kegs, the protruding ends of shoe-boxes, and the counters that stretched around three sides of the room. Here were related again all those stock anecdotes which have come down from an antiquity inconceivably remote, but which in every village are yet told as having happened three or four miles away, and three or four years ago, to the intimate friend of the narrator's uncle. The frequency of such assemblies takes off something of their zest; where everybody knows all his neighbor's history and has heard everybody else's favorite story, a condition of mental equilibrium ensues, and there is no exchange of electricities. The new-comer, or the man who has been away, is a heaven-send in a village; he stirs its stagnant intellect as a fresh breeze, and is for the time the hero of every congregation of idlers.

Such a man on this evening was Dave Sovine, the son of a settler from one of the Channel Islands. Four years ago, when but sixteen years old, Dave had unluckily waked up one summer morning at daybreak. Looking out of the little window in the end of the loft of his father's house, he had contemplated with disgust a large field of Indian corn to be "plowed out" that day under a June sun. So repulsive to his nature was the landscape of young maize and the prospect of toil, that he dressed himself, tied up his spare clothes in a handkerchief, and, taking his boots in his hand, descended noiselessly the stairway which was in the outside porch of the house. Once on the ground, he drew on his boots and got away toward the Wabash, where he shipped as cook on a flat-boat bound for New Orleans. No pursuit or inquiry was made by his family, and the neighbors suspected that his departure was not a source of regret. At Shawneetown the flat-boat was suddenly left without a cook. Dave had been sent up in the town with a little money to lay in supplies of coffee and sugar; instead of coming back, he surreptitiously shipped as cabin-boy on the steamboat Queen of the West, which was just leaving the landing, bound also for the "lower country." Sovine had afterward been in the Gulf, he had had adventures in Mexico, and he had contrived to pick up whatever of evil was to be learned in every place he visited. He had now come home ostensibly "to see the folks," but really to gratify his vanity in astonishing his old acquaintances by an admirable proficiency in deviltry. His tales of adventure were strange and exciting, and not likely to shrink in the telling. The youth of Moscow listened with open-mouthed admiration to one who, though born in their village, had seen so much of the world and broken all of the commandments. For his skill at cards they soon had not only admiration but dread. He had emptied the pockets of his companions by a kind of prestidigitation quite incomprehensible to them. He seemed to play fairly, but there was not a loafer in Moscow who had not become timid about playing with Dave; the long run of luck was ever on his side. It was much more amusing to his companions to hear him, with ugly winks and the complacent airs of a man who feels sure that he had cut his eye-teeth, tell how he had plucked others in gambling than to furnish him with new laurels at their own expense.

On this particular evening Dave Sovine lounged on one of the counters, with a stack of unbleached "domestic" cloth for a bolster, while his bright patent-leather shoes were posed so as to be in plain view. Thus comfortably fixed, he bantered the now wary and rather

11

impecunious "boys" for a game of poker, euchre, seven-up, or anything to pass away the time. George Lockwood, as representing the proprietors of the store, sat on a ledge below the shelves with his feet braced on a box under the counter. He was still smarting from his discomfiture with Rachel Albaugh, and he was also desirous of investigating Dave Sovine's play without risking his own "fips" and "bits" in the game. So, after revolving the matter in his mind as he did every matter, he said to Dave, with a half-sinister smile:

"Tom Grayson's upstairs in Blackman's office. Maybe you might get up a game with him. He plays a stiff hand, and he a'n't afraid of the Ole Boy at cards, or anything else, for that matter."

"You call him down," said Dave, winking his eye significantly, and involuntarily disclosing a vein of exultant deviltry which made the cool-blooded Lockwood recoil a little; however, George felt that it would be a satisfaction to see Tom's pride reduced.

Lockwood got down off the ledge in a sluggish way, and walked around the end of the counter to the stove-pipe which ran from the box-stove in the store up through the office above.

"I say, Tom!" he called.

"What?" came out of the pipe.

"Dave Sovine says he can beat you at any game you choose. Come down and try him."

Grayson was bending over a law-book with only a tallow candle for light. Studying the law of common carriers was, in his opinion, dull business for a fellow with good red blood in his veins. He heard the murmur of conversation below, and for the last half-hour he had longed to put the book up beside its sheepskin companions on the shelves and join the company in the store. This banter decided him.

"I'll come down a little minute and try just three games and no more," he said. Then he closed the book with a thump and went down the outside stairway, which was the only means of egress from the law-office, and was let into the back door of the store by George Lockwood. He got an empty soap-box and set it facing the nail-keg on which Dave Sovine had placed himself for the encounter. A half-barrel with a board on top was put between the players, and served for table on which to deal and throw the cards; the candle rested on the rusty box-stove which stood, winter and summer, midway between the counters. Lockwood snuffed the candle and then, with an affectation of overlistlessness, placed himself behind Sovine, so as to command a view of his cards and of all his motions.

Tom had prudence enough to insist on playing for small stakes of a twelve-and-a-half-cent bit at a game;—his purse was not heavy enough for him to venture greater ones. At first the larger number of games fell to Grayson, and his winnings were considerable to one who had never had more than money enough for his bare necessities. He naturally forgot all about the law of common carriers and the limit of three games he had prescribed himself.

Dave cursed his infernal luck, as he called it, and when the twelfth round left Tom about a dollar ahead, he gave the cards a "Virginia poke" whenever it came his turn to cut them; that is to say, he pushed one card out of the middle of the pack, and put it at the back. By this means Dave proposed to "change the luck," as he said; but George Lockwood, who looked over Dave's shoulder, was not for a minute deceived by this manœuvre. He knew that this affectation of a superstition about luck and the efficiency of poking the cards was only a blind to cover from inexpert eyes the real sleight by which Dave, when he chose, could deal himself strong hands. Even the Virginia poke did not immediately bring a change, and when Tom had won a dozen games more than Dave, and so was a dollar and a half ahead, and had got his pulses well warmed up, Dave manifested great vexation, and asked Grayson to increase the stakes to half a dollar, so as to give him a chance to recover some of his money before it was time to quit. Tom consented to this, and the proportions of winnings passed to the other side of the board. Dave won sometimes two games in three, sometimes three in five, and Tom soon found a serious inroad made in the small fund of thirteen dollars which he had earned by odd jobs writing and even by harder and homelier work. This money had been hoarded toward a new suit of clothes. He began to breathe hard; he put up his hard-earned half-dollars with a trembling hand, and he saw them pass into Sovine's pocket with a bitter regret; he took his few winnings with eagerness. Every lost half-dollar represented a day's work, and after every loss he resolved to venture but one more, if the luck did not change. But how could he endure to quit defeated? He saw before him weeks of regret and self-reproach; he felt a desperate necessity for recovering his ground. As the loss account mounted, his lips grew dry, the veins in his forehead visibly swelled, and the perspiration trickled from his face. He tried to hide his agitation under an affectation of indifference and amusement, but when he essayed to speak careless words for a disguise, his voice was husky and unsteady, and he kept swallowing, with an effort as though something in his throat threatened him with suffocation. Dave noted these signs of distress in his adversary with a sort of luxurious pleasure; he had in him the instincts of a panther, and the suffering inflicted on another gave an additional relish to his victory.

Lockwood watched the play with a sharp curiosity, hoping to

penetrate the secret of Sovine's skill. He felt, also, a certain regret, for he had not expected to see Tom quite so severely punished. At length Tom's last dollar was reached; with a flushed face, he held the coin in his trembling hand for a moment, and then he said bravely: "It might as well go with the rest, if I lose this time," and he laid it down as a single stake, hoping that luck would favor him.

When Dave had pocketed this he leaned back and smiled with that sort of ruthless content that a beast of prey feels when he licks his chops after having enjoyed a meal from his lawful prey.

Tom's losses were relatively great; it was a kind of small ruin that had suddenly overtaken him. A month of writing, if he had it to do, would not have replaced the money, nor was his a nature that could easily brook defeat. The very courage and self-reliance that would have stood him in admirable stead in another kind of difficulty, and that in other circumstances would have been accounted a virtue, were a snare to him now.

"Look here, Dave," he said, with a voice choked by mortification, "give me a chance to win a little of that back," and he laid his pocket-knife on the table.

"Tom, you'd better quit," said three or four voices at once. But Dave rather eagerly laid a half-dollar by Tom's knife and won the knife. He liked this chance to give a certain completeness to the job. Then Tom laid out his silk handkerchief, which he also lost—for the games all went one way now.

"Come, Tom, hold on now," said the chorus.

But Tom was in the torment of perdition. He glared at those who advised him to desist. Then, in a mixture of stupor and desperation, he placed his hat on the board against a dollar and lost that; then he stripped the coat from his back and lost it, and at last his boots went the same way. When these were gone, having nothing further to wager without consigning himself to aboriginal nakedness, he sat in a kind of daze, his eyes looking swollen and bloodshot with excitement.

"Come, Dave," said Lockwood, "give him back his clothes. You've won enough without taking the clothes off his back."

"That's all you know about it," said Dave, who noted every token of Tom's suffering as an additional element in his triumph. "That may be your Illinois way, but that isn't the way we play in New Orleans. Winnings is winnings where I learnt the game." And he proceeded to lay Tom's things in a neat pile convenient for transportation.

"Aw! come now, Dave," said one and another, "'t a'n't the fair thing to send a fellow home to his folks barefooted and in his shirt-sleeves."

14

But Dave smiled in supercilious contempt at this provincial view of things, and cited the usages of the superior circles to which he had gained admission.

Lockwood at length lent Tom the money to redeem his garments, and the necessity which obliged him to borrow from the man who had got him into the scrape was the bitterest of all the bitter elements in Tom's defeat. He went out into the fresh air and walked home mechanically. His dashing, headlong ways had already partly alienated his uncle, and the only hope of Tom's retaining his assistance long enough to complete his law studies lay in the chance that his relative might fail to hear of this last escapade. It was clear to Tom without much canvassing of the question that he could not borrow from him the money to replace what he had gotten from Lockwood to redeem his clothes. He entered the garden by the back gate, climbed up to the roof of the wood-shed by means of a partition fence, and thence managed to pull himself into the window of his own chamber as stealthily as possible, that his uncle's family might not know that he had come home at half-past twelve. He stood a long while in the breeze at the open window watching the shadows of clouds drift over the moonlit prairie, which stretched away like a shoreless sea from the back of his uncle's house. He could not endure to bring his thoughts all at once to bear on his affairs; he stood there uneasily and watched these flitting black shadows come and go, and he gnashed his teeth with vexation whenever a full sense of his present misery and his future perplexities drifted over him.

He shut the window and went to bed at last, and by the time daylight arrived he had turned over every conceivable expedient. There was nothing for him but to accept the most disagreeable of all of them. He would have to draw on the slender purse of his mother and Barbara, for Lockwood's was a debt that might not be put off, and he could see no present means of earning money. He purposed to make some excuse to go home again on Saturday. It would be dreadful to meet Barbara's reproaches, and to see his mother's troubled face. How often he had planned to be the support of these two, but he seemed doomed to be only a burden; he had dreamed of being a source of pride to them, but again and again he had brought them mortification. Had he been less generous or more callous he would not have minded it so much. But as it was, his intolerable misery drove him to castle-building. He comforted himself with the reflection that he could make it all right with the folks at home when once he should get into practice. Barbara should have an easier time then. How often had he drawn drafts on the imaginary future for consolation!

# III

## PAYING THE FIDDLER

"You didn't mean no harm, Tommy," said Mrs. Grayson, "I know you didn't." She was fumbling in the drawer of a clothes-press, built by the side of the chimney in the sitting-room of the Grayson farm-house in Hubbard township. She kept her money in this drawer concealed under a collection of miscellaneous articles.

Tom sat looking out of the window. Ever since his gambling scrape he had imagined his mother's plaintive voice excusing him in this way. It was not the first time that he had had to be pulled out of disasters produced by his own rashness, and it seemed such an unmanly thing for him to come home with his troubles; but he must pay Lockwood quickly, lest any imprudent word of that not very friendly friend should reach his uncle's ears. Nothing but the fear of bringing on them greater evil could have scourged him into facing his mother and sister with the story of his gambling. Once in their presence, his wretched face had made it evident that he was in one of those tight places which were ever recurring in his life. He made a clean breast of it; your dashing dare-devil fellow has less temptation to lie than the rest of us. And now he had told it all,—he made it a sort of atonement to keep back nothing,—and he sat there looking out of the window at the steady dropping of a summer rain which had pelted him ever since he had set out from Moscow. He looked into the rain and listened to the quivering voice of his disappointed mother as she rummaged her drawer to take enough to meet his debt from the dollars accumulated by her own and Barbara's toil and management—dollars put by as a sinking fund to clear the farm of debt. But most of all he dreaded the time when Barbara should speak. She sat at the other window of the room with her face bent down over her sewing, which was pinned to her dress at the knee. She had listened to his story, but she had not uttered a word, and her silence filled him with foreboding. Tom watched the flock of bedraggled and down-hearted chickens creeping about under the eaves of the porch to escape the rain, and wondered whether it would not be better to kill himself to get rid of himself. His mother fumbled long and irresolutely in the drawer, looking up to talk every now and then, mostly in order to delay as long as possible the painful parting with her savings.

"I know you didn't mean no harm, Tommy; I know you didn't; but it's awful hard on Barb'ry an' me, partin' with this money. Dave

16

Sovine's a wicked wretch to bring such trouble on two women like us, that's had such a hard time to git on, an' nobody left to work the place. Out uv six children, you an' Barb'ry's all that's left alive. It's hard on a woman to be left without her husband, an' all but the two youngest children dead."

Here she stopped ransacking the drawer to wipe her eyes. She gave way to her grief the more easily because she still lacked resolution to devote her earnings to filling up the gap made by Tom's prodigality. And in every trouble her mind reverted involuntarily to the greater tribulations of her life; all rills of disappointment and all rivers of grief led down to this great sea of sorrow.

"You're the only two't's left, you two. Ef you'd just keep out uv bad comp'ny, Tommy. But," she said, recovering herself, "I know you're feelin' awful bad, an' you're a good boy only you're so keerless an' ventersome. You didn't mean no harm, an' you won't do it no more, I know you won't."

By this time Mrs. Grayson's trembling hands, on whose hardened palms and slightly distorted fingers one might have read the history of a lifetime of work and hardship, had drawn out a cotton handkerchief in which were tied up thirty great round cumbersome Spanish and Mexican dollars, with some smaller silver. This she took to a table, where she proceeded slowly to count out for Tom the exact amount he had borrowed to redeem his clothes,—not a fi'-penny bit more did she spare him.

At this point Barbara began to speak. She raised her face from her work and drew her dark eyes to a sharp focus, as she always did when she was much in earnest.

"It don't matter much about us, Tom," she said, despondently. "Women are made to give up for men, I suppose. I've made up my mind a'ready to quit the school over at Timber Creek, though I do hate to."

"Yes," said her mother, "an' it's too bad, fer you did like that new-fangled study of algebray, though I can't see the good of it."

"I don't want to hurt your feelings," Barbara went on, "but maybe it'll do you good, Tom, to remember that I've got to give up the school, and it's my very last chance, and I've got to spin and knit enough this winter to make up the money you've thrown away in one night. You wouldn't make us trouble a-purpose for anything,—I know that. And, any way, we don't care much about ourselves; it don't matter about us. But we do care about you. What'll happen if you go on in this heels-over-head way? Uncle Tom'll never stand it, you know, and your only chance'll be gone. That's what'll hurt us all

17

'round—to give up all for you, and then you make a mess of it—in spite of all we've done."

"You're awful hard on me, Barb," said Tom, writhing a little in his chair. "I wish I'd made an end of myself, as I thought of doing, when I was done playing that night."

"There you are again," said Barbara, "without ever stopping to think. I suppose you think it would have made mother and me feel better about it, for you to kill yourself!"

"Don't be so cuttin' with your tongue, Barb'ry," said her mother, "we can stand it, and poor Tom didn't mean to do it."

"Pshaw!" said Barbara, giving herself a shake of impatience, "what a baby excuse that is for a grown-up man like Tom! Tom's no fool if he would only think; but he'll certainly spoil everything before he comes to his senses, and then we'll all be here in the mud together;—the family'll be disgraced, and there'll be no chance of Tom's getting on. What makes me mad is that Tom'll sit there and let you excuse him by saying that he didn't mean any harm, and then he'll be just as gay as ever by day after to-morrow, and just as ready to run into some new scrape."

"Go on, Barb, that's hitting the sore spot," said Tom, leaning his head on his hand. "Maybe if you knew all I've gone through, you'd let up a little." Tom thought of telling her of the good resolutions he had made, but he had done that on other occasions like this, and he knew that his resolutions were by this time at a heavy discount in the home market. He would liked to have told Barbara how he intended to make it all up to them whenever he should get into a lucrative practice, but he dreaded to expose his cherished dreams to the nipping frost of her deadly common sense.

He looked about for a change of subject.

"Where's Bob McCord?" he asked.

"It was a rainy day, and he's gone off to the grocery, I guess," said Mrs. Grayson. "I'm afeerd he won't come home in time to cut us wood to do over Sunday."

Tom had intended to ride back to Moscow and pay his debt this very evening. But here was a chance to show some little gratitude—a chance to make a beginning of amendment. He did not want to stay at home, where the faces of his mother and Barbara and the pinching economy of the household arrangements would reproach him, but for this very reason he would remain until the next day; it would be a sort of penance, and any self-imposed suffering was a relief. The main use that men make of penitence and the wearing of sackcloth is to restore the balance of their complacency. Tom announced his intention to see to the Sunday wood himself; putting his uncle's horse in the stable, he went

18

manfully to chopping wood in the rain and attending to everything else that would serve to make his mother and sister more comfortable.

# IV

# LOCKWOOD'S PLAN

George Lockwood, being only mildly malicious, felt something akin to compensation at having procured for Tom so severe a loss. But he was before all things a man secretive and calculating; the first thing he did with any circumstance was to take it into his intellectual backroom, where he spent most of his time, and demand what advantage it could give to George Lockwood. When he had let all the boys out of the store at a quarter past twelve, he locked and barred the door. Then he put away the boxes and all other traces of the company, and carried his tallow candle into his rag-carpeted bedroom, which opened from the rear of the store and shared the complicated and characteristic odors of the shop with a dank smell of its own; this last came from a habit Lockwood had when he sprinkled the floor of the store, preparatory to sweeping it, of extending the watering process to the rag-carpet of the bedroom. His mind gave only a passing thought of mild exultation, mingled with an equally mild regret, to poor Tom Grayson's misfortune. He was already inquiring how he might, without his hand appearing in the matter, use the occurrence for his own benefit. Tom had had presence of mind enough left to beg the whole party in the store to say nothing about the affair; but notwithstanding the obligation which the set felt to protect one another from the old fogies of their families, George Lockwood thought the matter would probably get out. He was not the kind of a man to make any bones about letting it out, if he could thereby gain any advantage. The one feeling in his tepid nature that had ever attained sufficient intensity to keep him awake at night was his passion for Rachel Albaugh; and his passion was quite outside of any interest he might have in Rachel's reversionary certainty of the one-half of John Albaugh's lands. This, too, he had calculated, but as a subordinate consideration.

He reflected that Rachel might come to town next Saturday,

19

which was the general trading-day of the country people. If she should come, she would be sure to buy something of him. But how could he tell her of Tom's unlucky gambling? To do so directly would be in opposition to all the habits of his prudent nature. Nor could he bethink him of a ruse that might excuse an indirect allusion to it; and he went to sleep at length without finding a solution of his question.

But chance favored him, for with the Saturday came rain, and Rachel regretfully gave over a proposed visit to the village. But as some of the things wanted were quite indispensable, Ike Albaugh was sent to Moscow, and he came into Wooden & Snyder's store about 4 o'clock in the afternoon. George Lockwood greeted him cordially, and weighed out at his request three pounds of ten-penny nails to finish the new corn-crib, a half-pound of cut tobacco to replenish the senior Albaugh's pipe from time to time, a dollar's worth of sugar, and a quarter of a pound of Epsom salts,—these last two for general use. He also measured off five yards of blue cotton drilling, six feet of half-inch rope for a halter, and two yards of inch-wide ribbon to match a sample sent by Rachel. Then he filled one of the Albaugh jugs with molasses and another with whisky, which last was indispensable in the hay harvest. These articles were charged to John Albaugh's account; he was credited at the same time with the ten pounds of fresh butter that Isaac had brought. George Lockwood also wrapped up a paper of "candy kisses," as they were called, which he charged Ike to give to Rachel from him, but which he forgot to enter to his own account on the day-book.

"By the way, Ike," he said, "did you know that Dave Sovine got back last week?"

"Yes," said Ike; "I hear the Sovine folks made a turrible hullabaloo over the returned prodigal,—killed the fatted calf, and all that."

"A tough prodigal he is!" said Lockwood, with a gentle smile of indifference. "You'd better look out for him."

"Me? Why?" asked Ike. "He never had any grudge ag'inst me, as I know of."

"No," said Lockwood, laughing, "not that. But he's cleaned all the money out of all the boys about town, and he'll be going after you country fellows next, I guess. He's the darnedest hand with cards!"

"Well, he won't git a-holt of me," said Ike, with boyish exultation. "I don't hardly more 'n know the ace f'um the jack. I never played but on'y just once; two or three games weth one of the harvest hands, four years ago. He was showin' me how, you know, one Sunday in the big hay-mow, an' jus' as I got somethin' 't he called high low jack, the old man took 't into his head to come up the ladder to see what was goin' on. You know father's folks was Dunkers, an' he don't believe in cards. I got high low jack that time, an' I won't fergit it the longest day I live." Ike grinned a little ruefully at the recollection. "Could n' draw on my roundabout fer a week without somebody helpin' me, I was so awful sore betwixt the shoulders. Not any more fer me, thank you!"

"It'u'd be good for some other young fellows I know, if they'd had some of the same liniment," said Lockwood, beginning to see his way clear, and speaking in a languid tone with his teeth half closed. "Blam'd 'f I didn't see Sovine, a-settin' right there on that kag of sixp'ny nails the other night, win all a fellow's money, and then his handkerchief and his knife. The fellow—you know him well—got so excited that he put up his hat and his coat and his boots, an' Dave took 'em all. He's got some cheatin' trick ur 'nother, but I stood right over 'im an' I can't quite make it out yet. I tried to coax 'im to give back the hat an' coat an' boots; but no, sir, he's a regular black-leg. He wouldn't give up a thing till I lent the other fellow as much money as he'd staked ag'inst them."

"Who wuz the other fellow?" asked Ike Albaugh, with lively curiosity.

"Oh! I promised not to tell"; but as Lockwood said this he made an upward motion with his pointed thumb, and turned his eyes towards the office overhead.

"W'y, not Tom?" asked Ike, in an excited whisper.

"Don't you say anything about it," said George, looking serious. "He don't want his uncle's folks to know anything about it. And besides, I haven't mentioned any name, you know"; and he fell into a playful little titter between his closed teeth, as he shook his head secretively, and turned away to attend to a woman who, in spite of the rain, had brought on horseback a large "feed-basket" full of eggs, and three pairs of blue stockings of her own knitting, which she wished to exchange for a calico dress-pattern and some other things.

But Lockwood turned to call after the departing youth: "You won't mention that to anybody, will you, Ike?"

"To b' shore not," said Ike, as he went out of the door thinking how much it would interest Rachel.

Ike Albaugh was too young and too light-hearted to be troubled with forebodings. Rachel might marry anybody she pleased "f'r all of him." It was her business, and she was of age, he reflected, and he wasn't her "gardeen." At most, if it belonged to anybody to interfere, "it was the ole man's lookout." But the story of Tom Grayson's losing all his money, and even part of his clothes, was something interesting to tell, and it did not often happen to the young man to have the first of a bit of news. A farm-house on the edge of an unsettled prairie is a dull place, where all things have a monotonous, diurnal revolution and a larger annual repetition; any event with a parabolic or hyperbolic orbit which intrudes into this system is a godsend; even the most transient shooting-star of gossip is a relief. But this would be no momentary meteor, and Isaac saw in the newly acquired information something to "tease Rache with," and teasing one's sister is always lawful sport. He owed her some good-natured grudges; here was one chance to be even with her.

Ike got home at half-past six, and Rachel had to spread for him a cold supper, chiefly of corn-bread and milk. He gave her the ribbon and the little package of square candy kisses from Lockwood. Rachel sat down at the table opposite her hungry brother, and, after giving him a part of the sweets, she amused herself with unfolding the papers that inclosed each little square of candy and reading the couplets of honeyed doggerel wrapped within.

"Did you hear anything of Tom?" Rachel asked.

"Yes."

"What was it?"

"Oh! I promised not to say anything about it."

"You needn't be afraid of making me jealous," said the sister, with a good-natured, half-defiant setting of her head on one side.

"Jealous? No, it's not anything like that. You ain't good at guessin', Sis; girls never air."

"Not even Ginnie Miller," said Rachel. She usually met Ike's hackneyed allusions to the inferiority of girls by some word about Ginnie. It was plain her brother was in a teasing mood, and that her baffled curiosity would not find satisfaction by coaxing. She knew well enough that Ike was not such a fool as to keep an interesting secret long enough for it to grow stale and unmarketable on his hands.

"Let it go,—I don't care," she said, as she got up and moved about the kitchen.

"You would, if you knew," said Ike.

"But I don't, and so there's an end of it"; and she began to hum a sentimental song of the languishing sort so much in vogue in that day. The melancholy refrain, which formed the greater part of this one, ran:

"Long, long ago, long ago."

It is one of the paradoxes of human nature that young women with all the world before them delight in singing retrospective

22

melodies about an auld-lang-syne concerning which, in the very nature of the case, they cannot well know anything, but in regard to which they seem to entertain sentiments so distressful.

"It wasn't so very long ago, 'nuther," said Ike, whose dialect was always intensified when there were harvest hands on the place.

"What wasn't?" said Rachel, with her back to him.

"Why, Tom's scrape, of course."

"Was it a very bad one? Did he get took up?" Rachel's face was still averted, but Ike noted with pleasure that her voice showed a keen interest in his news.

"Oh, no, 't's not him that ought to be took up; it's Dave Sovine."

Rachel cleared her throat and waited a few seconds before speaking again.

"Did Dave hurt Tom much?" she asked, groping after the facts among the various conjectures that suggested themselves.

"Well, yes," said Ike, with a broad grin of delight at his sister's wide guessing; but by this time he was pretty well exhausted by the strain put upon his feeble secretiveness. "Yes, hurt him? I sh'd say so!" he went on. "Hurts like blazes to have a black-leg like Dave win all yer money an' yer knife, 'an yer hankercher, an' yer hat an' coat an' boots in the bargain. But you mus'n't say anything about it, Sis. It's a dead secret."

"Who told you?"

"Nobody," said Ike, feeling some compunction that he had gone so far. "I just heard it."

"Who'd you hear it from?"

"George Lockwood kind uh let 't out without 'xactly sayin' 't wuz Tom. But he didn't deny it wuz Tom."

Having thus relieved himself from the uncomfortable pressure of his secret, Ike got up and went out whistling, leaving Rachel to think the matter over. It was not the moral aspect of the question that presented itself to her. If Tom had beaten Sovine she would not have cared. It was Tom's cleverness as well as his buoyant spirit that had touched her, and now her hero had played the fool. She had the wariness of one who had known many lovers; her wit was not profound, and she saw rather than contrived the course most natural to one of her prudent and ease-loving temperament; she would hold Tom in check, and postpone the disagreeable necessity for final decision.

# V

# THE MITTEN

Next to Tom's foreboding about his uncle was the dread of the effect of his bad conduct on Rachel. On that rainy Saturday afternoon he thought much about the possibility of making shipwreck with Rachel; and this led him to remember with a suspicion, foreign to his temper, the part that Lockwood had taken in his disgrace. By degrees he transferred much of his indignation from Sovine to George Lockwood. He resolved to see Rachel on his way back to town, and if possible by a frank confession to her to forestall and break the force of any reports that might get abroad. The bold course was always the easiest to one of so much propulsiveness. He remembered that there was a "singin'," as it was called in the country, held every Sunday afternoon in the Timber Creek school-house, half-way between his mother's house and the Albaugh's. This weekly singing-school was attended by most of the young people of the neighborhood, and by Rachel Albaugh among the rest. Tom planned to stop, as though by chance, at the gathering and ride home with the ever adorable Rachel.

When Tom reached the school-house, Bryant, the peripatetic teacher of vocal music, was standing in front of his class and leading them by beating time with his rawhide riding-whip. Esteeming himself a leader in the musical world, he was not restricted to the methods used by musicians of greater renown. It is easy for ignorance to make innovation,—the America of a half century ago was seriously thinking of revising everything except the moral law. While Noah Webster in Connecticut was proposing single-handed to work over the English tongue so as to render it suitable to the wants of a self-complacent young nation, other reformers as far west as St. Louis were engaged in improving the world's system of musical notation. Of the new method Bryant was an ardent propagator; he made much of the fact that he was a musical new light, and taught the "square notes," a system in which the relative pitch was not only indicated by the position of the notes upon the clef, but also by their characteristic shapes. Any simpleton could here tell "do" from "me" at sight.

In the "Missouri Harmonist" the lines and spaces were decorated with quavers and semi-quavers whose heads were circles, squares, and triangles; Old Hundred becoming a solemn procession of one-legged and no-legged geometric figures. But Bryant understood his business too well to confine his Sunday classes of young people to Sunday tunes. When Tom, after tying his horse to the inner corner of a rail-fence, pushed back the school-house door, creaking on its wooden hinges, the four divisions of the class were chasing one another through a "round," the words of which ran:

> "Now, Lawrence, take your bag,
> And go right straight to mill,
> And see, m—y b—o—y,
> That not a bit you spill!"

This kind of music was naturally popular. Such a service relieves the tedium of a Sunday afternoon, and has something of the charm a dog finds in pursuing his own tail.

Some of the members of the class turned their heads and their vocal mouths towards the door when Tom came in, but in the midst of this jangle of voices singing different portions of the same air most of them had all they could do to keep their time by waving their heads or thumping their toes on the puncheon floor, while they alternately looked at their books and at Bryant, who thrashed away with his whip, his lips seeming to say, though the words were inaudible in the general din:

"Up, down, right, left, up," as he perpetually made right angles in the air. Rachel was in the act of drawing the word "boy" to the full length of a long note with a hold after it, but she looked up long enough to recognize the new arrival; then she dropped her eyes to the book again and gave the most severe attention to Bryant and the square notes thereafter, not once looking at Tom to the end. From this unwonted absorption in her music, Tom inferred that Rachel had somehow heard of his misconduct and was offended. But her charms enchanted him more than ever now that they were receding from him, and with a characteristic resolution he determined not to give her up without a sharp endeavor to regain his lost ground.

When the "singing" "let out," Tom availed himself of the first moment of confusion, while Rachel stood apart, to ask permission to go home with her, in the well-worn formula which was the only polite and proper word to use for the purpose; for it is strange how rigidly certain exact forms were adhered to among people where intercourse was for the most part familiar and unconventional.

"May I see you safe home?" he asked, as he had often asked before, but never before with trepidation.

"No," said Rachel, with an evident effort, and without looking at Tom's face.

Such an answer is technically known as "the sack" and "the

mitten," though it would take a more inventive antiquary than I to tell how it got these epithets. But it was one of the points on which the rural etiquette of that day was rigorous and inflexible, that such a refusal closed the conversation and annihilated the beau without allowing him to demand any explanations or to make any further advances at the time. Tom was not of the sort easily snuffed out. He had to ride past Rachel's house, and it would be an addition to his disappointment that everybody would see his discomfiture. So he answered.

"Well, I'll lead up your horse for you anyhow," and he went out before she could make up her mind to refuse him, and brought the sorrel filly alongside a tree-stump left standing in front of the school-house for a horse-block. The rest had by this time either mounted and gone, or were walking away afoot. Rachel felt a secret admiration for his audacity as she sprang into her saddle, while Tom held her bridle and adjusted the stirrup to her foot.

"What have I done, Rachel?"

"You know, well enough." Her voice was low and tremulous. She had dismissed other favorites, but never before had she found in herself so much reluctance.

"Do you mean my gambling with Dave Sovine?" said Tom, driving, as usual, point-blank at the very center of things.

"Yes."

"Who told you?" He still held on to her bridle-rein with his left hand,—somewhat as a highwayman does in romances.

"Oh! I guess everybody knows. Ike heard it yesterday, from George Lockwood or somebody."

"It was Lockwood got me into it," said Tom, shutting his teeth hard. "If you'd let me go home with you, I could explain things a little."

But those who are enervated by the balmy climate of flattery naturally dread a stiff breeze of ridicule. Rachel Albaugh did not like to bear any share of the odium that must come on Tom when his recklessness, and, above all, his bad luck, should become known. She drew the rein that Tom held, until he felt obliged to let it go, and said "No."

"I have got what I needed," said Tom, making the best of his defeat.

"What?" asked Rachel.

"Oh! one mitten isn't of any use alone; you've given me a pair of them."

Tom felt now the exhilaration of desperation. He gayly mounted his horse, and bade Rachel a cheerful good-bye as he galloped past her; then, when he had overtaken a group of those ahead of Rachel, he reined up and turned in the saddle, leaning his left hand on the croup, while he joked and bantered with one and another. Then he put his horse into a gallop again.

When he was well out of hearing, Henry Miller, who was one of the party, remarked to his companions that he didn't know what was up, but it seemed to him as though Tom Grayson had got something that looked like a mitten without any thumb. "That's one more that Rache's shed," he remarked. "But when she gets a chance to shed me she'll know it."

As Tom rode onward toward the village his spirits sank again, and he let his horse break down into an easy trot and then into a slow walk.

It was no longer Sovine that he cursed inwardly. George Lockwood, he reflected, had called him away from the Law of Common Carriers to play a little game with Dave, and it was Lockwood who had reported his discomfiture to the Albaughs. He put these things together by multiplication rather than by addition, and concluded that Lockwood, from the first, had planned his ruin in order to destroy his chances with Rachel, which was giving that mediocre young man credit for a depth of forethinking malice he was far from possessing.

Monday morning Tom went into Wooden & Snyder's store on the way to his office above. Lockwood had just finished sweeping out; the sprinkling upon the floor was not dry; it yet showed the figure 8s which he had made in swinging the sprinkler to and fro as he walked. The only persons in the store were two or three villagers; the country people rarely came in on Monday, and never at so early an hour. One frisky young man of a chatty temperament had stopped to exchange the gossip of the morning with George; but meaning to make his halt as slight as possible, he had not gone farther than the threshold, on which he now balanced himself, with his hands in his pockets, talking as he rocked nervously to and fro, like a bird on a waving bough in a wind. Another villager had slouched in to buy a pound of nails, with which to repair the damage done to his garden fence by the pigs during Sunday; but as he was never in a hurry, he stood back and gave the first place to a carpenter who wanted a three-cornered file, and who was in haste to get to his day's work. When Lockwood had attended to the carpenter, Tom beckoned him to the back part of the store, and without saying a word counted out to him the money he had borrowed.

Something in Tom's manner gave Lockwood a sneaking feeling that his own share in this affair was not creditable. His was one of those consciences that take their cue from without. Of independent moral judgment he had little; but he had a vague desire to stand well in the judgment of others, and even to stand well in his own eyes when judged by other people's code. It was this half-evolved conscience that made him wish—what shall I say?—to atone for the harm he had but half-intentionally done to Tom? or, to remove the unfavorable impression that Tom evidently had of his conduct? At any rate, when he had taken his money again, he ventured to offer some confidential advice in a low tone. For your cool man who escapes the pitfalls into which better and cleverer men often go headlong is prone to rank his worldly wisdom, and even his sluggish temperament, among the higher virtues. Some trace of this relative complacency made itself heard perhaps in Lockwood's voice, when he said in an undertone:

"You know, Tom, if I were you, I'd take a solemn oath never to touch a card again. You're too rash."

This good counsel grated on the excited feelings of the recipient of it.

"I don't want any advice from you," said Tom in a bitter monotone.

I have heard it mentioned by an expert that a super-heated steam-boiler is likely to explode with the first escape of steam, the slight relief of pressure precipitating the catastrophe. Tom had resolved not to speak a word to Lockwood, but his wounded and indignant pride had brooded over Rachel's rejection the livelong night, and now the air of patronage in Lockwood drew from him this beginning; then his own words aggravated his feelings, and speech became an involuntary explosion.

"You called me down-stairs," he said, "and got me into this scrape. Do you think I don't know what it was for? You took pains to have word about it go where it would do me the most harm."

"I didn't do any such thing," said Lockwood.

"You did," said Tom. "You told Ike Albaugh Saturday. You're a cold-blooded villain, and if you cross my path again I'll shoot you."

By this time he was talking loud enough for all in the store to hear. The villager who wanted nails had sidled a little closer to the center of the explosion, the young man tilting to and fro on the threshold of the front door had come inside the store and was deeply engaged in studying the familiar collection of pearl buttons, colored sewing-silks, ribbons, and other knick-knacks in the counter showcase, while the carpenter had forgotten his haste, and turning about stood now with his tool-box under his arm, looking at Tom Grayson and Lockwood with blunt curiosity.

"That's a nice way to treat me, I must say," said Lockwood, in a kind of whine of outraged friendship. "You'd 'a' gone home

28

bareheaded and in your shirt-sleeves and your stocking-feet, if 't hadn't 'a' been fer me."

"I'd 'a' gone home with my money in my pocket, if you and Dave Sovine hadn't fixed it up between you to fleece me. I 'xpect you made as much out of it as Dave did. You've got me out 'v your way now. But you look out! Don't you cross my track again, George Lockwood, or I'll kill you!"

In a new country, where life is full of energy and effervescence, it is much easier for an enraged man to talk about killing than it is in a land of soberer thinking and less lawlessness. The animal which we call a young man was not so tame in Illinois two generations ago as it is now. But Tom's threat, having given vent to his wrath, lowered the pressure: by the time he had made this second speech his violence had partly spent itself, and he became conscious that he was heard by the three persons in the store, as well as by Snyder, the junior proprietor, who stood now in the back door. Tom Grayson turned and strode out of the place, dimly aware that he had again run the risk of bringing down the avalanche by his rashness. For if Tom was quickly brought to a white-heat, radiation was equally rapid. Long before noon he saw clearly that he had probably rendered it impossible to keep the secret of his gambling from his uncle. All the town would hear of his quarrel with Lockwood, and all the town would set itself to know to the utmost the incident that was the starting-point of a wrath so violent.

If Tom had not known by many frosty experiences his uncle's unimpressionable temper, he would have followed his instinct and gone directly to him with a frank confession. But there was nothing to be gained by such a course with such a man.

# VI

## UNCLE AND NEPHEW

Thomas Grayson the elder was one of those men who contrive to play an important part in a community without having any specific vocation. He had a warehouse in which space was sometimes let for the storage of other people's goods, but which also served to hold country produce whenever, in view of a probable rise in the market, he chose to enter the field as a cash buyer in competition with the "storekeepers," who bought only in exchange for goods. Sometimes, in the fall and the winter, he would purchase hogs and cattle from the farmers and have them driven to the most promising market. He also served the purpose of a storage reservoir in the village trade; for he always had money or credit, and whenever a house, or a horse, or a mortgage, or a saw-mill, or a lot of timber, or a farm, or a stock of goods was put on the market at forced sale, Grayson the elder could be counted on to buy it if no better purchaser were to be found. He had no definite place of business; he was generally to be found about the street, ready to buy or sell, or to exchange one thing for another, whenever there was a chance to make a profit.

He had married late; and even in marrying he took care to make a prudent investment. His wife brought a considerable addition to his estate and no unduly expensive habits. Like her husband, she was of a thrifty disposition and plain in her tastes. The temptations to a degree of ostentation are stronger in a village than in a city, but Mrs. Grayson was not moved by them; she lent herself to her husband's ambition to accumulate. Not that the Graysons were without pride; they thought, indeed, a good deal of their standing among their neighbors. But it was gratifying to them to know that the village accounted Grayson a good deal better off than some who indulged in a larger display. The taking of Tom had been one of those economic combinations which men like Grayson are fond of making. He knew that his neighbors thought he ought to do something for his brother's family. To pay the debt on the farm would be the simplest way of doing this, but it would be a dead deduction from the ever-increasing total of his assets. When, however, Barbara had come to him with a direct suggestion that he should help her promising brother to a profession, the uncle saw a chance to discharge the obligation which the vicarious sentiment of his neighbors and the censure of his own conscience imposed on him, and to do it with advantage to himself. He needed somebody "to do choores" at his house; the wood had to be sawed, the cow had to be milked, the horse must be fed, and the garden attended to. Like most other villagers, Grayson had been wont to look after such things himself, but as his wealth and his affairs increased, he had found the chores a burden on his time and some detraction from his dignity. So he, therefore, took his namesake into his house and sent him to the village school for three years, and then put him into the office of Lawyer Blackman, to whom he was wont to intrust his conveyancing and law business. This law business entailed a

30

considerable expense, and Thomas Grayson the elder may have seen more than a present advantage in having his nephew take up the profession under his protection. But the young man's unsteadiness, late hours, and impulsive rashness had naturally been very grievous to a cool-headed speculator who never in his life had suffered an impulse or a sentiment to obstruct his enterprises.

Of domestic life there was none in the house of Thomas Grayson, unless one should give that name to sleeping and waking, cooking and eating, cleaning the house and casting up accounts. With his wife Grayson talked about the diverse speculations he had in hand or in prospect, and canvassed his neighbors chiefly on the business side of their lives, pleasing his pride of superior sagacity in pointing out the instances in which they had failed to accomplish their ends from apathy or sheer blundering. The husband and wife had no general interest in anything; no playful banter, no interesting book, no social assemblage or cheerful game ever ameliorated the austerity of their lives. The one thread of sentiment woven into their stone-colored existence was a passionate fondness for their only child Janet, a little thing five years old when Tom came into the house to do chores and go to school,—a child of seven now that Tom was drifting into trouble that threatened to end his professional career before it had been begun. Janet was vivacious and interesting rather than pretty, though her mass of dark hair, contrasting with a fair skin and blue eyes, made her appearance noticeable. Strict in their dealings with themselves and severe with others, Janet's father and mother did not know how to refuse her anything; she had grown up willful and a little overbearing; but she was one of those children of abundant imagination and emotion that sometimes, as by a freak of nature, are born to commonplace parents. Those who knew her were prone to say that "the child must take back"; for people had observed this phenomenon of inheritance from remote ancestors and given it a name long before learned men discovered it and labeled it atavism.

A fellow like Tom, full of all sorts of impetuosities, could not help being in pretty constant conflict with his uncle and aunt. On one pretext or another he contrived to escape from the restraints of the house, and to spend his evenings in such society as a village offers. A young man may avoid the temptations of a great city, where there are many circles of association to choose from; but in a village where there is but one group, and where all the youth are nearly on a level, demoralization is easier. Tom had a country boy's appetite for companionship and excitement; he had no end of buoyant spirits and cordial friendliness; and he was a good teller of amusing stories,—so that he easily came to be a leader in all the

31

frolics and freaks of the town. His uncle administered some severe rebukes and threatened graver consequences; but rebukes and threats served only to add the spice of peril to Tom's adventures.

The austerity of acquisitiveness is more tedious to others, perhaps, than the austerity of religious conviction. To a child like Janet, endowed with passion and imagination, the grave monotony of the Grayson household was almost unbearable. From the moment of Tom's coming she had clung to him, rejoicing in his boyish spirits, and listening eagerly to his fund of stories, which were partly made up for her amusement, and partly drawn from romances which he had somewhat surreptitiously read. When he was away, Janet watched for his return; she romped with him in defiance of the stiff proprieties of the house, and she followed him at his chores. She cherished a high admiration for his daring and rebellious spirit, often regretting that she was not a boy: it would be fine to climb out of a bedroom window at night to get away to some forbidden diversion! On the other hand, the unselfish devotion of Tom to the child was in strange contrast with the headlong willfulness of his character. He made toys and planned surprises for her, and he was always ready to give up his time to her pleasure.

It is hardly likely that Grayson would have borne with his nephew a single year if it had not been for Janet's attachment to him. More than once, when his patience was clean tired out, he said to his wife something to this effect:

"I think, Charlotte, I'll have to send Tom back to his mother. He gets nothing but mischief here in town, and he worries me to death."

To which Mrs. Grayson would reply: "Just think of Janet. I'm afraid she'd pine away if Tom was sent off. The boy is kind to her, and I'm sure that's one good thing about him."

This consideration had always settled the question; for the two main purposes of life with Grayson and his wife were to accumulate property and to gratify every wish of their child. Having only one sentiment, it had acquired a tremendous force.

# VII

## LOCKWOOD'S REVENGE

When Tom, after his violent speech on that unlucky Monday morning, had gone out of Wooden & Snyder's store, George Lockwood turned to Snyder, the junior partner, and said, with his face a little flushed:

"What a fool that boy is, anyhow! He came in here the other night after the store was shut up and played cards with Dave Sovine till he lost all the money he had. I tried my best to stop him, but I couldn't do it. He went on and bet all the clo'es he could spare and lost 'em. I had to lend him the money to get 'em back. It seems Tom's girl—John Albaugh's daughter—heard of it, and now he will have it that I went in partnership with Sovine to get his money, and that I wanted to get Rachel Albaugh away from 'im."

"You oughtn't to have any card-playing here," said Snyder.

"I told the boys then that if they come in here again they mustn't bring any cards."

"Tom's a fool to threaten you that way. You could bind him over on that, I suppose," said Snyder.

"I s'pose I could," said George.

But he did nothing that day. He prided himself on being a man that a body couldn't run over, but he had his own way of resisting aggression; he was not Esau, but Jacob. He could not storm and threaten like Tom; there was no tempest in him. Cold venom will keep, and Lockwood's resentments did not lose their strength by exposure to the air. The day after Tom's outburst, Lockwood, having taken time to consider the alternatives, suggested to Snyder, that while he wasn't afraid of Tom, there was no knowing what such a hot-head might do. Lockwood professed an unwillingness to bind Tom over to keep the peace, but thought some influence might be brought to bear on him that would serve the purpose. Snyder proposed that Lockwood should go to see Tom's uncle, but George objected. That would only inflame Tom and make matters worse. Perhaps Snyder would see Blackman, so that Lockwood need not appear in the matter? Then Blackman could speak to Grayson the elder, if he thought best.

The calculating temper, and the touch of craftiness, pliancy, and tact in Lockwood served the ends of his employers in many ways, and Snyder was quite willing to put his clerk under obligations of friendship to him. Therefore, when he saw Tom go out of the office, Snyder mounted the stairs and had an interview with Blackman. As the lawyer was intrusted with all the bad debts and pettifogging business of Wooden & Snyder, any suggestion from a member of the firm was certain to receive attention. Snyder told the lawyer that Lockwood didn't want to drag Tom before a squire, and suggested that Blackman could settle it by getting the uncle to give the fellow a good admonition. He offered the suggestion as though it were quite on his own motion, he having overheard Tom's threat. The hand of George Lockwood was concealed; but it was only Lockwood who knew how exceedingly vulnerable Tom's fortunes were on the side of his relations with his uncle. That evening Blackman sat in Grayson's sitting-room. He was a man with grayish hair, of middle height, and rather too lean to fill up his clothes, which hung on his frame rather than fitted it; and if one regarded his face, there seemed too little substance to quite fill out his skin, which was not precisely wrinkled, but rather wilted. Grayson had turned around in his writing-chair and sat with one leg over the arm, but Blackman had probably never lolled in his life: he was possessed by a sort of impotent uneasiness that simulated energy and diligence. He sat, as was his wont, on the front rail of the chair-seat, as though afraid to be comfortable, and he held in his hand a high hat half full of papers, according to the custom of the lawyers of that day, who carried on their heads that part of their business which they could not carry in them. Blackman told the story of Tom's gambling as he had heard it, and of his threatening Lockwood, while the brows of Tom's uncle visibly darkened. Then the lawyer came to what he knew would seem to Grayson the vital point in the matter.

"You know," he said, "if George Lockwood was a-mind to, he could bind Tom to keep the peace; though I don't s'pose Tom meant anything more than brag by talking that way. But it wouldn't be pleasant for you to have Tom hauled up, and to have to go his bail. I told Snyder I thought you could fix it up without going before the squire." Blackman passed his heavily laden hat from his right hand to his left, and then with the right he nervously roached up his stiff, rusty hair, which he habitually kept standing on end. After which he took a red silk handkerchief from his hat and wiped his face, while Grayson got up and walked the floor.

"I shouldn't like to have to go anybody's bail," said the latter after awhile; "it's against my principles to go security. I suppose the best thing would be to send him back to the country to cool off."

Blackman nodded a kind of half assent, but did not venture any further expression of opinion. He rose and deposited his silk handkerchief in a kind of coil on the papers in his hat, and then bent

34

his head forward and downward so as to put on the hat without losing its contents; once it was in place he brought his head to a perpendicular position, so that all the mass of portable law business settled down on the handkerchief, which acted as a cushion between Blackman's affairs and his head.

Tom came in as Blackman went out, and something in the manner of the latter gave him a feeling that he had been the subject of conversation between the lawyer and his uncle. He went directly to his room, and debated within himself whether or not he should go down and interrupt by a frank and full confession the discussion which he thought was probably taking place between Mr. and Mrs. Grayson. But knowing his uncle's power of passive resistance, he debated long—so long that it came to be too late, and he went to bed, resolved to have the first of it with his uncle in the morning.

There was a very serious conference between the two members of the Grayson firm that evening. Mrs. Grayson again presented to her husband the consideration that, if Tom should go away, she didn't see what she was to do with Janet. The child would cry her eyes out, and there'd be no managing her. Grayson sat for some time helpless before this argument.

"I don't see," he said at length, "but we've got to face Janet. We might as well teach her to mind first as last." It was a favorite theory with both of them that some day Janet was to be taught to mind. So long as no attempt was made to fix the day on which the experiment was to begin, the thought pleased them and did no harm. But this proposition to undertake the dreadful task at once was a spurt of courage in Thomas Grayson that surprised his wife.

"Well, Mr. Grayson," she said, with some spirit, "the child's as much yours as she's mine; and if she's to be taught to mind to-morrow, I only hope you'll stay at home and begin."

To this suggestion the husband made no reply. He got up and began to look under the furniture for the boot-jack, according to his custom of pulling off his boots in the sitting-room every night before going to bed.

"You see, Charlotte," he said deprecatingly, when he had fished his boot-jack out from under the bureau, "I don't know what to do. If I keep Tom, Lockwood'll have him before the squire, and I'll have to pay costs and go bail for him."

"I wouldn't do it," said Mrs. Grayson promptly. "We can't afford to have the little we've got put in danger for him. I think you'll have to send him home, and we'll have to get on with Janet. I'm sure we haven't any money to waste. People think we're rich, but we don't feel rich. We're always stinted when we want anything."

The consideration of the risk of the bail settled the matter with both of them. But, like other respectable people, they settled such questions in duplicate. There are two sets of reasons for any course: the one is the real and decisive motive at the bottom; the other is the pretended reason you impose on yourself and fail to impose on your neighbors. The minister accepts the call to a new church with a larger salary; he tells himself that it is on account of opportunities for increased usefulness that he changes. The politician accepts the office he didn't want out of deference to the wishes of importunate friends. A widower marries for the good of his children. These are not hypocrites imposing on their neighbors; that is a hard thing to do, unless the neighbors really wished to be humbugged in the interest of a theory. But we keep complacency whole by little impostures devised for our private benefit. It is pleasant to believe that we are acting from Sunday motives, but we always keep good substantial week-day reasons for actual service. These will bear hard usage without becoming shiny or threadbare, and they are warranted not to lose their colors in the sunshine.

"I'm sure," said Grayson, "Tom gets no good here. If anything will do him any good, it will be sending him to the country to shift for himself. It'll make a man of him, maybe." No better Sunday reason for his action could have been found.

"I think it's your duty to send him home," said his wife, who was more frightened the more she thought of the possible jeopardy of a few hundred dollars from the necessity her husband would be under of going Tom's bail. "A boy like Tom is a great deal better off with his mother," she went on; "and I'm sure we've tried to do what we could for him, and nobody can blame us if he will throw away his chance."

Thus the question was doubly settled; and as by this time Mr. Grayson's boots were off, and he had set them in the corner and pushed the boot-jack into its place under the bureau with his foot, there was no reason why they should not take the candle and retire.

But when morning came Grayson was still loth to face the matter of getting rid of Tom, and especially of contending with Janet. Tom found no chance to talk with him before breakfast, for the uncle did not come out of his bedroom till the coffee was on the table, and he was so silent and constrained that Tom felt his doom in advance. Janet tried to draw her father and then her mother into conversation, but failing, she settled back with the remark, "This is the crossest family!" Then she made an attempt on Tom, who began by this time to feel that exhilaration of desperation that was usually the first effect of a catastrophe on his combative spirit, for no man could be more impudent to fate than he. When Janet playfully stole a biscuit from his plate, he pretended to search for it everywhere, and then set in a breakfast-table romp between the two which exasperated the feelings of Grayson and his wife. When they rose from the table the uncle turned severely on his nephew, and said: "Tom——"

But before he could speak a second word, the nephew, putting Janet aside, interrupted him with:

"Uncle, I should like to speak with you alone a minute."

They went into the sitting-room together, and Tom closed the door. Tom was resolved to have the first of it.

"Uncle, I think I had better go home." Tom was looking out of the window as he spoke. "I got into a row last week through George Lockwood, who persuaded me to play cards for money with Dave Sovine. I don't want to get you into any trouble, so I'm off for Hubbard Township, if you don't object. There's no use of crying over spilt milk, and that's all there is about it."

"I'm very sorry, Tom, that you won't pay attention to what I've said to you about card-playing." The elder Grayson had seated himself, while Tom now stood nervously listening to his uncle's voice, which was utterly dry and business-like; there was not the slightest quiver of feeling in it. "I've got on in the world without anybody to help me, but I never let myself play cards, and I've always kept my temper. You never make any money by getting mad, and if you're going to make any money, it's better to have people friendly. Now, I have to stand a good deal of abuse. People try to cheat me, and if I take the law they call me a skinflint; but I shouldn't make a cent more by quarreling, and I might lose something. I can't keep you, and have you go on as you do. I've told you that before. You'd better go home. Town will ruin you. A little hard work in the country'll be better, and you won't be gambling away the last cent you've got with a loafer like Dave Sovine, and then threatening to shoot somebody, as you did young Lockwood day before yesterday. Just think what you are coming to, Tom. I've done my best for you, and you'll never be anything but a gambler and a loafer, I'm afraid."

These hard words sounded harder in the level and self-complacent voice of the senior Grayson, who spoke slowly and with hardly more intensity than there would have been in his depreciation of a horse he was trying to buy. "Just think what you're coming to," he repeated, because he felt that the proper thing to do under the circumstances was to give Tom a good "talking to," and he couldn't think of anything more to say.

"I don't need you to tell me what I'm coming to," replied Tom, tartly; "I'm coming to the plow-handle and the grubbing-hoe. I'm sorry to give you trouble, but what I feel meanest about is mother and poor Barbara. I know what a fool I've been. But I'm no more a gambler and a loafer than you are. It'll take me longer to work into the law by myself, but I'll get there yet, and you'll see it."

This was Tom's only adieu to his uncle, on whom confessions of wrong and expressions of gratitude, had he felt like uttering them, would have been wasted. Tom went to his room, thumping his feet defiantly on the stairs. He made a bundle of his clothes, while his uncle sneaked out of the house to avoid a collision with his little daughter, the only person of whom he was afraid.

Tom told his Aunt Charlotte good-bye with a high head; but when it came to Janet, he put both arms about the child and drew her to him with a fond embrace.

"You shan't go away, Tom," she said, disengaging herself. "What are you going for? Did they say you must?" By "they" Janet meant her parents, whom she regarded as the allied foes of poor Tom. She looked indignantly at her mother, who had turned her back on this scene of parting.

"I'm going to help my mother," said Tom; "she's poor, and I oughtn't to have left her."

He again embraced the child, who began to cry bitterly. "What shall I do when you're gone?" she sobbed on his shoulder. "This house won't be fit to live in. Such a lot of old pokes!" And she stamped her feet and looked poutingly at her mother.

Tom disengaged himself from her intermittent embraces, and went out with his bundle in his hand.

He went first to the law-office, and sat his bundle on a chair, and addressed himself to Blackman, who had already arrived, and who was apparently much preoccupied with his writing.

"Mr. Blackman, I've made a fool of myself by gambling, and Uncle Tom has concluded I can't stay with him any longer. I don't much wonder at it either. But I do hate to give up the study. Couldn't you give me something to do, so that I could earn my board at your house?"

"No," said the lawyer, looking off horizontally, but not at Tom. "I was just going to tell you I couldn't keep you in the office. You've got altogether too much gunpowder for a lawyer. Better get into the regular army, Tom; that would suit your temper better." Then, after a moment's pause, he added: "I've got young sons, and your example might ruin them if you should come to my house to live." And he leaned forward as though he would resume his writing. These were sound and logical reasons that Blackman gave for not keeping Tom, and the lawyer was sincere as far as he went. But had he discovered by this time that Tom's mind was clearer and more acute than his own, and that if Tom should come to the bar with his uncle's backing he would soon be a formidable rival?

"Besides," resumed the lawyer, as Tom turned reluctantly away, "it's better for you to go to the country. George Lockwood will have you bound over to keep the peace if you stay, and now you're out with your uncle, who's going your bail?"

"Always George Lockwood," Tom thought, as he took up his bundle.

"Good-bye, Mr. Blackman!" Tom's voice was husky now. But when he descended the stairs he went down the village street with a bold front, telling his old cronies good-bye, answering their questions frankly, and braving it out to the last. Put the best face upon it he could, his spirit was bitter, and to a group of old companions who followed him to the "corporation line," at the edge of the village, he said, almost involuntarily:

"George Lockwood got me into this scrape to upset me, and he's purty well done it. If he ever crosses my path, I'm going to get even with him."

Such vague threats do not bind one to any definite execution, and they are a relief to the spirit of an angry man.

Having broken with his uncle, Tom must walk the long ten miles to his mother's farm in Hubbard Township. Before he got there his head was down; the unwonted fatigue of his journey, the bitter sense of defeat, the dark picture his imagination made of his mother's disappointment and of the despair of the ambitious Barbara took all the heart out of him.

When he reached home he strode into the house and sat down without saying a word.

"Has Uncle Tom turned you off?" asked Barbara, faltering a little and putting down her knitting. She had been dreading this end of all her hopes.

"Yes," said Tom; "and I wish to the Lord I was dead and done for." And he leaned his head on his left hand.

"Oh, my poor boy!" began Mrs. Grayson, "and you didn't mean no harm neither. And you're the only boy I've got, too. All the rest dead and gone. They's no end of troubles in this world!"

Tom's shoulders were heaving with feeling. After a moment or two of silence, Barbara went over and put her hand on him.

"Pshaw, Tom! what's the use of giving up? You're a splendid fellow in spite of all, and you'll make your way yet. You only needed a settler, and now you've got it. It won't look so bad by next week. You'll take a school next winter, and after that go back to study law again."

Then she quietly went to the clothes-press by the chimney and got out a hank of yarn, and said to Tom:

"Here, hold this while I wind it. I was just wishing you were here when I saw my ball giving out. That's like you used to do for me. Don't you remember? Mother, get Tom something to eat; he's tired and hungry, I expect."

And choking down the disappointment which involved more than Tom suspected, the keen, black-eyed girl wound her yarn and made an effort to chat with Tom as though he had come home on a visit.

As the last strands were wound on the ball, Tom looked at his sister and said:

"Barbara, you're one of a thousand. But I know this thing's thundering hard on you. I'm going to try to make it up to you from this time. I wish to goodness I had half of your steady sense."

# VIII

## BARBARA'S PRIVATE AFFAIRS

From childhood Barbara's ambition had centered in Tom; it was her plan that the clever brother should give standing to the family by his success in life. If Tom could only be persuaded to be steady, he might come to be a great man. A great man, in her thinking, was a member of the State legislature, or a circuit judge, for example: to her provincial imagination the heights above these were hazy and almost inaccessible. The scheme of a professional career for Tom had been her own, in conception and management; for though her brother was nearly two years her senior, she, being prudent and forecasting, had always played the part of an elder. Tom's undeniable "brightness" was a great source of pride to her. In spite of his heedless collisions with the masters, he was always at the head of his classes; and it seemed to Barbara the most natural thing in the world that she, being a girl, should subordinate herself to the success of a brother so promising. She had left school to devote herself to the house and the cares of the farm, in order that Tom might be educated—in the moderate sense of the word then prevalent. The brother was far from being ungrateful; if he accepted

40

his sister's sacrifices without protest, he repaid her with a demonstrative affection and admiration not often seen in brothers; and there were times when he almost reverenced in her that prudence and practical wisdom in which he found himself deficient.

It was only during this summer that Barbara had been seized with independent aspirations for herself; and perhaps even these were not without some relation to Tom. If Tom should come to be somebody in the county, she would sit in a reflected light as his sister. It became her, therefore, not to neglect entirely her own education. To go to Moscow to a winter school was out of the question. Every nerve was strained to extricate the farm from debt and to give a little help, now and then, to Tom. It chanced, however, that a student from an incipient Western college, intent on getting money to pay his winter's board bills, had that summer opened a "pay school" in the Timber Creek district school-house, which was only two miles from the Grayson farm.

Those who could attend school in the summer were, for the most part, small fry too young to be of much service in the field, and such girls, larger and smaller, as could be spared from home. But the appetite for "schooling" in the new country was always greater than the supply; and when it was reported that a school was "to be took up" in the Timber Creek school-house, by a young man who had not only "ciphered plumb through the Rule of Three," but had even begun to penetrate the far-away mysteries of Latin and algebra, it came to pass that several young men and young women, living beyond the district limits, subscribed to the school, that they might attend it, even if only irregularly;—not that any of the pupils dreamed of attacking the Latin, but a teacher who had attained this Ultima Thule of human learning was supposed to know well all that lay on the hither side of it. The terms of a "pay school," in that day, were low enough,—a dollar and twenty-five cents was the teacher's charge for each pupil for thirteen weeks; but the new schoolmaster had walked from home to avoid traveling expenses, the log school-house cost him no rent, and he had stipulated that he should "board 'round" in the families of his patrons, so that the money he received from twenty pupils was clear profit, and at the price of living in those primitive times would pay his board at college for six months.

Barbara, for one, had resolved to treat herself to a dollar and a quarter's worth of additional learning. The Timber Creek school-house was on the road leading to the village of Moscow; she could therefore catch a ride, now and then, on the wagon of some farmer bound to the village, by mounting on top of a load of wood, hay, or potatoes; and often she got a lift in the evening in a neighbor's empty wagon rattling homeward from town, or for a part of the way by sitting in the tail of some ox-cart plying between forest and prairie; but more frequently she had to walk both in going and coming, besides working early and late at her household duties.

Hiram Mason was the name of the new teacher whom the pupils found behind the master's desk on the first day of school. He was the son of a minister who had come out from New England with the laudable intention of lending a hand in evangelizing this great strapping West, whose vigorous and rather boisterous youth was ever a source of bewilderment, and even a cause of grief, to the minds of well-regulated Down-easters. The evangelists sent out aimed at the impossible, even at the undesirable, in seeking to reproduce a New England in communities born under a different star. Perhaps it was this peninsular trait of mind that prevented the self-denying missionaries from making any considerable impression on the country south of the belt peopled by the current of migration from New England. The civilization of the broad, wedge-shaped region on the north side of the Ohio River, which was settled by Southern and Middle State people, and which is the great land of the Indian corn, has been evolved out of the healthier elements of its own native constitution. But it was indebted to New England, in the time of its need, for many teachers of arithmetic and grammar, as well as for the less-admirable but never-to-be-forgotten clock-peddlers and tin-peddlers from Connecticut, who also taught the rustics of southern Ohio, Indiana, and Illinois things they had never dreamed of before, and took high pay for the instruction. Young Mason, though he had mostly grown up in the new country, and would have scorned the name of Yankee, had got from his father that almost superstitious faith in the efficacy of knowledge which, in the North-eastern States, has been handed down from generation to generation, and which has produced much learning and some pedantry. Mason was of middle stature, good breadth of shoulder, prominent, broad forehead, and brows that overhung his eyes, but were rather high above them. He had a well-set chin and a solid jaw; his mouth was too large to be handsome and was firmly closed; his gait was strong, straightforward, resolute, and unhurried. There were little touches of eccentricity in him: he had a way of looking at an interlocutor askance, and his habitual expression was one of mingled shyness and self-contained amusement. The religious enthusiasm of his father had been transmuted in him to a general earnestness of character, which was veiled under a keen perception of the droll side of life, derived from a mother of Southern extraction. His early-and-late diligence in study was the wonder of the country, but the tastes and aspirations that impelled him to so much toil rarely found utterance in any confessions, even to his nearest friends. Reserved as he was, the people could never complain that he held himself above them. A new-country youth, the son of a minister on slender pay, Hiram understood how to extend a helping hand, when occasion required, in any work that might be going on. At school, when the young master saw the boys playing at the boisterous and promiscuous "soak about," he would sometimes catch the contagion of the wild fun, and, thrusting his "Livy" into the desk, rush out of the door to mix in the confusion, throwing the yarn ball at one and another with a vigor and an accuracy of aim that doubled the respect of his pupils for him. But when once he had extricated himself from the mélée, and had rapped on the door-frame with his ruler, crying, "Books, books!" the boy who a minute before had enjoyed the luxury of giving the master what was known in school-boy lingo as a "sockdolager," delivered full in the back, or even on the side of the head, did not find any encouragement to presume on that experience in school-hours.

The new master's punishments usually had a touch of his drollery in them; he contrived to make the culprit ridiculous, and so to keep the humor of the school on his side. A girl who could not otherwise be cured of munching in school had to stand in front of the master's desk with an apple in her teeth; a boy who was wont to get his sport by pinching his neighbors, and sticking them with pins, was forced to make no end of amusement for the school in his turn, by standing on the hearth with a cleft stick pinching his nose out of shape. It was soon concluded that there was no fun in "fooling" with a master who was sure to turn the joke on the offender.

The older pupils who occupied the "writing bench," in front of a continuous shelf-like desk fixed along the wall, spent much of their time in smuggling from one to another fervid little love notes, which, for disguise, were folded like the "thumb-papers" that served to protect their books from the wear and tear of their over-vigorous thumbs, and from soiling. By passing books from one to another, with such innocent-looking square papers in them, a refreshing correspondence was kept up. This exchange of smuggled billets-doux was particularly active when Rachel Albaugh was present. As for the love-letters thus dispatched, they were fearfully monotonous and not worth the pains of capture by a schoolmaster. Some were straightforward and shameless declarations of admiration and affection in prose scrawls, but a very common sort was composed entirely of one or another of those well-worn doggerel couplets that have perhaps done duty since the art of writing became known to the Anglo-Saxons.

"If you love me as I love you,
No knife can cut our love in two,"

was a favorite with the swains of the country school-house; but

"The rose is red, the violet's blue,
Sugar's sweet, and so are you,"

had a molasses-like consistency in its alliterative lines that gave it the preference over all other love poems extant.

Amongst these unblushing scribblers of love doggerel and patient cutters and folders of many sorts of thumb-papers, whose fits of studying, like chills and fever, came on only "by spells," Barbara sat without being one of them. The last chance for education was not to be thrown away; and Mason soon singled out this rather under-sized, sharp-eyed girl, not only as the most industrious and clever of the pupils in the Timber Creek school, but as a person of quite another sort from the rest of them. When he was explaining anything to a group of half-listless scholars, her dark eyes, drawn to beads, almost startled him with their concentrated interest. She could not be taught in any kind of classification with the rest; her rate of progress was too rapid. So finding that Barbara studied all through the recess time, he undertook to give her extra instruction while the others were on the playground. The most agreeable minutes of his day were those in which he unfolded to her the prosaic principles of Vulgar Fractions, of Tare and Tret, and of the Rule of Three. This last was the great and final goal, and it was attained by few of those who attended an intermittent country school in that time. To reach it was to become competent to teach school. Barbara, with the help of the master, who directed her to save time by omitting some of the rubbish in Pike's Arithmetic, was soon in sight of this promised land of the Rule of Three, and it became a question of reviewing the book once more, when she should be through with it, so as to take rank among those who would certainly "do every sum in the book."

"Why not take up algebra?" said the teacher to her, during a long noon recess as they sat side by side at his desk poring over a slate full of figures.

"Do you think I could learn it?" she asked.

"You could learn anything," he said; and the assurance gave Barbara more pleasure than any commendation she had ever received. But she did not know what to reply. To go beyond the arithmetic would be, according to the standard of the country, to have a liberal education, and she was ambitious enough to like that.

But where would she get the money to buy a text-book? She didn't wish to confess her scruple of economy. It was not that she was ashamed of her poverty, for poverty might be said to be the prevailing fashion in the Timber Creek country; but it would be bringing to Mason's attention her private affairs, and from that she shrank with an instinct of delicacy for which she could not have given any reason. Yet there sat Mason, leaning back and waiting for her to reply to his question. After a few moments she mustered courage to ask timidly:

"Would the book cost much?"

"I wouldn't buy any book just now," said the master, seeing the drift of her thoughts. He went to one corner of the school-room, and, standing on the bench, pushed aside one of the boards laid loosely over the joists above. It was here, in the dark loft, that he kept the few articles not necessary to his daily existence in boarding 'round. Reaching his hand up above the boards, he found a copy of a school text-book on algebra, and brought it down with him, rapping it against his hand and blowing the dust off it.

"Use that for a while," he said.

"Oh, thank you!" said Barbara, taking hold of the book with a curious sense of reverence, which was greatly increased as she turned the leaves and regarded the symbols, whose nature and use were quite inconceivable to her. Here was a knowledge beyond any that she had ever dreamed of looking into; beyond that of any schoolmaster she had ever known, except Mason. "It looks hard," she said, regarding him.

"Take it home and try it," he replied, as he took up his ruler to call the scholars to books.

A closer companionship now grew up between the master and the pupil. Both of them anticipated with pleasure the coming of recess time, when the new study could be discussed together. Henceforth the boys looked in vain for Mason to take a turn with them in playing soak-about.

To a man of high aims nothing is more delightful than to have a devoted disciple. Even the self-contained Mason could not be quite unmoved in contemplating this young girl, all of whose tastes and ambitions flowed in the same channel with his own, listening to him as to an oracle. If he had not been so firmly fixed in his resolve that he would not allow any woman to engage his affections before he had completed his college course, he might have come to fall in love with her. But all such thoughts he resolutely put aside. Of course, teaching her was a delight; but who could help feeling delight in teaching such a learner? Moreover, he was particularly fond of algebra. But he could hardly lay all of his enjoyment to his

45

liking for algebra, or his pleasure in teaching a quick-witted pupil. He could not make himself believe that it was his enjoyment of algebraic generalizations that made his hand tremble whenever he returned a slate or book to Barbara Grayson.

Barbara, for her part, was too intent on her work to think much about anything else. She had more than once caught sight of the furtive, inquiring glance of her teacher on her face before he could turn his eyes away; she was pleased to note that his voice had a tone in addressing her that it had not when he spoke to the others; and she took pleasure in perceiving that she was beyond question the favorite pupil. But Barbara was averse to building any castles in the air which she had small chance of being able to materialize.

One evening, as she was going briskly toward home, she was overtaken by Mason, who walked with her up hill and down dale the whole long rough new-country road through the woods, carrying her books, and chatting about trivial things as he had never done before. He contrived, half in pleasantry, but quite in earnest, to praise her diligence, and even her mind. She had hardly ever thought of herself as having a mind. That Tom had such a gift she knew, and she understood how important it was to cultivate his abilities. But she was only Tom's sister. It seemed to her a fine thing, however, this having a mind of her own, and she thought a good deal about it afterward.

When Hiram Mason reached the place where Barbara was accustomed to leave the main road, in order to reach her home by a shorter path through a meadow, he got over the fence first and gave her his hand, though he wondered afterward that he had had the courage to do it. Barbara had climbed fences and trees too, for that matter, from her infancy, and she was in the habit of getting over this fence twice a day, without ever dreaming that she needed help. But a change had come over her in this two-miles' walk from school. For the first time, she felt a certain loneliness in her life, and a pleasure in being protected. She let Mason take her hand and help her to the top of the fence, though she could have climbed up much more nimbly if she had had both hands free to hold by. Hiram found it so pleasant helping her up, by holding her hand, that he took both her hands when she was ready to jump down on the meadow side of the fence, and then, by an involuntary impulse he retained her right hand in his left a bare moment longer than was necessary. A little ashamed, not so much of the feeling he had shown as of that he had concealed, he finished his adieux abruptly, and, placing his hands on the top rail, vaulted clean over the fence again into the road. Then he thought of something else that he wanted to say about Barbara's new study of algebra,—something of no consequence at all, except in so far as it served to make Barbara turn and look at him once more. The odd twinkling smile so habitual with him died out of his face, and he looked into hers with an eagerness that made her blush, but did not make her turn away. Blaming himself for what seemed to him imprudence, he left her at last and started back, only stopping on the next high ground to watch her figure as she hurried along through the meadow grass, and across the brook, and then up the slope toward the house.

There were several other evenings not very different from this one. The master would wait until all the pupils had gone, and then overtake Barbara. He solaced his conscience by carrying a book in his pocket, so as to study on the way back; but he found a strange wandering of the mind in his endeavors to read a dead language after a walk with Barbara. He still held to his resolution, or to what was left of his resolution, not to entangle himself with an early engagement. What visions he indulged in, of projects to be carried out in a very short time after his graduation, belong to the secrets of his own imagination; all his follies shall not be laid bare here. But to keep from committing himself too far, he drew the line at the boundary of Mrs. Grayson's farm,—the meadow fence. He gave himself a little grace, and drew the line on the inside of the fence. He was firmly resolved never to go quite home with his pupil, and never to call at her house. So long as he stopped at the fence, or within ten, or say twenty, or perhaps thirty, feet of it he felt reasonably safe. But he could not, in common civility, turn back until he had helped her to surmount this eight-rail fence; and indeed it was the great treat to which he always looked forward. There was a sort of permissible intimacy in such an attention. He guarded himself, however, against going beyond the limits of civility—of kindly politeness—of polite friendship; that was the precise phrase he hit on at last. But good resolutions often come to naught because of its being so very difficult to reckon beforehand with the involuntary and the uncontrollable. The goodman of the house never knows at what moment the thief will surprise him. One evening Mason had taken especial pains to talk on only the most innocent and indifferent subjects, such as algebra. On this theme he was the schoolmaster, and he felt particularly secure against any expression of feeling, for x, y, and z are unknown quantities that have no emotion in them. Though Barbara was yet in the rudiments of the study, he was trying to make her understand the general principles involved in the discussion of the famous problem of the lights. To make this clear he sat down once or twice on logs lying by the roadside, and wrote some characters on her slate showing the relation of a to b in any given case, while Barbara sat by and looked

47

over his demonstrations. But in spite of these delays, they got to the fence before he had finished, and the rest was postponed for another time. It didn't matter so much about the lights after all, whether they were near together or far apart; it does not matter to lights, but there are flames much affected by proximity. As Mason helped Barbara down from the fence, his passion, by some sudden assault, got the better of his prudence, and looking intently into the eyes shaded by the sun-bonnet, he came out with:

"It's all the world to a fellow like me to have such a scholar as you are, Barbara."

The words were mild enough; but his eager manner and his air of confidence, as he stood in front of her sun-bonnet and spoke, with his face flushed, and in a low and unsteady voice, made his speech a half confession. Startled at this sudden downfall of his resolution, he got back over the fence and went straight away, without giving her a chance to say anything; without so much as uttering a civil good-bye. The precipitation of his retreat only served to lend the greater significance to his unpremeditated speech.

Mrs. Grayson complained that there was "no sense in a girl's studyin' algebra, an' tryin' to know more 'n many a good schoolmaster ever knowed when I was a girl. Ever since Barbary's been at that new-fangled study, it's seemed like as if she'd somehow'r nuther gone deranged. She'll say supper's ready when they ain't knife nur fork on the table; an' she's everlastin'ly losin' her knittin'-needles an' puttin' her thimble where she can't find it, or mislayin' her sun-bonnet. Ef her head was loose, she'd be shore to leave that around somewheres, liker'n not."

If Hiram Mason's half-involuntary love-making had not brought Barbara unmeasured pleasure she would not have been the normal young woman that she was. He filled all her ideals, and went beyond the highest standard she had set up before she knew him. She was not the kind of a girl that one meets nowadays; at least, that one meets nowadays in novels. She did not have a lot of perfectly needless and inconceivably fine-spun conscientious scruples to prevent the course of her fortune from running smoothly. She did find in herself a drawing back from the future which Mason's partiality had brought within the range of her vision. But her scruple was only one of pride; she exaggerated the superiority of an educated family, such as she conceived his to be, and she reflected that the Graysons were simple country people. She felt in herself that she could never endure the mortification she would feel, as Hiram's wife, if the Masons should look down on her good but unlettered mother, and say or feel that Hiram had "married below him." If, now, Tom should come to something, the equation would be made good.

But the very day after Mason had spoken so warmly of the comfort he found in such a pupil was that disagreeable Saturday on which Tom had come home plucked in gambling, to ask for money enough to pay the debt he had incurred in redeeming his clothes. Was it any wonder that Barbara spoke to him with severity when she found her cherished vision becoming an intangible illusion? Tom would make no career at all at this rate; and to yield to Hiram Mason's wooing would now be to bring to him, not only the drawback of a family of humble breeding and slender education, but the disgrace of a rash, unsteady, and unsuccessful brother, whose adventures with gamblers would seem particularly disreputable to a minister's family. There was no good in thinking about it any more. Her pride could never bear to be "looked down on" by the family of her husband. It would be better to give it up at once—unless—she clung to this possibility—unless Tom should turn out right after all. The necessity for surrendering so much imminent happiness did not surprise her. She had always had to forego, and no prospect of happiness could seem quite possible of realization to an imagination accustomed to contemplate a future of self-denial. None the less, the disappointment was most acute, for she must even give up the school, and try, by spinning yarn, by knitting stockings, and by weaving jeans and linsey, to make up the money taken out of their little fund by Tom's recklessness.

On the next Monday, and the days following, she staid at home without sending any word to the schoolmaster. She held to a lurking hope that Tom's affairs might mend, and she be able, by some good luck, to resume her attendance on the school for a part of the remainder of the quarter. But when on Wednesday Tom's haggard face appeared at the door, and she read in it that all her schemes for him had miscarried, she knew that she must give up dreaming dreams which seemed too good to be innocent. There was nothing for her but to give herself to doing what could be done for Tom. It was lucky that the poor fellow did not suspect what it cost her to put a smooth face on his disasters.

# IX

# BY THE LOOM

On Monday, Mason saw with regret that Barbara was not at school. On Tuesday he felt solicitous, and would have made inquiry if it had not been for an impulse of secretiveness. By Wednesday he began to fear that his words spoken to her at the meadow fence had something to do with her absence. He questioned the past. He could not remember that she had ever repelled his attentions, or that she had seemed displeased when he had spoken his fervent and unpremeditated words. Aware that his bearing toward Barbara had attracted the observation of the school, he did not summon courage to ask about her until Thursday. Then when the voluble Mely McCord came to him before the beginning of the afternoon session, to ask how she should proceed to divide 130 by 9, he inquired if Barbara was ill.

"No, I don't 'low she's sick," responded Mely. "I sh'd 'a' thought she'd tole you, 'f anybody, what't wuz kep' 'er"; and Mely laughed a malicious little snicker, which revealed her belief that the master was in confidential relations with his algebra scholar. "She thinks the worl'n'all of the school an' the master." Mely gasped a little as she ventured this thrust, and quickly added, "An' of algebray—she's that fond of algebray; but I sh'd thought she'd 'a' tole you what kep' 'er, ur'a' sen' choo word. But I 'low it's got sumpin' to do weth the trouble in the family."

Mely made what the old schoolmasters called a "full stop" at this point, as though she considered it certain that Mason would know all about Barbara's affairs.

"Trouble? What trouble?" asked the master.

"W'y, I 'low'd you'd 'a' knowed," said the teasing creature, shaking her rusty ringlets, with a fluttering, half-suppressed amusement at the anxiety she had awakened in Mason's mind. "Hain' choo h-yeard about her brother?"

"No; which brother? The one that's in Moscow?"

"W'y, lawsy, don'choo know't she hain't got nary nuther one? The res' 's all dead an' buried long ago. Her brother Tom lost 'is sitooation along of gamblin' an' the like. They say he lost the boots offviz feet an' the coat offviz back." Here Mely had to give vent to her feelings in a hearty giggle; Tom's losses seemed to her a joke of the best, and all the better that the master took it so seriously. "I 'low it's cut Barb'ry up more'n a little. She sot sech store by Tom. An' he is smart, the smartest feller you'd find fer books an' the like. But what's the use a-bein' so smart an' then bein' sech a simple into the bargain? I say."

Mason did not like to ask further questions about Barbara's family affairs. He could hardly bear to hear Mely canvass them in this unsympathetic way. But there was one more inquiry that he made about Tom.

"Does he drink?"

"Mighty leetle. I 'xpect he takes a drop ur two now an' then, jest fer company's sake when he's a-cavortin' 'roun' weth the boys. But I 'low he hain't got no rale hankerin' fer the critter, an' he's that fond of Barb'ry 'n' 'is mother, an' they're so sot on 'im, that he would n' noways like to git reg'lar drunk like. But he's always a-gittin' into a bad crowd, an' tryin' some deviltry'r nuther; out uv one scrape an' into t'other, kind-uh keerless like; head up an' never ketchin' sight 'v a stump tell he's fell over it, kerthump, head over heels. His uncle's been a-schoolin' 'im, an' lately he's gone 'n' put 'im weth Squire Blackman to learn to be a lawyer; but now he's up 'n' sent him home fer a bad bargain. Ut's no go't the law, an' he won't never stan' a farm, yeh know. Too high-sperrited."

Possessed of a share of Mely McCord's stock of information about Barbara's troubles, Hiram Mason saw that his resolution against calling on his pupil at her own house would have to go the way of most of his other resolutions on this subject. He set himself to find arguments against keeping this one, but he was perfectly aware, all the time, that his going to the Graysons' would not depend on reasons at all. He reflected, however, that Barbara's trouble was a new and unforeseen condition. Besides, his regulative resolutions had been so far strained already that they were not worth the keeping. It is often thus in our dealings with ourselves; we argue from defection to indulgence.

Mely McCord felt sure of having the master's company after school as far as she had to go on the road leading to the Graysons'. But he went another way to Pearson's, where he was boarding out the proportion due for three pupils. Mrs. Pearson had intermitted the usual diet of corn-dodgers, and had baked a skilletful of hot biscuits, in honor of the master; she was a little piqued that he should absorb them, as he did, in a perfectly heartless way, and she even apologized for them, asserting that they were not so good as usual, in the vain hope that the master would wake up and contradict her. As soon as the early supper was over Hiram left the house, without saying anything of his destination. He took a "short cut" across a small prairie, then through the woods, and across Butt's corn-field, until he came out on the road near the place at

51

which he had several times helped Barbara over the fence. By her path through the meadow he reached the house just as the summer twilight was making the vault of the sky seem deeper and mellowing all the tones in the landscape. In that walk Mason's mind had completely changed front. Why should he try to maintain a fast-and-loose relation with Barbara? She was in need of his present sympathy and help. Impulses in his nature, the strength of which he had never suspected, were beating against the feeble barriers he had raised. Of what use was this battle, which might keep him miserable awhile longer, but which could end in but one way? As he walked through the narrow meadow path, in the middle of which the heavy overhanging heads of timothy grass, now ready for the scythe, touched one another, so that his legs brushed them aside at every step, he cast away the last tatters of his old resolves. The dams were down; the current might flow whither it listed. He would have it out with Barbara this very evening, and end the conflict.

It is by some such only half-rational process that the most important questions of conduct are usually decided—sometimes luckily; in other cases, to the blighting of the whole life. Is it not rather a poor fist of a world after all, this in which we live, where the most critical and irrevocable decisions must be made while the inexperienced youth is tossed with gusts of passion and blinded by traditional prejudices or captivated by specious theories? The selection of wives and vocations, the two capital elements in human happiness and success, is generally guided by nothing higher than the caprice of those whose judgments are in the gristle. Often the whole course of life of the strong, clear-seeing man yet to come is changed forever by a boy's whim. The old allegorists painted the young man as playing chess with the devil; but chess is a game of skill. What the young man plays is often a child's game of pitch and toss, cross or pile, heads or tails, for stakes of fearful magnitude. Luckily for Hiram, as you and I know from our present acquaintance with Barbara, nothing more disastrous than disappointment was likely to happen to him from his inability to keep his mortifying resolves. The abandonment of them had simplified his feelings and brought him present relief. When he knocked on the jamb of the open front door of the Grayson farm-house, and was invited to come in by the mother, there was a wholeness in his feelings and purposes to which he had been a stranger for weeks.

"Barb'ry," said Mrs. Grayson as she entered the kitchen, after giving Hiram a chair, "here's the master come to see you. I 'low he thought you mought be sick ur sumpin'."

Barbara sat perched on the loom-bench, with her back to the

52

web she had been weaving. Just now she was peeling, quartering, and coring summer apples to dry for winter stores. She untied her apron and went from the kitchen into the sitting-room, where Mason was looking about, as was his habit, in a quizzical, half-amused way. He had noted the wide stone fire-place, the blackness of whose interior was hidden by the bushy asparagus tops which filled it, and the wooden clock on the unpainted mantel-piece, which had a print of the death-bed of George Washington impaneled in its door. A stairway winding up in one corner gave picturesqueness to the room; diagonally across from this was a high post bed; there were some shuck-bottom chairs, a splint-bottom rocking-chair, and a bureau with a looking-glass on top. The floor was covered with a new rag-carpet, and the comfortable, home-like sentiment excited in Hiram's mind by the general aspect of the room was enhanced by a hearth cricket, which, in one of the crevices of the uneven flag-stones, was already emitting little vibrant snatches like the black fiddler that he was, tuning up for an evening performance.

The sight of Mason dissipated for the moment the clouds that darkened Barbara's thoughts; she saw blue sky for the first time since Tom's first return. It was a pleased and untroubled face that met his gaze when she extended her hand to him.

"Howdy, Mr. Mason!"

Mason fixed his eyes on her in his odd fashion, half turning his head aside, and regarding her diagonally.

"Well, Barbara, you're the lost sheep," was his greeting. "I was afraid you wouldn't come back to the flock if I didn't come into the wilderness and look you up."

"There's been such a lot of things to do this week," she answered hurriedly, "I didn't know how to get time to go to school."

This was truthful, but it was far from being frank, and it was not on these terms that Mason wished to meet her. His first thought was to put her more at ease.

"Can't we sit out on the porch?" he said; "I'm warm with walking." And he lifted two of the chairs and carried them to the covered porch. There would soon be no light outside but what came from the night sky, and what a dim candle in the sitting-room, when it should be lighted, might manage to spare through the open door. Hiram had a notion that in this obscurity he could coax Barbara out of the diplomatic mood into the plain indicative. But before they had sat down he had changed his plan.

"Hold on," he said, more to himself than to her; and added, "What were you doing when I came?"

"Only peeling some apples to dry."

53

"Let me help you; we'll have an apple-peeling all to ourselves."

"No," said Barbara, hesitatingly; but Mason went through the sitting-room and, opening the kitchen door, thrust his head through and said:

"Mayn't I sit out there and help Barbara peel apples, Mrs. Grayson?"

"You may do what you like, Mr. Mason," said the old lady, pleased with his familiarity; "but peelin' apples ain't jest the kind of work to set a schoolmaster at."

"Schoolmasters a'n't all of them so good for nothing as you think. Come on, Barbara, a little apple-peeling will make it seem like home to me; and this living 'round in other people's houses has made me homesick."

Barbara came out and took her old place on the loom-bench, beside the great three-peck basket of yellow apples. Her seat raised her considerably higher than Mason, who occupied a low chair. In front of Barbara was another chair, on which sat a pan to hold the quarters of apples when prepared for drying; on one of the rungs of this Barbara supported her feet. The candle which Mrs. Grayson lighted shed a dim yellow light from one end of the high smoke-blackened mantel-shelf, which extended across the chimney above the cavernous kitchen fire-place. The joists of the loft were of heavy logs, and these, and the boards which overlaid them, and all the woodwork about this kitchen, were softened and sombered by the smoke that had escaped from the great, rude chimney; for the kitchen was the original log-cabin built when Tom's father, fresh from Maryland, had first settled on the new farm; the rest of the house had grown from this kernel.

The mother, who had not dreamed of any relation between Barbara and Hiram Mason more friendly than that of master and pupil, was a little surprised at the apparently advanced stage of their acquaintance; but she liked it, because it showed that the schoolmaster was not "stuck up," and that he understood that "our Barb'ry" was no common girl. Tom looked in at the open outside door of the kitchen after a while, and was pleased. "Barb deserved a nice beau if ever anybody did," he reflected, and it might keep her from feeling so bad over his own failures. Not wishing to intrude, and wearied to exhaustion with his first day of farm-work since his return, he went around to the front door and through the sitting-room upstairs to bed. When the mother had finished "putting things to rights" she went into the sitting-room, and the apple-peelers were left with only the loom, the reel, and the winding-blades for witnesses.

They talked of school, of their studies, and of many other

54

things until the great basket of apples began to grow empty while the basket of parings and corings was full. The pan of apple-quarters having overflowed had been replaced by a pail, which was also nearly full, when, after a playful scuffle of hands in the basket, Hiram secured the last apple and peeled it. Then laying down his knife, he asked:

"You'll be back at school next week?"

Barbara had been dreading this inquiry. She wished Mason had not asked it. She had heartily enjoyed his society while they talked of things indifferent, but the question brought her suddenly and painfully back into the region of her disappointment and perplexities.

"I'm afraid I can't come any more. Things haven't gone right with us." The wide spaces between her words indicated to her companion the effort it cost to allude to her affairs.

Mason was more than ever puzzled. By what means could he establish such a ground of confidence between them as would enable him to enter into her difficulties and give her, at the least, the help of his sympathy and counsel? There seemed no way so good as that by direct approach.

"Barbara," he said, drawing his chair nearer to the loom-bench and leaning forward toward her, "won't you please tell me about your affairs, if—if you can do it? I don't want to intrude, but why can't you let me be your best friend and—help you if I can?"

This speech had a different effect from what Mason had intended. Barbara's pride resented an offer of help from him. Of all things, she did not wish to be pitied by the man she was beginning to love. He would always think of her as lower than himself, and she had too much pride to relish anything like the rôle of Cophetua's beggar maid.

"I can't do it, Mr. Mason; there's nothing anybody can do." She spoke with her eyes downcast. Having ventured so much and gained nothing, Mason leaned back in his chair and turned his head about to what a photographer would call a "three-quarters position," and looked at Barbara from under his brows without saying anything more. He was like a pilot waiting for the fog to lift. This silent regard made Barbara uneasy. She could not help feeling a certain appreciation of his desire to help her, however disagreeable it might be to her feelings. Perhaps she was wrong to repel his confidence so abruptly.

"I suppose you know about poor Tom?" she said, making so much concession to his kindness, but half swallowing the rapidly spoken words.

"Yes," said Hiram; "I heard he had got into a scrape such as

55

many a bright boy gets into. A village like Moscow is a hard place for a boy raised in the country. But he'll pull out of that."

It lifted a weight from Barbara's mind that Mason did not take a too serious view of Tom. She wished, however, that he would not look at her so long in that askance fashion.

"Did the trouble cost you much money?" he ventured to inquire after a while.

"Well, no, not much for some folks, but a good deal for us; we're rather poor, you know." There is a pride that conceals poverty; there is a greater pride that makes haste to declare it, feeling that only hidden poverty is shameful. "You know father was a smart man in some ways," Barbara continued, "but he hadn't any knack. He lost most of his money before he came to Illinois; and then when he got here he made the mistake, that so many made, of settling in the timber, though very little of the prairie had been taken up yet. If he hadn't been afraid of the winters on the prairie, we might have been pretty well off; but it's been a hard struggle opening a farm in the woods. Then we have had nothing but misfortune. My father died of a congestive chill, and then my three brothers and my sister died, and Tom and I are all that's left to mother. And there are doctor's bills to pay yet, and a little debt on the farm."

"Yes, yes," said Hiram, wounded in thinking of the pain he was giving Barbara in forcing her to speak thus frankly of the family troubles. "I know what it is. Poverty and I are old acquaintances; regular old cronies. She's going to stand by my side till I graduate, anyhow; but as I have known her ever since I was born, I can afford to laugh in her face. There's nothing like being used to a thing."

Barbara made no reply to this. Mason sat and looked at her awhile in silence. There was no good in trying to help her on his present footing. He leaned forward, resting his elbow on the loom-bench by her side.

"Look here, Barbara," he said, with abrupt decision, "let's, you and me, go in partnership with our poverty some day, and see what'll come of it. I suppose, so far as money is concerned, the equations would be about equal without the trouble of figuring it out."

Barbara looked at her hands in her lap with her eyes out of focus, and made no reply. After a while Hiram spoke again.

"Did I—make you mad, Barbara?" He used the word "mad" in the sense attached to it in that interior country, meaning angry.

"No, not mad," said Barbara. "Not that—but—I don't know what to say. I don't believe what you propose can ever be."

Mason waited for her to explain herself, but she did not seem

56

to be able to get her own consent. At length he got up and went to the mantel-piece and took down Barbara's slate.

"Let's talk about algebra awhile," he said.

Barbara was fond enough of algebra, but it seemed droll that Mason, with an unsettled proposition of marriage on hand, should revert to his favorite study. She could not see what he was writing, but when he passed the slate to her, she read:

$$a = \text{another lover.}$$
$$b = \text{objections to H. Mason.}$$
$$c = \text{interfering circumstances.}$$
$$x = a + b + c.$$

"Now," said Mason, when she looked up, "I'd like you to help me to get the exact value of x in this little equation. It's a kind of fortune-telling by algebra. We must proceed by elimination; you may strike out such of the letters on the right side of the last equation as do not count for anything."

But instead of proceeding as the master suggested, Barbara, whose reserve was partly dissipated by her amusement, took the pencil that he offered her, and after a moment's reflection wrote below:

$$a = 0$$
$$b = 0$$
$$x = c$$

"I never saw an equation more to my taste," said Hiram. "If it's only circumstances, then circumstances and I are going to fight it out. You think there are things that will keep us from making an equation between Barbara and Hiram?"

"There wouldn't be any equation," she said, looking out of half-closed eye-lids, as she always did when speaking with feeling. "Your family is an educated one, and your father and mother wouldn't approve of us. Mother never had any chance to learn, and her talk is very old-fashioned, but she's just as good as good can be, all the same. Tom's unsteady; I hope he'll get over that yet; but your father and mother and your sisters wouldn't like it."

"Yes, they would, if they knew you," said Mason, with enthusiasm; "and, besides, I don't see that I'm bound to get their consent."

"But that wouldn't change matters," persisted Barbara, despondingly. "If they didn't like it, it wouldn't be nice."

"Don't you bother about my happiness, Barbara. If I have you, do you think anything else will trouble me?" He got up and snuffed the candle with his fingers like the brave man that he was.

"I'm not bothering about you at all," said Barbara. "I'm not so good as you think I am. I let you take care of yourself in this matter; you're strong, and such things won't worry you." She was picking at her dress as she spoke. "Ever since you said what you did when you helped me over the fence last,"—Barbara took a long breath as she thought of that scene; she had often retraced all its details in her memory,—"I've known that you felt so toward me that you would face any thing. But I—I couldn't bear it if your folks should look down on me and I be—your wife." It was hard to say the last words; they sounded strangely, and when they were uttered, the sound of them put her into a trepidation not altogether disagreeable.

"Look down on you?" said Hiram, with a vehemence Barbara had never known him to manifest before. "Do you think my folks are such idiots? They don't meet a person like you often enough to get the habit of looking down on such."

"But you don't know women folks," said Barbara.

"I know my family better than you do, and you've got mighty curious notions about them and about yourself. You've always lived here in the woods, and you don't know what you're worth."

He lifted the empty apple-basket out of the way and sat down by her.

"Now, Barbara, you say you know how I feel toward you. You are the girl of all girls in the world for me. And now you won't spurn me, will you?" he said entreatingly.

Barbara's lips quivered and she seemed about to lose control of herself. However, after a little period of silence and struggle, she suppressed her feelings sufficiently to speak:

"I couldn't spurn you," she said. Then, after another pause: "Maybe you don't care any more for me than I do for you. But I'm in such trouble—that I can't tell what to say. Won't you wait and give me a little time? Things may be better after a while."

"How long shall I stay away? A week?" Mason's voice had a note of protest in it.

"Don't be hurt," she said, lifting her eyes timidly to his. "But I'm in such a hard place. Let me have two weeks or so to think about it, and see how things are going to turn." It was not that Barbara saw any chance for a change of circumstances, but that she could not resolve to decide the question either way, and wished to escape from her present perplexity by postponement.

"Just as you say," said Mason, regretfully; "but I tell you, Barbara, it's two weeks of dead lost time."

Then he got up and held out his hand to her.

"Good-bye, Barbara."

"Good-bye, Mr. Mason."

"Oh, call me Hiram! It's more friendly, and you call all the other young men by their first names."

"But you're the master."

"I'm not the master of you, that's clear. Besides, you've left school." He was holding her hand in gentle protest all this time.

"Well, good-bye—Hiram!" said Barbara, with a visible effort which ended in a little laugh.

Mason let go of her hand and turned abruptly and walked out of the door, and then swiftly down the meadow path. Barbara stood and looked after him as long as she could see his form; then she slowly shut and latched the kitchen door and came and covered with ashes the remaining embers of the fire, and took the candle from the mantel-piece and went through the now vacant sitting-room to her chamber above.

# X

# THE AFFAIR AT TIMBER CREEK CAMP MEETING

When Tom Grayson found himself suddenly stranded on the farmstead in Hubbard Township he went to work to learn again the arts half forgotten during his three-years' absence in Moscow. It was necessary to put his soft hands to the plow, and to burn his fair face in the hot sun of the hay-field. With characteristic heedlessness of results he set out, on the very first day after his return, to mow alongside the stalwart hired man, Bob McCord, the father of Mely. Bob lived in a little cabin not far from the Grayson place, and since Tom left the farm he had done most of the work for Mrs. Grayson. He was commonly known as "Big Bob," because he had a half-brother of sinister birth who was older than himself, but a small man, and who for distinction was "Little Bob." Big Bob fulfilled his name in every dimension. His chest was deep, his arms were gigantic in their muscularity, and no man had ever seen his legs show signs of exhaustion. His immense muscles were softened in outline by a certain moderate rotundity; his well-distributed adipose was only one of many indications of his extraordinary physical thriftiness. In more than one stand-up fight he had demonstrated his right to the title of champion of the county. Yet he was a boyishly good-natured man, with no desire to hurt anybody, and he never fought from choice. But every rising fisticuffer within half a hundred miles round had heard of Bob's strength, and the more ambitious of these had felt bound to "dare" him. It was not consonant with the honor of such a man as Bob to "take a dare"; so against first one and then another aspiring hero he had fought, until at length there was none that ventured any more to "give a dare" to the victor of so many battles. His physical perfections were not limited to mere bull strength: no man had a keener eye or a steadier hand; none could send a rifle-ball to its mark with a more unerring aim. Had he lived in the days of the Saxon invasion of England, McCord would have stood high on the list of those renowned for exploits of strength and daring, the very darling hero of the minstrel. Our own Indian wars of the seventeenth and eighteenth centuries brought renown to just such men as he, semi-barbarian path-makers for the advance of civilization. He had lagged a generation late. In the peaceful time, when strength of muscle was secondary to mental power, and when a sure aim was no longer important for the defense of one's life, nor the chief means for winning one's meat, the powerful Bob McCord saw degenerate men, whom he could have held at arms-length, prevail over him in the struggle for subsistence. For though he was capable of hard work he could never endure steady application; his nature was under mortgage to adventurous ancestors, the ancient Indian-fighters and scouts of the Appalachian country, and those more remote forefathers, the untamed emigrants who had been almost expelled from the Scottish border in the time of the Stuarts, to help resettle the devastated north of Ireland, to say nothing of the yet wilder Irish women with whom they had mated. Nothing less than the sound of the cup scraping on the bottom of the family meal-box would impel Bob to work. Every wind that came from the great sea of grass to the westward brought him the whir of the wings of prairie-hens; dreams of bear-hunting filled his mind whenever he looked into the recesses of the woods. At sight of the rising moon his hunter's soul imagined the innumerable deer which at that hour come from their coverts to graze on the prairies. Every stream tantalized him with the thought of darting perch, and great prowling cat-fish hidden beneath its surface, and challenging him to catch them if he could. If, as we are taught to believe, the manliness of the English aristocracy and that of the American apery is only kept alive by outdoor sports, how much their superior in surplus manhood must such a man as Bob McCord be! In his estimation no days were counted a part of human life except those passed in circumventing and taking the wild creatures of the woods or the prairie, and those others spent in the rude fun of musters, barbecues, elections, corn-shuckings, wood-choppings, and like assemblages, where draughts from a generous big-bellied bottle, with a twisted neck, alternated with athletic feats, practical jokes, and tales as rude as the most unblushing of those told by pious pilgrims to Canterbury in the old religious time.

It was alongside this son of Anak that Tom set himself to do a full day's work at the start. The severity of labor accorded well with his pungent feeling of penitence. Big Bob regarded him as he might any other infant, not unkindly; he even had a notion that the Widow Grayson and her children were in some sense under his care, and he did not wish any harm to come to the boy, but a practical joke was too good a thing to be missed. For two hours and a half, on that morning of Tom's appearance in the field with a scythe, Bob did not once stop to take the usual rests. Tom felt inevitable exhaustion coming on, though he cut a much narrower swath than his companion. McCord's herculean right knee was bare, having that morning forced itself through his much-bepatched trousers of butternut-dyed cotton cloth. While swinging his wider-sweeping scythe at a desperate rate, he kept telling Tom stories of adventure and the well-worn joe-millers of the log-cabin firesides, never seeming to notice the poor fellow's breathless endeavors to keep up or his ever-narrowing swath. Only when at length he turned and looked at Tom's face and perceived that the persistency of his will might carry him too far, he said, as with his scythe he picked some bunches of good grass from the edge of an elder patch and cast a wistful glance at the jug standing in a cool fence corner:

"Looky h-yer, Tom, you're a-gittin' kind-uh white-like about the gills, un 'f you try to keep up weth me, yer hide 'll be on the fence afore night."

"I know that," said Tom, who found himself so thoroughly beaten that there was no use in denying it.

"Well, hang yer scythe on that air red-haw over there un take a leetle rest, un then try a pitch-fork awhile. I 'lowed I'd see what sort uv stuff you've got, seein's you wuz so almighty gritty. A bigger man'n you couldn't hold agin me"; and Bob let the amusement he felt at Tom's discomfiture escape in a long hearty chuckle, rising at length into a loud laugh, as he reversed his scythe and fell to whetting it, making the neighboring woods ring with the tune he beat on the resonant metal,—a kind of accompaniment to the briskness of his spirit.

61

And now Barbara appeared bringing the snack that was commonly served to the mowers in the forenoon. Bob hung up his scythe, and, having taken some whisky, joined the exhausted Tom under the shady boughs of a black walnut. Barbara uncovered her basket, which contained an apple-pie to be divided between the two and a bottle of sweet milk. Tom had stretched himself in sheer exhaustion on a swath of hay.

"You foolish boy," said Barbara. "You've gone at your work too brash. You ought to be ashamed of yourself. Here, take some of this pie; and don't you work so hard the rest of the day."

"Tom," said Bob, speaking with his mouth full of pie, "'f I had the eddication you've got, you wouldn't ketch me in this yere hot sun. I'd take a school. What's eddication good fer, anyhow, ef 't ain't to git a feller out uh the hot sun?"

But for the present Tom resolved to stick faithfully to his toil. As the days wore on, and he became accustomed to the strain, he found the work a sedative; he was usually too tired to think much of his disappointment. Only the face of Rachel Albaugh haunted his visions in lonely hours, and at times a rush of indignant feeling towards George Lockwood disturbed his quiet.

In the early days of August there came a time of comparative leisure. The summer harvests were over, and the fields of tall corn had been "laid by" after the last plowing. Then Illinois had a breathing spell; and shutting up its house, and hitching up its horse, and taking all the children, it went to visit its "relations," staying a week at a place. Farmers frequented the town to meet old friends and get the better of them in swapping horses; and in this time of relaxation came the season of Baptist Associations and Methodist Camp-meetings and two-days' Basket Meetings—jolly religious picnics, where you could attend to your soul's salvation and eat "roas'in' ears" with old friends in the thronged recesses of the forests, among a people who were perhaps as gregarious as any the world has ever produced. Children looked forward to this gypsying with eagerness, and adults gave themselves over to it with the abandon of children. What night-scenes there were! Within the oval of tents at a camp-meeting two great platforms were raised on posts six or eight feet high and covered with earth; on these were built blazing bonfires, illuminating all the space inclosed by the tents and occupied by the enthusiastic assembly, which, as one great chorus, made the wide forest vocal with a tide of joyous or pathetic song. But there were two poles to the magnetism of a camp-meeting. In the region of outer blackness, quite beyond the reach of any illumination from platform bonfires or pulpit eloquence, there were also assemblies of those who were attracted by the excitement, but to whom the religious influences were a centrifugal force. Here jollity and all conceivable deviltry rejoiced also in a meet companionship.

The Great Union Camp-Meeting was held in the first half of August on the Timber Creek camp-ground, only a mile and a half from the Grayson place. The mother and Barbara went every evening and came back with accounts of the attendance, of the old friends encountered, and of the sermons of favorite preachers. They told how "powerfully" the elder had preached, and how the eloquent young preacher, who was junior on the next circuit, had carried all before him in a pathetic exhortation. But Tom showed no desire to attend. He was slowly sinking into a depression quite unusual with him. He had been accustomed to the excitement of the town, and the prospect of a life of dull routine on a farm ate into his spirit like a biting rust. Barbara amused him with stories of the camp-meeting; she told him of the eccentric German exhorter whose broken English she mimicked, and of the woman she had heard relate in a morning "speaking-meeting" that, when convinced of the sin of wearing jewelry, she had immediately taken off her ear-rings and given them to her sister. These things lightened his spirit but for a moment; he would relapse soon into the same state of mental lassitude, or more acute melancholy. Barbara endeavored to cheer him with projects; he could take a school the next winter, and with the money earned pay his board somewhere in town and take up the study of law again. But all of Barbara's projects were moderate and took full account of difficulties. Tom had little heart for a process that demanded plodding and patient waiting; nor did any of Barbara's suggestions hold out any prospect of his recovering his ground with Rachel, which was the thing he most desired.

One evening, as he finished a supper which he had eaten with little relish and in silence, he pushed back his chair and sat moodily looking into the black cave of the kitchen fire-place, where the embers were smoldering under the ashes. Then when his mother had left the kitchen, and Barbara was clearing away the plates, he said:

"The more I think of it, the worse I feel about George Lockwood. The tricky villain got me into that scrape and then told all about it where he knew it would do me the most harm. I'd just like to shoot him."

"You'd better shoot him and get yourself hanged!" said Barbara with impatience. "That would mend matters, wouldn't it?"

"'T wouldn't matter much to me," said Tom. "This country life doesn't suit me; I'd just as well be out of it, and they do say hanging is an easy way of dying." This last was spoken with a grim smile.

"I suppose you don't think of us," said Barbara.

"I'm more trouble than good to you and mother."

"And now if you would only commit a crime"—Barbara was looking at him with a concentrated gaze—"that would put an end to all mother's sorrows; she would soon die in torture, and I would be left alone in the world to be pointed at by people who would say in a whisper: 'That's the sister of the fellow that was hanged.'" And Barbara caught her breath with a little gasp as she turned away.

"Oh, don't talk that way, Barb! Of course I don't mean to do anything of the sort. It's a kind of relief to talk sometimes, and I do feel bitter enough."

Barbara turned sharply on him again and said: "That's just the way to get to be a murderer—keep stirring up your spite. After a while the time'll come when you can't control yourself, may be, and then you'll do something that you only meant to think about."

Tom shuddered a little and, feeling uncomfortable under Barbara's gaze, got up and started away. But Barbara followed him and caught hold of his arm, and pulled him around till she could look in his face, and said, with more feeling than she liked to show:

"Look here, Tom! Give me your word and honor that you'll put all such thoughts out of your mind."

"Of course I will, Sis, if you think there's any danger."

"And come and go over to the camp-meeting to-night with mother and me. It'll do you good to see somebody besides the cows."

"All right," said Tom, shaking himself to get rid of his evil spirit, and remembering, as he went out to harness old Blaze-face to the wagon, that he would stand a chance of catching a glimpse of Rachel in the light of the torches.

The preaching was vigorous and stirring, and the exhorter, who came after the preacher, told many pathetic stories, which deeply moved a people always eager to be excited. The weird scene no doubt contributed by its spectacular effect to increase the emotion. The bonfires on the platforms illuminated the circle of white tents, which stood out against the wall of deep blackness in the forest behind; the light mounted a hundred feet and more through the thick branches of lofty beech and maple trees, and was reflected from the under side of leaves quivering in the breeze. The boughs and foliage, illuminated from below, had an unreal and unworldly aspect. No imagery of the preacher could make the threatened outer darkness of the lost so weird to the imagination as this scene, in which the company of simple-minded people found themselves in the presence of a savage Nature, and in a sphere of light bounded on every hand by a blackness as of darkness primeval.

Tom paid little attention to the eloquence of the preacher or to the tearful words of him who came after. At first he was interested and even excited by the scene; he watched the flickering of the great shadows of the tree trunks as the platform fires rose and fell; but presently he set himself to searching under the large straw bonnets for a face. He knew well that the sight of that face could not make him happy, but he seemed driven by some evil impulse to seek for it. If Rachel was there he did not find her. When the exhorter had closed his artless string of disconnected anecdotes with an equally artless appeal, and a hymn was announced, Tom whispered to Barbara that he would go and see if the horse was all right, and would meet her at the door of the Mount Zion tent when meeting should "let out." Then as the congregation rose, he went out by a passage between two of the tents into the woods. The "exercises" lasted a full hour longer, and it was half-past ten before the presiding elder gave the benediction. Barbara and her mother went to the door of the Mount Zion tent, where they stood watching the moving people and waiting for Tom. Mely McCord, who was to ride home with them, was talking in her fluent way to Barbara when an excited man rushed into the space within the tents, and, finding himself obstructed by the groups of people in the aisles, ran hurriedly across the boards that served for backless benches until he reached the great rude pulpit. He addressed a word to the white-haired presiding elder, who was at that moment standing on the steps of the stand, engaged in shaking hands with old friends from all parts of his district. Then the new-comer seized the tin horn that hung against a tree, and which was used to call the people to meeting. With this in his hand he mounted the rude board rostrum and blew a long, harsh blast. Part of the people out of curiosity had stopped talking when he made his appearance, and when the strident tin horn ceased, there was a momentary murmur and then the stillness of death, except for confused cries of excitement in the remote outer regions, which now became audible. Then the man on the platform said, in a breathless voice:

"A man has been killed in the woods outside of the camp-ground. The murderer has fled. The sheriff is wanted!"

"Here he is!" cried some voices, and the sheriff stood up on a bench and waved his hand to the messenger, who came down and communicated in a few words what he knew of the murder. The sheriff then hurriedly departed.

"Sit down there, mother," gasped Barbara. "Mely, you stay by mother."

Then Barbara's slight form pushed through the crowd, until her progress was arrested by a dense knot of eager inquirers that

65

encompassed the man who had brought the news. It was quite impossible to get within twenty feet of him, or to hear anything he was saying; but bits of intelligence percolated through the layers of humanity that enveloped him. Barbara could only wait and listen. At last a man a little nearer the radiating center said in reply to the query of one who stood next to her:

"It's George Lockwood, that clerks for Wooden & Snyder down 't Moscow, that is killed, but I can't find out who 't wuz done it."

Barbara's heart stood still within her for a moment. Then dreading to hear more, she pushed out of the ever-increasing crowd and reached her mother.

"Come, mother; we must get home quick."

"What's the matter, Barb'ry? Who's killed?" asked Mely McCord.

"I don't know anything, only we must get home. Quick, mother!" she was impelled by instinct to save her mother as long as possible from the shock she felt impending. But it was of no use.

"What's the matter, Sam; can you make out?" cried a man near her to one just emerging from the crowd about the messenger.

"W'y, they say as Tom Grayson's shot an' killed a feller from Moscow, an' Tom's made off, an' can't be found. They's talk of lynchin' him."

Mrs. Grayson's lips moved; she tried to speak, but in vain; the sudden blow had blanched her face and paralyzed her speech. It was pitiable to see her ineffectual effort to regain control of herself. At length she sank down on a shuck-bottom chair by the door of the tent.

"Yer's some smellin'-salts," said a woman standing by, and she thrust forward her leathery hand holding an uncorked bottle of ammonia.

"He didn't do it," murmured Mrs. Grayson, when she had revived a little. "Our Tommy wouldn't do sech a thing. Go up there,"—and she pointed to the pulpit,—"you go up there, Barb'ry, an' tell the folks 't our Tommy never done it."

"Come, mother; let's go home," said Barbara faintly, for all her energy had gone now.

"I'll go with you," said Mely.

But Mrs. Grayson did not wish to go; she was intent on staying in order to tell the folks that Tommy "never, never done sech a thing."

She yielded at length to the gentle compulsion of Barbara and Mely and the neighbors who gathered about, and got into the wagon. Mely, who knew every inch of the road, took the reins, and

66

drove slowly toward the Grayson house, picking a way among the stumps, roots, and holes of the new road.

# XI

# FRIENDS IN THE NIGHT

The ride seemed to Barbara almost interminable. If she could have left her half-distracted mother she would have got out of the wagon and run through the fields, in hope of finding Tom and knowing from him the whole truth, and making up her mind what was to be done. When at length the wagon reached the gate in front of the Grayson house, Bob McCord was in waiting. He had heard that a bear had been seen on Broad Run, and had left the camp-meeting early, intent on a departure before daylight in pursuit of that "varmint." He had known nothing of the shooting, but he told Barbara that, when he came near the Grayson house, he had seen Tom run across the road and into the house,—and that Tom came out again almost at once, and reached the gate in time to meet the sheriff and give himself up. The sheriff had dismounted one of the men with him, and putting Tom in the saddle they had gone toward Moscow on a gallop. Bob wasn't near enough to hear what Tom had said when the sheriff took him; but knowing that something must be wrong, he had waited for the return of the wagon.

It was some relief to the tension of Barbara's feelings to know that Tom was now in the hands of the lawful authorities and well on his way to Moscow, where he would be out of the reach of the angry crowd that was surging to and fro around the camp-meeting.

But there followed the long night of uncertainty. The mother sat moaning in her chair, only rousing herself enough now and then to assure some newly arrived neighbor that "poor Tom never done it." Barbara confided only to Mely McCord the very faint hope she entertained that Tom was not guilty. She couldn't believe that he would break his solemn promise, made that very evening. But in her secret heart she could not get over the fact that George Lockwood was lying in the woods stark and dead, and no one was so likely to have killed him as her impetuous brother.

About 1 o'clock, the dreadful monotony of the night was

67

dreadfully broken by the arrival of the deputy-sheriff. He spoke in an unsympathetic, official voice, but in a manner externally respectful. He must search Tom's room; and so, taking a candle, he went to the room alone, and soon came back bringing an old-fashioned single-barrel, flint-lock pistol, of the kind in use in the early part of the century. It had belonged to Tom's father, and the officer had found it in one of the drawers in the room. Barbara sat down and shut her eyes as the deputy passed through the sitting-room with the weapon, but Mrs. Grayson called the officer to her.

"I say, Mister—I don't know your name. Let me speak to you."

"Yes, ma'am," said the man, "My name's Markham"; and he came and stood near her.

"Air you the son of Lijy Markham?" Mrs. Grayson always identified people by recalling their filiation, and she could not resist this genealogical tendency in her mind even in the hour of sorest trial.

"Yes," said the officer.

"Well, now, what I want to say is that Tommy didn't kill that man. I'm his mother, an' I had ought to know, an' I tell yeh so. You hadn't ought to 'a' took 'im up fer what he didn't do."

Markham was puzzled to know what to reply, but he answered presently:

"Well, the court'll find out about it, you know, Mrs. Grayson." The man's official stiffness was a little softened by the tones of her heart-broken voice.

Barbara never could tell how she got through the hours from half-past 10 to 3 o'clock. Neighbors were coming and going—some from a desire to be helpful, others from curiosity, but Mely remained with them. Bob McCord was too faithful to leave the Graysons when he might be needed but it was impossible for him to remain awake from mere sympathy. When Markham was gone, he lay down on the end of the porch farthest from the door, and slept the sleep of the man of the Bronze Age. His fidelity was like that of a great dog—he gave himself no anxiety, but he was ready when wanted.

At 3 o'clock Barbara said to Mely: "I can't stand it a minute longer; I can't wait for daybreak. Wake up your father and ask him to hitch up Blaze. I'm going to see Tom as quick as I can get there. I ought to have started before."

"I'm a-goin' too," said Mrs. Grayson.

"No, mother; you stay. It's too much for you."

"Me, Barb'ry?" The mother's lip quivered, and she spoke in a tremulous voice, like that of a pleading child. "Me stay 't home an' my Tommy—my boy—in jail! No, Barb'ry; you won't make me stay 't home. I'm goin' t' Moscow, ef it kills me. I must. I'm his mother, Barb'ry. He's the on'y boy 't 's left. All the rest is dead an' gone. An' him in jail!"

"Pap! pap! you wake up!" Mely was calling to her father lying there asleep, and Barbara came and stood in the door, fain to hasten Bob McCord's slow resurrection from the deeps of unconsciousness and at the same time to escape from the sight of her mother's despair.

As Bob got up and comprehended the urgent request that the horse be harnessed immediately, Barbara's attention was drawn to a man coming swiftly down the road in the moonlight. The figure was familiar. Barbara felt sure she recognized the new-comer; and when, instead of stopping to fumble for the gate-bolt, he rested his hands on the fence alongside and sprang over, she knew that it was Hiram Mason, whom she had not seen since the evening, nearly two weeks before, when they had peeled apples together. It would be hard to say whether pleasure or pain predominated in her mind when she recognized him.

By the time Mason got over the fence Bob McCord had gone to the stable, and Mely had reëntered the house. Barbara went forward and met Hiram on the steps to the porch.

"Poor, dear Barbara!" were his words as he took her hand. At other times her pride had been nettled by his pity, but her desolate soul had not fortitude enough left to refuse the solace of his tender words.

"I came the very moment I heard," he said. "I was staying away down at Albaugh's, and Ike was the only one of them on the camp-ground. He was so excited, and so anxious to see and hear, that he didn't get home till 2 o'clock. And only think I was sleeping quietly and you in such trouble!"

"You mustn't come in," said Barbara. "We're a disgraced family, and you mustn't come in here any more."

"What notions!" answered Hiram. "I'm here to stay. Let me ask your mother." He took hold of her arms and put her aside very gently and pushed on into the house, where Mely was pinning on Mrs. Grayson's wide cape preparatory to her ride to Moscow.

"Mrs. Grayson—" said he.

"W'y, ef 't ain't the master!" she interrupted in a trembling voice. "Mr. Mason, Tommy never killed that man, an' he hadn't ought to 'a' been took up."

"Mrs. Grayson, won't you let me stay with you a few days, now you're in trouble, and help you through?"

The old lady looked at him for a moment before she was able to reply.

"It ain't fer a schoolmaster an' a preacher's son to come here, now folks'll be a-sayin' 't we're—'t we're—murderers." This last word, uttered with tremulous hesitation, broke down her self-control, and Mrs. Grayson fell to weeping again.

"I'm going to stay by you awhile, and we'll see what can be done," said Mason. "They've taken your boy, and you'll let me fill his place a little while, won't you, now?"

"God bless you, my son!" was all the weeping woman could say; and Barbara, who had followed Hiram into the room and stood behind him while he talked to her mother, turned her face to the dark window and wept heartily for the first time in this sorrowful night.

"You'd jest orter 'a' heerd the master a-talkin' to Mrs. Grayson," said Mely McCord afterward. "He stood there lookin' at her with his head turned kind-uh cornerin'-like, un his words was so soft-like un pitiful;—lawsey! ef he did n' make me feel jes like 's ef my heart wuz a-comin right up into my mouth."

Bob McCord led old Blaze up in front of the gate, and all in the house went down to the road.

"Mr. McCord," said Mason, "I want to drive that wagon."

"I don't b'lieve you kin do this fust piece uv road with nothin' but a weakly moonshine," said Bob.

"Oh, yes! I've been over it a good many times." Only Barbara knew how often Hiram had traversed it.

When the schoolmaster had helped Mrs. Grayson and Barbara into the wagon, and while Mely was assisting them to adjust themselves, he went to the horse's head, where McCord was standing, and said in a low voice:

"They told me there was a rush to lynch him last night; and Ike Albaugh says that Jake Hogan, who worked for them this last harvest-time, told him at the camp-ground that the Broad Run boys were going to make another of their visits to Moscow to-night if the coroner's inquest was against Tom. Now, Tom may be innocent; and he ought to have a fair show anyhow."

"I'd better see to that!" said Bob. "I 'low I'll jest drop in amongst 'em over onto the run, kind-uh accidental-like, afore dinner-time to-day, an' throw 'em off, one way er 'nother, ez the case may be."

Mrs. Grayson was seated in a chair placed in the springless wagon for her comfort, while Hiram and Barbara sat on a board laid across from one side to the other of the wagon. They departed out of sight slowly, Mason guiding the horse carefully over the rough ground in the obscurity of a moonlight not yet beginning to give way to the break of day.

# XII

# A TRIP TO BROAD RUN

As the wagon disappeared, Bob called to his daughter, who had been left in charge.

"Mely! Mely! You jes stir up the kitchen fire there, honey, un bile me a cup of coffee, agin I go home un fetch my gun wi' the dogs, un come back." (Bob knew there was no coffee at home.) "I'm a-goin' over onto Broad Run arter bears."

"Aw, now, pap, you're all-ays off fer a hunt at the wrong time. Don' choo go away now, un the folks in sech a world uh trouble. Un besides, mammy hain't got anough to eat in the house to do tell you come back." All this Mely said in a minor key of protest, which she had learned from her mother, who was ever objecting in a good-natured, pathetic, impotent way to her husband's thriftless propensities.

"I know what I'm up to, Mely. They's reasons, un the schoolmaster knows'em. You keep your tongue still in yer head, honey. On'y be shore to remember, 'f anybody axes about me, 't I'm arter bears. Jes say't bears uz been seed over onto Broad Run, un't pap couldn't noways keep still, he wuz so sot on goin' over 'n' sayin' howdy to 'em. That'll soun' like me, un folks 'll never mistrust."

"But mammy hain't akchelly got anough fer the children to eat," responded Mely.

"Well, I 'low to fetch some bear meat home, un you kin borry some meal from Mrs. Grayson's bar'el tell I git back. 'F they knowed what kind uh varmints I wuz arter over there, they wouldn't begrudge me nuthin', Sis. Come, now, hump yer stumps; fer I'll be back in a leetle less'n no time."

And Bob went off in the darkness. In about a dozen minutes he returned with his powder-horn slung about his shoulders over his hunting-shirt and carrying his rifle. He was closely followed by Pup, Joe, and Seizer, his three dogs, whose nervous agitation, as they nosed the ground in every direction, contrasted well with the massive stride of their master. Having swallowed such a breakfast as Mely could get him out of Mrs. Grayson's stores, and put a pone of cold corn-bread into the bosom of his hunting-shirt, McCord was off for the Broad Run region at the very first horizon-streak of daybreak. Though game was but a secondary object in this expedition, he could not but feel an exhilaration which was never wanting when he set out in the early morning with his gun on his shoulder and in the congenial companionship of his dogs. Hercules or Samson could hardly have rejoiced in a greater assurance of physical superiority to all antagonists. The most marked trait in Bob's mental outfit was the hunter's cunning, a craft that took delight in tricks on man and beast. The fact that he was akin to some of the families on Broad Run enhanced the pleasure he felt in his present scheme to get the better of them. He would "l'arn the Broad Run boys a thing or two that'd open their eyes." His great plump form shook with merriment at the thought. Plovers rose beating the air and whistling in the morning light as he passed, and the dogs flushed more than one flock of young prairie-chickens, which went whirring away just skimming the heads of the grass in low level flight, but Bob's ammunition was not to be spent on small game this morning. By 7 o'clock the increasing heat of the sun made the wide, half-parched plain quiver unsteadily to the vision. The sear August prairie had hardened itself against the heat—the grass and the ox-eyes held their heads up without sign of withering or misgiving: these stiff prairie plants never wilt—they die in their boots. But the foliage of the forest which Bob skirted by this time appeared to droop in very expectation of the long oppressive hours of breathless heat yet to come. In this still air even the uneasy rocking poplar-leaves were almost stationary on their edge-wise stems.

Steady walking for more than three hours had brought Bob to the outskirts of the Broad Run region, and had sobered the dogs; these now sought fondly every little bit of shade, and lolled their tongues continuously. The first person that Bob McCord encountered after entering the grateful region of shadow was one Britton—"ole man Britton," his neighbors called him. This old settler led a rather secluded life. Neither he nor his wife ever left home to attend meetings or to share in any social assembly. They had no relatives among the people of the country, and there was a suspicion of mystery about them that piqued curiosity. Some years before, a traveler, in passing through the country, gave out that he recognized Britton, by his name and features, as one whom he had known in Virginia, where he said Britton had been an overseer and had run away with his employer's wife. The neighbors had never accepted the traveler's story in this way; though they were ready to believe that the woman might have run away with Britton. When Bob came in sight of him the saturnine old man was standing looking over the brink of a cliff into a narrow valley through which coursed the waters of Broad Run, steadying himself meanwhile by a sapling. Bob, following his first impulse, deposited his gun, beckoned his close-following little dog back, and crept stealthily towards Britton, keeping a tree between him and the old man when he could. Arrived in reach he made a spring, and laying firm hold of his victim by grasping him under the arms, he held him for a moment over the edge of the precipice. Then he brought him back and set him safely down as one might a child, and said innocently:

"W'y, Mr. Britton, I do declare, 'f I hadn't'a' cotcht you, you'd'a' fell off!"

The shriveled old man drew back to a safe distance from the brink, and tried to force his insipid face into a smile, but he was pale from the deadly fright. Big Bob rubbed his legs and gave way to a spasm of boisterous boyish laughter.

"Seed any bear signs 'round about, Mr. Britton?" he said, when his laugh had died into a broad grin.

"No."

"What wuz you lookin' over the cliff fer?"

"Zeke Tucker. He's workin' fer me, an' he's been gone all the mornin' arter my clay-bank hoss. I'm afeard sumpin's happened."

"'F I find him I'll set the dogs onto him an' hurry him up a leetle," said Bob, laughing again and going on, intent now on encountering Zeke, alone, for purposes of his own.

Then, when he had gone a little way, he stopped and looked back at the retreating old man, and grinned as he noted the doleful way in which his over-large trousers bagged behind.

"Mr. Britton," he called, "which way'd Zeke go?"

"Up the crick; the hoss is up thar sumers."

Having secured this information, Bob went on, descending the cliff to the valley through which Broad Run rattled its shallow waters—a valley so broken and rugged as to render it almost unfit for cultivation. This glen was settled, as such regions are wont to be, by a race of "poor whiteys," or rather by a mixture of people belonging to two stocks originally different. The one race was descended from the lowest of the nomads, vagrants, and other poverty-stricken outcasts that had been spirited away from England by means legal and illegal, to be sold for a long term into bondage in the American colonies; the other, from the roughest wing of the great Scotch-Irish immigration of the last century—the hereditary borderers who early fought their way into the valleys and passes of the Alleghanies. Equally thriftless in their habits, and equally without any traditions of their origin, members of these two tribes mingled easily. The people in whom the Scotch-Irish blood preponderates are more given to violence, but their humor, their courage, and their occasional bursts of energy indicate that they have a chance of emerging from barbarism; while the poor whiteys of English descent are most of them beyond the reach of evolution, foreordained to extinction by natural selection, whenever the pressure of overpopulation shall force them into the competition for existence.

With that instinctive unthriftiness which is the perpetual characteristic of the poor whitey in all his generations, the Broad Run people had chosen the least inviting lands within a hundred miles for their settlement, as though afraid that by acquiring valuable homes they might lose their aptitude for migration; or afraid, perhaps, that fertile prairies might tempt them to toil. The convenience of a brook by their doors, and a wood that was uncommonly "handy," had probably determined their choice. Then, too, the circumjacent cliffs gave them a sense of being shut in from prairie winds, and put some limit to the wanderings of their half-starved "critters." For the rest, their demands upon the land were always very modest—a few bushels of "taters," for roasting in the ashes; a small field of maize, for roasting-ears, hominy, and corn-dodgers; and such pumpkins and beans as could be grown intermingled with the hills of corn, were about all that one of these primitive families required, beyond what could be got with a gun or a fishing-line. The only real luxuries affected were onions and melons—"ing-uns un watermillions," in Broad Run phrase. Their few pigs and cows ran at large, and lived as they could. Oxen they rarely owned, but whenever a man was in the least prosperous he was sure to possess a single inferior saddle-horse, though he sometimes had no saddle but a blanket girt with a surcingle. A horse was kept at the service of neighbors; for, like other savages, the Broad Run people were hospitable and generous to members of their own tribe, and the only economy they understood was that of borrowing and lending, by which a number of families were able to make use of the same necessary articles. This happy device, for example, enabled one circulating flat-iron to serve an entire neighborhood.

The Broad Run people entertained a contempt for the law that may have been derived from ancestors transported for petty felonies. It seemed to them something made in the interest of attorneys and men of property. A person mean enough to "take the law onto" his neighbor was accounted too "triflin'" to be respectable; good whole-souled men settled their troubles with nature's weapons,—fists, teeth, and finger-nails,—and very rarely, when the offense was heinous and capital, with bullets or buckshot. Men who were habitually disgraceful in any way—as, for example, those who could not get drunk without beating their wives—were punished, without the delay of trial, by the infliction of penalties more ancient than statutes, such as ducking, riding on a rail, whipping, or sudden banishment. Hanging by lynch-law was reserved for the two great crimes of horse-stealing and murder.

They put the killing of George Lockwood into the category of grudge-murder, since he was shot at night "without giving him a show for his life." But the shooting did not immediately concern Broad Run, and Broad Run folks would not have felt themselves responsible for seeing justice done, if it had not been for concurring circumstances. Lynch law is an outbreak of the reformatory spirit among people of low or recent civilization. Like other movements for reform, it is often carried by its own momentum into unforeseen excesses. It had happened recently that two brothers, thieves of the worst class, who had infested the country and had long managed to escape from the law, had been sent to prison for four years. They were believed to be guilty of an offense much blacker than the robbery for which they were sentenced; but the murder of a strange peddler had escaped notice until the body had been discovered two years after the crime, and the crime could not then be brought home by legal evidence. Their attorney, a lawyer notorious for chicanery, had, by appeal, got a new trial on account of some technical error in the proceedings of the lower court. The county had already been heavily taxed to defray the expense of convicting them, and the people were exasperated by the prospect of a new expense with the possible escape of the criminals. Public expenses, it is true, sat lightly on Broad Run; the taxes levied on its barren patches and squalid cabins were not considerable, but Broad Run made much of the taxes it did pay, and it caught the popular indignation, and was indignant in its own prompt and executive fashion. The very night before the new trial was to begin, the doors of the jail were forced, and the two prisoners were shot to death by a mob. On the jail door was left a notice, warning the attorney of the criminals to depart from the county within thirty hours, on pain of suffering a like fate. Though Broad Run got most of the credit for this prompt vindication of justice, the leaving of this legible notice upon the door was taken as evidence of the complicity of some whose education was better than that of the settlers at the Run. This execution had taken place but three months before the shooting of George Lockwood, and the mob was like a were-wolf. Perhaps I ought rather to liken it to those professional reformers who, having abolished slavery, or waved their hats while others abolished it, proceed to inquire for the next case on the docket, and undertake forthwith to do away with capital punishment or the marriage relation. Having found its local self-complacency much increased by success in discovering a method cheaper and more expeditious than those of the courts, Broad Run was readily inclined to apply its system of criminal jurisprudence to a new case.

But this local reformatory tendency, like many large movements of the sort, was very capable of lending itself to the promotion of personal aims and the satisfaction of private grudges. One of Tom Grayson's rash boyish exploits, soon after he took up his abode with his uncle in town, had been to avenge himself for an affront put upon him the year before by Jake Hogan of Broad Run. Jake, while working as a hired man for Butts, the next neighbor to the Graysons, had taken the side of his employer in the long-standing quarrel between the Buttses and the Graysons about pigs in the corn-field and geese in the meadow, "breachy" horses and line fences. Jake had gone so far one day as to throw Tom, then a half-grown boy, into the "branch." A boy's memory of such events is good, and when Jake rode into Moscow, a year later, in company with his sweetheart to see the circus, Tom repaid the old grudge by taking the stirrups from Jake's saddle and dropping them into the public well; so that the consequential Jake had the mortification of escorting a giggling Broad Run girl to her home with his lank legs and his big boots dangling, unsupported, against the flanks of his horse. Hogan would have beaten Tom, if he had not received an intimation that this would perhaps involve the necessity of his settling the matter a second time with big Bob McCord. But he laid up his grudge, and from that time he had taken pleasure in testifying to his settled conviction that Tom "wouldn' never come t' no good eend." He always lent emphasis to this sinister prediction by jerking his head back, with the self-confident air of a man who knows what he knows. From the moment of the shooting of Lockwood, when Jake found that Tom was on the direct road to the gallows, he began to twit all his cronies.

"Hain't I all-ays said so? Go to thunder! D'yeh think Jake Hogan don't know a feller as the rope's already got a slip-knot onto?" And he would jerk his chin back, and stiffen his neck, as he defiantly waited for a reply.

Not content with exulting in successful prophecy, Jake got a notion from the first that it devolved on him now to see that this young scapegrace should not fail of merited punishment. His neighbors at the Run, having boasted much of the value of what they called "Broad Run law," were willing to add a leaf to their laurels as reformers of the county; and he counted also on finding recruits among the loafers on the outskirts of the camp-meeting, if the coroner's jury should return a verdict adverse to Tom.

Bob McCord was able to conjecture something of this state of affairs from the slender information the schoolmaster had given him. During all his morning's walk to Broad Run, Bob's thoughts had chiefly revolved about plans for circumventing Hogan. His first crude scheme was to join the reformers in their little excursion, and then mislead or betray them; but his friendly relations with the Graysons were too well known to Jake for this to be possible. It was not until the old man Britton had mentioned Zeke Tucker that there occurred to Bob's inventive mind a proper agent for his purpose. Wishing to have his coming known, he steered his course near to the rickety cabin of Eleazar Brown, or, as he was commonly called, "Ole Lazar Brown."

"G'-mornin', S'manthy," Bob called to Lazar Brown's daughter, at the same time giving his head a little forward jerk,—the very vanishing point of a bow,—but without stopping his march. S'manthy had buried two husbands, and had borne eight white-headed children, but she had never been called by any other name than S'manthy. Just now she was "batting" clothes on a block in front of the house, turning a wet garment over with her left hand from time to time, and giving it the most vindictive blows with a bat held in her right.

"Y' ain't heern nothin' 'v no bears a-cap'rin' 'round h-yer lately, eh?' Bob asked, relaxing his gait a little.

"They say as they's a b'ar been seed furder upt the run, un I 'low you mout fine some thar ur tharabouts," replied the woman, intermitting her batting a moment and pushing back her faded pink sun-bonnet. "But wha' choo doin' away f'om home, I'd thes like to know, when they's so much a-goin' on in your diggin's? They say you've had a murder 'n' all that."

"I don't talk, S'manthy. I'm a-lookin' fer bears. They 's times when yo'd orter hole onto yer tongue with both uh yore han's."

Bob quickened his stride again and was soon out of sight among the scrubby trees of the rugged valley.

"I say, daddy!" called S'manthy, when Bob had had time to get out of hearing; "looky h-yer, daddy!"

Old Lazar Brown, in answer to this call, came and stood in the door, taking his cob-pipe from his mouth with his shaky hand and regarding his daughter.

"Big Bob McCord's thes gone along upt the run a-hunt-in' fer b'ars," said S'manthy. "Un they say as the feller that killed t' other feller las' night's the son uh the woman 't 'e works fer. Bob's the beatinest hunter! Ef Gaberl wuz to toot his horn, Bob'd ax him to hole on long anough fer him to git thes one more b'ar, I'll bet."

Lazar Brown had shaking-palsy in his arms, and, being good for nothing else, could devote his entire time to his congenial

77

pursuits as gossip and wonder-monger of the neighborhood. Having listened attentively to S'manthy, he shook his head incredulously.

"Yeh don't think ez he's arter b'ars, do yeh, S'manthy? Bob's got some trick er 'nother 'n 'is head. W'y, thes you look, he mus' uh le't home afore daybreak. Now, Bob'd natterly go to the carner's eenques' to-day, whar they'll be a-haulin' that young feller up that shot t' other feller las' night. Big Bob's got some ornery trick 'n 'is head." Here Lazar Brown stopped to replace his pipe in his mouth. He was obliged to use both hands, but after two or three attempts he succeeded. "Looky h-yer, S'manthy, you thes keep one eye out fer Bob; I 'low he'll go down the run towurds ev'nin'. He'll be orful dry by that time, fer he's one of the driest fellers. Thes you tell him 't I've got a full jug, un ax him in, un we'll kind-uh twis' it out uh'im. I 'low I'll go 'n find Jake."

Lazar returned to the house, knocked the ashes out of his pipe and refilled it. Then with some difficulty he succeeded in taking a live coal from the ashes; holding it in the leathery palm of his shaking left hand, he got it deposited at last on the corn-cob bowl of his pipe. As soon as this operation of firing-up was completed, he set out in a trotty little walk, glad to have news that would make the neighbors hearken to him.

Meantime Bob McCord, having passed out of sight of S'manthy in his progress up the creek, had faced about and come back through the bushes to a point overlooking Lazar Brown's cabin, where, in a dense patch of pawpaws, he stood in concealment. This movement greatly perplexed the old dog Pup, who stood twitching his nose nervously, unable to discover what was the game that had attracted his master's eye. When at length Bob saw Lazar start off down the run, he smote his knee with his hand and gave vent to half-smothered laughter.

"Tuck like the measles!" he soliloquized. "Un it'll spread too. See 'f it don't! Come, Pup—bears! bears! ole boy!"[1]

The dogs took the hint and ceased their nosing about the roots of trees for squirrels, and in beds of leaves and bunches of grass for

---

[1] Why it was that Bob said "bears," and did not say "b'ars," as some of his class did, I do not know. Broad as his dialect was, it was perceptibly less aberrant than that of Lazar Brown's family, for example. It is impossible to trace the causes for local and family variations of speech; nor is a word always pronounced in the same way in a dialect,—it varies in sound sometimes, when more or less stress is put upon it. The varieties are here set down as they existed, except that print can never give those shades of pronunciation and inflection that constitute so large a part of the peculiarities of speech, local, personal and temporary.

hares. They began to make large circles through the trees about Bob, who moved forward as the center of a sort of planetary system, the short-legged dog keeping near the center, while Pup ranged as far away as he could without losing sight of his master,—the remote Uranus of the hunt. Joe, having "tairrier" blood in him, ran with his nozzle down; but long-legged Pup, with a touch of greyhound in his build, carried his head high and depended on his eyes. The fact that Tom Grayson's life was at stake afforded no reason, in Bob's view, for giving over the pursuit of bears. Nor did he hunt in serious earnest merely because there was neither bread nor meat at home. A cat will catch mice for the mere fun of it, and with Bob the chase was ever the chief interest of life. But Bob did not forget his other errand; while the dogs were seeking for bears, he was eagerly scanning the bushes in every direction for Zeke Tucker. Half a mile above Lazar Brown's he encountered Zeke, carrying a blind-bridle on his arm, and still looking in vain for Britton's stray horse.

"Hello, Zeke! the very feller I wuz a-lookin' fer. Don't ax me no questions about what I'm a-doin' over h-yer, an' I won't tell you no lies. Let's set down a minute on that air hackberry log."

The writer of a local guide-book to the city of Genoa recounts, among the evidences of piety exhibited by his fellow-citizens, the hospital built by them for those "la quale non è conceduto di bearsi nel sorriso di un padre." Zeke was one of those to whom, in the circumlocution of the Genoese writer, had not been granted the benediction of a father's smile. Such unfortunates were never wanting in a community like Broad Run, but no one had ever thought of building an asylum for them, though there were many ready to make them suffer the odium of sins not their own. From that unexpected streak of delicacy which is sometimes found in a rough man of large mold, Bob McCord had always refrained from allusion to the irregularity of Zeke's paternity, and had frequently awed into silence those who found pleasure in jibing him. This had awakened in Zeke a grateful adhesion to Bob, and in the young man's isolation among his neighbors and his attachment to himself Bob saw a chance to secure an ally.

"Zeke," said McCord, when once they were seated on the hackberry log, "you 'n' me's all-ays been frien's, hain't we?"

"Toobshore, Bob! they hain't no man a-livin' I'd do a turn fer quicker."

"Well, now, you tell me this: Is Jake Hogan a-goin' to town weth the boys to-night?"

"I hadn't no ways orter tell, but I 'low 't 'e is."

"You a-goin' along?"

"I dunno. 'F you don't want me to, I don't reckon ez I shall."

79

"Yes, but I'd ruther you 'd go. I don't want that air fool boy hung 'thout a fair stan'-up trial, 'n' I may as well tell you 't I don't mean he shall be nuther, not 'f I have to lick Jake Hogan tell his ornery good-fer-nothin' hide won't hold shucks. But don't choo tell him a word 't I say."

"Trust me." Zeke was pleased to find himself in important confidential relations with a man so much "looked up to" as Bob McCord. "Jake 's been the hardest on me 'v all the folks, un they 's been times when I 'lowed to pull up un cl'ar out for the Injun country, to git shed uv 'im. I wish to thunder you would lick him 'thin 'n inch 'viz life. He's a darn-sight wuss 'n git out."

"Looky h-yer, Zeke; I'll tell you how you kin git even with Jake. You jest go 'long weth the boys to-night, wherever they go. I'm goin' to fix it so's they won't do nuthin' to-night. You're livin' 't ole man Britton's now, ainch yeh?"

"Yes."

"Well, you git off fer half a day f'om Britton's, un go to the eenques' this arternoon, un fine out all you kin. Arter supper, you go over to the groc'ry; un jest as soon's you fine out whech way the wind sets, you've got to let me know. 'T won't do fer me to be seed a-talkin' to you, ur fer me to loaf aroun' Britton's. But ef Jake makes up his mine to go to Moscow, you light a candle to-night un put it in the lof' where you sleep, so 't 'll shine out uv a crack on the south side uv the chimbley, in the furder eend uv the house."

"But his mine 's already made up," said Zeke.

"They's time to change afore night. Ef he's goin' to Perrysburg——"

"Perrysburg? They ain't no talk uv Perrysburg," said Zeke.

"They may be," answered Bob. "Un ef Perrysburg's the place, you put the candle at the leetle winder on the north side uv the chimbley. Un when I shoot you put out the candle, un then I'll know it's you, un you'll know 't I understan'. You see, 't won't do fer me to stop any nearder 'n the hill, un I'll wait there till I see your candle. Then you go weth Jake." Here Bob got up and strained his longsighted eyes at some object in the bushes on the other side of the brook. "Is yon hoss yourn, on t' other side of the branch?"

"I don't see no hoss," said Zeke.

"Well, you watch out a minute un you'll ketch sight uv 'im. He's gone in there to git shed of the flies."

"That's our clay-bank, I believe," said Zeke, getting up and carefully scanning the now half-visible horse.

"Mine! you hain't seen nor heern tell of me, un you b'long to Jake's crowd weth all your might."

With these words Bob set out again for his bear-hunt, while

the barefoot Zeke waded through the stream, which was knee-deep, and set himself to beguile Britton's clay-bank horse into standing still and forfeiting his liberty.

# XIII

## A BEAR HUNT

Bob McCord had that quick, sympathetic appreciation of brute impulses which is the mark of a great hunter. Given a bear or a deer in a certain place, at a certain hour of the day, and Bob would conjecture, without much chance of missing, in which direction he would go and what he would be about. In a two-hours' beating-up the ravine he found no traces of bears. He then faced almost about and bent his course to where the illimitable western prairie set into the woods in a kind of bay. Why he thought that on a hot day like this a bear might be taking a sunning in the open grass I cannot tell; he probably suspected Bruin of an excursion to the corn-fields for "roas'in' ears." At any rate his conjecture was correct. Pup, beating forward in great leaps, with his head above the grass, caught sight of a female bear making her way to a point of timber farther down the run known as Horseshoe Neck. When the bear saw the dogs she quickened her leisurely pace into a lumbering gallop. Pup's long legs were stretched to their utmost in eager leaps which presently brought him in front of her; Joe, when he came up, annoyed her at the side; and stout little Seizer, watching the chance whenever she was making an angry lunge at Pup, would bravely nip her heels and so make her turn about. Before she could get her head fairly around the fiste would turn tail and run for his life. Bob tried to get within range before the bear should disappear in the forest, but as soon as she saw herself near the timber she charged straight for it, refusing to strike at Pup, and wholly disregarding the barking of bob-tail Joe, or the proximity to her heels of Seizer. She quickly disappeared from sight in the underbrush, and the embarrassed dogs came near losing her. A few moments too late to get a shot, McCord came running to the woods at the point of her entrance. He examined the brush and listened a moment.

"She's gone up stream," he said, "bound to make her hole at Coon's Den, 'f I don't git there fust."

He returned to the prairie and ran breathlessly along the edge of the woods for the better part of a mile; then he dashed into the timber, and pushing through the brush until he reached a cliff, he clambered down and stood with his back to the head of a ravine tributary to the valley in which Broad Run flowed. He was breathless, and his flimsy lower garments had been almost torn off him by the violence of his exertion and the resistance of underbrush and rocks; in fact, raiment never seemed just in place on him; the vigorous form burst through it now on this side, and now on that. Hearing the dogs still below him, he knew that he had come in time to intercept the progress of the bear toward the heap of rocky débris at the head of the ravine. Once in these fastnesses, no skill of hunter or perseverance of dogs would have been sufficient to get her out.

The bear was soon in sight, and Bob saw that the nearly exhausted dogs were taking greater risks than ever. Little Seizer was particularly venturesome, and was so much overcome with heat and fatigue, and so breathless with barking, that it was hard for him to get out of the way of the bear's retorts. "She'll smash that leetle ijiot the very nex' time, shore," muttered Bob with alarm; and though he knew the range to be a long one, he took aim and fired. Unluckily the infuriated Seizer gave the bear's heel a particularly savage bite, and at the very instant of Bob's pulling the trigger she turned on the little dog, and thus caused the ball to lodge in her right shoulder just as she was striking out with her left paw. She barely reached the dog, and failed to crush him with the full weight of her arm, but she lacerated his side and sent him howling out of the fray. Now, wounded and enraged, she recognized in the hunter her chief enemy; and, neglecting the dogs, she rushed up the ravine toward McCord. Bob poured a large charge of powder into his gun, and, taking a bullet from his pouch, he felt in his pocket for the patching. A moment he looked blankly at the oncoming bear and muttered "Gosh!" between his set teeth. There was not a patch in his pocket. He had put some pieces of patching there in the darkness of the morning before leaving home, without remembering that his pocket was bottomless. He stood between a wounded bear and her cubs, and there was no time for deliberation. He might evade the attack if he could succeed in getting up the cliff where he had come down, but in that case she would reach her hole and he would lose the battle. He promptly tore a piece from the ragged leg of his trousers, and, wrapping his ball in it, rammed it home. Then he took a cap from a hole in the stock of his gun and got it fixed just in time to shoot when the bear was within a dozen feet of him. Uncultivated man that he was, he had the same refined pleasure in the death-throes of his victim that gentlemen and ladies of the highest breeding find in seeing a frightened and exhausted fox torn to pieces by hounds with bloody lips.

Bob's first care was to look after Seizer, who was badly wounded, but whose bones were whole. The afternoon had passed its middle when he shot the bear, and by the time he had cared for the dog and dressed his game the sun was low and McCord was troubled lest he should have delayed too long the execution of his stratagem for the confusion of Jake Hogan.

Another man might have been considerably embarrassed to dispose of the bear. But Bob proceeded first to divest it of every part that was of little value. Then he hoisted the carcass to his shoulder and tossed the bear-skin on top. Taking up his rifle and balancing his burden carefully before starting, he went swaying to and fro down the ravine, choosing with care the securest places among the rocks to set his feet in. It was thus that Samson went off with the great gates of Gaza. McCord was a primitive, Pelasgic sort of man, accustomed to overmatch the ferocities of Nature with a superior strength and cunning. Lacking the refinement and complexity of the typical modern, this antique human is more simple and statuesque; even the craft of such a man has little involution. There was joy in his bloody victory over the most formidable beast in his reach that was virile and unalloyed by ruth or scruple—a joy like that which vibrates in the verses of Homer.

It was a good mile to Lazar Brown's, where Bob hoped to find a horse to take his bear home. When at length he stopped to unshoulder his burden on a salient corner of old Lazar's rail fence, sunset had begun to bless the overheated earth.

"Got a b'ar, did n' choo?" said Old Lazar, who was in wait for Bob.

"To be shore, Uncle Lazar. Whadje expeck?"

"Come in, Bob, wonch yeh? I got a fresh jug full uv the critter yisterday, un I 'low you're purty consid'able dry agin this time. You purty much all-ays air dry, Bob."

"Well, Uncle Lazar, I am tol'able dry un no mistake. I hain't had nuthin' to drink to-day 'ceppin' jes branch water, un clear water's a mighty weak kind uv a drink fer a pore stomick like mine. 'N, I'm hungry too. Don' choo 'low S'manthy could rake up a cole dodger summers about?"

"Oh, stay tell she gits you some supper."

"No, Uncle Lazar; I could n' stop a minute noways. They hain't got nary thing t' eat 't our house. Len' me your mare to git this 'ere varmint home?"

"I could n', Bob. I'm thes uz willin' to 'commodate ez anybody kin be, but I've promised the mar' to one uv the boys to-night—to—to go a-sparkin' weth."

"Oh, sparkin' kin wait. What's a feller want to go sparkin' a Friday night fer? Tell him to wait tell Sunday, so 's the gal 'll have a clean dress on."

"But I've gi'n my word, Bob."

"Your word hain't no 'count, un you don't fool me, Uncle Lazar," said Bob, with a broad grin. "Your mare's a-goin' to town to-night, un ef she sh'd git a bullet-hole put into her who'd pay the funeral ixpenses?"

This consideration went for a good deal with Lazar.

"I say, Bob," he said, coming closer and speaking low, "is they goin' to be shootin' to-night?"

"Uv course they is, un plenty uv it. Don' choo know't the sheriff's gi'n bonds, un 'f 'e lets a prisoner go he's got to pay the damages? Un them town fellers is sot agin lynchin'." Seeing S'manthy in the cabin door straining her attention to the utmost, Bob spoke loud enough to reach her ears. "Lookey h-yer, Uncle Lazar," he went on; "d'you reckon 't that feller that's a-goin' to git your mare shot to-night 'll gin you a whole quarter uv bear-meat fer the use an' the damages ef she's shot?"

This last hint had the desired effect.

"'T ain't no use a-talkin', Daddy," S'manthy called out; "I hain't a-go'n' to let a'ole frien' like Bob Mcord pack that-ar great big b'ar all the way over to Timber Crick on his shoulders ez long 's my name's S'manthy. Un I hain't a-go'n' to have the mar' shot. So thar 's 'n eend auv it." S'manthy's common "uv" or "uh" for "of" became "auv" when she wished to be particularly emphatic and full-mouthed in a declaration.

"Good fer you, S'manthy," said Bob. "You sh'll have the best leg this critter's got. Take yer ch'ice."

A rusty ax was brought out, and Bob stopped a moment to examine its serrated edge. "I say, Uncle Lazar, ez this a' ax ur a saw? From the aidge uv it I sh'd call it a saw, but the back uv it is sumpin like a' ax." Then with a laugh he proceeded to cut off a liberal quarter of the bear, while S'manthy's ten-year-old tow-headed boy was sent to "ketch up the mar'," which was nibbling grass on the farther side of a patch of broad-leaved cotton-weeds. When the quarter of bear-meat had been hung up at the north end of the cabin, Lazar got out his jug and Bob began to satisfy the longings of his colossal thirst, while S'manthy set out on the poplar table which stood in the middle of the floor some "Kaintucky corn-dodger," as she called it; and despite Bob's protest against staying till she could cook some supper, she put a bit of fat salt pork in the skillet to fry. Meantime the old man plied Bob with more whisky, both before and after eating. When he thought it time for this to have taken effect, he began to try to satisfy his own curiosity.

"D'joo h-yer about the carner's eenquest, Bob?" he said cautiously, feeling his way toward his point.

"No, I didn't. You see, I hain't seed nobody but the bear, un she wuz the ign'rantest critter. Could n't tell me nuthin'." And Bob laughed at his own wit, as was his custom. "How 'd it go?" Bob had wanted to ask this question, but he wished to let Uncle Lazar begin.

"Well, I hyern f'om Raphe Jackson, thes now, that the jury said 's Lockwood come to 'is final eend ut the han's uv Tom Grayson, ur sumpin like that; un they said 't wuz reg'lar bloody murder in the fust degree. My! ef that wuz n't a mad crowd! They made a rush fer Grayson, but the depitty shurriff 'd got 'im away. Ef they 'd 'a' cotcht him they would n't 'a' made two bites uv him."

"You don't say!" Bob was a little stunned. He had not thought of Tom's being at the inquest. He felt that perhaps in coming away he had made a mistake that had come near to being a fatal one.

"They wuz thes a-howlin', Raphe said, un they had n't lef' the place when he come away. They wuz made madder by the way the young scoundrel stood up un declared 't he did n' know nuthin' about the murder, arter 't wuz proved on him, plain 's the nose on a man's face, an' the dead man a-layin' right thar afore 'is own eyes."

Bob was in a brown study, and nothing was said on either side for half a minute. It made Bob uncomfortable to reflect that he had come near losing the game at the outset.

"I 'low 't 'll go hard weth the young feller to-night."

This roused McCord from the reverie produced from his surprise.

"I reckoned the boys'u'd be a-goin' to Moscow to-night," he said; and added, "Let 'em go!" And then he laughed as though he knew something.

"Say, Bob," said Uncle Lazar, whose curiosity was piqued beyond endurance, "what's in the wind? What wuz it fotcht you all the way over h-yer un the eenquest a-goin' on so closte to your house?"

"Had n' got no meat," said Bob, with a wink.

"They's sumpin more'n that ar. You've got sumpin ur nuther on Jake, I'll bet."

"I 'ke speck you know a whole lot, Uncle Lazar," said Bob. "I sh'd think you'd jest right up un guess now."

"Well, I can't seem to."

"Well, I'm not a-goin' to let 't out, Uncle Lazar, 'thout this 'ere whisky uh yourn's a leetle too powerful fer me."

Bob did not fear the whisky: it was rare that whisky could get the better of such a frame as his; and, moreover, he was inured to it. He only threw out this hint to persuade his host to be more liberal in dispensing it.

But it appeared that Lazar's liberality with his whisky was probably exhausted; and Bob rose to go, affecting to be unsteady on his legs.

"Seddown, Bob; seddown, while I see about the mar'.'"

"Well, I 'low I will, Uncle Lazar. That air whisky uh yourn has sort-uh settled into my feet a leetle."

Lazar went out to see if the boy had brought the horse, making a signal to his daughter to try her skill at coaxing Bob to tell. Meantime Bob ogled S'manthy, who, like Delilah, was debating how she could win this Samson's secret. Presently he said, in a half-tipsy tone:

"S'manthy, you 'n' me wuz all-ays good frien's, wuz n't we?"

"Toobshore, Bob."

"I used to think you wuz some at a hoe-down; you wuz the best-lookin' un the liveliest dancer uv all. How you did slam-bang the floor!"

S'manthy smiled in her faded way. "Bob, that's all saf'-sodder, un you know it. Say, Bob, ef you're sech a frien' why on yerth don' choo tell a-body what fotcht you over h-yer to-day?"

"Aw, well, I'd tell, on'y I'm afeared you'd go un let out."

"Not me. 'T a'n't like me to blab."

"Well, I don' mine tellin' you, S'manthy, 'f yeh won't tell the ole man tell mornin'.'"

"Oh! I'd never tell him. He'd go potterin' all over Broad Run Holler weth it, fust thing."

"'S the bes' joke," said Bob, rubbing his knees exultingly; "but I'm afeared you'll tell," he added, rousing himself.

"'Pon my word 'n' honor, I won't. Nobody'll ever git 't out uh me." And S'manthy emphasized this assurance by a boastful nodding of the head forward and to one side.

"Well, 'f you think you kin keep the sekert overnight—Don' choo tell no livin' critter tell mornin'.'"

"I hain't no hand to tell sekerts, an' you 'd orter know that, Bob."

"Well, you jes let Jake 'n' his crowd go to Moscow to-night," said Bob, chuckling in a semi-tipsy, soliloquizing tone. "I come over to make shore they wuz a-goin', un I wuz to let the sher'f know ef they had got wind uv anything. I saw Markham, the deppitty, about

86

one o'clock this mornin', un he tole me he 'd look arter the eenques' un I mus' keep a lookout over h-yer. Jake 'll have a rousin' time, un no mistake."

"Shootin'?" queried S'manthy, with eagerness.

"Naw! I wuz on'y a-lettin' on about shootin' to fool Uncle Lazar. Hain't got no needcessity to shoot. Better 'n that! Gosh!"

"Goin' to take the young feller away?"

"I 'low they did n't never take him back to Moscow arter the eenques'."

"Tuh law! You don't say? Whar 've they tuck 'm to?"

"I sha'n't tell," said Bob. "I sha'n't tell even you, S'manthy."

"Perrysburg?"

"You all-ays wuz some at guessin'. But I sha'n't say nary nuther word, on'y he 's whar Jake won't find him ef he goes to Moscow. They went summers, un that's anough. Perrysburg jail 's ruther stronger 'n ourn, I'll say that. 'T wuz all fixed, 'fore I lef' home, to run him off afore the verdick wuz in, un not to keep to the big road nuther, so 's Jake would n' git wind uv 'em. Don't you whisper Perrysburg to a livin' soul. You jes' let Jake go down to Moscow! I'm comin' over 'n the mornin' to fetch your mare home un git my little Seizer that 's got to stay h-yer to-night, un then I'll fine out how they come out." And Bob chuckled as he left the house, only turning back to say:

"You keep closte, S'manthy, ur you'll spile it all. 'F you do tell, I won't never forgive yeh."

Bob now went out and down to the brookside, where he cut up and stripped three or four leatherwood bushes, and tied the tough, fibrous bark into one strong rope. With this he girded the bear to the horse's back, meantime resisting all of old Lazar's inquiries about the reason for his coming. At length he walked off in the dusk, unsteadily leaning against the horse on which the bear-meat was tied, and was soon out of sight.

"Bob won't tell me," said the old man plaintively, as he came into the house.

"He won't, won't he?" demanded S'manthy, with exultation in her voice. "You don' know how. Takes me to git at a sekert."

"Did he tell you, S'manthy?" Uncle Lazar looked a little crest-fallen.

"In course he did. Think I couldn' make him tell? W'y, I kin thes twis' Big Bob 'roun' my little finger."

"Well, what on yerth did he come over yer fer, S'manthy?"

"I promised not to tell you."

"To be shore you did. But you're a-goin' to."

"Yes; but you'll let it out, un then what'll Bob say to me?"

"What'll Jake say to you fer lettin' yer mar' go off, when one uv his boys had the promise? Un what 'll the folks say when they find out you knowed, un let 'em be fooled by Big Bob? You 've got to tell, S'manthy, ur else have all the' Holler down on yeh. Besides, you could n' keep that sekert tell bed-time, noways, un you know you couldn'. 'T ain't in you to keep it, un you might thes ez well out weth it now ez arter awhile."

"Aw, well, Daddy, Bob didn' say much, on'y ut Jake wouldn' fine the feller that done the shootin' when he got to Moscow."

"Tuh law!" exclaimed the old man, waiting with open eyes for more.

"He wuz tuck off, afore the eenques' wuz over, to Perrysburg, un Bob come over to see 't Jake didn' git no wind uv it. That 's all they is to it. Un you need n' go un tell it, h-yer an' yan, nuther."

S'manthy knew well that this caution was of no avail. But by tacking the proviso to the information, she washed her hands of responsibility, and convinced herself that she had not betrayed a secret. It was an offering that she felt bound to make to her own complacency.

Uncle Lazar, for his part, made no bones. He only tarried long enough to set his pipe to smoking.

Bob McCord had stopped in the growing darkness under the shade of a box elder, a little beyond the forks of the road. He presently had the satisfaction of seeing the head of the old man as he trotted away through the patch of stunted corn toward a little grocery, which was located where the big road crossed Broad Run Hollow, and which was the common center of resort and intelligence for the neighborhood.

## XIV

## IN PRISON

Hiram Mason managed with difficulty to drive the first two miles of forest road—over roots and stumps, through ruts and mud-holes, and with no light but that of a waning moon. When he reached Timber Creek bridge he got down and led the horse on its unsteady floor. Then came, like a dark spot in the pale moonlight, the log school-house, which reminded him that he was running away from his day's work. He stopped at the new log-house of John Buchanan, a Scotch farmer who had been one of his predecessors, and called him up to beg him to take his place. Buchanan, whose knowledge was of the rudimentary kind, had ceased to teach because he had not been able to meet the increased demands of the patrons of the school; it was a sort of consolation to his thwarted ambition to resume the beech-scepter if only for a day.

When Buchanan's house had been left behind, the road passed into an outskirt of small poplars, and then finally shook off this outer fringe of forest and lay straight away over the dead level of the great prairie. By the time the wagon reached this point the dawn was beginning to reveal the landscape, though as yet the world consisted only of masses of shadow interspersed with patches of a somber gray. But the smooth road was sufficiently discernible for Hiram to put the horse into a trot, which afforded no little relief to the impatient Barbara. Up to this time they had traveled in silence, except for the groans and sighs of Mrs. Grayson. But at length Barbara took the lead.

"I can't believe that Tom did that shooting," she said to Mason. "He promised me after supper last night that he would put all hard feelings against George Lockwood out of his mind. Tom is n't the kind of a fellow to play the hypocrite. Oh, I do hope he is innocent!"

"So do I," said Mason.

"To be sure he is," said Mrs. Grayson, with a touch of protest in her voice.

Barbara had detected a note of effort in Hiram's reply, that indicated a prevailing doubt of Tom's innocence, and she did not speak again during the whole ride. When they entered the village, Mason drove first to the sheriff's house, and went in, leaving Barbara and her mother in the wagon. Sheriff Plunkett had not yet had his breakfast. He was a well-built man, of obliging manners, but with a look of superfluous discreetness in his face. Mason explained in few words that the mother and sister of Tom Grayson, who had not seen him since the shooting of Lockwood, were at the door in a wagon and wished to be admitted to the jail. The sheriff regarded Mason awhile in silence; it was his habit to examine the possible results of the simplest action before embarking in it. He presently went upstairs and came down bringing with him the jail keys. Mason drove the wagon to the jail, tied the horse to a tree, and suggested to Mrs. Grayson and Barbara that it would be better for him to go in first. He had a vague fear that there might be something in Tom's situation to shock the feelings of his mother and sister. The sheriff had walked briskly along the wagon track in the middle of the street to avoid the dew-laden grass on either side of the road. When he came to the door of the jail he said in an undertone as he shoved the great iron key into the door:

"Tom's in the dungeon."

"Why did you put him in the dungeon?" asked Mason.

"We always put prisoners accused of murder in there."

"You might put an innocent man in that place," said Mason.

"Well, there ain't much doubt about Tom's being guilty; and anyways the jail's so weak that we have to put anybody accused of murder in the dungeon, where there ain't any outside windows."

By the time he had finished this speech, Plunkett had admitted Mason and himself to the jail and locked the outside door behind them. The prison was divided into two apartments by a hall-way through the middle. The room to the left, as one entered, was called the dungeon; it was without any light except the little that came through at second-hand from the dusky hall by means of a small grating in the door; the hall itself was lighted by a simple grated window at the end farthest from the outside door.

When the sheriff had with difficulty opened the door of the dungeon, he could not see anything inside.

"Tom, come out," he called.

Mason was barely acquainted with Tom, but he was shocked to see the fine-looking fellow in handcuffs as he came to the door, blinking his eyes at the light, and showing a face which wounded pride and anxiety had already begun to make haggard.

"Mr. Mason, I didn't expect to see you," said Tom. "Did you hear anything from mother and Barbara?"

"They're outside," said Mason. "I thought I'd just take your place at home for a few days."

The sheriff had gone along the hall to open the door leading into the room on the side opposite the dungeon. Tom regarded Mason a moment in silence, and presently said with emotion:

"How can I make anybody believe the truth? They'll say that a man who'd kill another would lie about it. I believe I should n't care so much about the danger of being hung, if I could only make a few people know that I did n't kill George Lockwood. I can't make you believe it, but I'm not guilty." As he said this, Tom dropped his eyes from Mason's face, and an expression of discouragement overspread his own.

"You certainly don't seem like a guilty man," said Hiram.

"The worst of it is," said Tom, as they followed the sheriff into the eastern room of the jail, "I can't think, to save my life, who 'twas that could have done the shooting. I don't know of any enemy that

90

Lockwood had, unless you might have called me one. I hated him and talked like a fool about shooting, but I never seriously thought of such a thing."

The eastern room of the wretched little jail was about fifteen feet wide and twenty feet long. In it were confined from time to time ordinary prisoners and occasionally lunatics, without separation on account of character or sex. Fortunately Tom had the jail now to himself.

The sheriff, who in those days was also the jailer, locked Mason and Tom in the eastern room while he opened the outside door and admitted Mrs. Grayson and Barbara to the hall. Then he locked the front door behind them and proceeded to unlock the door of the eastern room. Barbara ran in eagerly and threw her arms about Tom.

"Tell me truly, Tom," she whispered in his ear, "did you do it? Tell me the solemn truth, between you and me."

"Before God Almighty, Barb," he answered, "I didn't shoot George Lockwood, and I didn't even see him on the camp-ground. I wasn't in that part of the woods, and I hadn't any pistol."

"Tom, I believe you," said Barbara, sobbing on his shoulder. Wondering that her brother did not return her embrace, she looked down and saw his handcuffs, and felt, as she had not before, the horror of his situation.

Mrs. Grayson now gently pushed Barbara aside and approached Tom.

"I didn't do it, mother," said Tom; "I didn't do it."

"Of course you did n't, Tommy; I never thought you did—I just knew you couldn't do it." And she put her trembling arms about him.

Hiram had gone into the corridor from motives of delicacy.

"Couldn't you move him into the east room?" he said to the sheriff. "It's too bad to have to lie in that dungeon, without air, and in August too. And is it necessary to keep his handcuffs on?"

"Well, you see, it's the regular thing to put a man into the dungeon that's up for murder, and to put handcuffs on. The jail's rather weak, you know; and if he should escape—I'd be blamed."

Mason went into the dark room and examined the dirty, uncomfortable cot, and felt of the damp walls. Then he returned to the east room just as Tom was explaining his flight from the camp-ground.

"I saw a rush," he said, "and I went with the rest. A man was telling in the dark that George Lockwood had been shot, and that they were looking for a fellow named Grayson and were going to hang him to the first tree. I ran across the fields to our house, and

91

by the time I got there I saw that I'd made a mistake. I ought to have come straight to Moscow. I went into the house and came out to go to Moscow and give myself up, but I met the sheriff at the gate."

"The first thing is the inquest," said Mason. "Have you thought about a lawyer?"

"There's no use of a lawyer for that," said Tom. "My fool talk about killing Lockwood is circumstantial evidence against me, and I'll certainly be held for trial—unless the real murderer should turn up. And I don't know who that can be. I've puzzled over it all night."

"You studied with Mr. Blackman, I believe," said Mason. "Couldn't you get him to defend you?"

"I don't know that I want him. He's already prejudiced against me. He wouldn't believe that I was innocent, and so he couldn't do any good."

"But you've got to have somebody," said Barbara.

"I've been over the whole list," said Tom, "and I'd rather have Abra'm than anybody else."

"Abra'm 'll do it," said Mrs. Grayson; "I kin git him to do it. He's a little beholden to me fer what I done fer him when he was little. But he's purty new to the law-business, Tommy."

"Abra'm Lincoln's rather new, but he's got a long head for managing a case, and he's honest and friendly to us. The circuit court begins over at Perrysburg to-morrow, and he'll like as not stop at the tavern here for dinner to-day. You might see him, mother."

"Tom! Tom!" The voice was a child's, and it came from the outside of the window-grating. A child's fingers were clutched upon the stones beyond the grating; and before Tom could answer, the brown head of Janet Grayson was lifted to the level of the high, square little window, and her blue eyes were peering into the obscurity of the prison.

"Tom, are you there? Did they give you any breakfast?" she faltered, startled and ready to cry at finding herself calling into a place so obscure and apparently so void.

"O Janet! is that you?" said Tom, putting his face to the grating. "You blessed little soul, you! But you must n't come to this dreadful place." And Tom tried to wipe his eyes with his sleeve.

"Yes, but I am sorry for you, Cousin Tom," she said, dropping to the ground again and turning her head on one side deprecatingly; "and I was afraid they wouldn't give you enough to eat. Here's three biscuits." She pulled them out of her pocket with difficulty and pushed them through the grating.

"Thank you, thank you," said Tom. "You are a dear loving little darling. But see here, Janet, you'd better not come here any more; and don't call me cousin. It's too bad you should have to be ashamed of your cousin."

"But I will call you cousin, an' I don' care what they say. Are you in there, too, Barbara? You didn't kill anybody, did you?"

"No; neither did Tom," said Barbara, leaning down to the window.

"Janet," said Tom, "d' you tell Uncle Tom and Aunt Charlotte that I didn't shoot anybody. They won't believe you, but it's a fact."

Janet had heard the news at the breakfast-table. Sheriff Plunkett, wishing to conciliate so influential a person as Thomas Grayson the elder, had sent him word very early of the unfortunate predicament in which Tom found himself, and had offered to comply with any wishes Mr. Grayson might express concerning his nephew, so far as the rigor of the law allowed. To steady-going people like the Graysons the arrest of Tom on such a charge was a severe blow; and his execution would compromise for all time their hitherto unsullied respectability in their little world. They drank their breakfast coffee and ate their warm biscuit and butter and fried ham and eggs with rueful faces. The comments they made on Tom's career were embittered by their own share of the penalty. Janet had listened till she had made out that Tom was in jail for killing somebody. Then, after hearing some rather severe remarks from her parents about Tom, she burst into tears, rose up and stamped her feet in passion, and stormed in her impotent, infantile way at her father and mother and the people who had locked up Tom in jail. When the first gust of her indignation had found vent, she fled into the garden to cool off, as was her wont. After awhile she came back and foraged in the kitchen, where she pounced upon three biscuits which had been left on a plate by the fire to keep them warm. With these she had made off through the back gate of the garden, thence down the alley and across the public square to the jail.

Meantime a lively discussion was carried on in the house.

"We've got to do something for Tom, I suppose," said Mrs. Grayson, after the question of his blameworthiness was exhausted. "He's your nephew, and we can't get around that. Goodness knows he's given us trouble enough, and expense enough, already." It was a favorite illusion with the Graysons that they had spent money on Tom, though he had earned all he had received.

"Yes," said Grayson reluctantly; "it'll be expected of us, Charlotte, to stand by him. He's got no father, you know. And I suppose George Lockwood was aggravating enough."

"The Lord knows I'm sorry for Tom; he was always good to Janet." This reminded Mrs. Grayson of her daughter, and she went

93

to the open door of the dining-room and called, "Janet! O Janet! It's curious how she stands by Tom. She's off in the sulks, and won't answer a word I say. I suppose you'll have to go his bail," she said with apprehension.

"No, it's not bailable. They don't bail prisoners charged with capital offenses."

"That's a good thing, anyhow. I hate to have you go security."

"I suppose Martha'll be able to pay the lawyers," said Thomas Grayson. "She won't expect us to do any more for Tom. It's bad enough to have to stand the disgrace of it."

"Janet! Janet! O Janet!" called Mrs. Grayson anxiously. "I declare, I'm uneasy about that child; it's nearly half an hour since she went out. I wish you'd go and have a look for her."

But at that moment Janet rushed in breathless through the kitchen.

"O Pa! I've been over to the jail to see Tom."

"You've been to the jail!" said Grayson, recoiling in his heart from such an experience for Janet.

"Yes, an' they've put Barbara and Aunt Martha in there too, along with Tom." She was bursting with indignation.

"Thomas," said Mrs. Grayson, as she gathered up the hitherto neglected breakfast plates, "Martha and Barbara have come from home this morning."

"I suppose so," said Grayson, looking out of the window.

"Now it's not going to do for us to let them go without coming here to breakfast," said the wife. "People will say we're hardhearted; and when they once get to talking there's no knowing what they won't say. They might blame us about Tom, though the Lord knows we did our best for him."

"Will you go and ask Martha and Barbara to come over?" said Grayson, with a sneaking desire to escape the disagreeable duty.

"I can't bear to," said his wife. "I hate to go to the jail and see Tom there. Besides, if they're coming I must make some coffee."

Grayson stood still and looked out of the window.

"Will they let them come if you ask 'em?" inquired Janet.

"Let who come?" said her father abstractedly.

"Aunt Martha and Barbara and Tom."

"Of course they'll not keep your Aunt Martha nor Barbara. They haven't killed anybody."

"Neither has Tom. He told me to tell you he hadn't."

"I suppose they all talk that way. 'T ain't like Tom to lie about anything though. He generally faces it out, rain, hail, or shine. I wish to goodness he could prove that he didn't kill George. Where are you going, Janet?"

94

"To fetch Aunt Martha and Barbara. I wish they'd let Tom come too."

Grayson spent as much time as possible in getting his hat and looking it over before putting it on. Then, when he could think of no other pretext for delay, he started as slowly as possible, in order to give Janet time to fetch his relatives away from the jail before he should encounter them. Janet found her aunt coming out of the prison in order to allow the sheriff to go to breakfast.

"Aunt Martha," cried Janet, "Ma wants you an' Barbara to come to breakfast. She sent me to tell you."

"I don't like to go there," said Barbara to her mother in an undertone.

But Mason, who was behind, perceiving Barbara's hesitation, came up and whispered: "You'd better go, Barbara. Tom will need all the help he can get from your uncle's position. And I'll take the horse and put him into your uncle's stable."

## XV

## ABRAHAM LINCOLN

The village of Moscow was founded by adventurous pioneers while yet Napoleon's Russian expedition was fresh in all men's minds, and took from that memory its Russian name, which, like most other transplanted names of the sort, was universally mispronounced. The village had been planted in what is called an "island," that is, a grove surrounded by prairie on every side. The early settlers in Illinois were afraid to seat themselves far from wood. As it stands to-day the pretty town is arranged about a large public square, neatly fenced, and with long hitching-rails on all four sides of it. The inside of the square is trimly kept, and is amply shaded by old forest-trees—the last survivors of the grove that formed the "island." Moscow contains a court-house, which is pretentious and costly, if not quite elegant, besides other public buildings. On the streets facing this park-like square nearly all the trade of the thriving country-town is carried on. But in the time of Tom Grayson's imprisonment the public square was yet a rough piece of woods, with roots and stumps still obtruding where underbrush and trees had been cut out. There was no fence, and there were no hitching-rails. The court-house of that day was a newish frame building, which had the public-grounds all to itself except for the jail, on one corner of the square. Facing the square, on the side farthest from the jail, stood the village tavern. One half of it was of hewn logs, which marked it as dating back to the broad-ax period of the town's growth; the other half had been added after the saw-mill age began, and was yet innocent of paint, as were the court-house and several other of the principal buildings in the town. In front of the tavern was a native beech-tree, left behind in the general destruction. Under it were some rude benches which afforded a cool and favorite resort to the leisurely villagers. One of the boughs of this tree served its day and generation doubly, for besides contributing to the shadiness of the street-corner, it supported a pendant square sign, which creaked most dolefully whenever there was wind enough to set it swinging in its rusty iron sockets. The name of the hotel was one common to villages of small attainments and great hopes; the sign bore for legend in red letters: "City Hotel, R. Biggs."

To the City Hotel there came, on this first day after Tom's arrest, one of those solitary horsemen who gave life to nearly every landscape and mystery to nearly every novel of that generation. This horseman, after the fashion of the age, carried his luggage in a pair of saddle-bags, which kept time to his horse's trot by rapping against the flaps of his saddle.

"Howdy, Cap'n Biggs," said the traveler to the landlord, who was leaning solidly against the door-jamb and showing no sign of animation, except by slowly and intermittently working his jaws in the manner of a ruminating cow.

"Howdy, Abe," was the answer. "Where yeh boun' fer?"

"Perrysburg," said the new arrival, alighting and stretching the kinks out of his long, lank limbs, the horse meanwhile putting his head half-way to the ground and moving farther into the cool shade. Then the horseman proceeded to disengage his saddle-bags from the stirrup-straps, now on one side of the horse and then on the other.

"Have yer hoss fed some corn?" In asking this question Captain Biggs with some difficulty succeeded in detaching himself from the door-post, bringing his weight perpendicularly upon his legs; this accomplished he sluggishly descended the three door-steps to the ground and took hold of the bridle.

"What's this I hear about Tom Grayson, Cap'n?" said the new-comer, as he tried to pull and wriggle his trousers-legs down to their normal place.

96

"Oh, he's gone 'n' shot Lockwood, like the blasted fool he is. He wuz blowin' about it afore he lef' town las' month, but nobody reckoned it wuz anything but blow. Some trouble about k-yards an' a purty gal—John Albaugh's gal. I s'pose Tom's got to swing fer it, 'nless you kin kinder bewilder the jury like, an' git him off. Ole Mis' Grayson's in the settin'-room now, a-waitin' to see you about it."

Captain Biggs lifted his face, on which was a week's growth of stubby beard, to see how his guest would take this information. The tall, awkward young lawyer only drew his brow to a frown and said nothing; but turned and went into the tavern with his saddle-bags on his arm, and walking stiffly from being so long cramped in riding. Passing through the cool bar-room with its moist odors of mixed drinks, he crossed the hall into the rag-carpeted sitting-room beyond.

"Oh Abra'm, I'm that glad to see you!" But here the old lady's feelings overcame her and she could not go on.

"Howdy, Mrs. Grayson. It's too bad about Tom. How did he come to do it?"

"Lawsy, honey, he didn't do it."

"You think he didn't?"

"I know he didn't. He says so himself. I've been a-waitin' here all the mornin' to see you, an' git you to defend him."

The lawyer sat down on the wooden settee by Mrs. Grayson, and after a little time of silence said:

"You'd better get some older man, like Blackman."

"Tom won't have Blackman; he won't have nobody but Abe Lincoln, he says."

"But—they say the evidence is all against him; and if that's the case, an inexperienced man like me couldn't do any good."

Mrs. Grayson looked at him piteously as she detected his reluctance.

"Abra'm, he's all the boy I've got left. Ef you'll defend him I'll give you my farm an' make out the deed before you begin. An' that's all I've got."

"Farm be hanged!" said Lincoln. "Do you think I don't remember your goodness to me when I was a little wretch with my toes sticking out of my ragged shoes! I wouldn't take a copper from you. But you're Tom's mother, and of course you think he didn't do it. Now what if the evidence proves that he did?"

Barbara had been sitting in one corner of the room, and Lincoln had not observed her in the obscurity produced by the shade of the green slat curtains. She got up and came forward. "Abra'm, do you remember me?"

"Is this little Barby?" he said, scanning her face. "You're a young woman now, I declare."

There was a simple tenderness in his voice that showed how deeply he felt the trouble that had befallen the Graysons.

"Well, I want to say, Abra'm," Barbara went on, "that after talking to Tom we believe that he doesn't know anything about the shooting. Now you'd better go and see him for yourself."

"Well, I'll tell you what, Aunt Marthy," said he, relapsing into the familiar form of address he had been accustomed to use toward Mrs. Grayson in his boyhood; "I'll go over and see Tom, and if he is innocent, as you and Barby think, we'll manage to save him or know the reason why. But I must see him alone, and he mustn't know about my talk with you."

Lincoln got up, and laying his saddle-bags down in one corner of the room went out immediately. First he went to inquire of Sheriff Plunkett what was the nature of the evidence likely to be brought against Tom. Then he got the sheriff to let him into the jail and leave him alone with his client. Tom had been allowed to remain in the lighter apartment since there was no fear of his escape on this day, when all the town was agog about the murder, and people were continually coming to peer into the jail to get a glimpse of the monster who in the darkness had shot down one that had helped him out of a gambling scrape.

Lincoln sat down on the only stool there was in the room, while Tom sat on a bench.

"Now, Tom," said the lawyer, fixing his penetrating gaze on the young man's face, "you want to remember that I'm your friend and your counsel. However proper it may be to keep your own secret in such a situation as you are, you must tell me the whole truth, or else I cannot do you any good. How did you come to shoot Lockwood?"

"I didn't shoot Lockwood," said Tom brusquely; "and if you don't believe that it's no use to go on."

"Well, say I believe it then, and let's proceed. Tell me all that happened between you and that young man."

Tom began where this story begins and told all about turning the Bible at Albaugh's; about the gambling in Wooden & Snyder's store and how he was led into it; about his visit to Hubbard Township to get money to pay Lockwood, and Rachel's revelation of Lockwood's treachery in telling Ike. Then he told of his anger and his threatening, his uncle's break with him, and his talk with Barbara the evening before the murder; and finally he gave a circumstantial account of all that happened to him on the camp-ground, and of his flight and arrest.

98

"But," said Lincoln, who had looked closely and sometimes incredulously at Tom's face while he spoke, "why did you take a pistol with you to the camp-meeting?"

"I did not. I hadn't had a pistol in my hands for a week before the shooting."

"But Plunkett says there's a man ready to swear that he saw you do the shooting. They've got a pistol out of one of your drawers, and this witness will swear that you used just such an old-fashioned weapon as that."

"Good Lord, Abe! who would tell such an infernal lie on a fellow in my fix? That makes my situation bad." And Tom got up and walked the stone-paved floor in excitement. "But the bullet will show that I didn't do it. Get hold of the bullet, and if it fits the bore of that old-fashioned pistol I won't ask you to defend me."

"But there wasn't any bullet." Lincoln was now watching Tom's countenance with the closest scrutiny.

"No bullet! How in creation did they kill him, then?"

"Can't you think?" He was still studying Tom's face.

"I don't know any way of killing a fellow with a pistol that's got no bullet unless you beat his brains out with the butt of it, and I thought they said George was shot."

"So he was. But, Tom, I've made up my mind that you're innocent. It's going to be dreadful hard to prove it."

"But how was he killed?" demanded Tom.

"With buckshot."

Tom stood and mused a minute.

"Now tell me who says I did the shooting."

"I never heard of him before. Sovine, I believe his name is."

"Dave Sovine? W'y, he's the son of old Bill Sovine; he's the boy that ran off four years ago, don't you remember? He's the black-leg that won all my money. What does he want to get me hanged for? I paid him all I owed him."

Lincoln hardly appeared to hear what Tom was saying; he sat now with his eyes fixed on the grating, lost in thought.

"Tom," he said at length, "who was that strapping big knock-down fellow that used to be about your place—hunter, fisherman, fist-fighter, and all that?"

"Do you mean Bob McCord?"

"That must be the man. Big Bob, they called him. He's friendly to you, isn't he?"

"Oh, yes!"

"Well, you have Big Bob come to see me next Tuesday at the tavern, as I go back. I'll be there to dinner. And if you are called to the inquest, you have only to tell the truth. We won't make any fight before the coroner; you'll be bound over anyhow, and it's not best to show our hand too soon."

With that he took his leave. When he got out of the prison he found Mrs. Grayson and Barbara waiting to see him.

"Well, Aunt Marthy," he said, "it don't seem to me that your boy killed that fellow. It's going to be hard to clear him, but he didn't do it. I'll do my best. You must get all Tom's relations to come to the trial. And have Big Bob McCord come to see me next Tuesday."

The influence of Tom's uncle, judiciously directed by Hiram Mason, secured for the accused permission to remain in the light room of the prison in the day-time with manacles on, and to sleep in the dungeon at night without manacles. And the influence of Janet secured from Tom's aunt the loan of the clean though ancient and well-worn bedding and bed-linen that had been afforded him during his stay in his uncle's house. This was set up in the dark room of the jail in place of the bed that had been a resting-place for villains almost ever since the town was founded.

Understanding that Tom was to be taken to the coroner's inquest that afternoon, Hiram tried to persuade the sheriff to take him to Perrysburg jail at night for safety; for he had no knowledge of Bob McCord's plan for sending the mob there. But Plunkett refused this. He knew that such a change might offend Broad Run in case it should take a notion to enforce law in its own way, and Broad Run was an important factor in an election for county officers. Plunkett felt himself to be a representative sheriff. The voters of Broad Run and others of their kind had given him his majority, and he was in his place to do their will. Elevation to office had not spoiled him; he recognized in himself a humble servant of the people, whose duty it was to enforce the law whenever it did not conflict with the wishes of any considerable number of his "constituents." To his mind it did not appear to be of much consequence that a man who deserved hanging should receive his merited punishment at the hands of a mob, instead of suffering death according to the forms of law, after a few weeks or months of delay. But he was too cautious to reveal to Mason the true state of his mind; he only urged that the removal of Tom to Perrysburg would be an act of timidity that might promote the formation of a mob while it would not put Tom out of their reach; and this Mason could not deny.

# XVI

## THE CORONER'S INQUEST

The murder of George Lockwood furnished a powerful counter-excitement, which quite broke the continuity of religious feeling, and lacked little of completely breaking up the camp-meeting. Hundreds of men and women thronged about the place of the shooting and discussed all the probable and possible details of the affair, of which several versions were already current. The coroner ordered the body removed to a large barn in the neighborhood; whereupon the people rushed thither to get a sight of the dead man, for there is no source of excitement so highly prized by the vulgar as the ghastly. At 3 in the afternoon the barn was crowded. The people jostled one another closely upon the wide threshing-floor, and the wheat-mow alongside contained, among others, at least twenty women whose appetite for the horrible had led them to elbow their way early to this commanding situation. The hay-mow at the other end of the floor was full of men and boys, and the high girders were occupied by curious spectators, perched like rows of chimney-swifts at the time of autumnal flitting. More adventurous youth had managed to climb even into the dizzy collar-beams under the comb of the barn, to the dismay of the mason-swallows whose young were sheltered in adobe houses attached to the rafters. There were heads, and pendant legs, and foreshortened arms enough in the upper part of the barn to suggest a ceiling-fresco of the Last Judgment by an old Italian master. Other curious people had crowded into the horse stables below the wheat-mow, and were peering over the manger into the threshing-floor and intermingling their heads with those of the beasts of the stall, much as the aforementioned old Italian painters mix up brute and human faces in their Nativity pieces. The crowd upon the floor itself stretched out of the wide-open double doors on each hand, beyond which there was a surging mass of people blindly gravitating toward the center of excitement, though all the proceedings were invisible and inaudible to them.

On two boards supported by kegs and boxes lay the lifeless body of Lockwood. The pitiful sight of the pallid face and the eyes sunken in their sockets exasperated the spectators. Between the body and the hay-mow the coroner took his place on the only chair in the barn; at the opposite side of the corpse the jury was seated on improvised benches. Markham, the sheriff's deputy, assisted by a

101

constable, kept back the press, whose centripetal force threatened at every movement to overwhelm the innocent jurymen.

As a matter of course, the first witness sworn was a doctor. Coroners begin at the beginning by first proving that the deceased is duly dead, and so within their jurisdiction; and by finding out by just what means the knife, rope, poison, or pistol ball severed the thread of existence. The human passion for completeness is as much prone to show itself in law proceedings as in art performances; coroners' inquests like to go down to the physiological principles that underlie the great fact of practical importance, and to inquire what was the name and function of the particular artery the severance of which put an end to consciousness in a set of ganglia which, with their complicated adjuncts, constitute what we call a man. It was in this case settled very promptly that the unfortunate deceased came to his death by a charge of buckshot. I shall not entertain the reader with the anatomical particulars, although these proved to be of the most pungent interest to the auditory at the inquest, and were scientifically expounded in every cross-roads grocery in the county for months afterward. There are old men in Illinois who haven't got done explaining the manner of it yet. But the important thing was accomplished when the coroner and his jury were convinced that the man was not only apparently, but scientifically, and therefore legally, dead; thus a basis was laid for the subsequent proceedings.

It is one of the strong points of a coroner that he knows nothing about what is held to be competent testimony,—nothing of the strict laws of relevancy and irrelevancy. He therefore goes to work to find out the truth in any way that seems good to him, without being balked by that vast network of regulations which are sure to embarrass the best endeavors of a more learned court. Markham was sworn immediately after the doctor had finished. It was his business to identify Tom's pistol. I fancy a lawyer might have insisted that no foundation had been laid for this testimony; but to the coroner it seemed the most orderly way, immediately after proving that Lockwood had been killed, to show the weapon with which he might have been killed. Markham swore to finding this pistol in Tom's room; and the ocular proof of the existence of such a weapon, in juxtaposition with the ghastly evidence before them of Lockwood's violent death, went far to establish Tom's guilt in the minds of the people. Then other witnesses swore to Tom's presence on the camp-ground; and two young men from Moscow had heard him threaten, some weeks before, that he would shoot George Lockwood.

It was just when the evidence of these two was finished that the people on the threshold of the south door of the barn began to sway to and fro in a sort of premonitory wave-motion, for outside of the door Sheriff Plunkett, having just arrived from Moscow with Tom Grayson, was battling with the condensed crowd in an endeavor to reach the presence of the coroner.

"You can't git through, Sher'f," said one man. "This crowd's so thick you could bore a nauger into it."

But the sheriff's progress was aided by the interest of the people in Tom. They could not resist turning about to look at him, and every movement displaced some human molecules; so that Plunkett, aided by the respect shown to him as an officer, was able to push a little farther in at every budge. But the people were not content with looking at Tom.

"You've got to swing fer it, you young rascal," said one man as Tom passed.

"Coward to shoot a man in the dark!" muttered another.

And ever as in this slow progress Tom came nearer to the center he felt the breath of the mob to be hotter. When he got within the door there was a confused rustle among the people on the threshing-floor, a murmur from those who jostled one another in the hay-mows, and a sound of indignation from the people seated on cross-beams and clinging to girders; mutterings even came down from those lodged like overhanging angels in the dizzy collar-beams, fast by the barn-swallows' nests. Such excited crowds are choruses who wait for some one to give them the key; the pitch of the first resolute voice determines the drift of feeling. If somebody had called out at this moment for fair play, the solvent feeling of the crowd might have crystallized about this one. But indignation got tongue first.

"Hang him!" The words came from the corner of the threshing-floor farthest from the coroner, and in an instant the tide of feeling ran swiftly to that side. Tom recognized the harsh voice, and realized his danger in perceiving that the resentful Jake Hogan was leading those who sought to lynch him.

When the sheriff, with Grayson, had penetrated to the neighborhood of the coroner, the inquest was continued by calling David Sovine. This young man, with stylish trousers strapped down to patent-leather shoes, came forward chewing tobacco and affecting a self-confident swagger. He took the oath nonchalantly.

"Tell us what you know of the murder of George Lockwood," said the coroner.

"Well, me an' George had been together, an' we parted. He was goin' to-wards his horse an' me to-wards the camp-meetin'. I was about twenty foot, or maybe twenty-five foot, away from 'im

103

when along come Tom Grayson an' says, says he, 'I'm boun' to git even with you wunst fer all.' I looked aroun', an' Tom was aimin' his pistol. George Lockwood says, says he, 'Don't shoot me, Tom'; but Tom he up an' fired, an' George jist keeled over like, an' never said another word. Tom run off as fast as his legs could carry him. I run up to George, an' he was layin' there dead 's a door-nail. Then the crowd come a-runnin', an' that's about all I know about it."

"D' you remember the pistol?"

"Yes."

"Was it like this?"

"Yes; an ole-fashioned big bore single-barrel like that, I should say."

"That'll do. You can stand aside," said the coroner.

"Hang him!" cried Jake Hogan; and there were other cries that showed how swiftly and terribly the current was setting in the direction indicated by Jake.

Tom Grayson was sworn.

"Now," said the coroner, "you don't have to criminate yourself. If you cannot answer any question asked of you without criminating you, you can decline to give an answer."

For how many ages have Anglo-Saxons made their criminal law ridiculous by this rule!

"Now," the coroner went on, "tell us just what you know about the shooting at the camp-meeting."

"I don't know anything at all about it," said Tom with agitation. "I haven't seen George Lockwood since I quarreled with him in Moscow till I saw him here." And he pointed with a trembling finger to the stark form of the man he had hated.

"Lie!" cried Hogan. The coroner called, "Order!"

"Aw!" said one of the women in the wheat-mow. "To think he could have the impedence to hole up his head an' talk that away un the corpse right there afore his eyes!"

"Do you know that pistol?" asked the coroner.

Tom took it up and looked at some marks on the butt of it.

"It's mine," he said.

"Did you have it at the camp-meeting?"

"No, nor any other."

"You are not obliged to criminate yourself," said the coroner again; "but didn't you see Lockwood killed?"

"No," said Tom. "It's all a lie that Dave Sovine swore to, and he knows it. I wasn't on that part of the ground."

"Hang him!" interjected Hogan.

"The bah-y is awful plucky, upon me sowl," said Magill, who

104

was standing on a plow-beam in order to see over the heads of the crowd. "It would be a pity to hang a man of such good stuff."

"The bare-faced villain!" growled the man next to him, and the unfavorable impression evidently had sway with the crowd. When people have once made up their mind as to how a thing has happened, they do not like to have their fixed notions disturbed. Tom's heart sank; he could see that the chance for his getting back to the jail alive was growing smaller. Hiram Mason had attached himself to Tom and the sheriff, and had elbowed his way to the front in their wake; the people, supposing that he had some official function, made way for him. He now got the ear of the sheriff.

"If you don't get Tom away at once he'll be lynched," he said.

"I know it; but I don't know what to do," said Plunkett. "If I make any move, I'll fetch the crowd down on Tom."

"Get him down into the cow-stable under the barn, and let Markham take him off. You stay here and they won't suspect that he's gone."

There was something pitiable about the sheriff's inability to make a decision at a critical moment. He looked at the angry crowd, who were paying little attention to the testimony of unimportant witnesses, and he looked at the coroner. He didn't like to bear the responsibility of having a prisoner taken from his hands; still more he disliked to offend so many voters.

"Settle it with Markham and the coroner," he said, sneaking out of the decision he could not bring himself to make.

"Mr. Markham," whispered Hiram, "the sheriff wants you and me to get Tom off. I'll get the horses ready, and you and Tom are to come out through the cow-stable. Speak to the coroner about it, and don't let the crowd see it. If we don't get him away before this thing breaks up he'll never get to town alive."

"All right," said Markham. "I'll be in the cow-stable with Tom when you're ready."

Jake Hogan had already gone out to muster his men, and Hiram was very impatient at the long time it took him to work his way outward. He was a little annoyed when Magill, getting down from the plow-beam, stopped him to whisper:

"I say, you're Tom's friend. Now what can I do for the bah-y? I s'pose he's guilty, but I don't want to see such a bowld gintleman as he is lynched by such a set of howlin' blackguards as these."

"Go over there and stand in front of Tom, so that the people won't see him and Markham when they get down into the cow-stable."

Having whispered this between his teeth, Mason painfully worked his way out of the door, while Magill pushed forward toward

105

the coroner. For Magill the people made way as best they could, supposing that the clerk was one of the functionaries without whom the performance could not proceed. The coroner had acceded to Markham's proposition and was contriving to protract the session. Magill called Sheriff Plunkett to him and made that worthy stand in unimportant conversation with him, so that they two covered from all observers first Markham's descent and then Tom's. The deputy sheriff and then his prisoner had to climb over a hay-rack and thence down to the ground. The cow-stable was beneath that end of the barn which jutted over a hill-side descending to a brook. As nothing was to be seen from this stable, there was nobody in it but a few boys.

When Mason came to say that he was ready, Markham passed out with his prisoner and down the hill-side to the bed of the brook, where Mason had brought the deputy's horse and old Blaze. Tom had been brought to the inquest in a wagon; but as it was necessary to avoid the main road, Mason had unharnessed Blaze for Tom to ride. As the hoofs of the horses clattered down over the stones in the bed of the stream, Tom felt as a man might who had but just eluded the coils of a boa-constrictor. In a little while the two were galloping over the open prairie toward Moscow by by-roads.

The prisoner's absence was observed; but, as the sheriff remained, it was not at first suspected that he had got entirely away. People looked for him and inquired of one another where "they had put him." At length the testimony was all in, and the case was given to the jury. These "good men and true," as the old English law supposes them to be, retired for consultation; that is, they changed places with the coroner and stood with their faces toward the wall in the corner and their backs toward the crowd, which now buzzed like a nest of indignant bumble-bees. After a few minutes, the jury turned and their foreman read the verdict:

"We find that George Lockwood came to his death by being shot with buckshot, fired from a pistol by Thomas Grayson, Junior, and we recommend that the said Thomas Grayson be committed to answer to the charge of murder."

When this formal condemnation had been read, the passions of the crowd broke over all bounds, and the words of the coroner, formally ordering the commitment of the prisoner, were not heard. Cries of "Hang him! Hang him to the first tree!" mingled with curses, broke forth. Men swung themselves down from the high beams and there was a rush from the mows, while the women among the wheat-sheaves drew back in terror as they might have done in a rising hurricane. The crowd surged hither and thither about the outside of the barn, and surrounded the sheriff and the coroner, demanding the prisoner. It was more than five minutes after the verdict was in before it was believed that Tom had been taken away, and then the mob were bewildered by the certainty that nobody had seen him taken down the Moscow road. Foiled in their purpose, they fell away, and the tide of passion began to ebb. But the more determined rallied about Hogan, and agreed to meet him at the Broad Run grocery after dark, to make arrangements for a trip to the county-seat during the night.

# XVII

# A COUNCIL OF WAR

As soon as Zeke had eaten the frugal supper of mush and milk that Mrs. Britton set out for him, he sought the dilapidated little Broad Run grocery. The building was of logs, and had a pair of deer's antlers over the door for a sign that it was in one sense a public house. The low door, with its threshold on the level of the ground, the one square, dingy little window, and the shabby stick chimney, in the chinks of which the clay plaster was cleaving, gave the place a run-down expression. In looking at the building, one got a notion that it would like to slink away if it could. Zeke found nobody in but the proprietor, a boozy-headed looking man, with his hands usually in his trousers' pockets, and his swollen eye-lids never wide open. The stock of groceries was small; two barrels of corn-whisky and one of molasses were the dominant elements; a quart cup and some glasses stood on a dirty unpainted poplar counter, beside a pair of scales. The whole interior had a harmonious air of sloth, stupidity, and malpropriety; and its compound odors were as characteristic as indescribable. Zeke waited about awhile, wondering that no one should have come to the rendezvous.

"Where's Jake Hogan?" he enquired of the "grocery-keeper."

"I dunno."

Zeke had anticipated this answer. The man never did know anything but the price of his liquors. It was the safest way for one who kept such a resort and heard so many confidences, and it was a way of answering questions that required the least exertion.

107

"But I wuz to meet him here."

"Oh, you wuz!" Then, after awhile, he asked, "Been over to his house?"

"No."

The grocery-keeper did not say any more, but Zeke conjectured that the meeting had adjourned to Jake Hogan's cabin for greater privacy. Zeke made his way over there with much stumbling, for the night was rather a dark one in the woods. The cabin which was now owned and occupied by Hogan was, like most of the Broad Run dwellings, built of round logs with the bark on; that is to say, the bark had been left on when the house was built, but years of rain and sun had peeled off about half of it, and left the house spotted and ragged. There was but one room, and one might enter this without ceremony, for the door stood wide open, though not on account of hospitality. This door was made of heavy puncheons and had originally hung on wooden hinges, but the uppermost hinge had come off six months before, and though Jake had "'lowed to fix it" nearly every day since, it had not been repaired, for Hogan was a public-spirited citizen, deeply interested in politics, and in reformatory movements like the present one for hanging Tom Grayson; and it was not to be expected that such a man could, in the nature of things, spare time to put a paltry hinge on a door, when grave questions were always likely to be mooted at the grocery. So every morning the clumsy door was lifted aside; at bed-time it was with difficulty partly hoisted and partly shoved back into its place. If the night was very warm, the ceremony of closing the door was omitted. Locks were not necessary in a neighborhood like Broad Run, where honesty was hardly a virtue, there being so little temptation to theft. Jake's house contained a rude home-made bedstead of poles, and two or three stools of the householder's own manufacture. Hogan "'lowed" some day to make one or two more stools and a table. At present, he and his wife patiently ate from skillet and pot, until the table should be made. It was something to have conceived the notion of a table, and with that Jake rested. There was a large fire-place built of sticks and clay; it had stones for andirons and was further furnished with a pot, not to mention a skillet, which stood on two legs and a stone and had lost its handle. Jake always 'lowed he'd get a new skillet; but he postponed it until he should have more money than was absolutely needful to buy indispensable clothes and whisky with. There was also a hoe, on which Mrs. Jake baked cold water hoe-cakes when she had company to supper. For shovel, a rived clapboard had been whittled into a handle at one end. Some previous owner had been rich enough and extravagant enough to have the four-light window glazed, but all the panes were now broken. An old hat, too shabby even for Jake to wear, filled the place of one of the squares of glass; the rest of the sash was left open for light and ventilation.

Secure as Jake and his party felt from legal interference, they had chosen to retire to this cabin instead of remaining at the grocery. This secrecy was rather an involuntary tribute of respect for the law than an act of caution. Mrs. Hogan, whose household duties were of the lightest, had been sent away, and into Jake's cabin a party of twenty had crowded, so far as was possible for them to get in. Some stood outside of the door, and Zeke had to find a place at the broken window in order to hear what was going on. This was a muster of the leaders and the center of the party; one of the "boys" had been sent to the camp-ground to seek recruits who were not to be trusted in this council of war. The recruits were notified to assemble at the cross-roads "'twix midnight un moon-up."

The first that Zeke made out was that Jake was relieving his mind in a little speech:

"D' yeh know they've gone un set up the k-yards onto us, boys? Soon's Uncle Lazar h-yer tole me't Bob McCord ud come over h-yer a-huntin', I know'd he wuz arter sumpin' ur nother besides b'ars. Bob's purty tol'able cute, but he a'n't the on'y cute feller in the worl'. Me'n' Uncle Lazar jes laid fer 'im. Ketch Jake Hogan asleep, won' cheh! Uncle Lazar, thar, when he seen Bob a-comin' down the run weth a b'ar on 'is shoulder, he jes' soaks 'im weth whisky, un then 'im un S'manthy worms it out 'v 'm what he wuz a-loafin' over yer fer un not at the eenques'. He would n' noways tell Uncle Lazar, but he's kind-uh fond uv S'manthy, un she's smart, S'manthy is. She jes' kind-uh saf-sawdered 'im un coaxed 'im up, tell he could n' keep it in no longer, bein' a leetle meller, un he tole 'er 't 'e wuz a-spying aroun' so's to let the shurruff know 'f we'd got wind uv 'is plans, un 't 'e expected to have the larf on Jake to-morry. But Uncle Lazar 'n' me 've got that fixed up, un Bob wuzn't more'n out-uh sight afore Uncle Lazar wuz a trit-trottin' 'n 'is way, yeh know, fer Jake Hogan's. Bob's a-comin' over to-morry to fetch back Uncle Lazar's mar' un have the larf onto us. But he took jes' one too many pulls at Lazar's jug." Here Jake paused to vent a laugh of self-complacency and exultation.

"Thunder 'n' light'in', Jake," called out one of the party who stood outside of the door, beyond the light of the flickering blaze on the hearth, "what did Bob tell S'manthy? Why don' choo tell us, anyways? You're a long time a-gittin' to the p'int. The business afore this yer meetin' is to hang Tom Grayson to a short meter toon. Now you tell me, what's Uncle Lazar's whisky-jug got to do weth that? What's the needcessity uv so much jaw?"

"Don' choo fret the cattle now," said Jake. "You want to know

109

what Bob tole S'manthy? W'y ut the shurruff was a-sendin' Tom Grayson f'om the eenques' over to Perrysburg jail to git him out-uh your way. I 'low that's got sumpin' to do weth the business afore the meetin' hain't it?"

"Maybe he wuz a-foolin' S'manthy," said the interlocutor, in a voice a little subdued.

"Maybe he wuzn't," retorted Jake.

"He wuz drunk ez a fool," piped up Uncle Lazar in a quivering treble. "He mus' 'a' tuck 'most a quart out-uh my jug, un he could n' stan' straight w'en 'e went away. He tuck keer never to say Perrysburg to me, but he talked about shootin' you-all down at Moscow, jes zif shootin'-irons wuz a-goin' to skeer sech a devilish passel uv fellers ez you-all. I could n' git nuthin' more out 'v 'm. But I seed all the time 't they wuz sumpin' kinday kep' in, like. He on'y let on to S'manthy arter I'd gone outay doors, un when he wuz thes chock full un one over. Un he tied S'manthy up so orful tight about it, she kinday hated to tell me, un I had to thes tell 'er 't she mus'."

"Jes y'all look at the case," said Jake, with a clumsy oratorical gesture. "Tom's uncle's one uv them ar rich men what always gets the'r own way, somehow ur nuther. That's what we're up fer. Ef we don't settle this yer business by a short cut acrost the woods, they'll be a pack uv lawyers a-provin' that black's white, un that killin' hain't no murder noways, un Tom'll git off 'cause he's got kin what kin pay fer the law, un buy up the jury liker'n not. A pore man don' stan' no kind uv a chance in this yer dodrotted country. Down in North Kerliny, whar I come from, 't wuz different. Now I say sass fer the goose is—"

"Aw, well, what's sass got to do weth the question, Jake? We're all in favor uv the pore man, cause that's us," said his opponent, from outside the door.

"Well," retorted Jake, "what would ole Tom do for young Tom 't this time? Ainh? Jes you screw up yer thinkin' machine, ef you've got ary one, un tell me that. Wouldn' he jes nat'rally get the shurruff to put out to Perrysburg weth 'im, un then git a change uv venoo, un then buy up a jury un a passel uv dodrotted lawyers un git 'im off; ur else hire some feller to break open the jail un sen' the young scamp to t' other side of the Mississip'? It stan's to nater 't Tom Grayson's in Perrysburg jail to-night."

"Un it stan's to nater," said one of the company, "that Broad Run's a-goin' to make a frien'ly visit to the nex' county to-night. Un it stan's to nater we're goin' to settle Hank Plunkett's hash at the next 'lection fer shurruff."

"Now yer a-talkin' sense," cried another of the crowd.

As soon as it was clear that the meeting was in favor of going

110

to Perrysburg, the gathering began to break up, some of the men feeling by this time a strong gravitation towards the grocery. Zeke went to Jake Hogan and explained that he "mus' be a-goin'."

"You know," he added, "I've ruther got to steal my hoss. The ole man Britton mout lemme have one ef the ole woman'd let him. But I know she jest nat'rally won't. So I'd better go back un git to bed, then when the folks is asleep I'll crawl out."

# XVIII

## ZEKE

Two things lay heavy on Zeke Tucker's mind as he hastened toward Britton's. For the life of him he could not tell whether Perrysburg was the destination to which Bob wished to send Jake, or whether Jake might not be right in supposing that Bob had incautiously betrayed his own secret. But this was Bob's affair; what troubled him most was to devise a way by which he could get possession of a piece of candle. Mrs. Britton would not allow a hired man to have a light. "Any man that could n' feel 'is way into bed mus' be simple," she said.

Zeke found the old people out of bed later than usual. Mrs. Britton had been churning, and the butter "took a contrary streak," as she expressed it, and refused to come until she and the old man had churned alternately for two hours. She was working the butter when Zeke came in and sat down. Watching his chance, he managed to snatch a tiny bit of candle-end that had been carefully laid up on the mantel-piece. But when Mrs. Britton's lighted candle flickered in its socket, she went to get the piece that was already in Zeke's pocket.

"I declare to goodness," she said, as she fumbled among the bits of string and other trumpery on the shelf, "where's that piece of candle gone to? Do you know, Cyrus?"

This question was addressed to her husband, who never did know where anything she wanted "had gone to." But she always gave vent to her feelings by asking him, and he always answered, as he did now, with an impassive "No."

"Zeke, d' you see that short piece of candle that was here on the shelf?"

Zeke rose and affected to look for it.

"I don't see nothin' uv it," he said at length.

"Well, if the rats ain't a-gittin' no better fast. Who'd a' believed they'd 'a' got up on the shelf?" So saying, she reluctantly lighted a fresh candle to take her butter to the spring.

By the time she was well out of the back door, Zeke, with one eye on the lethargic Britton, who was now a-doze in his chair, raked a hot coal from the ashes, and blowing it to a flame lighted his bit of candle with it. Then he quickly climbed to the loft, and opening the window-shutter put the candle in the glassless window on the side of the chimney toward Perrysburg. He was shivering for fear the old woman would see the light, though she was at the other end of the house, and he was yet more afraid that Bob would not see it before it should burn out. Hearing, at length, the crack of Bob's rifle, he extinguished the expiring wick and slipped down the ladder without arousing the slumbering old man.

"I expect they's another man shot," said Mrs. Britton, when she came back. If she had ever been a planter's wife her pronunciation had probably degenerated, though her archaic speech was perhaps a shade better than the "low down" language of Broad Run.

"Why?" asked Zeke.

"Oh! I heerd a gun go off, un guns ain't common at 9 o'clock at night. An' I thought I saw a flicker uv light in our loft jus' now, but it went out as soon as the gun went off. It made me feel creepy, like the house was ha'nted." And she again began to look on the mantel-piece for the lost bit of candle which she was loath to give up.

"I'm a-goin' to bed," said Zeke, "ghos's ur no ghos's"; and he again mounted the ladder. After he had lain on the bed with his clothes on for an hour, keeping himself awake with difficulty, he felt sure that the old couple below stairs must be sound asleep. He softly opened the square window, the wooden shutter of which made no sound, as it swung on hinges of leather cut from an ancient boot-top. Then he climbed out on the projecting ends of the sticks which composed the chimney, and cautiously descended to the ground.

"Cyrus!" said Mrs. Britton to her husband; "didn't you hear that noise?"

"What noise?"

"That scratchin' kind-uh noise inside of the chimbley."

"No, I don't hear nothin'"; and the old man made haste to resume his sleep where he had left off.

"I do believe this house is ha'nted," sighed Mrs. Britton to herself.

The next morning when she woke up she called out, according to her wont, to the hired man in the loft: "Zeke! Zeke! O Zeke!"

She got no reply. Vexed of all things that a hired man should lose a minute of time, she called again in vain. A minute later she was about to get up and go to the ladder so as to be better heard, when there came to her the sound of Zeke chopping wood at the back door.

"Well, ef the world ain't a-comin' to 'n end, when Zeke Tucker gits up an' goes to choppin' of 'is own accord!"

When Zeke came in to breakfast, she said: "You're out bright and airly this mornin'."

"Yes; I could n' sleep."

"D' you hear that scratchin' in the chimbley?"

"Ya-as," said Zeke, with hesitation. He was relieved that the conversation should be broken at this point by the entrance of the old man from the stable.

"Zeke," said Britton, as he drew his chair to the table, "what's the matter with ole Gray?"

"I never noticed nothin' when I gin him 'is oats. But 't wuzn't fa'rly light then."

"He's been rode. They's sweat marks onto him, un the saddle's wet yet."

The old woman put down her knife and fork. "That's witch-work," she said. "First, the butter wouldn't come, then I lost that piece of candle; un it's tee-totally gone too. Now rats don't never git up onto that shelf. Then I see a flicker of light in the loft while I was puttin' away the butter, an' you 'n' Zeke a-settin' h-yer by the fire. Then I wuz waked up by that scritch-scratchin' soun' in the chimbley, fer all the world like somebody a-climbin' down into the room, though they wa'n't nobody clum down, fer I listened. It kep' Zeke awake all night an roused 'im out airly this mornin'. Th' ain't nothin' short of witch-work gits Zeke up an' sets him to choppin' wood 'thout callin'. An' it's been a-ridin' ole Gray. Maybe the ghost of that feller that wuz shot over 't the camp-meetin' 's a-ha'ntin' roun' the country, like. I don' b'lieve it'll ever be quiet tell the feller that shot 'im's hung."

The old man was very taciturn, and Zeke could not divine whether he was impressed by his wife's mysterious "it," or whether, suspecting the truth about old Gray, he thought best to say nothing. For if anything should set Mrs. Britton going she would not stop scolding for days, and Britton knew well that Zeke would not be the chief sufferer in such a tempest.

As soon as he had eaten his breakfast Zeke went out to dig early potatoes in Britton's farther field. About 9 o'clock a clod of earth came flying past his legs and broke upon his hoe. He turned to look, and saw another one thrown from the corn-field near by ascending in a hyperbolic curve and then coming down so near to his head that he moved out of the way. He laid down his hoe and climbed the fence into the corn-field, which at this time of the year was a dense forest of green stalks higher than a man's head. Bob McCord was here awaiting Zeke. He had left Lazar Brown's horse tied in a neighboring papaw patch.

"Did you go to Perrysburg?" began Bob.

"Yes," said Zeke. "You played it onto 'em good. I wuz ruther more 'n half fooled myself. I 'lowed sometimes ut maybe S'manthy had come it over you."

Bob laughed all through his large frame.

"When we got to Perrysburg un come to wake up the shurruff he wuz skeered, un ast what 't wuz we wuz arter.

"'That murderer,' says Jake Hogan, like a ghos' fum behin' his false-face.

"'What murderer?' says the shurruff. 'They hain't no murderer in the jail.'

"'They hain't, sonny?' says Jake, weth sech a swing. 'You ketch us with yer dodrotted foolin',' says he; 'we hain't the kind to be fooled. We know what we're about afore we begin, we do. We hain't the sort to be tuck in by lawyers nur nobody else,' says he.

"'I tell you they hain't no murderer h-yer,' says the shurruff, says he.

"'Tie 's han's, boys,' says Jake, in Jake's way, yeh know, like as if he wuz king uv all creation."

"Weth Eelenoys throwed in like a spool uv thread, to make the bargain good," suggested Bob, losing all prudence and giving way to a long, unrestrained peal of laughter.

"Jes' so," said Zeke. "When we come to the jail un got the door open they wuzn't nobody thar but Sam Byfiel', the half-crazy feller that wuz through h-yer last ye'r a-playin' his fool tricks, un a man name' Simmons, as had stole half a cord uh wood. Simmons was that skeered when we come in, 't 'e got down on 'is knees un begged, un whined, un sniffled, un says, 'Boys,' says he, 'I hain't noways purpared to die. Don't hang me, un I won't never steal nothin' ag'in,' says he."

"I'll bet Byfiel' wuzn't skeered," said Bob.

"Not him. He'd been a-playin' the angel Gaberl about Perrysburg weth a long tin horn, blowin' it into people's winders at midnight, just to skeer 'em un hear 'em howl, un the watchman had

114

jugged him. Jake says, says he, 'Sam Byfiel', tell us whar that air murderer is.' Jake put 'is voice away down in 'is boots,—it sounded like a mad bull a-bellerin'. But Sam jest lif's Jake's false-face, this away, un peeps under, un says, 'Jake Hogan,' says 'e, 'I knowed it mus' be you by yer big-feelin' ways. It's mighty hard fer a man that's a nateral born to make a fool uv hisself; but, Jake, I'll be derned ef you hain't gone un done it this time.'

"'Hain't Tom Grayson h-yer?' says Jake.

"'No,' says Byfiel'. 'Somebody's been a-greenin' on you, Jake; Tom hain't never been h-yer,' says he.

"'Aw, you're a lunatic, Sam,' says Jake.

"'Ditto, brother,' says Byfiel'.

"The shurruff's folks had run out, un 'bout this time they'd began to raise the neighbors, un somebody run to the Prisbaterian church un commenced to pull away on the new church bell, 't a man Down East sent 'em. We thought we'd better be a-lightin' out mighty soon. But time we wuz in our saddles crack went a gun fum behin' the court-house. I s'pose 't wuz shot into the air to skeer us; but Jake, like a fool, out weth his pistol un shot back. The Perrysburg people wuz like a bee-gum that's been upsot. The people was now a-runnin', some one way un some t'other, un more guns wuz fired off fum summers,—we never stopped to eenquire fum whar, tell we'd got safe acrost the county line. One uv them guns must 'a' been a rifle, un it must 'a' been shot in bloody yarnest, fer I heerd the bullet whiz."

"You never stopped to say good-bye!" said Bob.

"Not me! Ole Gray wuz the very fust hoss that pulled hisself acrost the corporation line. I didn' seem to feel no interest in stayin', noways."

"What's Jake goin' to do nex' thing?" asked Bob, not yet recovered from his merriment.

"Wal, about half the fellers rode straight on home un wouldn't talk to Jake at all, 'cept maybe to cuss 'im now un then fer a fool, on'y fit to hole a snipe-bag fer Bob McCord. They swore they wuz done go'n' under sech as him. But Jake ain't the kind to gin it up; he says 'f 'e kin get a dozen he's boun' to go a Sunday night when they'll be lots of fellers about the camp-meetin', un some uh them'll go too, maybe."

"We'll have to see about that," said Bob, getting up. "But you stick to Jake, closte ez a cuckle-burr."

"All right," said Zeke, remembering his potato patch and looking ruefully at the ascending sun as he hurried back to his work.

Bob went on his way and returned the horse to Lazar Brown's

115

house; but Uncle Lazar was nowhere to be seen, and S'manthy was evidently out of humor.

"S'manthy, yer 's yer hoss," said Bob.

"Wal, you thes let 'im loose thar; I hain't got no time to bauther."

"How'd the boys come out las' night down 't Moscow?"

"Aw, I don' know, un I don' keer, neither. You're a low-lived passel uh loafers, all uh yeh, big an' leetle."

"W'y, S'manthy! You wuz that sweet las' night."

S'manthy was in a hurry about something, but she showed her irregular teeth as she disappeared around a corner of the cabin, looking back over her shoulder to say:

"You'e a purty one, hainch yeh, now?"

Bob's face shone with delight as he went on up the run to look for the bear's cubs. He succeeded in killing one of them and capturing the other alive, but he had to take them and his wounded dog home afoot. It seemed too great a venture to ask S'manthy to lend the horse a second time.

# XIX

# THE MYTH

Jake's leadership had received a severe blow, and Bob could hardly believe that he would be able to muster a company again. But Hogan's vindictiveness and persistence rendered it probable that he would not rest in his present ridiculous position without making an effort to redeem himself, even if he had to act with a small party.

"You see," Bob explained to Mason that Saturday night, "Jake's got the most p'ison kind uv hold-on you ever seed. He's shore to try't over, fust or last."

"He won't let you fool him again," said Mason.

Bob smiled and picked up a chip, which he began to whittle as an aid to reflection.

"It would be a juberous thing to try again. But I'm goin' to see Pete Markham in the mornin'. He'll go apast h-yer to the camp-meetin', fer he's a Methodis' by marriage,—that is, his wife's a member, un that makes Pete feel 'z if he wuz a kind-uv a member-

116

in-law. Un Pete knows mighty well 't when the time comes roun' fer him to run fer office, it'll be worth while to know pussidin' elders, un circus-riders, un locus' preachers, un exhausters, un all sorts uv camp-meetin' people. Pete's jes' as shore to go to camp-meetin' a Sunday mornin' 'z a bear is to eat honey when he comes acrost a tumble-down bee-tree."

The next morning Bob stood in his shirt-sleeves leaning over Mrs. Grayson's gate and watching the people that rode to the great Sunday assembly at the Union camp-ground. Many a staid plow-horse, with collar-marks on his shoulders, had been diligently curried and brushed to transform him into a stylish saddle-nag; and many a young man, with hands calloused by ax-helve and plow-handle, rode to-day in his Sunday best with a blooming girl by his side, or behind him, and with the gay heart of a troubadour in his breast. Fresh calico dresses, in which the dominant tint was either a bright pink or a positive blue, were flaunted with more pride than a princess feels in her lace and pearls. The woman who has worked and schemed and skimped to achieve her attire knows the real pleasure and victory of self-adornment.

The early comers of this Sunday-morning procession are, in the main, Methodists going to eat bread and water with the brethren in the 9 o'clock love-feast assembly, to sing together the touching songs of fellowship, and to tell, and to hear told, the stories of personal trials and sorrows,—to taste the pleasure of being one of a great company wrought to ecstasy by a common religious passion. But as the summer sun mounts higher, the road is more and more thronged with a miscellaneous company. For at 11 o'clock the presiding elder, a great man of all the country round, will preach one of his favorite sermons, and all the world—believers and scoffers, doctors and lawyers, and judges and politicians—will be there to hear him marshal in new forms the oft-repeated arguments in favor of the divine origin of Christianity, or the truth of the Arminian system of Wesley, and to admire the dramatic effect of his well-told anecdotes and the masterly pathos of his peroration. The people no longer go in couples; there are six and even ten in a group. And how well they sit their saddles! There is no "rising to the trot," in the ungraceful fashion of New York and Boston gentlemen and ladies who have put away the tradition of ancestors of unrivaled horsemanship, to adopt from England an ugly custom excusable only in a land of fox-hunting. You might find girls in their teens in this company who ride with grace and dash over difficult roads, and who could learn nothing worth their while from a riding-master,— for to ride perfectly consists chiefly in riding as naturally and unconsciously as one walks, and that is rarely given to any but those that are to the saddle born. But besides saddle-horses there are wagons, for wherever there is a prairie, wheels come early. One or two families not yet out of a pioneer state of existence go creaking painfully along in ox-carts; and there are barefoot boys skurrying afoot across fields to save distance. Everybody feels bound to go. The attraction of a crowd is proportioned to its greatness, like all other gravitation, and this one will drain the country dry of people. Scarcely any one stays at home, as you see. There are little children in the wagons and on the croups of the saddle-horses, while some supernumerary ones are held in place on the withers; it is in this way that the babies get their first lessons in horsemanship. At half-past 10 o'clock the roads are beclouded with dust that drifts to leeward, turning the green blades of the corn-field to gray and grizzling the foliage of the trees. All along the road there is the sound of voices in many keys—but all with a touch of holiday buoyancy in them. There is that universal interchange of good feeling which is only found in communities that have no lines of social cleavage. Everybody is talking to everybody,—about the weather, the crops, the latest weddings, the most recent deaths, and, above all, the murder at the camp-meeting. To this topic every party drifts when the Grayson farm-house comes in sight, if not before. Wild stories are repeated of Tom's profligacy, and of the causes that led to the feud between him and Lockwood. As the people come nearer to the house their voices fall into a lower tone, and they ride by the front gate in almost entire silence, scanning the house with eager curiosity, as though trying to penetrate the chagrin of those within. They all nod to Bob; it is the common and indispensable civility of the country. Bob nods to all in turn and grunts in a friendly way at those with whom he is acquainted; but to his best friends he gives a cheerful "Howdy!"

At length the deputy sheriff, Markham, appears, riding alongside of his wife. She is also escorted on the other side by Magill, the county clerk, who is saying the pleasantest things he can think of to her. When Markham arrives at a point nearly opposite the gate, Bob does not nod, but gives his head a significant jerk backward and to the left,—a laconic invitation to stop a moment, rendered the more explicit by the utterance in a low tone of a single word, "Pete!" Markham draws rein and stops to hear what Bob has to say; and Mason, who has come out on the porch at that moment, descends to the gate to talk with Magill and Mrs. Markham, who have also pulled up. The whole five are presently engaged in conversation in one group, while the horses amuse themselves by thrusting their dusty noses through the cracks of the fence to nibble at such blades of grass as are within their reach. The sight of the deputy sheriff and the county clerk in front of the Grayson house piques yet more the curiosity of the passers-by, who wonder what those privileged folks can be talking about.

"You cannot do that," Markham said presently, in reply to a suggestion that came from Mason. "It's no use talking to the sheriff about moving Tom to Perrysburg. He's made up his mind not to move him; and if he did move him, Perrysburg wouldn't be a safe place."

"The shairiff seems to have one eye on Broad Run, ainh Pate?" said Magill chaffingly.

But Pete Markham neither smiled nor said anything in reply.

"It's a shame something can't be done for Tom," said Mason. "He's got a right to a fair trial; and we think he's innocent."

"I'll do anything I can," said Markham, whose memory had been haunted by the appealing face of Mrs. Grayson ever since his domiciliary visit in search of Tom's pistol.

"I'm not caring much whether he's innocent or not, meself," said Magill. "May be Lockwood aggravated 'im an' naded puttin' out of the way. All I say is, Tom faced that crowd the other day like a man, an' he's a born gintleman in me own istimation; an' I'd niver let a gintleman be hung by a gang of blackguards, if I could help it."

"Broad Run don't vote for you, Magill," said Markham.

"You wouldn't ixpict it to vote for a man with a clane shirt on, now would ye?"

"Well," said Bob, "I've been a-thinkin' that ef Pete could make people b'lieve that they wuz another man wanted fer the shootin', it would sort uh muddle Jake's plans fer a while, un by that time liker'n not Abe Lincoln'll find out who the rale murderer is."

"Tell me what's the color of his hair, Pate?" said Magill. "Then I'll help you foind him."

"Well," drawled Markham, turning a little sidewise in the saddle to rest himself, and looking perfectly serious and secretive, "I haven't found out about his hair,—he wore a straw hat, you know. But he was a youngish fellow, with foxy whiskers under his chin."

"Middlin' small?" suggested Magill, with a faint pucker of drollery about the corner of his mouth.

"Yes," said Markham, biting the butt of his beech switch meditatively. "Ruther under the average, I should say, without being small."

"One eye a leetle crossed?" Bob McCord inquired, laughing.

"Right eye a little out," said Markham, waving his hand outwardly. "He had quarreled with Lockwood a good while ago and owed him a grudge. That's the man."

"Know his name?" put in Magill.

119

"N-o. That's one thing we're trying to find out. He come from off East where Lockwood used to live. We've got to try to find if anybody knows which way he went when he left the camp-meetin' that night, and if anybody can tell just where he come from."

"Oh! I understand now what you're after," said Magill. "There'll be a plinty will remimber the man when you come to spake about him. Don't you say what you want him fer. L'ave all explinations to me. I'm not responsible, an' I'll let out the saycrits of the shairiff's office."

The passers-by had grown visibly fewer in the last few minutes, and now the belated ones rode for the most part in a rapid trot or a gallop. Mrs. Markham began to warn her husband that there would not be a seat left; so the horses' heads were drawn up, and the trio set forward with a nod of good-bye to Bob and the schoolmaster.

Markham went to work in all seriousness to get information about the imaginary young man with red whiskers under his chin and an outward cast in one eye who had been seen on the ground the night of the murder. Magill took occasion to remark that if the praycher 'd only 'a' known what Markham was looking for, and all about the rale facts of the murder, he mightn't have held Tom up for an awful warnin' to the young that mornin'. But he supposed it did not matter whether you had the roight fellow or the wrong one, if you were only praychin'. Some of those who heard the clerk describe the smallish man with the red goatee and one eye out a little, thought they could remember having seen a man answering to this description; but as they could not give any information tending to secure his arrest, Magill did not think it worth while communicating their knowledge to Markham. But he quoted their sayings and surmises to the next persons he spoke to; so that, without ever straining his conscience to the point of positively asserting the substantive existence of such a red-whiskered young man with a squint, he had almost come to believe in him by the time the day was over.

The story reached Broad Run in two or three forms before night, and served to throw Jake's forlorn hope into confusion. But Magill did not think best to leave the Broad Run people to the mercy of rumor in so important a matter. He rode up to the grocery about half-past 5 in the afternoon, and having hitched his horse to a neighboring dogwood, he walked in with a good-evening to the group at the door. Going up to the counter he called up the whole party to drink with him, as became an Irish gentleman of generous spirit, who was, moreover, a prudent politician. But Broad Run had never taken a fancy to Magill; there was a ceremoniousness about his attempts to flatter them which did not harmonize with their rough-and-ready ways. If he had said, "Come, boys, liquor up!" they would have thought his manner perfect; but he bowed blandly to Jake Hogan, and said, "Have something to drink, won't you?" and so to the rest. They mentally condemned him as "too all-fired fine in his ways and too much dressed up for a free country." But they did not neglect the opportunity to drink at somebody else's expense. Jake Hogan was the more ready to accept such hospitality because he had been feeling a little depressed since his unlucky trip to Perrysburg. And now this story which he had heard of another man who might be the murderer had destroyed what chance he had of mustering a party for Moscow; for Jake's most devoted partisans did not like to run any risk of hanging the wrong man.

"Mr. Magill," said Jake, after he had turned his whisky-glass nearly to the perpendicular in the endeavor to extract the last drop, "what's this yer story about Tom's not being the ginooine murderer? I don't take no stock in the yarn, fer my part."

"Well, it ain't best to say anything about it till they get the other man," said Magill, assuming a close look. "I hear they're purty hot on his track."

"What kind of a lookin' creetur wuzzy?" asked Bijy Grimes, an oldish man with an effeminate chin and soft, fair cheeks which contrasted strangely with his slovenly and unkempt appearance. Bijy had drunk his liquor, and now sat resting on a keg with his mouth dropped wide open; it was a way he had of listening.

"Well, I don't know anything only what I hear," said Magill. "I'm not the shairiff, you know. The story goes that he was a man with a red goatee—"

"Un what fer sized man?" asked Bijy.

"Rather under-sized, and with one eye a little walled," said Magill.

"I'm darned ef 't ain't the wery man I seed," said Bijy, who never failed to know something about everything. "He wuz comin' towurds the camp-meetin' that wery arternoon. Dern!" and he shut his mouth, and got to his feet in excitement. "I kind-uh suspicioned 'im too," he added.

"Well, I don't know anything," said the clerk; "but if they catch that stranger and prove it on him,—mind, I say, if they prove it,— count me for one that will help get the world rid of him by Broad Run law, as they call it. But I've got to get on home, gintlemen. Good-bye, gintlemen, and good luck to you all!" So saying, Magill bowed respectfully.

The rest nodded their heads and said good-bye.

"He's too orful slick," said Jake, when Magill had gone.

"Makes me kind uv sick. Now I like a man ut talks out like a man, you know; without so much dodrotted saf-sawder, un so on. He ain't none uh my kind, Magill hain't."

## XX

## LINCOLN AND BOB

Fast by the "City Hotel" in Moscow stood a beech-tree, as we have said, and under this tree were two or three benches. This umbrageous spot was the cool and favorite loafing-place of the villagers, the trysting-place for making bargains or meeting friends. The ground was beaten by many feet to the hardness of a floor, and the village boys delighted to play marbles in this convenient spot. Their cries of "rounses," "taw," "dubs," "back licks," and "vent" might often be heard there before and after school hours. On one of these benches under the beech-tree Bob McCord had an interview with Tom Grayson's lawyer, according to appointment, on the day of Lincoln's return from court at Perrysburg.

"What's this about lynching Tom?" Lincoln inquired. "A lot of fellows rode into Perrysburg looking for him last Thursday night."

"Yes," said Bob, with a hearty chuckle: "I put 'em onto that air track myself. They wuz comin' down h-yer, but I made 'em think 't Tom wuz moved to Perrysburg."

"Are they going to try it again?" asked Lincoln.

"Not right off; they're sort-uh discairaged like. A few uv 'em wuz cocked un primed to come a Sunday night,—sech uv 'em as hadn't gin it up arter ridin' over to Perrysburg,—but we fooled 'em ag'in. Pete Markham, the depitty sher'f, jes' sidled over to camp-meetin' un let on 't he wuz a-lookin' fer somebody what knowed sumpin' about a young feller weth red whiskers un one eye a leetle crossed, like. Magill, the clerk, went over to camp-meetin' un down onto the Run, un gin it out on the sly like zif he could n' keep in, that they'd diskivered the tracks uv a young feller from another k-younty weth red whiskers, un so on, that had done the shootin'. The story run like a perrary fire in a high wind un sort-uh mixed 'em up in the'r minds, like. I've got it fixed so as they can't come down

122

unbeknownst to me; un ef wust comes to wust, w'y, I've got my eye sot onto a crowbar."

"A crowbar? What would you do with a crowbar, Bob?" asked Lincoln, with a puzzled contraction of the brows. "You wouldn't try to whale the whole crowd with it, would you?"

"W'y, Abe, I 'low ef a rale tight pinch comes, to try a tussle weth that air jail. I don't know's I could prize out one uv them air iron grates, but ef 't wuz to come to that, I'd try to git Tom out uv harm's way. You say the word un I'll find some way to let 'im out anyhow."

"No, no; don't do that. If he runs away he'll be caught, and then he'll be sure to be lynched, or hanged. Let me try the law first, and then it'll be time enough to use crow-bars afterward if I fail. Do you know Dave Sovine?"

"When I see 'im. He's an ornery kind uv a cuss. I don't know 's he rickollecks me."

"So much the better if he doesn't. You must get him to tell you all about the shooting—his story of it. Get him to tell more than was brought out at the inquest. Make him explain it, and find out if he's going to clear out before the trial."

"I heern tell 't he won't talk," said Bob. "The prosecutin' attorney's shut 'im up tight 'z bees-wax, they say."

Lincoln mused awhile. "If the prosecuting attorney has shut him up, you must open him. Contrive some way to get his story and find out what he means to do."

But it was not easy to encounter Dave in these days. Since he had acquired notoriety, as the only witness of the murder, he had been seized with an unprecedented diffidence, and kept himself out of public gaze. The boys about the village conjectured that he was "laying low for big game." Bob, however, had no objection to waiting for Sovine's coming. He liked this lurking for prey as a cat likes the watching at a mouse-hole. Besides, loafing of any sort suited Big Bob's genius. He could sit astride a barrel on the shady side of a grocery for hours with no sense of exhaustion. More than one day McCord had passed in this way, when at last Dave Sovine came in sight, walking rather hurriedly and circumspectly toward the center of the village. Bob was in the middle of a hunting yarn which he was lazily telling to another loafer on the next barrel as he whittled a bit of hickory stripped from one of the hoops in front of him. Without betraying any excitement, he astonished his companions by bringing the long-drawn story to an abrupt conclusion. Then dismounting from his barrel he sauntered across the street in such a way as to encounter Dave and to fall in with the direction in which the latter was going.

123

"Hot day!" Bob said, as he intersected Dave's course at an acute angle.

"Yes," answered the other.

"How's the corn crap out your way?"

"Dunno," said Dave.

"Goin' to be in town long?" Bob persisted.

To this Dave made no response. He only turned off abruptly at the street-corner and left Bob behind.

"A feller might as well try to git sugar-water by tappin' a dead sycamore as to git anything out uv him," Bob said to himself, as he turned and took the road toward Hubbard Township.

As he walks homeward over the level prairie, which westwardly has no visible limit, Bob can only think of one way to persuade Sovine to talk, and that way is out of the reach of a man so impecunious as he. It is in vain that you thrust your great fists down into the pockets of your butternut trousers, Bob. You know before you grope in them that there is no money there. You have felt of them frequently to-day and found them empty; that is why you are going home thirsty. Money will not be persuaded to remain in those pockets. Nevertheless, all the way home Bob mechanically repeats the search and wonders how he will get money to carry out his plan. He might go to Lincoln, but he has an instinctive feeling that Lincoln is what he calls "high-toned," and that the lawyer might see an impropriety in his new plan. By the time he passes into his own cabin he knows that there is no other way but to get the money from Mrs. Grayson. No easy task, Bob reflects. Mrs. Grayson has never shown any readiness to trust Bob McCord's business skill.

But the next morning he takes the path to the Grayson house, walking more and more slowly as he approaches it, with head dropped forward and fists rammed hard into his pockets, while he whistles doubtfully and intermittently. Now and then he pauses and looks off scrutinizingly. These are the ordinary physical signs of mental effort in this man. In seeking a solution of any difficulty he follows his habits. He searches his pockets, he looks for tracks on the ground, he scans the woods.

He approaches the back of the Grayson house and is relieved to see Barbara alone in the kitchen, spinning.

"You see, Barb'ry," he said, as he half ducked his head in entering the door,—"you see, I'm in a fix."

"Won't you take a chair, Mr. McCord?" said Barbara, as she wound the yarn she had been spinning on the spindle and then stopped the wheel.

"No, I'm 'bleeged to yeh, I won't sed down," he replied,

holding himself awkwardly as with a sense that indoors was not a proper or congenial place for him.

"Abe Lincoln sot me a sum un I can't noways git the answer. He wanted me to git out uh that air Dave Sovine a full account uh the lie he's a-goin' to tell agin Tommy. But I can't git at it noways. The feller won't talk to me. I've thought uv ketchin' 'im by himself un lickin' 'im till 'e'd let it out, but I'm afeerd Abe 'u'd think ut that 'u'd flush his game afore he wuz ready to shoot. They ain't on'y jest one other way, un that's to gamble weth Dave un coax his secret that away. But you see I'm so oncommonly pore this year 't I couldn't gamble at a cent a game 'thout he'd trust me, un he wouldn't do that, I 'low."

After cross-questioning Bob a little, Barbara went into the sitting-room to her mother and Bob went to the outer door to breathe the open air while he waited. Barbara's mother positively refused to let go of a dollar of her precious little hoard of silver.

"D' you think, Barb'ry, 't I'd let a shif'less kind uv a man like Big Bob have my money to gamble it away to that Sovine? No, I won't, and that's all there is about it. Dave got a lot uv my money a-gamblin' with Tommy, an' he don't git no more uv it, that's as shore as my name's Marthy Grayson. They don't no good come uv gamblin' noways, an' I can't bear that Dave Sovine should git some more uv our money, an' him a-tryin' to swear away Tommy's life."

Barbara stood still a minute to give her mother's indignation time to spend itself. Then she said:

"Well, poor Tom'll have to die, I suppose, if you can't bring yourself to give Bob something to help Abraham save him."

Mrs. Grayson stood for several seconds in self-conflict. Then she replied, "Well, Barb'ry, you always will have your way." Saying this she turned irresolutely toward her money-drawer. "I s'pose I'd jest as well give up first as last. How much does Bob want?"

"Ten dollars 'll be enough, he thinks."

"Ten dollars! Does he think I'm made out of money? Now, looky here, Barb'ry; I'm not a-goin' to give him no sech amount. Here's five, an' you tell him I won't spare another red cent."

Barbara took the silver pieces and went out to Bob.

Possessed of funds, Bob again set out to meet Dave. This time he could not wait for Dave to come to town, but boldly sallied out along the road past the house of Sovine's father. How could he wait? His pockets and his fingers were burned by the possession of so much hard cash. He felt obliged to take it out and count it once or twice, and to make an inspection of his pockets, which had a treacherous way of coming into holes under the strain of the big, muscular hands, so often rammed into their depths for purposes of meditation.

After walking past the Sovine house once or twice without encountering Dave, he sat down by a prairie brook, the gentle current of which slipped noiselessly along, dragging its margins softly against the grass, whose seed-laden heads at this season of the year hung over into the water, the matted blades lying prone upon the unbroken surface:—their tips all curved in one way mark the direction of the gentle stream. Bob reclined on the low bank, where he was concealed from the road by a little yellow-twigged water-willow, the only thing within a mile or two that could be called a tree.

After awhile Dave Sovine, sauntering, ruminating tobacco, and looking warily about, as was his way, came slowly along the road. When he caught sight of Bob he started, and paused irresolutely as though about to retreat. But seeing that Bob was looking at him, he recovered himself and came toward the reclining figure. Truth to tell, Dave was lonesome in retirement, and the sight of Bob had awakened a desire to talk.

"Have you seed a man go a-past h-yer weth a bag of wheat on his hoss?" queried Bob. "I'm a-waitin' h-yer to buy a half-bushel uv seed wheat fer fall sowin' fom a feller what's a-comin' in fom t' other eend uv the k-younty."

The story was impromptu, and Bob had no time to fill in details. Dave looked at him suspiciously, and only replied by shaking his head. By way of confirming his theory of the reason for his waiting, Bob idly jingled the silver coins in his pocket as he talked about the crops and the relative advantage of living in the timber, where you can raise winter wheat, or out on the perrary. The sound of tinkling silver caught Dave's ear, as it was meant to.

"Play a game of seven-up?" said Dave languidly.

"You're too good a hand fer me," answered Bob with affected wariness.

"Oh! we'll only try small stakes. Luck's ag'inst me here lately"; and he pulled out a well-worn pack of cards without waiting for Bob to reply.

"No; ef I play, I want to play weth my k-yards," said Bob, who had a lurking hope of winning, notwithstanding Dave's reputation.

"I don't mind where the cards come from," said Dave, as he took Bob's pack, which was in a worse state than his own. Then, with habitual secretiveness, he said, "Let's go into the corn-field."

They crossed the road and climbed into the corn-field, seating themselves on the edge of the unplowed grassy balk between the corn and the fence. Here they were hidden and shaded by the broad-leaved horse and trumpet weeds in the fence-row. As was to be expected, Bob won rather oftener than he lost at first. After a while the luck turned, and Bob stopped playing.

"You'd better go on," said Dave.

"I d' know," answered Bob; "I'm about as well off now as I wuz in the beginnin'. I 'low I'd better hold up."

"Aw, no; let's go on. You might make sumpin."

"Well," said Bob, running the ends of the cards through his fingers, "ef you'll tell me jest how that air shootin' tuck place, I will."

"I don't keer to talk about that," said Dave, with a nonchalant air, that hardly concealed his annoyance. "The prosecuting attorney thought I'd better not."

"I wuzn't at the eenques'," Bob pleaded, "un they's so many stories a-goin' that I want to h-yer it f'om you."

"Oh, I know you," said Dave. "You think I haven't got my eye-teeth cut yet. You have been a-layin' for me and I know what you are here fer. Do you think I don't see through your winter wheat? I know you're on Tom's side."

"Well, in course I am," said Bob, roused to audacity by his failure to deceive. "But it mout be jest as well fer you to tell me. Un maybe a leetle better. It mout be the very k-yard fer you to throw at this p'int in the game." And Bob's face assumed a mysterious and suggestive look as he laid his cards on the grass and leaned forward regarding Dave.

"Well," said Dave, in a husky half-whisper, letting his eyes fall from Bob's, "I'll tell you what: I don't really keer to have Tom hung, un I've been feelin' bad un wishin' I could git out ov it. Ef I had anuff money to go to New Orleans like a gentleman, I'd just light out some night, and give Tom a chance for his life."

"Maybe you mout git the money," said McCord, picking up his cards. "But your story wouldn' hang him nohow, I 'low." Here Bob laid down a half-dollar for a new game, and Dave covered it.

"Of course, if I stay he's got to swing," said Dave; and by way of proving this to Bob, he told his story of the shooting with some particularity, while he proceeded to win one half-dollar after another almost without interruption. "Now," he said, when he had told the story and answered Bob's questions, "you can see that's purty tolerable bad. I sh'd think they'd ruther I'd clear out. An' if somebody'd give you a hundred dollars an' you'd let me play three or four games of poker with you some fine day I'd make tracks, an' the prosecuting attorney'd have to get along without me."

By this time all of the five dollars that Barbara had furnished, except the last twenty-five-cent piece, had passed from Bob's reluctant hands to Dave Sovine's greedy pockets. This one quarter of a dollar Bob had prudently placed in the great pocket of his hunting-shirt, that he might have something to fill his stone jug with. For though he was devoted to the Graysons' side of the controversy, Bob McCord could hardly be called a disinterested philanthropist; and he held that even in serving one's friends one must not forget to provide the necessaries of life.

"You're awful good on a game," said Bob, with a rueful face. "You've cleaned me out, by hokey; I'll see ef I can't git you that hundred dollars, so's you kin win it. But it'll take time fer the Widder Grayson to raise it, I 'low."

"Oh! they ain't no partik'lar hurry," said Dave, cheerfully counting over his winnings and stowing the silver about in his pockets as a ship-master might distribute his ballast. "Only if I don't get the money I'll have to stay h-yer an' go to court, I guess." And Dave hitched up his trousers and walked off with the air of a man who has a master-stroke of business in view.

Lincoln came to town the next week and Bob told him the story, while Lincoln made careful notes of Dave's account of the shooting.

"He says ef Widder Grayson'll let me have a hunderd dollars, un I'll let him play draw poker fer it, he'll light out fer parts onknown."

"Oh! he wants pay, does he?" And the young lawyer sat and thought awhile. Then he turned full on Bob and said:

"Could I depend on you to be in court at the trial without fail, and without my sending a subpœna?"

"Oh, I'll be there un nowheres else," said Bob. "You needn't soopeeny me. I'll come 'thout callin', foller 'thout tollin', un stan' 'thout hitchin'."

"Now if Dave Sovine comes after you for that hundred dollars, you'd better put him off, as easy as you can. If we should buy him off we wouldn't want to give the prosecution time to fetch him back."

Bob thought he saw a twinkle in Lincoln's eye as he said this; a something in his expression that indicated more than he said. But though he looked at the lawyer curiously, he got no further light. That evening, as Bob passed the Grayson farm-house, he told the anxious Barbara something about it, and added: "Abe Lincoln's powerful deep. He's got sumpin ur nuther in 'is head 't I can't noways see into. I don't half believe 't 'e means to buy up that low-lived scoundrel arter all. He acts like a man that's got a deadfall all sot, un is a-tryin' to honey-fugle the varmint to git 'im to come underneath."

And Barbara took what comfort she could out of this assurance.

128

# XXI

## HIRAM AND BARBARA

To Barbara, indeed, the unrelieved apprehension and suspense of those long, hot August days were almost intolerable. The frequent excursions to the Moscow jail, to carry some tidbits of home cookery, or some article for Tom's personal comfort, afforded a practical outlet to feeling and a relief from the monotony of passive suffering, but these journeys also brought sharp trials of their own to Barbara's courage and self-control. She might not betray to Tom or to her mother how much she suffered; it was for her to support both the one and the other.

Doubtless it would have been a relief could she have told Hiram Mason all the dreadful apprehensions that haunted her during the long, sleepless nights. But from the hour of Mason's entering the house he had avoided confidential relations with Barbara. Before and after school Hiram attended to all those small cares that about a farm-house usually fall to the lot of a man. Gentle and considerate to Mrs. Grayson and Barbara, he preserved toward the latter a careful reserve. He could not resume the subject discussed the evening they had peeled apples by the loom; it seemed out of the question that he should talk to Barbara of such things while her mind was engrossed with the curse of Cain impending upon her brother. He might have sought to renew the matter under cover of giving her a closer sympathy and a more cordial support in her sorrows, but he saw in her demureness only the same sensitive pride that had shrunk from his advances; and he knew that this pride had been wounded to the quick by the family disgrace. Moreover, to urge his claims as a lover at such a time would cover all his services to the family with a verdigris of self-interest; and he thought that such advances would add to Barbara's distress. In making them he would be taking an unfair advantage of the obligations she might feel herself under to him, and the more he thought of it the more he abhorred to put himself in such an attitude. So he daily strengthened his resolution to be nothing but Mrs. Grayson's next friend while he remained under her roof, and to postpone all the rest until this ordeal should be past.

In many ways he was able to be helpful to the two troubled women. He stood between them and the prying curiosity of strangers, answering all questions about the family, about Tom, and about the case. He was their messenger on many occasions, and he went with them every Saturday or Sunday to Moscow. But at other times Barbara saw little of him except at the table, and he avoided all conspicuous attentions to her. Even Mely McCord, though often at the house, could find no subject for chaff in the relations of the two. When the matter was under discussion among the young gossips at the Timber Creek school-house, Mely declared she "did n' 'low they wuz anything in the talk about the master un Barbary,—he did n' pay Barbary no 'tention 't all, now 't 'e 'd got every chance." If Mason had been a person of less habitual self-repression he would not have been able to house his feelings so securely; but this man came of an austere stock; self-control was with him not merely habitual, it was hereditary.

Hiram had besides a battle of his own to fight. The Monday morning after the killing of Lockwood, as he went to the school-house, he was met in the road by Lysander Butts, next neighbor to the Graysons—a square-built man with a cannon-ball head. Butts was from the hill country of New Jersey, a man of narrow prejudices and great obstinacy.

"Looky here, Mr. Mason," he said, "d' you think now that a schoolmaster ought to take up for a rascal like Tom Grayson, that's a gambler, and I don't know what, and that's killed another fellow, like a sneak, in the dark?"

"I have n't taken up for Tom any more than to want him to have fair play," said Mason. "But I thought that the poor old lady needed somebody to be her friend, and so I went there, and am going to do what I can for her."

"Well, I know the Graysons mighty well, first and last, this many a ye'r, and they're all cut off of the same piece; and none of them is to be overly trusted, now you mind that."

"You have a right to your opinion," said Hiram; "but I am Mrs. Grayson's friend, and that is my lookout."

"Mrs. Grayson's friend?" said Butts, with a sneer. "Mrs. Grayson, ainh? As if you could make me believe it was the mother you're defending. It's Barbary you're after."

Mason colored as though accused of a crime. Then, recovering himself, he said: "It's very impudent of you to be meddling, Mr. Butts. So long as I behave myself, it's none of your business." And he went on toward the school.

"None of my business, ainh? You'll find out whose business it is mighty shortly," Butts called after Hiram.

The quarrel between the Buttses and the Graysons dated back to their first settlement in Illinois. Butts had regularly cut wild hay on the low-lying meadow between the two farms. Fond of getting something for nothing, he gave out among his neighbors that this forty acres was his own, but he put off entering it at the Land Office. When Tom Grayson's father entered his farm he found this piece blank and paid for it. From that time Butts had been his enemy, for there was no adjunct to a farm in the timber so highly prized as a bit of meadow. When once near neighbors in the country have quarreled their proximity is usually a guarantee that they will never be reconciled;—there are so many occasions of offense between people who must always be eating off the same plate. It was universally known that "the Buttses and the Graysons couldn't hitch." Where two of their fields joined without an intervening road they had not been able even to build a line fence together; but each man laid up a rail fence on the very edge of his own land, and the salient angles of the two hostile fences stood so near together that a half-grown pig could not have passed between. This is what is called, in the phrase of the country, a "devil's lane," because it is a monument of bad neighborhood.

When Mason reached the school-house that morning Angeline Butts had her books and those of her younger brother and two younger sisters gathered in a heap, and the rest of the scholars were standing about her, while she did her best to propagate the family antagonism to the master. The jealousy of Lysander Butts's family had been much inflamed by Barbara's swift success in study. Angeline had never been able to get beyond the simple rules of arithmetic; her feeble bark had quite gone ashore on the sandy reaches of long division. The Buttses were therefore not pleased to have Barbara arrive at the great goal of the Rule of Three, and even become the marvel of the neighborhood by passing into the mysterious realm of algebraic symbols. For Angeline's part she "couldn't see no kind-uv good, noways you could fix it, in cipherin' with such saw-bucks." Figgers was good enough for common folks, she said, and all this gimcrack work with x's and y's was only just a trick to ketch the master. For her part she wouldn' fool away time settin' her cap for sech as him, not if he was the only man in the world.

When Tom was arrested for murder, the Buttses felt that their day had come. Folks would find out what sort of people the Graysons were now; and what would become of all Barbary's fine match with the master? Hey? But when, on the very day after the shooting, Angeline came home bursting with indignation, that the master'd gone and took up his board and lodging at the Graysons', and had put John Buchanan into his place for a day and gone off down to the jail with the Graysons, their exasperation knew no bounds. Butts rose to the occasion, and resolved to take his children out of the school. No man that countenanced murder could teach

Butts's children. It is the inalienable right of the free-born American citizen to relieve his indignation by taking his children from school, and by stopping his newspaper.

When Mason entered the school-room after his encounter with the father he was not surprised to find the whole battalion of Butts infantry drawn up in martial array, while Angeline held forth to the assembled pupils on the subject of the master's guilt in countenancing Tom Grayson, and the general meanness of the whole Grayson "click," living and dead. When the auditors saw Hiram come in they fell away to their seats; but Angeline, pleased to show her defiance of the master, who could no longer punish her, stood bolt upright with her bonnet on until the school had been called to order. The younger Buttses sat down from habitual respect for authority, and the brother pulled off his hat; but Angeline jammed it on his head again, and pulled him to his feet. She might have left before the school began; but she preferred to have a row, if possible. So when the school had grown quiet, she boldly advanced to the space in front of the master's desk, with the younger and more timid Buttses slinking behind her.

"Mr. Mason, father's goin' to take me out of school," she said.

"So he told me."

"He wants us to come right straight home this morning."

"Well, you know the road, don't you?" said Hiram, smiling. "If he's in a hurry for you, I should have thought you might have been there by this time."

This reply set the school into an audible smile. Angeline grew red in the face, but the master was standing in silence waiting for her to get out, and the scholars were laughing at her. There was nothing more to be said, and nothing for it but to be gone or burst. In her irritation she seized her youngest sister, who was shamefacedly sneaking into Angeline's skirts, and gave her a sharp jerk, which only added a fresh impulse to the titter of the scholars, and Angeline and her followers were forced to scuffle out of the door in confusion.

Lysander Butts was not a man to give over a struggle. Conflict was his recreation, and he thought he could "spite the master" not only by refusing payment for the tuition his children had already received, but by getting the Timber Creek district to shut Mason out of their school-house. There were those in the district who resented Mason's friendship for the Graysons, but they were not ready to go so far as Butts proposed. And in asking Buchanan to teach school for him a single day Mason had unwittingly made friends against the time of trouble; for the old schoolmaster now took the young man's part, and brought over to his side the three Scotch families in the district, who always acted in unison, as a sort of clan. Butts was at a serious disadvantage in that he lived beyond the limits of the Timber Creek district. "What does he want to come a-maiddlin' wi'us fer?" Buchanan demanded of the Timber Creekers. "Let 'im attaind to the beesness of his own deestrict, and not go to runnin' his wee crookit daivils' lanes doun here." Such arguments, with the help of Mason's good-nature, his popularity with the pupils, and his inflexible determination to keep his own gait, caused the opposition to weaken and die out gradually without doing serious damage to the school.

To this favorable issue the friendly influence of the Albaugh family, who were outside of the district on the other side from Butts, contributed something. With Rachel Albaugh Mason became better acquainted through her interest in Tom's fate. She sought a conversation with the master almost every day to gain information about the case. The placidity of her face was not ruffled by solicitude, the glory of her eyes was not dimmed by tears. But interest in Tom's fate there surely was. It did not greatly matter to her whether Tom had committed the deed or not: in any case he was a bold and daring fellow who had lifted himself out of the commonplace, and who was proportionately interesting to Rachel's imagination.

But the people generally did not see things through the eyes of a romantic young woman. They were for the most part dead against Tom, and the adverse tide set more and more strongly against him when the long August days had worn themselves away and September with its bursts of storm had come in. If Tom had shot Lockwood in a street affray there would have been a disposition to condone the offense, seeing there was "a girl in the case," a circumstance that goes for much in the minds of pioneer people; for girls and horses are two things accounted well worth fighting for in a new country. Some philosophers explain this by saying that both the one and the other are means of ascent in the scale of civilization. But the fact is, that new-country people set much more store by their horses and their sweethearts than they do by civilization, for which, in the abstract, they care but little. They also esteem courage very highly. But to shoot a man in the dark as Lockwood had been shot was cowardly, and cowardice was in itself almost ground enough for hanging a man.

This increased momentum in the popular feeling against Tom could not escape the knowledge of Mason, to whom people talked with some freedom, but he managed to conceal it from Barbara and Mrs. Grayson. His situation indeed was becoming more and more difficult. He foresaw that the maintenance of his present attitude toward Barbara might soon become impossible. To be always near to her, and yet to keep himself so aloof, was more than even his nature would bear. Above all, to see her consumed by sorrow and to be afraid to speak the tenderest word of sympathy was torment. The very aspect of her suffering face set his nerves in a tremor; it became difficult for him to say good-morning to her with composure. There is the uncontrollable in all of us; and self-contained as Hiram was, he came upon the uncontrollable in himself at last.

He had reached the closing days of his school term, though it yet lacked a fortnight of the September "court week" at Moscow. It was his purpose to remain and see the Graysons through their trouble: what would become of his own trouble, when Tom's fate should have been settled one way or the other, he could not foretell. And he was, moreover, filled with the worst forebodings in regard to the issue of the trial. He came home from school a little earlier than usual on the last day but one of his school session, and fearing to trust himself too much in Barbara's presence, he had gone past the house directly to the barn, to do those night and morning things which are classed as chores or "choores," according to the accent of the region in which you chance to hear the word. On entering the barn he was surprised to find Barbara sitting on the "draw-horse" or shaving-bench. She had fled to the threshing-floor, with the belief that she was seeking for eggs, but really to find relief in tears that she could not shed in the house without opening the great deep of her mother's sorrows. She had remained longer than she intended, weeping heartily, with no witness but the chattering swallows in the rafters above, and old Blaze-face, who looked placidly at her from behind the bars of his hay-rack.

The sight of Barbara alone in the dusky light of the threshing-floor awakened in Hiram an inexpressible longing to tell her of all there was in his heart; the vision of Barbara in tears was too much for his resolution. He went forward and sat down by her; he involuntarily put his right arm about her shoulders, and drew her to him in a gentle embrace; he took her handkerchief in his left hand and wiped the tears from her cheeks and said softly:

"Dear Barbara, now don't cry any more; I'm so sorry for you."

Barbara sat still; whether displeased or not Hiram could not tell, for she did not say a word. She neither accepted nor refused his embrace. Hiram felt a powerful impulse to say more, but he suddenly remembered that Barbara's grief had no relation to him, and it seemed hateful that he should intrude his own feelings and hopes upon her in her all-engrossing sorrow, and he feared to offend again a pride so sensitive as he knew hers to be. But he allowed himself once more to draw the silent Barbara toward him

134

with a gentle pressure; then, with a resolute effort at self-control, he climbed into the mow to pitch down some hay for old Blaze. This duty he performed as quickly as possible, blindly intent on returning to Barbara once more. But when he came down again Barbara had gone, and he sat down on the draw-horse where she had been, and remained there long, all alone but for the swallows flitting in and out through the openings between the lower ends of the rafters, and gossiping from one mud-built nest to another. In this time he asked himself questions about his conduct in the difficult days yet to come, and tried to reproach himself for the partial surrender he had made to his feelings; though now he had given so much expression to his affection, he could not for the life of him repent of it.

If he had known how much strength this little outbreak of sympathy on his part had given to Barbara, his conscience would have been quite at ease. Even Mrs. Grayson was sustained by the girl's accession of courage. In the darkest days that followed, Barbara liked to recall Hiram's voice soothing her, and begging her not to weep; and with blushes she remembered the pressure of his gentle embrace about her shoulders. This memory was a check to the bitterness of her grief. But Hiram had lost confidence in himself. There were yet two more weeks to be passed, and unless he should desert Barbara in her trouble, he would have to spend these weeks in unceasing conflict.

The next day was the last of the school-term, and according to immemorial usage, the last Friday afternoon of a school-term was spent in a grand spelling-match, in which others than the regular pupils of the school were free to engage. It was while this orthographical scrimmage was going on that the county clerk, Magill, sprucely dressed, and ruddy-faced as ever, rode up to the school-house. He spent many of his days in riding about the county, palavering the farmers and flattering their wives and daughters, and, by his genial Irish manners, making friends against the time of need. Who could tell whether it might not also be worth while to make friends with the grown-up and growing-up pupils of the Timber Creek school; there would be elections after these boys came to vote. Besides, he remembered that Rachel Albaugh was one of Mason's postgraduate scholars, and it was not in such a connoisseur of fine women to miss an opportunity of seeing the finest in the county. So he went in and sat for an hour on the hard bench with his back against the stone jamb of the great empty fire-place, and smilingly listened to the scholars wrestling with the supreme difficulties of Webster's Elementary; such, for example, as "incomprehensibility," and other "words of eight syllables accented on the sixth." By the time the spelling-match was over and the school was ready to be dismissed he had evolved a new plan relating to his own affairs. In making friends and electioneering no one could excel Magill; but for attending to the proper work of his office he had neither liking nor aptitude, and the youth he kept there, though good enough at building fires and collecting fees, was not competent to transcribe a document. The records were behind, and he needed some one to write them up. He was too prudent to take into the office any man who in after years could use the experience that might be gained and the knowledge of his own dilatory habits that might be acquired there to supplant him. It occurred to him now that it would be a good stroke to engage Mason, who was not likely ever to be a resident of the county, and who could therefore never become a rival.

While these thoughts were in Magill's mind, Hiram was indulging in a few words of that sort of sentiment to which schoolmasters are prone when the parting time comes. When the children were dismissed they formed themselves into two rows on the outside of the school-house door, according to an antique and, no doubt, Old-World custom still lingering in some rural places at that time. When the master made his exit the boys were on his right and the girls were on his left,—probably because of Eve's indiscretion in the garden of Eden. Between the two rows Hiram marched slowly, with a quizzical look on his face, as the boys, to the best of their knowledge and ability, bowed to him, and the girls, with an attempt at simultaneousness, dropped "curcheys" of respect. Magill stood in the door and smiled to see some of the boys bend themselves to stiff right angles on their middle hinges, while others grinned foolishly and bobbed their heads forward or sidewise, according to the string they chanced to pull. The performances of the other row were equally various; some of the girls bent their knees and recovered themselves all in one little jerk, while others dropped so low as to "make tubs" of their dress-skirts. When these last honors had been paid, the scholars broke ranks and started for their homes.

As Magill put one foot into the stirrup he said: "Mason, how would yeh like to come down to Moscow an' help me write up me books? I'm a good dale behoind; an' ef you like to come for a wake or two an' help me to ketch up, I'll give yeh four bits a day an' yer board at the tavern."

Hiram's finances were so straitened that this offer of fifty cents a day was very welcome to him. How could he serve the Graysons better than to be where he could see Tom every day, and look after his interest in any contingency that might arise? This and

136

the recollection of his embarrassing situation in the Grayson household quickly decided him; and as the condition of Magill's office was distressing, he promised to come to town in time to begin by 9 o'clock the next morning.

That evening he explained the matter to Barbara and her mother at the supper table; and before bed-time he had arranged with Bob McCord to look after the "critters," as Bob called them. The next morning Hiram was off by daybreak. Bob McCord took him half-way with old Blaze,—for the rest, he "rode shank's mare," as the people say,—and by 9 o'clock he was trying to thread the labyrinth of confusion in Magill's office.

To Barbara it seemed the greatest good fortune to have Mason near to Tom, but the table was intolerably lonely when only two sorrow-smitten women sat down together.

## XXII

## THE FIRST DAY OF COURT

The eventful morning at the opening of the "fall term" of the court of Moscow came at length. Mrs. Grayson again put her house into the care of her neighbor Mely McCord, and she arranged that Bob McCord should stay at home so as to feed the cattle that night and the next morning. It was thought that Tom's trial would take place on the second day. Mrs. Grayson and Barbara drove into Moscow early on the first day of court, that they might give Tom all the sympathy and assistance possible.

On that very first forenoon the grand jury heard such fragments of evidence as the public prosecutor thought necessary to bring before them, and found an indictment against Thomas Grayson, Junior, for murder in the first degree. In the prevailing state of public opinion a true bill would almost have been found if no evidence had been before them. Delay in such cases was not to be thought of in that time of summary justice; dilatory postponements were certainly not to be expected in a court presided over, as this one was, by Judge Watkins. He was a man approaching sixty years of age, with a sallow, withered face; a victim to hot biscuit and dyspepsia; arbitrary and petulant, but with deep-set, intelligent black eyes. Though his temper was infirm, his voice crabbed, and his administration of justice austere and unrelenting, he was eminently just, and full of the honorable if somewhat irascible pride of a Virginian with a superstitious reverence for his "family." Judge Watkins came of an ancestry who were famous only for courageously holding up their heads and doing nothing that they considered unworthy of gentlemen. Their greatest pride was that they had always been proud. The judge's coat hung loosely on his frame, and his trousers were generally drawn up in wrinkles so as to show the half of his boot-legs. His garments were, moreover, well worn and rather coarse; like his planter ancestors, he never fancied that dress could add anything to the dignity of a gentleman. The substantial distinction of a gentleman, in his estimation, consisted in being of a "good family," and in preferring to lose one's life rather than to lie, and to take another man's life rather than to suffer the reproach of falsehood or cowardice. It was characteristic of a Virginian of this type to have something like a detestation for clothes, except in so far as they served for decency and warmth; all the great difference which separated a respected gentleman from a despised fop lay in this fierce contempt for appearances. Judge Watkins left fine coats and gold watches for those who needed such decorations; he clothed himself in homespun and family pride.

When the indictment was read, the judge, looking from under his overhanging, grizzled eyebrows, said, "When can we try this case?" The counsel on both sides knew that he intended to dispatch this disagreeable business promptly. As he put the question, Judge Watkins looked first at Allen, the prosecuting attorney, and then at Lincoln.

"We are ready, your Honor," said the prosecuting attorney, a little man with a freckled face and a fidgety desire to score a point on every occasion. "I hope there'll be no delay, your Honor. The defense knew six weeks ago that a true bill would be found. They've had time enough to prepare, and I hope we shall be able to go on."

The judge listened impatiently to this, with the air of a man who has heard so much clap-trap that it has become nauseous to him. Indeed, before Allen had completed his little speech Judge Watkins had turned quite away from him and fastened his deep-set eyes on young Lincoln, who rose to his feet without succeeding in getting himself quite straight,—this was always a matter of time with him,—and said in a grave, half-despondent way:

"Your Honor, we are ready."

"I'll set the case for to-morrow, then," said the judge, and added in a sharper key, "Sheriff, command silence!" This last injunction was prompted by an incontinent rustle of interest in the

138

court-room when the time for the murder trial was fixed for the next day. The judge's high-strung, irascible nerves, and his sense of the sacred dignity of his court, made him take offense at the slightest symptom of popular feeling.

The sheriff, who sat at the judge's left a little lower than the judge, now stood up and rapped with a mallet on the plank desk in front of him, and cried lustily, "Si—lence in court!"

And all was still again.

The judge's dignity would not admit of his addressing the commonalty, who, since they were neither members of the bar, court officers, witnesses, nor criminals, were beyond official recognition, but he said to the sheriff in a severe tone:

"Sheriff, you will arrest any person who makes any kind of disturbance in the court."

Then the business of the court went on. One after another of the spectators, whose interest was centered in the next day's session, rose and tip-toed softly out of the room. They did not all go at once, nor did any one of them go noisily. The judge had been known to fine a man for treading heavily, and those who wore squeaking boots were in misery until they were quite clear of the door.

## XXIII

## BROAD RUN IN ARMS

The popular imagination had made Tom into something monstrous. Visitors to the village went to the jail window to look at him, as one might go to look at a wild beast. Confinement, solicitude, and uncertainty had worn upon him. He shrank nervously into the darker corners of the jail to avoid observation. His mind was a very shuttlecock between the battledores of hope and fear. He knew no more than the public of the purposes or expectations of his lawyer. All that Lincoln would say to Tom or his friends was that the case was a difficult one, and that it was better to leave the line of defense wholly to himself. But in proportion as Tom's counsel was uncommunicative about his plans rumor was outspoken and confident, though not always consistent in its account of them. It was reported that Tom was to plead guilty to manslaughter; that Lincoln would try to clear him on the ground of justifiable homicide in self-defense; and that the lawyer had found a man willing to swear that he was in company with Tom on another part of the ground at the very time of the shooting. In any case, it was decided that Lincoln would move for a change of venue, for it was well understood that in Moscow the accused did not stand "a ghost of a chance."

As the time of the court session drew on, a new and more exciting report had got abroad. It was everywhere said that Dave Sovine had been bought off, and that he was to get his money and leave the country in time to avoid testifying. How the story was set a-going, or who was responsible for it, no one could tell. Dave Sovine's conferences with Bob McCord may have raised surmises, for as the time of the trial approached, Dave grew more and more solicitous to get the hundred dollars and be off. He even hinted to Bob that he might refuse to accept it, if it did not come soon. Bob McCord had his own notions about the report. He thought that either Sovine had incontinently let the matter out, which was hardly probable, or that Abe Lincoln for some reason wanted such a belief to be spread abroad. Secretive and tricky as Bob was, there was a finesse about Lincoln's plans which he could not penetrate, and which led him more than once to remark that Abe was "powerful deep for a young feller." Whether the rumor was launched for a purpose or not, it had had the effect of waking up Allen, the public prosecutor, who put a watch on Sovine's movements, and gave his chief witness to understand that any attempt of his to leave the country, by night or day, would bring about his immediate arrest.

The story that Sovine had been bought off produced another result which could not have been desired by either of the lawyers: it fanned to a blaze the slumbering embers of Broad Run. Jake Hogan's abortive expedition to Perrysburg had left resentment rankling in his manly bosom. He had reluctantly given over the attempt to redeem himself by making a raid on Moscow the Sunday night following, when Deputy Sheriff Markham had pretended to look up a hypothetical wall-eyed, red-whiskered man, who was believed to have had some reason for killing George Lockwood. It was, indeed, only by degrees that Broad Run came to understand that its dignity had been again trifled with. The first result of its indignation was that the Broad Run clan, attributing to Sheriff Plunkett all the humiliation put upon it, had unanimously resolved to compass his defeat at the next election. Plunkett, having heard of this, promptly took measures to avert the defection of his good friends on the Run. Markham, as the principal author of the

140

difficulty, was dismissed from his place of deputy on some trifling pretext. It did not cost Sheriff Plunkett serious pain to let him go; Markham was becoming too conspicuous a figure. It is the way of shrewd small men to cut down in time an apprentice who is likely to overtop the master. Then Plunkett told his brother-in-law to go out to Broad Run and explain things. Greater diplomatists than he have prepared to make use of irresponsible ambassadors when they had that to say which it might be necessary to repudiate. The brother-in-law was one of those men who like to take a hand in local politics, not for the sake of holding office themselves, but for the pleasure of intrigue for its own sake. He first sought Jake Hogan at his cabin, and sat and whittled with him on the wood-pile in the most friendly way, laughing at Jake's lank jokes, flattering his enormous self-love, and by every means in his power seeking to appease Hogan's wrath against the sheriff. The sheriff hadn't anything to do with running Tom off after the inquest, said the envoy,—Markham had done that. It was Markham who had peddled around the story of the man with red whiskers. Markham had got too big-feeling for his place. The sheriff saw that Markham was against the Broad Run boys, and so he put him out—dropped him like a hot potato, you know.

"Just consider," the brother-in-law urged, "how much Plunkett's done for the boys. He's refused tee-totally to let Tom go to Perrysburg. Plunkett ain't going to be dictated to by rich men like ole Tom Grayson. He knows who elected him. And he don't feel obliged to protect a murderer after the coroner's jury say's he's guilty."

"They's been talk of his shootin' if any reg'laters come around," said Jake.

"Him shoot?" answered the brother-in-law. "He's done everything he could not to put out the boys, and what 'u'd 'e shoot for? He ain't anxious to have the job of hangin' Tom Grayson. He's heard tell of sheriffs, 'fore now, that's felt themselves ha'nted as long's they lived, because they'd hanged a man. He ain't goin' to fight for the privilege of hangin' Tom, and he ain't the kind to do anythin' brash, and he ain't ag'inst good citizens like the boys on the Run—depend on that. Of course,"—here the brother-in-law picked up a new splinter and whittled it cautiously as he spoke,—"of course you know't the sheriff's give bonds. He's got to make a show of defending his prisoner. He's took 'n oath, you see, 'n' people expect him to resist. But if a lot of men comes, what can one man do? S'posin' they was to tie his hands, and then s'pose they was to say if he moved they'd shoot. What could he do?"

The envoy stopped whittling and looked at Jake, giving the slightest possible wink with one eye. Jake nodded his head with the air of a man who is confident that he is not such a fool as to be unable to take a hint enforced by half a wink.

"What does 'n oath amount to with a pistol at your head?" the brother-in-law inquired; "an' what's the use of bonds if your hands are tied? You can talk strong; that don't hurt anybody."

Jake nodded again, and said, "In course."

"If you was to hear about the sheriff's sayin' he'd ruther die than give up his prisoner, you can just remember that he's got to talk that way; he's under bonds, and he's swore in, and the people expect him to talk about doin' his dooty. But you're too old a hand to set much store by talk?"

"Well, I 'low I am," said Hogan, greatly pleased that his experience and astuteness were at length coming in for due recognition.

Then when Jake was pretty well mollified, the brother-in-law adjourned himself and Jake to the grocery, where he treated the crowd, and in much more vague and non-committal terms let all the citizens that resorted thither understand that Sheriff Plunkett was their friend, and that Pete Markham was the friend of the rich men and the lawyers. But he took pains to leave the impression that Tom would certainly meet his deserts at the hands of the court, for the sheriff desired to avoid the embarrassment of a mob if he could.

The sweetness of Jake Hogan's spirit had been curdled by his disappointment and reverses, but these overtures from the sheriff to him as a high-contracting power were very flattering and assuring. When, a little later, the startling intelligence reached that center of social and intellectual activity, the Broad Run grocery, that Dave Sovine had been bought off, Broad Run was aroused, and Jake Hogan left off sulking in his tent and resumed his activity in public affairs.

"Didn't I tell you," he asked, leaning his back against the counter and supporting himself on his two elbows thrust behind him, while one of his legs, ending in a stogy boot, was braced out in front of him, "you can't hang the nephew 'v a rich man in such a dodrotted country as this yer Eelenoys? Dave Sovine's bought off, they say, by an ornery young lawyer un that air Bob McCord." Jake was too prudent to apply any degrading adjectives to a man of Bob's size and renown. "Dave'll light out the day afore the trial with rocks in his pockets, un that air young coward'll git clean off. Where's yer spunk, I'd like to know? 'F you're go'n' to be hornswoggled by lawyers like that air long-legged Abe Lincoln, un skin-flints like ole Seven-percent Tom Grayson, w'y, you kin, that's all."

Jake, with his head thrown forward, looked sternly around on the group about him, and they seemed to feel the reproach of his superior aggressiveness. Bijy Grimes was rendered so uneasy by Jake's regard that he shut his mouth; and then, not knowing what better to do, he ventured to ask humbly, "What kin we do about it, Jake?" letting his mouth drop open again in token that he waited for a reply.

"Do?" said Jake contemptuously. "W'y, chain-lightnin', Bijy, what a thing, now, to ax! Show me two dozen, ur even one dozen, men that'll stan' at my back tell the blood runs, un I'll show 'em 't folks can't take a change of venoo out-uh the k-younty that knows all about the rascality into one that don't. I'll show 'em how to buy off witnesses, un I'll l'arn these yer dodrotted lawyers un rich men how to fool wreth the very bone un sinoo uv the land."

Notwithstanding the natural love of these men for a little excitement, they had been rendered somewhat unresponsive by Jake's failures. The most of them thought it best to go to town on the day of the trial and see how it would come out. But at 6 o'clock in the evening of the first day of court, Lew Baker, a farmer from the river valley beyond the Run, rode past the door of the grocery on his way home, and said a collective "Howdy" to the three or four who stood outside. Bijy Grimes, who was one of them, came out toward the middle of the road heading off the traveler.

"Hello, Lew! Any nooze about the trial?" he said, dropping his lower jaw from between his fat infantile cheeks and waiting for a reply, while the rest of the group moved up to hearing distance.

"Well, yes," said Baker, pulling up his horse and swinging himself round in the saddle so as to bring the most of his weight on the right stirrup, while he rested his left elbow on his left knee and his right hand on the horse's mane. "I heern tell, jest as I come away, that Dave what-ye-may-call-'im, the witness, had sloped, liker'n not. He hain't been seed aroun' for a right smart while, un they say he's gone off to New Urleans ur the Injun country. Moscow's stirred up about it."

"Tu-lah!" said Bijy. "They 'low he'll be got off, don't they!"

"They're shore sumpin's fixed, fer the young feller's lawyer hain't soopeenied a derned witness."

"Tu-lah!" said Bijy. "Is that a fack?"

"Shore 's shootin', they say. He's to be got off somehow, I s'pose."

"Tu-laws-a-massy!" broke out Bijy; and turning to his fellow-loafers he said, "That'll rile Jake purty consid'able, now won't it?"

It did stir up Jake when he heard of it. He promptly set to work to form a company to descend at once on Moscow and take the case out of the hands of the dodrotted lawyers. He could not at so late an hour get together more than twenty or twenty-five men from

143

Broad Run and the regions within warning distance. Some of these joined him only because they could not endure to have anything very exciting take place in their absence: it would entail the necessity of their hearing for the rest of their lives the account given of the affair by the participators, who would always value themselves on it. Some of the larger boys, whose aid had been rejected in the previous excursion because they were not accounted mature enough for such public responsibilities, were now admitted: the company would be small, and a boy is better than nobody in a pinch. S'manthy's oldest son, a tow-headed fellow of fifteen, was one of these, and he was sent over the hill to warn Zeke Tucker, who was still at Britton's, a mile away from the borders of what was distinctively called "the Run Neighborhood."

The September twilight was already fading when the lad presented himself in front of Zeke Tucker, who sat perched on top of a rail fence for rest and observation after his day's work. Mrs. Britton was making the house over-warm, and Zeke preferred the fresh air.

"I say, Zeke," said the breathless boy, "it's to come off to-night, un I'm a-goin', by hokey!"

"What's to come off to-night?"

"W'y, the hangin'—the hangin' of that young chap Tom down't Moscow; un I'm goin' to take grandad's ole flint-lock."

"Your grandad's ole flint-lock! You might as well take a stick," said Zeke.

"Oh! it'll go off ef you tech it off weth a coal of fire, but I don't 'low I kin find any coal to tech it off weth down thar," and S'manthy's son scratched his head thoughtfully. "But, anyways, it'll look like a gun in the night."

"Yes, un you'll look like a man, I s'pose. But what time's Jake goin'?"

"Twix' ten un 'leven. Donchoo be late."

"You tell Jake not to go, noways, wethout me," said Zeke, hoping by this to delay Jake's start.

# XXIV

# FIRST COME, FIRST SERVED

Zeke sat restless on the fence until S'manthy's boy, exultant that his manhood was to be recognized by his admission to the band, had gone out of sight in the direction of the grocery. Then Zeke sprang from the fence and started, as fast as legs could carry, along an old Indian trail, hoping by this disused and in some places obstructed short cut across the prairie to save a mile of the eight-miles' journey to Bob McCord's cabin. Bob was already abed when Zeke, badly blown by his rapid walking, knocked at the door.

"Who's there?" called Bob, emerging from his first heavy sleep.

"It's me—Zeke Tucker! Git up, quick, Bob! Jake Hogan's off at ten 'r 'leven, un it's nigh onto that a'ready." And Zeke impatiently rattled the door of the cabin, the latch-string of which had been drawn in to lock it.

Bob came down on the floor with a thump, and his few clothes were soon pulled on; then he came out and stood in the fresh air, on the "butt-cut" of a tulip-tree, or "flowering poplar," which, to compensate for the descent of the hill-side, had been laid against the bottom log of his cabin for a front-door step. Zeke explained to him how urgent the case was.

"Baub! don't you go 'n' go off down to Moscow to-night," called Mrs. McCord. "They hain't no airthly use in your botherin' yourself so much about other folkses business. You'd orter stay'n' look arter your own wife un childern." It was Mrs. McCord's invariable habit to object, in her plaintive and impotent fashion, to everything her husband proposed to do. She had not the slightest expectation that he would remain at home in consequence of anything she might say, nor did she care that he should; but she had a vocation to hold in check his thriftless propensities. This she tried to do by protests uttered indiscriminately against all his outgoings and his incomings, his downsittings and his uprisings.

"We ain't got no hoss," said Bob, replying to Zeke, and paying no heed to his wife. "Mrs. Grayson un Barb'ry 've gone un gone to town weth ole Blaze, so's to be weth Tom airly in the mornin'. What on yerth to do I don't noways see." Bob was standing with his fists in his pockets, looking off anxiously toward the horizon.

"Can't you git Butts's?" said Zeke.

"Thunder! No! Buttses un Graysons don't hitch. Butts don't

145

speak to none uv'em, un he hates Tom the wust, fer throwin' rocks at his geese when they got into the medder, un dauggin' his haugs out-uh the corn. They'd a leetle rather Tom'd be lynched un not. By blazes! I've got to git one of Butts's hosses right straight off. Buchanan's hoss is lame, un they hain't nary nuther one to be got this side uv Albaugh's, and that's too fur away. You go down to the branch un wait fer me, un I'll git Butts's little wagon. I 'low they'll be hoppin' mad 'f they fine out what I got it fer, but I've got to git it, 'f I have to steal it. They hain't no two ways about it."

"I don't think you'd ortuh go off that a-way, Baub," began Mrs. McCord again. "Un me more 'n half sick. I've been feelin' kind-uh slarruppy like fer two 'r three days. Un them air taters is to be dug, un Mely's gone away. You 'n' Zeke Tucker 'll make a purty fist uv it a-lickin' all Broad Run, now, wonch yeh? Wha' choo got to do weth Jake—"

But Bob did not hear the rest of it, nor was it ever uttered indeed. For Mrs. McCord, when she found that her husband had gone, did not think it worth while to finish her lamentations; she only drew a sigh of complacent long-suffering and submission to fate, and went to sleep.

Hardened sinner that he was, Big Bob felt a little twinge of shame as he made his way rapidly to Butts's house. His wife's set speech about being more than half sick, often as he had heard it, and little as he had ever heeded it, had now made a sufficient lodgment in his consciousness to suggest a way out of his difficulty; but it was a way which a loafer of the superior sort, such as Bob, might feel ashamed to take, knowing that such a scheme as he was concocting would be an outrage on all the sacred principles of good neighborhood—an outrage only to be justified by military necessity. All the way to Butts's, hurried as he was, his hands were ramming his trousers-pockets, after his fashion of groping there for a solution of his difficulties. It was the carrying over into other affairs the habitual research which the hunter makes for bullets, caps, patching, or jack-knife to meet the exigencies of the forest.

Arrived at the unpainted, new frame-house, which, being two feet longer and one foot broader than any other in the neighborhood, was the particular pride of the Butts family, he noted that all the lights were out, and after hesitating whether to capture the horse by stealth or by strategy, he went to the front door and rapped. The head of the proprietor came out of one of the lower windows with an abrupt "Who's there?" spoken with that irritation a weary man is prone to express when awakened from his first nap to attend to some one else's wants.

"I say, Mr. Butts," said Bob, pushing his hands harder against the bottoms of his pockets, "kin I git the loan uv one uv your hosses un your leetle wagon to fetch the doctor? My ole woman's purty bad; been sick ever sence the sun was 'n 'our high, un we can't git nothin' to do no good."

"What seems to be the matter?" said Butts, wishing to postpone an unpleasant decision.

Bob hesitated a moment: lying is a dangerous business unless it is carried on with circumspection. "Blamed 'f I know jest what it is. I suspicion it's the dyspepsy."

The name of dyspepsia was new to the country at that day, though the complaint was ancient enough, no doubt. Just what dyspepsy might be Bob did not know, but he hit on it as the vaguest term he could recall and one that had a threatening sound. It would not have served his purpose to have repeated Mrs. McCord's diagnosis of her own case, that she was "feelin' kind-uh slarruppy like." "Whatever 'tis, she don't think she kin git through till mornin' 'thout I git a doctor."

"Well, I doan know. The sorrel's lame; un I don't like to let the bay colt go noways, he's sech a sperrited critter."

Butts drew his head in at this point to consult with Mrs. Butts as to how he could evade lending the cherished bay colt.

"Looky h-yer, Mr. McCord," presently called Mrs. Butts, keeping her nightcapped head well out of sight as she spoke, "you don't want no doctor nohow." Mrs. Butts had come by virtue of superior credulity to hold the position of neighborhood doctress, and she was not friendly to regular physicians. "You jest take along with you a bottle of my new medicine, 't I call the 'Scatter Misery,' It's made out-uh roots an' yarbs, an' it's the best thing I know fer mos' every kind of complaint. It's good insides an' outsides. You rub the Scatter Misery onto the outsides un give her a swaller now un then insides. It'll fetch 'er 'roun' in an hour or two."

Bob felt himself fairly entangled in his own intrigue, but he gave his great fists another push into his trousers-pockets and said:

"I'm much obleeged, Mrs. Butts, but my ole woman tole me ez I wuzn't to come back 'thout a doctor; un ef you hain't got no critter you kin len' me, I mus' be a-gittin' 'long down to Albaugh's mighty quick. That's a powerful ways off, though. I wish I'd gone there straight un not come over h-yer."

This last was uttered in a tone of plaintive disappointment as Bob turned away, walking slowly and giving the family council time to change its mind.

"Aw, well, Bob," called Butts, after a conference with his wife, "I don't like to disobleege a neighbor. You kin have the bay colt; but you must drive slow, Bob. He's a young thing un the fidgetiest critter."

Bob would drive slow. He professed that he never drove faster 'n a slow trot, "nohows you can fix it." And he helped Butts to hitch up with no sense of exultation, but rather with a sneaking feeling of shame.

However, nothing troubled Bob long or deeply, and when he had passed the branch and taken in Zeke Tucker, and got out of the woods to the smooth prairie road beyond, he forgot his scruples and tried to find out just how much speed Butts's bay colt might have in him. Nor did he slacken pace even when he got into the village streets; but remembering how near it was to Jake's time, he held the horse swiftly on till he reached an alley-way behind some village stores. Telling Tucker to tie the horse, he got over the fence and laid hold of a rusty crowbar that he had long kept his mind fixed on. Putting this on his shoulder, he was soon at the jail.

"Tom!" he called, in a smothered voice, at the grated window on the east side. But all within was as silent as it was dark. For a moment Bob stood perplexed. Then he went to the grating at the back of the jail—the window that opened into the passage-way at the end opposite to the front door.

"Tom, where air you?" he called, putting his hands up on each side of his mouth, that his words might not be heard in the street.

"In the dungeon." Tom's voice sounded remote.

Bob spent no time in deliberating, but thrust the crowbar between the cross-bars of the iron grating. His first difficulty was similar to that of Archimedes, he could not get a fulcrum; or, as he expressed it less elegantly to Zeke, "he couldn't git no purchase onto the daudblasted ole thing." But by persistently ramming the point of the crowbar against the stone-work at the side of the window he succeeded at length in picking out a little mortar and bracing the tip of the crowbar against a projecting stone. He had great confidence in his own physical strength, but the grating at first was too much for him; the wrought-iron cross-bar of the window bent under the strain he put upon it, but it would not loosen its hold on the masonry. At this rate it would take more time than he could hope to have to push the bars apart enough to admit even Zeke's thin frame, and he could not hope to bend them far enough to let his own great body through. He therefore changed his mode of attack. Withdrawing his crowbar from the grating, he felt for a seam in the stones at the base of the window and then drove the point of the bar into this over and over again, aiming as well as he could in the dark and taking the risk of attracting the attention of some wakeful villager by the sound of his ringing blows. At length, by drilling and

148

prying, he had loosened the large stone which was in some sort the key to the difficulty. This accomplished, he made haste to insert the bar again into the grating, bracing its point as before in the seam he had already opened in the stone-work at the side of the window. Then, with his feet against the wall of the jail, he crouched his great frame and put forth the whole of his forces, thrusting his mighty strength against the crowbar, as blind Samson in his agony tugged at the pillars of the Philistine temple. In some colossal work of Michael Angelo's I have seen a tremendous figure so contorted, writhing in supreme effort. The mortar broke, some of the stones gave way at length, and one bar of the grating was wrenched reluctant from its anchorage in the wall below. Then, letting the crowbar fall, Bob seized the rod now loosened at one end and tore it quite out, and then threw it from him in a kind of fury. The process had to be repeated with each separate bar in the grating, though the breaking up of the wall about the window made each rod come more easily than the preceding one. When all had been removed he squeezed through the window-opening, feet first, and felt his way down the passage to the door of the dungeon, where Tom was anxiously waiting for his deliverer. Bob made what a surgeon would call a "digital examination" of the dungeon door, and found its strength to be such that to break it down would require the rest of the night, if, indeed, there was any hope of achieving it at all in a dark hall-way, too narrow to admit of a free use of the crowbar.

"Dern the luck!" said Bob, pausing a moment.

"What's the matter, Bob?" asked Tom anxiously.

But Bob did not seem to hear the question. "We must git a cole-chisel," was all he said; and he hastened to creep back out of the broken-up window.

"Whach yeh go'n' to do?" asked the waiting Zeke, as Bob emerged.

But Bob only said, "Come on, quick!" and started off in a swinging trot toward the village blacksmith shop, a low, longish, wooden building, barely visible in the darkness. He pulled at the door, but it was firmly closed with a padlock. Then he felt his way along the side of the building to a window-sash, which was easily taken out of its place.

"Heap uh use uh lockin' the door," he muttered, as he climbed in. "Blow up the belluses there un see ef you kin make a light."

Zeke, who had followed his leader, pumped away on the bellows in vain, for the fire in the forge had quite gone out, though the ashes were hot to Zeke's touch. Both of the men set to work to find a blacksmith's cold-chisel, feeling and fumbling all over the disorderly shop. As it often took the smith half an hour to find this particular tool, it would have been a marvel for two strangers to find it at all in the darkness.

"We'll have to gin up the c'nundrum," said Bob, with his hands again in his pockets. "Didn' you say as you 'lowed the sher'f was expectin' Jake?"

"Yes," answered Zeke. "Jake's got a kind-uv a secret urrangement weth Plunkett's brother-in-law. They hain't to be shootin'-work on nary side, but on'y jist a-plenty uv thunderin' loud talk fer the looks uv the thing. Jake's to make the derndest kind uv a row, un the sher'f's to talk about dyin' 'n 'is tracks un all that, you know. That 's some weeks ago't the sher'f s brother-in-law fixed all that up, un Jake, he tole us they wouldn' be no danger."

"Turn your coat wrong sides out," said Bob, turning his own. "Now tie your han'kercher acrost yer face, so 's to kiver all below yer eyes."

When these directions had been carried out Bob climbed out of the window, and stopped to put his hands into his pockets again and consider.

"Whach yeh go'n' to do?" asked Zeke.

But Bob only asked, "What'll we do fer pistols'?" and with that set himself to feeling all about the ground in front of the smith's shop, picking up and rejecting now a bit of a dead bough from the great sycamore under the friendly shade of which the smith did all his horse-shoeing, now a bit of a board, and again a segment of a broken wagon-tire, and then a section of a felloe. At last Bob came upon the broken wheel of a farmer's wagon, leaning against the side of the shop in waiting for repairs to its woodwork and a new tire. From this he wrenched two spokes and gave one of them to Zeke.

"There's your pistol, Zeke. Put it jam up agin Plunkett's head un tell him to hole still ur die. We've got to play Jake Hogan onto 'im un git the keys. Th' ain't nary nuther way."

As Bob passed the jail in going toward the sheriff's house he took along the crowbar. Plunkett lived in a two-story frame dwelling on the eastern margin of the village. Bob sent Zeke to run around it and pound on the back door and bang on every window with his wagon-spoke and his fists, while Bob himself dealt rousing blows on the front door with his crowbar. When Zeke had made the circuit of the house, Bob put the crowbar under the door.

"We mustn't wait fer him to open, he'll see how few we air," he whispered. "Prize away on this yer." Then, while Zeke lifted up on the bar, Bob hurled his whole bull weight against the door. The staple of the lock held fast, but the interior facing of the door-jamb was torn from its fastenings and fell with a crash on the floor, letting the door swing open. Not to lose the advantage of surprise, Bob and

Zeke pushed up the stairway, guided by the noise made by some one moving about. By the time they reached Plunkett's sleeping-room the latter had struck a light with steel and flint, and had just lighted a tallow-candle, which was beginning to shed a feeble glimmer on the bed, the rag-carpeted floor, the shuck-bottom chairs, and the half-dressed man, when Bob, coming up quickly behind him, blew the light out, and seizing Plunkett with the grip of a bear crowded him down to the floor with a smothered oath.

"Don't kill me, boys," said the sheriff in a hoarse whisper; for this rough usage frightened him a little, notwithstanding his good understanding with the mob.

"Say one word un you're a dead man," said Zeke Tucker, pressing the cold muzzle of his wagon-spoke close to the sheriff's head. These melodramatic words were, I am glad to say, a mere plagiarism. In the absence of anything better, Zeke repeated the speech of a highwayman in an old-fashioned novel he had heard Mrs. Britton read on Sunday afternoons. Then he added on his own account: "We won't have no tricks; d' yeh h'yer?"

"They's mor' 'n forty uv us," said Bob, "un we want them air keys right straight."

"If I had half a chance I'd ruther die than give 'em up,"—this was all that Plunkett could remember of the defiant speech he was to have made on this occasion,—"but there they air, at the head of my bed"; and a cold shudder went over him as Zeke again touched him ominously with the end of the wagon-spoke.

The sheriff's wife, though she had every assurance of the secret friendliness of the mob, now began to weep.

"Not a word!" said Bob, who was continually scuffling his feet, in order, like Hannibal and other great commanders, to make his forces seem more numerous than they were. "We won't hurt you, Mrs. Plunkett, ef you keep still; but ef you make a noise while we're gone, the boys outside might shoot."

The woman became silent.

"Some of our men'll be left to guard your house till our business is finished," said Bob to the sheriff, who lay limp on the floor, growing internally angry that the Broad Run boys should not show more respect for his dignity. "Don't you move or make any soun', fer yer life," added Bob when he reached the top of the stairs, down which he descended with racket enough for three or four.

As they left the house with the keys, Bob and Zeke gave orders in a low voice to an imaginary guard at the door.

All that Tom had made out was that the irruption of Bob McCord into the jail signified imminent danger to himself, and when Bob had gone out again, Tom's heart failed him. He stood still, with his fingers on the iron grating in the dungeon door. For this last night the sheriff had taken the additional precaution of leaving Tom's manacles on when he had locked him in the dungeon, and the lack of the free use of his hands added much to his sense of utter helplessness in the face of deadly peril. He could not see any light where he stood, gripping the bars and staring into the passage-way; but he could not endure to leave this position and go back into the darker darkness behind him. Confinement and anxiety had sapped the physical groundwork of courage. When he heard Bob and Zeke come past the jail on their return from the blacksmith shop he had made out nothing but the sound of feet, whether of friends or foes he did not know; and when the sounds died away, a horror of deadly suspense fell upon him. All black and repulsive possibilities became imminent probabilities in the time that he waited. Over and over again he heard men and horses coming, and then discovered that he was hearkening to the throbbing of his own pulse. At last he heard the key turning in the lock of the front door, and was sure that the enemy had arrived. It was not till Bob said, when he had got into the hall and was trying the keys in the dungeon door, "Quick, Tom, fer God Almighty's sake!" that his spirit, numb with terror, realized the presence of friends.

"What's the matter?" asked Tom, his teeth chattering with reaction from the long suspense.

"Jake Hogan'll be h-yer in less'n no time"; and with that Bob, having got the door open, almost dragged the poor fellow out, taking time, however, to shut the front door and lock it, and taking the keys with him, "fer fear somebody might git in while we're away," as he said laughing.

Once the jail was cleared, a new perplexity arose. Until this moment it had not occurred to Bob to consider what disposal he should make of the prisoner.

"What am I goin' to do weth you, Tom?" he demanded, when they stood concealed in the thick obscurity under an elm-tree on the side of the court-house opposite to the jail. "I wonder 'f you hadn' better light out?"

"Not without Abra'm says so," answered Tom, still shivering and feeling a strong impulse to run away in the face of all prudence.

"Looky h-yer, Tom; when I got the keys from the sher'f, I brought them all along. They 's the big key to the jail, un the key to the dungeon. Now, h-yer, I've got two more. It seems like as ef one uv 'em had orter onlock the east room of the jail, un liker 'n not t' other's the court-house key. S'pose'n I put you in there; they'll never look there in the worl'."

"I s'pose so," said Tom, "if you think it's safe." But in his

152

present state he shuddered at the idea of being left alone in the dark. "If Abra'm thinks I'd better not clear out, I'll be where I'm wanted in the morning, and they can't say I have run off," he added.

So Tom was locked in the court-house and left to feel his way about in the dark. He found, at length, the judge's bench, the only one with a cushion on it, and lay down there to wait for daylight, listening with painful attention to every sound in the streets. When at length he heard the tramp of horses and conjectured that Jake's party were actually looking for him, he could not overcome the unreasonable terror that weakness and suspense had brought upon him. He groped his way up the stairs and slunk into one of the jury rooms above for greater security.

# XXV

## LIKE A WOLF ON THE FOLD

Barbara, at her uncle's house, had not been able to go to bed. Tom's fate, she knew, would be decided the next day, and whatever of hope there might be for him was hidden in the mind of his lawyer. Mrs. Grayson had involuntarily fallen into a slumber, and the anxious Barbara sat by her in the darkness, wishing for the coming of the day, whose coming was nevertheless dreadful to her. The sound of a wagon rattling in another street startled her; she went to the window and strained her eyes against the darkness outside of the glass. Though she could not suspect that in the wagon was Bob McCord hurrying to the rescue of Tom, she was yet full of vague and indistinct forebodings. She wished she might have passed the night in the jail. A little after midnight she thought she heard a sound as of horses' feet: again she went to the window, but she could not see or hear anything. Then again she heard it: there could be no mistake now; she could make out plainly the confused thudding of many hoofs on the unpaved road. Presently, from sound rather than from sight, she knew that a considerable troop of horsemen were passing in front of her uncle's house. She left the room quietly, and spoke to her uncle as she passed his door; but without waiting for him she went out into the street and ran a little way after the horsemen, stopping, hearkening, turning this way and that in her indecision, and at length, after groping among the trees and stumps in the public square, reached the jail.

Jake Hogan had sent forward two men to watch the prison, while he with his main force surrounded Plunkett's house. The sheriff had obediently kept his place where Bob had laid him, in the middle of the floor, until he got into a chill. Then, as he heard no sound outside of the house, his courage revived, and he crept back into bed.

Jake had come prepared to play the bully, according to agreement, in order to save Plunkett's reputation for courage and fidelity, but he was disconcerted at finding the door of the house wide open; he had not expected that things would be made so easy. After stumbling over the fallen door-facing, he boldly mounted the stairs with as much noise as possible. Entering Plunkett's bedroom, he cried out in what he conceived to be his most impressive tones:

"Gin up the keys of that ar jail, ur your time has come."

"What air you up to now?" cried the sheriff, angry at this second visit. "You knocked me down and got the keys nigh on to an hour ago. Now what in thunderation does this hullabaloo mean, I want to know."

"Wha' choo talkin'?" said Jake. "We hain't on'y jest got yer."

"Only just got here?" said the sheriff, rising up in bed. "Only just come? Then there's another crowd that must 'a' done the business ahead of you. There was more 'n forty men surrounded this house awhile ago, and beat down my door, and come upstairs here in this room, and knocked me down and choked me black and blue and went off with the keys. I guess they've hung Tom and gone before this."

"Looky h-yer now, we don't want no more uv your tricks. We're the on'y party out to-night, sartin shore, un we're boun' to have them air keys ur die," said Jake, tragically. "You might's well gin 'em up fust as last, Hank Plunkett, un save yourself trouble."

"Well, if you want 'em, you'll have to look 'em up," said the sheriff. "I haven't got 'em, and I'll be hanged if I know who has. I was knocked down and nearly killed by a whole lot of men. Kill me, if you've got a mind to, but you won't find the keys in this house. So there now." And he lay back on his pillow.

"Come on, boys; we'll s'arch the jail. Un ef we've been fooled weth, Hank Plunkett'll have to pay fer it."

With that the Broad Run boys departed and the sheriff got up and dressed himself. There was a mystery about two lynching parties in one night; and there might be something in it that would affect his bond or his political prospects if it were not looked into at once. He resolved to alarm the town.

At the jail door Hogan encountered Barbara piteously begging the men to spare her brother's life.

"Looky h-yer," he said, in a graveyard voice, "this ain't no kind uv a place fer women folks. You go 'way."

"No, I won't go away. I'm Tom's sister and I won't leave him. You mustn't shoot him. He didn't kill George Lockwood."

"You mus' go 'way, ur you'll git shot yer own self," said Jake.

"Well, shoot me—d' you think I care? I'd rather die with Tom. I know your voice, Jake Hogan; and if you kill Tom you'll be a murderer, for he isn't."

"Take her away, boys," said Jake, a little shaken by this unexpected appeal. But nobody offered to remove Barbara. All of these rude fellows were touched at sight of her tears. It had not occurred to them to take into account the sister or the mother when they thoughtlessly resolved to hang Tom. But the path of the reformer is always beset by such thorns.

"Down weth that ar door!" cried Jake, not to be baffled in his resolution, and convinced by Barbara's solicitude that Tom was certainly within. There was reason for haste too, for the villagers were already stirring, and there might be opposition to his summary proceedings. But pompous commands have not much effect on heavy doors, and Jake found that this one would not down so easily as he hoped. Jake began pounding on it with the poll of an ax borrowed from a neighboring wood-pile, and meanwhile dispatched two men to break open the blacksmith shop and fetch a sledge-hammer. But S'manthy's boy, on his own motion, went around to the back of the jail with the purpose of trying the window. Finding it as Bob had left it, with the grating torn out, he entered the jail and penetrated to the dungeon, coming back presently to tell Jake that he had found the window out, the dungeon door open, and Tom "clean gone."

"Thunder!" said Jake, dropping his ax. "Who could they be? The shuruff says they wuz more 'n forty on 'em; so they couldn't be rescuers. They hain't ten men in the wide worl' 'at thinks Tom's innercent. Like 's not it's a lot uv fellers f'um the south-east of the k-younty, down towards Hardscrabble, whar Lockwood had some kin. They've hung him summers. Let's ride 'roun' un see ef we kin fin' any traces. Un ef Hank Plunkett has played a trick, we'll git squar' some day, ur my name hain't Hogan."

The men mounted and rode off. Barbara, who stood by in agony while Jake beat upon the door, and who had heard the report that Tom was gone, could not resist the despairing conclusion that he must have suffered death. In her broken-hearted perplexity she could think of nothing better than to hurry to the tavern where

155

Hiram Mason was a boarder. Half the people of the village were by this time in the streets, running here and there and saying the most contradictory things. Mason had been awakened with the rest, and by the time Barbara reached the tavern door, she encountered him coming out.

"W'y, Barbara! for goodness' sake, what brought you out? What has happened?" he said.

"O Mr. Mason! I'm afraid Tom's dead. I ran after Jake Hogan and his men when I heard them pass, and begged Jake to let Tom off. They tried to drive me away, but I staid; and when they got into jail, Tom wasn't there. Jake said that the sheriff said he had been taken away and lynched by more than forty men. Oh, if they have killed the poor boy!"

"Maybe it isn't so bad," said Hiram, as he took her left hand in his right and led her, as he might have led a weeping child, along the dark street toward her uncle's house. "Don't cry any more, Barbara!"

"I shouldn't wonder," he said, after a while, "if Bob McCord knows something of this."

"But we left him at home to-night," said Barbara; and then she began to weep again, and to say over and over in an undertone, "O my poor Tom!"

Mason could not say any more. He only grasped her hand the more firmly in his and walked on. Presently a wagon came across the walk just in front of them, issuing from an alley.

"That's Butts's wagon, and that's his bay colt, I do believe," said Barbara, looking sharply at the dark silhouette of the horse. "I know the way that horse carries his head. I wonder if Butts has been mean enough to have anything to do with this wicked business."

What Barbara saw was Zeke Tucker hastening to replace the horse in the stable, while Bob remained in town to keep a furtive watch over the court-house till morning. Mason thought he saw some one moving in the alley, and a detective impulse seized him.

"Stay here a moment, Barbara," he said, and letting go of her hand he ran into the alley and came plump upon the burly form of Bob McCord.

"It's all right, Mr. Mason," chuckled Bob. "Tom's safe 'n' soun' where they'll never find him. By thunder!" And Bob looked ready to explode with laughter; the whole thing was to him one of the best of jokes.

"Come and tell Barbara," said Mason.

Bob came out of the alley to where Barbara was standing near the white-spotted trunk of a young sycamore, and recounted briefly how he had fooled Butts, and how he had got the keys from

156

Plunkett. His resonant laughter grated on Barbara's feelings, but she was too grateful to him to resent the rudeness of his nature.

"Where is Tom?" Barbara asked.

"Oh! I'm a-playin' Abe Lincoln," said Bob in a whisper. "The fewer that knows, the better it'll be. Tom says he won't light out, unless Abra'm says to. Speak'n' of Abe Lincoln," he said, "I don't want to be seed weth him to-night. You go back, Mr. Mason, un tell Abe 't Tom's safe. Ef he thinks Tom's chances is better to stan' trial, w'y, he'll find 'im in the court-house to-morry when the court wants 'im, shore as shootin'. He's on'y out on bail to-night," said Bob, unwilling to lose his joke. "But ef Abe thinks Tom hain't got no chance afore a jury, let 'im jest wink one eye, kind-uh, un 'fore daybreak I'll have the boy tucked into a bear's hole 't I know of, un he kin lay there safe fer a week un then put out for Wisconsin, ur Missouri, ur the Ioway country. You go 'n' let Abe know, un I'll see Barb'ry safe home—she won't gimme the mitten to-night, I 'low." And Bob chuckled heartily; life was all so droll to this man, blessed with a perfect digestion and not worried by any considerable sense of responsibility.

Mason went up to Lincoln's room and awakened him to tell him the story of the night. The lawyer's face relaxed, and at length he broke into a merry but restrained laughter. He saw almost as much fun in it as Bob McCord had, and Mason felt a little out of patience that he should be so much amused over such a life-and-death affair.

"Tom doesn't want to be an outlaw," said Lincoln very gravely, when the question of Tom's going or staying was put to him. "I don't believe he could escape; and if he did, life would hardly be worth the having. There is only just one chance of proving his innocence, but I think he'd better stay and take that. Maybe we'll fail; if we do, it may yet be time enough to fall back on Bob and his bear's hole. By the way, where has Bob stowed Tom for the night?"

"Bob won't tell," said Mason. "He says he's playing Abe Lincoln; and the fewer that know, the better."

Lincoln laughed again, and nodded his head approvingly. "So he brings Tom to court in good time," he said.

Mason went out and encountered Bob in the street, and gave him Lincoln's decision. Then Hiram went and told Barbara about it, and sat with her and her mother until morning. A while before daybreak, finding the town free from any person disposed to molest Tom, Bob came to Barbara and had her make a cup of coffee and give him a sandwich or two. These he took out of the back gate of the Grayson garden and left them with Tom in the court-house.

The next morning at half-past 6 o'clock the lawyers of the

157

circuit took their seats at the breakfast-table in the meagerly furnished, fly-specked dining-room of the tavern, the windows of which were decorated with limp chintz curtains, and the space of which was entirely filled with the odors of coffee and fried ham, mingled with smells emitted by the rough-coat plastering and the poplar of the woodwork: this compound odor of the building was a genius of the place. The old judge, who sat at the end of the table opposite to that occupied by the landlady, spread his red silk handkerchief across his lap preparatory to beginning his meal, and looked up from under his overhanging brows at Lincoln, who was just taking his seat.

"What's this, Lincoln? I hear your client was carried off last night by a mob of forty or fifty men and probably hanged. And you don't even get up early to see about it."

"My client will be in court this morning, Judge," said the lawyer, looking up from his plate.

"What!"

"I am informed that he is in a safe place, and he will be ready for trial this morning."

"Where is he?" asked the judge, looking penetratingly at Lincoln.

"I should be glad to tell your Honor; but the fact is, I can't manage to find out myself."

Then one of the other lawyers spoke up. "Lincoln, from what you say, I suppose the first mob took Grayson to save him from the second. But I don't see how the Old Boy you raised forty men on your side. I wouldn't have believed that the poor devil had so many friends."

"I? I didn't raise any men. I was sound asleep, and didn't know a word about it until the row was all over."

After breakfast there was much discussion of the case among the lawyers standing in a group in the bar-room. What would Lincoln do? Why had he not moved for a change of venue? Why had he subpœnaed no witnesses? Would he plead necessary self-defense, or would Tom plead guilty and throw himself on the mercy of the governor?

The sheriff was very active in the latter part of the night in telling his story and in making a display of zeal. It was he who had taken time by the forelock in telling the judge all about the events of the night; how his door had been beaten in by a great mob; how he had been rudely knocked down and choked until he was almost insensible; and how pistols had been cocked and placed against his head. Then he told of the coming of the second mob. He did not

158

know which way Tom had been taken, or whether he had been hanged or not, but he had sent the deputy to make inquiries.

In making an examination of the prison after daylight, Sheriff Plunkett found the keys of the jail inside of the hall-way, as though they had been thrown in at the broken-down window. When he went to force the court-house door, the key belonging to it was found lying on the doorstep; and when on opening the door he saw Tom with his manacles on, awaiting him, his surprise was complete.

"I thought you'd been hung," he said.

"Not yet," said Tom, grimly.

"Say, where did that mob come from that got you out?"

"You can't question me," said Tom. "I'm not a witness to-day; I'm a prisoner."

Many of the excited people, moved by the restive longings of a vague curiosity, had followed the sheriff into the court-room, and the news of Tom's presence there soon spread throughout the village. There were already all sorts of contradictory and exciting rumors in the streets about the events of the preceding night; women let their breakfast coffee boil over while they discussed the affair across back fences; men almost forgot to eat anything in their eagerness for news; country people were flocking in by all the roads and listening to all sorts of contradictory tales told by the villagers. When it became known that Tom was alive and awaiting his trial there was a general rush to secure seats, and the court-room was filled long before the bell in its belfry had announced the hour for the trial to begin.

# XXVI

## CIRCUMSTANTIAL EVIDENCE

At last the sheriff's new deputy went up the court-house stairs, and pulled away on the rope that rattled the bell in the belfry—a bell that uttered its notes in irregular groups, now pausing for breath, and now sending one hurried stroke clattering hard on the heels of another. Its clanking had no more dignity than the words of a gossip eagerly tattling small news. While the bell was yet banging, Judge Watkins's iron-gray head and stooped shoulders appeared; he pushed his way slowly through the press, his brows contracted in impatience at finding even the physical progress of the court obstructed by the vulgar. The people squeezed themselves as nearly flat as possible in the endeavor to make way for his Honor, of whom they were as much in awe as school-boys of a stern master. Bob McCord, erect in the aisle, was an island in the very channel, and the most serious obstacle to the judge's passage; nor did it help things for Bob to turn sidewise, for he was equally obtrusive in all his dimensions. The judge was a good deal ruffled in his endeavors to pull by him.

"I wish I wuz littler, Jedge," said Bob, with a fearless laugh that startled the bystanders, "but I can't seem to take myself in another eench."

The dyspeptic judge was not without a sense of humor. It would be a derogation from his dignity to say that he smiled at Bob's apology; but certainly there was a little relaxation of his brows, and a less severe set to his lips, when he finally edged past and left the crowd to close around Big Bob again.

The judge began the session by ordering the sheriff to bring in the grand jury. This in turn was no easy task; but at length that body succeeded in descending the stairs, defiling through the aisle, and getting into the jury box. In a few words, precise and tart, the judge charged the grand jurymen to inquire into two lawless attacks which had been made on the sheriff during the night; into the conduct of the sheriff; and into the evidently insecure condition of the county jail. Then, when the members of the grand inquest had reluctantly made their painful way up the stairs to their room overhead, the judge called the case of The People of the State of Illinois versus Thomas Grayson, Junior, and there was a hush in the crowded court-room.

Tom sat regarding the crowd with such feelings as a gladiator doomed to mortal combat might have had in looking on the curious spectators in the Coliseum. Mrs. Grayson and Barbara had been provided with chairs within the bar; but on his mother and sister Tom did not dare to let his eyes rest. He saw, however, without looking directly at them, that little Janet was standing by Barbara, and that his uncle sat with crest-fallen face by his mother's side, and that his Aunt Charlotte had not come at all. Just outside of the bar, but immediately behind Mrs. Grayson, so as to form one of the group, stood Hiram Mason, erect and unblushing. One of the landmarks on which Tom's gaze rested oftenest was the burly form and round, ruddy face of Big Bob McCord, half way between the judge and the door. And at one of the open windows there presently appeared the lank countenance of Jake Hogan, who had climbed up

160

from the outside, with the notion that he was somehow bound to supervise the administration of public justice. He managed with difficulty to get perching-room on the window-sill. Into two of the raised back seats a group of women had squeezed themselves to their last density, and among them, singular and conspicuous as she always was, sat Rachel Albaugh. Tom's was not the only eye that observed her; the lawyers from other counties were asking one another who she was, and she had even attracted the attention of the judge himself; for a gallant interest in good-looking women lingers late in a Virginia gentleman, no matter how austere his mold. At a pause in the preliminary proceedings the judge spoke to the clerk, sitting just below and in front of him, at a raised desk.

"Magill, who is that girl?" he asked.

"Which one, Judge?" queried Magill, pretending to be in doubt.

"You needn't look so innocent. Of course I mean the one a modest man can't look at without being a little ashamed of himself. You know her well enough, I'm sure."

"I s'pose yer Honor manes John Albaugh's daughter," said Magill. "She's the one that's at the bottom of all this row, they say."

As soon as the judge heard that Rachel's beauty had something to do with the case in hand he fell back into his official reserve, as though he felt a scruple that to talk about her, or even to take note of her beauty, might be, in some sort, a receiving of evidence not properly before the court.

The jury was very soon impaneled, for in that day entire ignorance of the matter in hand was not thought indispensable to a wise decision. Lincoln made no objection to any of the names drawn for jurymen except that of Abijah Grimes, of Broad Run Township. The exclusion of Bijy's open countenance from the jury box was another blow to Jake Hogan's faith in the institutions of the land. His brow visibly darkened; here was one more sign that a rich man's nephew could not be punished, and that a poor man hadn't no kind uv a chance in sech a dodrotted country. No time was spent in an opening speech; the preliminary oratory, by which our metropolitan barristers consume the time of an indulgent court and make a show of earning their preposterous fees, was rarely indulged in that simpler land and time. The fees paid, indeed, would not have justified the making of two speeches.

No portion of the crowd tucked into the four walls of the Moscow court-house showed more interest in the trial than the members of the bar. The unsolved mystery that hung about Lincoln's line of defense, the absence of any witnesses in Tom's behalf, the neglect of all the ordinary precautions, such as the seeking of a change of venue, produced a kind of flurry of expectation inside of the bar; and the lawyers in their blue sparrow-tail coats with brass buttons, which constituted then a kind of professional uniform, moved about with as much animation as uneasy jay-birds, to which the general effect of their costume gave them a sort of family likeness. Their attention was divided, it is true; for when a member of the bar did succeed in settling himself into a chair, which he always canted back on its hind legs, he was pretty sure to get into a position that would enable him to get a glance now and then at the face of Rachel Albaugh, who was interesting, not only for her beauty, but on account of her supposed relation to the case actually before the court. Never had Rachel's lustrous eyes seemed finer, never had her marvelous complexion shown a tint more delicious; her interest in the case lent animation to her expression, and her attitude of listening set off the graceful turn of her features.

The prosecuting attorney called Henry Miller to prove that Tom had been irritated with Lockwood at Albaugh's, but Henry did what he could for Tom, by insisting that it didn't "amount to anything" as a quarrel; it was "only a huff," he said. The next witness called was the nervous young man who had stood balancing himself on the threshold of Wooden & Snyder's store when Tom had threatened Lockwood, in paying back the money borrowed to discharge his gambling debt. He was a habitual gossip, and the story lost nothing from his telling. He did not forget to mention with evident pleasure that Rachel Albaugh's name had been used in that quarrel. At this point Rachel, finding too many eyes turned from the witness to the high seat at the back of the room, lowered her green veil.

Then the carpenter who had bought a three-cornered file on the morning of Tom's outburst against Lockwood also swore to the details of that affair as he remembered them, and the villager who had come in to buy nails to repair his garden fence gave a third version of the quarrel; but Snyder, the junior proprietor of the store, told the incident as it was colored by his partisanship for Lockwood and in a way the most damaging to Tom. He swore that Lockwood was really afraid of Tom, and that at Lockwood's suggestion he had himself got Blackman to speak to Tom's uncle about it. The young men followed who had heard Tom say, as he left town after his break with his uncle, that George Lockwood was the cause of all his troubles, and that Lockwood "had better not get in his way again, if he knew what was good for him."

Lincoln sat out that forenoon without making a note, without raising an objection, without asking the witnesses a question, and

162

without a book or a scrap of paper before him. He did not break silence at all, except to waive the cross-examination of each witness. The impression made in Tom's favor by his voluntary appearance at the trial, when he might perhaps have got away, was by this time dissipated, and the tide set now overwhelmingly against him; and to this tide his self-contained lawyer had offered not the slightest opposition. It was a serious question even among the lawyers whether or not Lincoln had given up the case. But if he had given up the case, why did he not fight on every small point, as any other lawyer would have done, for the sake of making a show of zeal? To Allen, the public prosecutor, there was something annoying and ominous in Lincoln's silence; something that made him apprehensive of he knew not what.

When the court took its noon recess Barbara and her mother were in utter despondency. It seemed to them that Lincoln was letting the case go by default, while the prosecuting attorney was full of energetic activity.

"Abra'm," said Mrs. Grayson, intercepting Lincoln as he passed out of the bar with his hat drawn down over his anxious brows, "ain't ther' nothin' you kin do for Tom? Can't you show 'em that he never done it?"

"I'll do whatever I can, Aunt Marthy, but you must leave it to me." So saying, he quickly left her and pushed on out of the door, while his learned brethren gathered into a group within the bar, and unanimously agreed in condemning his neglect of every opportunity to break the force of the evidence against Tom. Why had he not objected to much of it, why had he not cross-questioned, why did he not ask for a change of venue yesterday?

When the sheriff and his deputy, at the close of this forenoon session, passed out of the court-house with Tom, there was a rush of people around and in front of them. Men and boys climbed up on wagons, tree stumps, and whatever afforded them a good view of the criminal. For the most part the people were only moved by that heartless curiosity which finds a pleasurable excitement in the sight of other people's woes, but there was also very manifest an increasing resentment toward Tom, and not a little of that human ferocity which is easily awakened in time of excitement and which reminds us of a sort of second cousinship that subsists between a crowd of men and a pack of wolves—or between a pack of men and a crowd of wolves.

When Tom found himself at length landed within the friendly prison walls, out of sight and hearing of the unfeeling crowd, he was in the deepest dejection. For what, indeed, that could happen now would be sufficient to turn back such a tide of popular

163

condemnation? Barbara came to him presently with a dinner more relishable than that which the sheriff was accustomed to serve to prisoners, and all the way to the jail idle people had strolled after her; and though no one treated her with disrespect, she could hear them saying, "That's his sister," and their voices were neither sympathetic nor friendly. When she set down the tray on one of the stools in front of Tom, she kept her eyes averted from his, lest he should detect the despondency that she knew herself to be incapable of hiding. On his part, Tom made a feint to eat the food, for Barbara's sake. But after examining first one tid-bit and then another, essaying to nibble a little first at this and then at that, he got up abruptly and left the whole.

"'T isn't any use, Barb," he said, huskily. "I can't eat."

And Barbara, knowing how much need her brother had for all his self-control, did not trust herself to speak, but took up the tray and went out again, leaving Tom, when the deputy had locked the door, sitting alone on the bench with his head between his hands.

# XXVII

# LIGHT IN A DARK PLACE

The people who had seats in the court-room were, for the most part, too wise in their generation to vacate them during the noon recess. Jake Hogan clambered down from his uncomfortable window-roost for a little while, and Bob McCord took a plunge into the grateful fresh air, but both got back in time to secure their old points of observation. The lawyers came back early, and long before the judge returned the ruddy-faced Magill was seated behind his little desk, facing the crowd and pretending to write. He was ill at ease; the heart of the man had gone out to Tom. He never for a moment doubted that Tom killed Lockwood, but then a sneak like Lockwood "richly desarved it," in Magill's estimation. Judge Watkins's austere face assumed a yet more severe expression; for though pity never interfered with justice in his nature, it often rendered the old man unhappy, and therefore more than usually irascible.

There was a painful pause after the judge had taken his seat and ordered the prisoner brought in. It was like a wait before a funeral service, but rendered ten times more distressing by the element of suspense. The judge's quill pen could be heard scratching on the paper as he noted points for his charge to the jury. To Hiram Mason the whole trial was unendurable. The law had the aspect of a relentless boa-constrictor, slowly winding itself about Tom, while all these spectators, with merely a curious interest in the horrible, watched the process. The deadly creature had now to make but one more coil, and then, in its cruel and deliberate fashion, it would proceed to tighten its twists until the poor boy should be done to death. Barbara and the mother were entwined by this fate as well, while Hiram had not a little finger of help for them. He watched Lincoln as he took seat in moody silence. Why had the lawyer not done anything to help Tom? Any other lawyer with a desperate case would have had a stack of law-books in front of him, as a sort of dam against the flood. But Lincoln had neither law-books nor so much as a scrap of paper.

The prosecuting attorney, with a taste for climaxes, reserved his chief witness to the last. Even now he was not ready to call Sovine. He would add one more stone to the pyramid of presumptive proof before he capped it all with certainty. Markham was therefore put up to identify the old pistol which he had found in Tom's room. Lincoln again waived cross-examination. Blackman felt certain that he himself could have done better. He mentally constructed the questions that should have been put to the deputy sheriff. Was the pistol hot when you found it? Did it smell of powder? Did the family make any objection to your search?—Even if the judge had ruled out such questions the jury would have heard the questions, and a question often has weight in spite of rulings from the bench. The prosecuting attorney began to feel sure of his own case; he had come to his last witness and his great stroke.

"Call David Sovine," he said, wiping his brow and looking relieved.

"David Sovine! David Sovine! David Sovine!" cried the sheriff in due and ancient form, though David sat almost within whispering distance of him.

The witness stood up.

"Howld up your roight hand," said the clerk.

Then when Dave's right hand was up Magill rattled off the form of the oath in the most approved and clerkly style, only adding to its effect by the mild brogue of his pronunciation.

"Do sol'm swear 't yull tell th' truth, th' 'ole truth, en nuthin' b' th' truth, s' yilpye God," said the clerk, without once pausing for breath.

Sovine ducked his head and dropped his hand, and the solemnity was over.

Dave, who was evidently not accustomed to stand before such a crowd, appeared embarrassed. He had deteriorated in appearance lately. His patent-leather shoes were bright as ever, his trousers were trimly held down by straps, his hair was well kept in place by bear's oil or what was sold, for bear's oil, but there was a nervousness in his expression and carriage that gave him the air of a man who has been drinking to excess. Tom looked at him with defiance, but Dave was standing at the right of the judge, while the prisoner's dock was on the left, and the witness did not regard Tom at all, but told his story with clearness. Something of the bold assurance which he displayed at the inquest was lacking. His coarse face twitched and quivered, and this appeared to annoy him; he sought to hide it by an affectation of nonchalance, as he rested his weight now on one foot and now on the other.

"Do you know the prisoner?" asked the prosecutor, with a motion of his head toward the dock.

"Yes, well enough"; but in saying this Dave did not look toward Tom, but out of the window.

"You've played cards with him, haven't you?"

"Yes."

"Tell his Honor and the jury when and where you played with him."

"We played one night last July, in Wooden & Snyder's store."

"Who proposed to Tom to play with you?"

"George Lockwood. He hollered up the stove-pipe for Tom to come down an' take a game or two with me."

"What did you win that night from Tom?"

"Thirteen dollars, an' his hat an' coat an' boots, an' his han'ke'chi'f an' knife."

"Who, if anybody, lent him the money to get back his things which you had won?"

"George Lockwood."

Here the counsel paused a moment, laid down a memorandum he had been using, and looked about his table until he found another; then he resumed his questions.

"Tell the jury whether you were at the Timber Creek camp-meeting on the 9th of August."

"Yes; I was."

"What did you see there? Tell about the shooting."

Dave told the story, with a little prompting in the way of questions from the lawyer, substantially as he had told it at the coroner's inquest. He related his parting from Lockwood, Tom's appearance on the scene, Tom's threatening speech, Lockwood's entreaty that Tom would not shoot him, and then Tom's shooting. In making these statements Dave looked at the stairway in the corner of the court-room with an air of entire indifference, and he even made one or two efforts to yawn, as though the case was a rather dull affair to him.

"How far away from Mason and Lockwood were you when the shooting took place?" asked the prosecutor.

"Twenty foot or more."

"What did Tom shoot with?"

"A pistol."

"What kind of a pistol?"

"One of the ole-fashion' sort—flint-lock, weth a ruther long barrel."

The prosecuting lawyer now beckoned to the sheriff, who handed down to him, from off his high desk, Tom's pistol.

"Tell the jury whether this looks like the pistol."

"'T was just such a one as that. I can't say it was that, but it was hung to the stock like that, an' about as long in the barrel."

"What did Grayson do when he had shot George, and what did you do?"

"Tom run off as fast as his feet could carry him, an' I went up towards George, who'd fell over. He was dead ag'inst I could get there. Then purty soon the crowd come a-runnin' up to see what the fracas was."

After bringing out some further details Allen turned to his opponent with an air of confidence and said:

"You can have the witness, Mr. Lincoln."

There was a brief pause, during which the jurymen changed their positions on the hard seats, making a little rustle as they took their right legs from off their left and hung their left legs over their right knees, or vice versa. In making these changes they looked inquiringly at one another, and it was clear that their minds were so well made up that even a judge's charge in favor of the prisoner, if such a thing had been conceivable, would have gone for nothing. Lincoln at length rose slowly from his chair, and stood awhile in silence, regarding Sovine, who seemed excited and nervous, and who visibly paled a little as his eyes sought to escape from the lawyer's gaze.

"You said you were with Lockwood just before the shooting?" the counsel asked.

"Yes." Dave was all alert and answered promptly.

"Were you not pretty close to him when he was shot?"

"No, I wasn't," said Dave, his suspicions excited by this mode

167

of attack. It appeared that the lawyer, for some reason, wanted to make him confess to having been nearer to the scene and perhaps implicated, and he therefore resolved to fight off.

"Are you sure you were as much as ten feet away?"

"I was more than twenty," said Dave, huskily.

"What had you and George Lockwood been doing together?"

"We'd been—talking." Manifestly Dave took fresh alarm at this line of questioning.

"Oh, you had?"

"Yes."

"In a friendly way?"

"Yes, tubby shore; we never had any fuss."

"You parted from him as a friend?"

"Yes, of course."

"By the time Tom came up you'd got—how far away? Be careful now."

"I've told you twiste. More than twenty feet."

"You might have been mistaken about its being Tom then?"

"No, I wasn't."

"Did you know it was Tom before he fired?"

"Tubby shore, I did."

"What time of night was it?"

"Long towards 10, I sh'd think."

"It might have been 11?"

"No, 't wusn't later'n about 10." This was said doggedly.

"Nor before 9?"

"No, 't wus nigh onto 10, I said." And the witness showed some irritation, and spoke louder than before.

"How far away were you from the pulpit and meeting-place?"

"'Twixt a half a mile an' a mile."

"Not over a mile?"

"No, skiercely a mile."

"But don't you think it might have been a little less than half a mile?"

"No, it's nigh onto a mile, I didn't measure it, but it's a mighty big three-quarters."

The witness answered combatively, and in this mood he made a better impression than he did on his direct examination. The prosecuting attorney looked relieved. Tom listened with an attention painful to see, his eyes moving anxiously from Lincoln to Dave as he wondered what point in Dave's armor the lawyer could be driving at. He saw plainly that his salvation was staked on some last throw.

"You didn't have any candle in your hand, did you, at any time during the evening?"

"No!" said Dave, positively. For some reason this question disconcerted him and awakened his suspicion. "What should we have a candle for?" he added.

"Did either George Lockwood or Tom have a candle?"

"No, of course not! What 'd they have candles for?"

"Where were the lights on the camp-ground?"

"Closte by the preachers' tent."

"More than three-quarters of a mile away from the place where the murder took place?"

"Anyway as much as three-quarters," said Dave, who began to wish that he could modify his previous statement of the distance.

"How far away were you from Lockwood when the murder took place?"

"Twenty feet."

"You said 'or more' awhile ago."

"Well, 't wusn't no less, p'r'aps," said Dave, showing signs of worry. "You don't think I measured it, do yeh?"

"There were no lights nearer than three-quarters of a mile?"

"No," said the witness, the cold perspiration beading on his face as he saw Lincoln's trap opening to receive him.

"You don't mean to say that the platform torches up by the preachers' tent gave any light three-quarters of a mile away and in the woods?"

"No, of course not."

"How could you see Tom and know that it was he that fired, when the only light was nearly a mile away, and inside a circle of tents?"

"Saw by moonlight," said Sovine, snappishly, disposed to dash at any gap that offered a possible way of escape.

"What sort of trees were there on the ground?"

"Beech."

"Beech-leaves are pretty thick in August?" asked Lincoln.

"Ye-es, ruther," gasped the witness, seeing a new pitfall yawning just ahead of him.

"And yet light enough from the moon came through these thick beech-trees to let you know Tom Grayson?"

"Yes."

"And you could see him shoot?"

"Yes."

"And you full twenty feet away?"

"Well, about that; nearly twenty, anyhow." Dave shifted his weight to his right foot.

"And you pretend to say to this court that by the moonlight that you got through the beech-trees in August you could even see that it was a pistol that Tom had?"

"Ye-es." Dave now stood on his left foot.

"And you could see what kind of a pistol it was?" This was said with a little laugh very exasperating to the witness.

"Yes, I could," answered Dave, with dogged resolution not to be faced down.

"And just how the barrel was hung to the stock?" There was a positive sneer in Lincoln's voice now.

"Yes." This was spoken feebly.

"And you twenty feet or more away?"

"I've got awful good eyes, an' I know what I see," whined the witness, apologetically.

Here Lincoln paused and looked at Sovine, whose extreme distress was only made the more apparent by his feeble endeavor to conceal his agitation. The counsel, after regarding his uneasy victim for a quarter of a minute, thrust his hand into the tail-pocket of his blue coat, and after a little needless fumbling drew forth a small pamphlet in green covers. He turned the leaves of this with extreme deliberation, while the court-room was utterly silent. The members of the bar had as by general consent put their chairs down on all-fours, and were intently watching the struggle between the counsel and the witness. The sallow-faced judge had stopped the scratching of his quill, and had lowered his spectacles on his nose, that he might study the distressed face of the tormented Sovine. Mrs. Grayson's hands were on her lap, palms downward; her eyes were fixed on Abra'm, and her mouth was half open, as though she were going to speak.

Barbara found it hard to keep her seat, she was so eager for Lincoln to go on, and Tom was leaning forward breathlessly in the dock; his throat felt dry, and he choked when he tried to swallow; it seemed to him that he would smother with the beating of his heart. But it was worth while to turn away from these more interested parties to look for a moment at the ruddy face of Bob McCord, which was puckered to a kind of focus with an expression that was customary with him in a moment of supreme interest, as when he was drawing a sure bead on a bear or deer. It was worth while to regard Rachel Albaugh, who had lifted the veil from her face radiant with interest. Lincoln appeared to be the only perfectly deliberate person in the room. He seemed disposed to protract the situation as long as possible. He held his victim on the rack and he let him suffer. He would turn a leaf or two in his pamphlet and then look up at the demoralized witness, as though to fathom the depth of his

170

torture and to measure the result. At last he fixed his thumb firmly at a certain place on a page and turned his eyes to the judge.

"Now, your Honor," he said to the court, "this witness," with a half-contemptuous gesture of his awkward left hand toward Sovine, "has sworn over and over that he recognized the accused as the person who shot George Lockwood, near the Union camp-meeting on the night of the 9th of last August, and that he, the witness, was standing at the time twenty feet or more away, while the scene of the shooting was nearly a mile distant from the torches inside the circle of tents. So remarkably sharp are this witness's eyes that he even saw what kind of pistol the prisoner held in his hands, and how the barrel was hung to the stock, and he is able to identify this pistol of Grayson's as precisely like and probably the identical weapon." Here Lincoln paused and scrutinized Sovine. "All these details he saw and observed in the brief space of time preceding the fatal shot,—saw and observed them at 10 o'clock at night, by means of moonlight shining through the trees—beech-trees in full leaf. That is a pretty hard story. How much light does even a full moon shed in a beech woods like that on the Union camp-ground? Not enough to see your way by, as everybody knows who has had to stumble through such woods." Lincoln paused here, that the words he had spoken might have time to produce their due effect on the judge, and especially on the slower wits of some of the jury. Meanwhile he turned the leaves of his pamphlet. Then he began once more: "But, may it please the court, before proceeding with the witness I would like to have the jury look at the almanac which I hold in my hand. They will here see that on the night of the 9th of last August, when this extraordinary witness"—with a sneer at Dave, who had sunk down on a chair in exhaustion—"saw the shape of a pistol at twenty feet away, at 10 o'clock, by moonlight, the moon did not rise until half-past 1 in the morning."

Sovine had been gasping like a fish newly taken from the water while Lincoln uttered these words, and he now began to mutter something.

"You may have a chance to explain when the jury get done looking at the almanac," said the lawyer to him. "For the present you'd better keep silence."

There was a rustle of excitement in the court-room, but at a word from the judge the sheriff's gavel fell and all was still. Lincoln walked slowly toward the jury-box and gave the almanac to the foreman, an intelligent farmer. Countrymen in that day were used to consulting almanacs, and one group after another of the jurymen satisfied themselves that on the night of the 9th, that is, on the morning of the 10th, the moon came up at half-past 1 o'clock. When all had examined the page, the counsel recovered his little book.

"Will you let me look at it?" asked the judge.

"Certainly, your Honor"; and the little witness was handed up to the judge, who with habitual caution looked it all over, outside and in, even examining the title-page to make sure that the book was genuine and belonged to the current year. Then he took note on a slip of paper of the moon's rising on the night of August 9 and 10, and handed back the almanac to Lincoln, who slowly laid it face downward on the table in front of him, open at the place of its testimony. The audience in the court-room was utterly silent and expectant. The prosecuting attorney got half-way to his feet to object to Lincoln's course, but he thought better of it and sat down again.

"Now, may it please the court," Lincoln went on, "I wish at this point to make a motion. I think the court will not regard it as out of order, as the case is very exceptional—a matter of life and death. This witness has solemnly sworn to a story that has manifestly not one word of truth in it. It is one unbroken falsehood. In order to take away the life of an innocent man he has invented this atrocious web of lies, to the falsity of which the very heavens above bear witness, as this almanac shows you. Now why does David Sovine go to all this trouble to perjure himself? Why does he wish to swear away the life of that young man who never did him any harm?" Lincoln stood still a moment, and looked at the witness, who had grown ghastly pale about the lips. Then he went on, very slowly. "Because that witness shot and killed George Lockwood himself. I move your Honor, that David Sovine be arrested at once for murder."

These words, spoken with extreme deliberation and careful emphasis, shook the audience like an explosion.

The prosecutor got to his feet, probably to suggest that the motion was not in order, since he had yet a right to a re-direct examination of Sovine, but, as the attorney for the State, his duty was now a divided one as regarded two men charged with the same crime. So he waved his hand irresolutely, stammered inarticulately, and sat down.

"This is at least a case of extraordinary perjury," said the judge. "Sheriff, arrest David Sovine! This matter will have to be looked into."

The sheriff came down from his seat, and went up to the now stunned and bewildered Sovine.

"I arrest you," he said, taking him by the arm.

The day-and-night fear of detection in which Dave had lived for all these weeks had wrecked his self-control at last.

"God!" he muttered, dropping his head with a sort of shudder. "'T ain't any use keepin' it back any longer. I—didn't mean to shoot him, an' I would n't 'a' come here ag'inst Tom if I could 'a' got away."

The words appeared to be wrung from him by some internal agony too strong for him to master; they were the involuntary result of the breaking down of his forces under prolonged suffering and terror, culminating in the slow torture inflicted by his cross-examination. A minute later, when his spasm of irresolution had passed off, he would have retracted his confession if he could. But the sheriff's deputy, with the assistance of a constable, was already leading him through the swaying crowd in the aisle, while many people got up and stood on the benches to watch the exit of the new prisoner. When at length Sovine had disappeared out of the door the spectators turned and looked at Tom, sitting yet in the dock, but with the certainty of speedy release before him. The whole result of Lincoln's masterful stroke was now for the first time realized, and the excitement bade fair to break over bounds. McCord doubled himself up once or twice in the effort to repress his feelings out of respect for the court, but his emotions were too much for him; his big fist, grasping his ragged hat, appeared above his head.

"Goshamity! Hooray!" he burst out with a stentorian voice, stamping his foot as he waved his hat.

At this the whole court-roomful of people burst into cheers, laughter, cries, and waving of hats and handkerchiefs, in spite of the sheriff's sharp rapping and shouts of "Order in court!" And when at length the people were quieted a little, Mrs. Grayson spoke up, with a choking voice:

"Jedge, ain't you a-goin' to let him go now?"

There was a new movement of feeling, and the judge called out, "Sheriff, order in court!" But his voice was husky and tremulous. He took off his spectacles to wipe them, and he looked out of the window behind him, and put his handkerchief first to one eye, then to the other, before he put his glasses back.

"May it please the court," said the tall lawyer, who had remained standing, waiting for the tempest to subside, and who now spoke in a subdued voice, "I move your Honor, that the jury be instructed to render a verdict of 'Not guilty.'" The judge turned to the prosecuting attorney.

"I don't think, your Honor," stammered Allen, "that I ought to object to the motion of my learned brother, under the peculiar circumstances of this case."

"I don't think you ought," said the judge, promptly, and he

proceeded to give the jury instructions to render the desired verdict. As soon as the jury, nothing loath, had gone through the formality of a verdict, the sheriff came and opened the door of the box to allow Tom to come out.

"O Tom! they are letting you out," cried Janet, running forward to meet him as he came from the dock. She had not quite understood the drift of these last proceedings until this moment.

This greeting by little Janet induced another burst of excitement. It was no longer of any use for the judge to keep on saying "Sheriff, command order in court!" All the sheriff's rapping was in vain; it was impossible to arrest and fine everybody. The judge was compelled to avail himself of the only means of saving the court's dignity by adjourning for the day, while Mrs. Grayson was already embracing her Tommy under his very eyes.

As for Barbara, overcome by the reaction of feeling, she sat still in passive happiness which she did not care to show to this crowd, whose late unfriendly manifestations toward Tom she could not yet quite forgive. Hardly conscious of what was passing around her, she did not observe that her mother had presently let go her hold on Tom, and that Tom had come near and was standing in front of her. Her natural reserve made her wish to avoid a scene in public, but there are times when natural reserve is not a sufficient barrier. Tom gently put his hand on her shoulder and said "Barb," then all sense of the presence of others was obliterated in an instant. The only fact that she took note of was that her brother was there before her with unmanacled hands, free to go where he listed and forever delivered from the danger that had hung over him so imminently. Of what she did you must not expect a description; embraces and kisses of joy would seem hysterical if set down here in black and white for readers of our time, who like the color washed out of a human passion before it is offered to them. No! no! let us turn away—we do not like such things. But those hearty Illinois folk who looked on that scene between Barbara and Tom, and whose quick sympathies made them part of it, did not feel the slightest disapproval when they saw the faithful sister put her arms about Tom's neck; and every one of her kisses they seconded with clapping of hands and cheers, and some of the people were even foolish enough to weep for sympathy.

174

# XXVIII

## FREE

The lawyers presently congratulated Lincoln, Barbara tried to thank him, and Judge Watkins felt that Impartial Justice herself, as represented in his own person, could afford to praise the young man for his conduct of the case.

"Abr'am," said Mrs. Grayson, "d' yeh know I kind uv lost confidence in you when you sot there so long without doin' anything." Then, after a moment of pause: "Abr'am, I'm thinkin' I'd ort to deed you my farm. You've 'arned it, my son; the good Lord A'mighty knows you have."

"I'll never take one cent, Aunt Marthy—not a single red cent"; and the lawyer turned away to grasp Tom's hand. But the poor fellow who had so recently felt the halter about his neck could not yet speak his gratitude. "Tom here," said Lincoln, "will be a help in your old days, Aunt Marthy, and then I'll be paid a hundred times. You see it'll tickle me to think that when you talk about this you'll say: 'That's the same Abe Lincoln that I used to knit stockings for when he was a poor little fellow, with his bare toes sticking out of ragged shoes in the snow.'"

Mrs. Grayson tried to say something more, but she could not.

Tom got his speech at length, when he saw the gigantesque form and big laughing red face of Bob McCord approaching him.

"Bob!" he said, "you dear old Bob! God A'mighty bless you, old fellow."

"I'm that tickled," said Bob, rocking to and fro with amusement. "Tom, you'd orto 'a' seed Jake Hogan's face. I watched it closte. Go to thunder! How it did git mixed about the time you wuz let out! I'm a-goin' to find 'im un see how he feels agin this time"; and Bob let go of Tom's hand and moved off through the crowd to look for Jake.

Tom took mechanically all the congratulations offered to him. Rachel came with the rest; there were some traces of tears about her long lashes as she beamed on Tom the full effulgence of her beauty and friendliness. Tom gave a little start when he saw her; then he took her hand, as he did that of the others, in a half-unconscious way. He was everybody's hero in the reaction of feeling, but he had been so near to the gallows within an hour that he had difficulty yet in appreciating the change.

175

"You'll come back into the office again, won't you, Tom?" said Blackman, in a spurt of good feeling.

"I don't know, Mr. Blackman. I must go home and rest, and be sure I'm alive, before I know what I shall do."

Tom's uncle had been utterly surprised by the turn affairs had taken, for he had never really doubted Tom's guilt. Now he was, for the first time, almost effusive; he gave himself credit that he had stood by his nephew.

"We'd like to have you back, Tom," he said; "and you'd be a general favorite now."

"I want to go home first, Uncle Tom, and get the place out of debt, so mother and Barb'll be easy in their minds. Then I don't know what I shall do. I don't feel as if I could ever come to town again without fetching mother with me. But I can't tell; I want to get out of this town; I hate the very sight of it. Come, Barb; do let's get off. Where's the horse? I want to get home, where I won't see any more of this crowd, and where I can be alone with you and mother."

Before they had made their way to the front door of the court-house the multitude outside had got firm hold of the fact of Tom's acquittal and the manner of it, and when he appeared they set up a shout; then there were cheers and more cheers. But Tom only looked worried, and sought to extricate himself from the people who followed him. At length he managed to get away from the last of them.

"You haven't ate anything to-day," said Janet, who clung to his hand and danced along by his side. "Come to our house to supper. I expect we'll have warm biscuits and honey."

"You dear little body!" said Tom. "I can't stop for supper to-night, Janet; I must go home with mother. I want to get out of the ugly town. I'll come and see you sometimes, and I'll have you out at the farm lots of times." He stopped to put his pale, trembling hand under her pretty chin; he turned her face up to his, he stooped and kissed her. But no entreaty could prevail on him to delay his departure. Not even the biscuits and honey on which Janet insisted. Hiram Mason helped him to hitch up old Blaze-face to the wagon. Then Tom turned to Hiram and grasped both his arms.

"You're going with us," he said abruptly.

"Not to-night, Tom. I'll come in a few days, when I've finished my writing in the clerk's office. I'll stop on my way home."

"I want to thank you, but I can't; confound it," said Tom.

"Never mind, Tom; I'm almost happier than you are."

"I'm not exactly happy, Mason," said Tom; "I've got that plaguey feeling of a rope around my neck yet. I can't get rid of it here in Moscow. Maybe out at the farm I shall be able to shake it off.

176

Janet, won't you run into the house and tell mother and Barbara to come out quick—I want to get away."

Tom had expected that Bob McCord would take a place in the wagon, but Bob was not so modest as to forego a public triumph. He first went and recovered the wagon-spoke from beneath the court-house steps, where he had hidden it the night before. This he put into the baggy part of his "wamus," or hunting-jacket—the part above the belt into which he had often thrust prairie-chickens when he had no game-bag. Then he contrived to encounter Jake Hogan in the very thick of the crowd.

"O Jake!" he called, "what's the price uh rope? How's the hangin' business a-gittin' along these days? Doin' well at it, ain't yeh?"

"Wha' joo mean?" asked Jake, as he half turned about and regarded Bob with big eyes.

"Seems like's ef you'd ort to be'n ole han' by this time, Jake. You sot the time fer Tom's funeral three deffer'nt nights: wunst you wuz a-goin' to have it over't Perrysburg, un wunst the Sunday night that Pete Markham throwed you off the track weth that air yarn about a wall-eyed man weth red whiskers, un wunst ag'in las' night. Ev'ry time you sot it they wuz some sort uv a hitch; it didn't seem to come off rightly. S'pose un you try yer hand on Dave Sovine awhile. They's luck in a change."

"I hain't had no han' in no hangin's nor nuthin' uh that sort," snarled Jake.

"You hain't? Jest you go un tell that out on Broad Run, sonny. Looky h-yer, Jake. I've got the evidence agin you, un ef you dare me I'll go afore the gran' jury weth it. I jest dare you to dare me, ef you dare."

But Jake did not dare to dare him. He only moved slowly away toward his horse, the excited crowd surging after him, to his disgust.

"Looky h-yer, Jake," Bob went on, following his retreat. "I want to gin you some advice as a well-wishin' friend un feller-citizen. Barb'ry knowed your v'ice las' night, un Barb'ry Grayson hain't the sort uv a gal to stan' the sort uv foolin' 't you've been a-doin' about Tom."

"Aw, you shet up yer jaw, now wonchoo?" said Jake.

"I say, Jake," said McCord, still pursuing the crest-fallen leader of Broad Run, while the crowd moved about Big Bob as a storm center. "I say there, Jake; liker 'n not Barb'ry'll stay in town to-night un go afore the gran' jury to-morry. Now ef I wuz you I'd cl'ar the county this very identical night. Your ornery lantern-jawed face wouldn' look half's han'some as Tom's in that air box in front uv the sher'f."

"You shet up!" said Jake.

"Come un shet me up, wonch you?" said Bob, rubbing his hands and laughing.

Jake had reached his horse now, and without another word he mounted and rode away. But Bob kept walking about with his fists in his pockets, his big elbows protruding, and his face radiant with mischief until Sheriff Plunkett came out of the court-house.

"I say, Sher'f," he called, "how many men'd you say they wuz in that air fust mob?"

"Nigh onto forty, I should think," said Plunkett; "but of course I can't just exactly say." And he walked away, not liking to be catechised. There was something mysterious about that mob, and he was afraid there might be something that would count in the next election.

"They had pistols, didn't they?" Bob continued, following him.

"Yes, to be sure," said Plunkett, pausing irresolutely.

"Now looky h-yer, Sher'f; I know sumpin about that air mob. They wuzn't but jest on'y two men in the whole thing. I don't say who they wuz"; and here Bob looked about on the crowd, which showed unmistakable signs of its relish for this revelation.

"Un as fer pistols, they did have 'em. I've got one of 'em h-yer." Bob here pulled the wagon-spoke from the depths of his hunting-shirt. "That's one of the identical hoss-pistols that wuz p'inted at your head las' night. Felt kind-uh cold un creepy like, didn't it now, Hank Plunkett, when its muzzle was agin yer head, un it cocked, besides? Ha-a! ha!"

The crowd jeered and joined in Bob's wild merriment.

"I'll have you arrested," said the sheriff severely. "You've confessed enough now to make the grand jury indict you."

"Fer what? Fer savin' the life uv a innercent man? That'd be a purty howdy-do, now wouldn't it? Un it would be a lovely story to tell at my trial, that the sher'f uv this yere county gin up his keys to two men, two lonesome men weth on'y wagon-spokes! He-e! An' the wagon-spokes cocked! A wagon-spoke's a mighty bad thing when it does go off, especially ef it's loadened with buckshot."

Plunkett came close to McCord, and said in an undertone loud enough to be heard by others: "Ah, Bob, I knowed it wuz your voice, un I knowed your grip. They ain't any other man in this county that can put me down the way you did las' night. But don't you tell Jake ur any of his crowd about it"; and he winked knowingly at Bob.

"Aw, go to thunder, now!" said Bob, speaking loudly and not to be cajoled into giving up his fun. "Sher'f, you can't come no gum games on me. By jeementley crickets, you wuz skeered, un that's all they is about it. You wilted so 't I wuz afeerd you'd clean faint away afore I could git out uv yeh where the keys wuz. Why didn't you hide Tom summers? You wuz afeerd Broad Run'd vote agin you, un you as good as tole Jake Hogan ut you wouldn' make no trouble when he come to lynch Tom."

"No, I didn't; I didn't have anything to say to Jake."

"Ef you take my case afore the gran' jury un I'm tried, I'll prove it on yeh. Now, Hank Plunkett, they's two things that'll never happen." Here Bob smote his right fist into his left palm. "One is 't you'll ever fetch my case afore the gran' jury. That's as shore's you're born. T' other is that you'll ever be elected ag'in! Wha'd joo turn off Pete Markham fer? Fer tryin' to save Tom, un to please Broad Run. Now you're come up weth, ole hoss. Markham'll be the nex' sher'f. You jest cut a notch in a stick to remember't Big Bob McCord tole you so. Ef 't hadn' been fer me 'n' Abe Lincoln you 'n' Jake, 'twext and 'tween yeh, 'd 'a' hung the wrong feller. Now I jest want to see you fetch me afore the court wunst. Ef you pester me too much, I'm derned 'f I don't go thar on m' own hook."

"You've been drinking, Bob," said Plunkett, as he hurried away; but the people evidently sided with McCord, whose exploit of mobbing the sheriff almost single-handed had made him more than ever the champion of the county.

That night Jake Hogan, afraid of arrest, succeeded in trading his cabin, with the front door still unhinged, and his little patch of rugged ground for a one-horse wagon and some provisions. Over the wagon he stretched his only two bed-sheets of unbleached domestic for covering. Before noon the next day, he had passed safely out of the county. The raw-boned horse, the rickety wagon, the impoverished and unwilling cow tied behind, the two yellow mongrel pups between the wagon-wheels, and the frowsy-headed wife alongside of him were token enough to every experienced eye that here was a poor whitey on his travels. To all inquiries regarding his destination, Jake returned:

"I'm boun' fer Messouri. Yeh see they hain't no kind of a chance fer a poor man in this yer daudrautted Eelinoys country."

Once an example of migration had been set, his neighbors grew restless also, and in a year or two nearly all of them had obeyed their hereditary instinct and followed him to Pike County in Missouri. The most of the Broad Run neighborhood is now included in a great grazing farm; here a few logs, there some tumble-down ruins of a stick-chimney, and in another place a rough stone hearth, only remain to indicate the resting-place for a few years of a half-nomadic clan, whose members or their descendants are by this time engaged, probably, in helping to rid the Pacific coast of its unchristian Chinese.

# XXIX

## THE CLOSE OF A CAREER

Dave Sovine's partial confession, which had served to acquit Tom, was sufficient at the next term of the court to condemn him, for no plea of accidental shooting could save him after he had tried to escape at the expense of another man's life. During his trial the motive for shooting Lockwood remained an inexplicable mystery. But when once Dave was convinced that his execution was inevitable and there was an end to all the delights of deviltry, he proceeded to play the only card remaining in his hand, and to euchre Justice on her own deal. Like other murderers of his kind he became religious, and nothing could be more encouraging to criminals than the clearness and fervor of his religious experience, and his absolute certainty of the rewards of paradise. His superiority in wickedness had made him the hero of all the green goslings of the village; his tardy conversion and shining professions made him an object of philanthropic interest to sentimental people and gave him the consolations of conspicuity to the last.

It was during this lurid sunset period of his unnecessary existence that Dave made confessions. These were not always consistent one with another; the capacity for simple and direct truth-telling is a talent denied to men of Sovine's stamp, nor can it be developed in a brief season of penitence. It is quite probable that Sovine failed to state the exact truth even when narrating his religious experiences. But by a comparison of his stories, with some elimination of contradictory elements, the main facts regarding the death of George Lockwood were made out with passable clearness. Being of a thrifty turn of mind, Lockwood had, by a series of careful observations, detected one of the principal tricks employed by Dave to win the money of the unwary. It had been Lockwood's purpose to play the trick back on Dave at some favorable opportunity, but this he found quite impossible. To bring himself to Dave's proficiency in manipulation no end of assiduous practice would be needful. There remained one other way in which he might utilize his discovery. It was an established rule in that part of the country that he who detected his opponent in the very act of cheating at cards might carry off the stakes.

When Lockwood went to the camp-meeting he put into his pocket a bit of candle, in order to have a game with Dave; and when on encountering him Dave proposed the game, the two went out

180

into the woods, remote from the meeting, Lockwood lighted his candle and they sat down on a log to play. Lockwood won at first and doubled the stakes at every game, until Dave, seeing that his pocket-money was running short, and the candle fast wasting in the breezes, concluded to sweep in the stakes with his favorite trick. George Lockwood exposed the cheat at the very instant, and put the stakes in his pocket. But Dave had received his education in its higher branches in the South-west of half a century ago, and he had no notion of suffering himself to be bankrupted so easily. He drew his pistol and demanded the stakes, following Lockwood with reiterated threats, until, in a moment of exasperation, he shot him. A crowd came quickly at the sound of the pistol, and Dave had the shrewdness not to run away and not to attempt to take any money from George Lockwood's person. Remembering Tom Grayson's threats, he declared, with his usual alertness in mendacity, that he had seen Grayson do the shooting, and thus diverted attention from himself.

He had no further thought at the time than to get out of a present difficulty; it was his purpose to leave the country before the trial should come on. But he found himself watched, and he imagined that he was suspected. He saw no chance to move without making sure of his own arrest; he became alarmed and unfitted for decision by the sense of his peril; as the trial approached, his nerves, shaken by dissipations, were unstrung by the debate within him. He saw ghosts at night and his sleep almost entirely forsook him. This horror of a doom that seemed perpetually to hang over him was greatly enhanced by the cross-examination to which he was subjected; from the first he misdoubted that Lincoln had penetrated his whole secret and possessed the means of making it known. And when he heard himself charged publicly with the murder and as publicly arrested, he believed that some evidence against him had been found; he did not draw the line between the charge and the proof, and the half confession escaped him in the first breakdown produced by sudden despair.

But at the last he spoke edifyingly from the scaffold, and died with as much composure and more self-complacency than Tom would have shown had he fallen a victim to Dave's rascality. What becomes of such men in another world is none of my business. But I am rather pleased to have them depart, be it to paradise, or purgatory, or limbo, or any other compartment of the world of spirits. In some moods I could even wish them a prosperous voyage to the Gehenna of our forefathers, now somewhat obsolescent, if only they would begone and cease to vex this rogue-ridden little world of ours.

# XXX

# TOM AND RACHEL

When Tom rode home from the trial with his mother and Barbara, his emotions were not just what one might expect; the events of the day and the tremendous strain on his nerves had benumbed him. He was only conscious that it gave him a great pleasure to leave the village behind, and to get once more upon the open prairie, which was glorified by the tints and shadows of the setting sun. The fields of maize, with their tassels growing brown and already too ripe and stiff to wave freely, and with their long blades becoming harsh and dry, so that the summer rustle had changed to a characteristic autumnal rattling, seemed to greet him like old friends who had visibly aged in his absence. Tom found his mind, from sheer strain and weariness, fixing itself on unimportant things; he noted that the corn-silk which protruded from the shucks was black, and that the shucks themselves were taking on that sear look which is the sure token of the ripeness of the ear within the envelope. Now and then he marked an ear that had grown so long as to push its nose of cob quite beyond the envelope. The stretches of prairie grass showed a mixture of green and brown; the September rains had freshened a part of the herbage, giving it a new verdure, but the riper stalks and blades had maintained their neutral colors. These things interested Tom in a general way, as marking the peaceful changes that had taken place in the familiar face of nature during his period of incarceration. What he felt in regarding these trifles was simply that he was alive and once more free to go where he pleased. He said little, and replied to the remarks of his mother and Barbara briefly, and he drove old Blaze-face at a speed quite unbecoming a horse at his time of life. The people whom he passed cheered him, or called out their well-meant congratulation, or their bitter remarks about Dave Sovine, but Tom on his part was not demonstrative; he even drove past Rachel Albaugh and her brother Ike with only a nod of recognition. To any remark of his mother and Barbara about Dave's villainy, and to any allusion to the case, he returned the briefest answers, giving the impression that he wished to get mentally as well as physically away from the subject. When he got home he asked for an old-fashioned country hoe-cake for supper, and he would have the table set out on the kitchen porch; he said it seemed so delightful to be permitted to go out-of-doors again. After supper he turned old Blaze into the pasture, with a notion that he too might prefer his liberty.

In reflecting on the events of the day, Barbara remembered with pleasure that Rachel had congratulated Tom. It made his vindication complete that the young woman who had refused his attentions when he was accused of nothing worse than foolish gambling had now taken pains to show her good-will in public. But when the question of a possible renewal of the relations between Tom and his old sweetheart came up in Barbara's mind, there was always a doubt. Not that there was anything objectionable about Rachel Albaugh. Barbara said to her mother over and over again, in the days that followed Tom's acquittal, that there was nothing against Rachel. If Rachel was not very industrious she was certainly "easy-tempered." In her favor it could be said that she had a beautiful face, and that she would be joint heiress with her brother to a large and well-improved prairie farm, to say nothing of her father's tract of timber-land.

After a while Barbara came to wish that Tom's old affection for Rachel might be kindled again. She did not like to see him so changed. He plodded incessantly at farm work, and he seemed to have lost his relish for society. If any one came to the house, he managed to have business abroad. He was not precisely gloomy, but the change in him was so marked that it made his sister unhappy.

"Why don't you go to see Rachel?" she asked, a week after the trial. Barbara was straining her eyes down the road, as she often did in those days. "Rachel would be glad to see you again, Tom, like as not."

"Maybe she would," answered Tom, as he picked up the pail and started to the spring for water by way of cutting off all further talk on the question.

The days went by without Tom's showing by any sign that he cared to see Rachel, and to Barbara's grief the days went by without Hiram Mason's promised arrival at the Graysons'. But there came presently a note from Hiram to Barbara, saying that he had been detained by the necessity he was under of finishing Magill's writing, and by the difficulty he found in getting his pay from the easy-going clerk for what he had done. But he hoped to stop on his way home in three or four days. This note was brought from Moscow by Bob McCord, who also brought Janet. The child had teased her father into letting her come out in Aunt Martha's wagon with Bob, whom she had seen driving past the house on his way in.

Janet spent her time in the country wholly with Tom. She followed him afield, she climbed with him into the barn lofts, she sat on the back of old Blaze when Tom led him to water, she went

183

into the forest when Tom went to fell trees for fire-wood, she helped him to pick apples, and she was as happy in all this as she would have been in the Elysian Fields.

"Cousin Tom," she said, the day after her arrival, as she leaned out of the high, open window of the hay-loft, "yonder's a lady getting down on the horse-block at the house."

Tom climbed up from the threshing-floor to the mow, and, standing well back out of sight in the gloom of the loft, he recognized Rachel Albaugh's horse. Then he went back again to his wheat-fanning on the threshing-floor.

"Aren't you going to go and help her?" said Janet, when Tom stopped the noisy fanning-mill to shovel back the wheat and to rake away the cheat.

"Pshaw!" said Tom. "A country girl doesn't need any help to get off a horse."

Rachel had come to call on Barbara, nor did she admit to herself that her visit had anything to do with Tom. But she found herself in an attitude to which she was unaccustomed. From the moment that Tom had been charged with murder her liking for him increased. The question of his guilt or innocence did not disturb her—except in so far as it jeoparded his life; he was at least a dashing fellow, out of the common run. And now that he had been acquitted, and was a hero of everybody, Rachel found in herself a passion that was greater than her vanity, and that overmastered even her prudence. She was tormented by her thoughts of Tom in the day, she dreamed of him at night. Tom would not come to her, and she felt herself at length drawn by a force she could not resist to go to him.

Barbara asked Rachel to stay to dinner, and promised that Tom would put away her horse as soon as he knew that she had come. This was but the common hospitality of the country, but Barbara hoped that Rachel's presence might evoke Tom's old buoyant self again. And so, while Barbara sat on the loom-bench weaving a web of striped linsey, Rachel sat near her, knitting. It appeared to Barbara that Rachel had undergone almost as great a change as Tom. She had lost her taciturnity. Her tongue kept pace with the click of her needles. She only broke the thread of her talk when she paused to take the end of one needle out of the quill of her knitting-case and put another in. Under color of sympathy for the Graysons in their troubles she talked of what was in her mind. How dreadful it must have been for Tom to be in jail! How anxious he must have been at the trial! How well he bore up under it all! How proud he must have been when he was acquitted! These and such remarks were web and woof of her talk, while Barbara was throwing

184

her nimble shuttle to and fro and driving the threads home with the double-beat of her loom-comb.

By half-past 11 the early farm dinner was almost ready, and Mrs. Grayson blew a blast on the tin horn which hung outside of the door, to let Tom and Janet know that they were to come in.

When Tom heard the horn he went and led Rachel's horse to the stable, after perching Janet in the saddle; and then he delayed long enough to shuck out and give him eight or ten ears of corn. After this he came to the house and washed his hands and face in the country way, with much splash and spatter, in a basin that sat on a bench outside of the door, and Janet washed hers, imitating to the best of her ability Tom's splattering way of dashing the water about. Then the two used the towel that hung on a roller in the kitchen porch, and Tom entered the kitchen with his clothes soiled by labor and with that look of healthful fatigue which comes of plentiful exercise in the open air.

"Howdy, Rachel? All well 't your house?" This was the almost invariable formula of country politeness, and it was accompanied by a faint smile of welcome and a grasp of her hand.

"Howdy, Tom?" said Rachel, cordially. "I hope you are well." Rachel regarded him a moment, and then let her eyes droop. Had Rachel discovered that her face was at its best when her long eyelashes were lowered in this fashion, or was the action merely instinctive?

"Oh, so-so!" answered Tom, uneasily, as he seated himself with the rest at the table. Rachel sat next to him, and he treated her with hospitable politeness, but she looked in vain for any sign of his old affection. She hardly once fairly encountered his eye during the meal. He seemed more indifferent to her attractions than she had ever known any man, old or young, to be. And yet she knew that her charms had lost nothing of their completeness. That very morning she had gone into the rarely opened Albaugh parlor and examined herself in the largest looking-glass in the house—the one that hung between the parlor windows, and that had a print of Mount Vernon in the upper panel of the space inclosed between the turned frames. Her fresh and yet delicate complexion was without a speck or flaw, her large eyes were as lustrous as ever, and there was the same exquisite symmetry and harmony of features that had made her a vision of loveliness to so many men. But Tom seemed more interested in his cousin, whom he kept laughing with a little childish byplay while talking to his sister's guest. Rachel felt herself baffled, and by degrees, though treated cordially, she began to feel humiliated. When dinner was finished by a course of pumpkin pie and quince preserves served with cream, Tom pushed back his chair and explained that he was just going to begin building some rail pens to hold the corn when it should be gathered and shucked, and that he could not allow himself the usual noon-time rest. The days were getting so short, you know. Would Rachel excuse him? Barbara would blow the horn so that he could put the saddle on Rachel's horse when she wanted it. But wouldn't she stay to supper?

Rachel declined to stay to supper, and she was visibly less animated after dinner than she had been before. The conversation flagged on both sides; Barbara became preoccupied with her winding-blades, her bobbins, and her shuttle, while Rachel was absorbed in turning the heel of her stocking. By half-past 1 o'clock the guest felt bound to go home; the days were getting shorter and there was much to be done at home, she remembered. The horn was blown, and Tom led her horse out to the block and helped her to mount. As he held her stirrup for her to place her foot, it brought to his memory, with a rush, her refusal to let him ride home with her from the Timber Creek school-house after the "singing." When he looked up he saw that Rachel's mind had followed the same line of association; both of them colored at this manifest encounter of their thoughts.

"I suppose I oughtn't to have said 'no' that day at the school-house." Rachel spoke with feeling, moved more by the desperate desire she felt to draw Tom out than by any calculation in making the remark.

"Yes, you ought," said Tom. "I never blamed you."

Then there was an awkward pause.

"Good-bye, Tom," said Rachel, extending her hand. "Won't you come over and see us sometime?"

"I'm generally too tired when night comes. Good-bye, Rachel"; and he took her hand in a friendly way. But this was one of those farewells that are aggravated by mental contrast, and Rachel felt, as she looked at Tom's serious and preoccupied face, that it was to her the end of a chapter.

Tom started up the pathway toward the house, but stopped half-way and plucked a ripe seed-pod from the top of a poppy-stalk, and rubbed it out between his two hands as he looked a little regretfully after Rachel until she disappeared over the hill. Then he turned and saw Barbara standing on the porch regarding him inquiringly.

"You aren't like yourself any more, Tom," she said.

"I know that," he answered, meditatively, at the same time filliping the minute poppy-seeds away, half a dozen at a time, with his thumb. "I don't seem to be the same fellow that I was three months ago. Then I'd 'a' followed Rachel like a dog every step of the way home."

"She's awfully in love with you, poor girl."

"Oh! she'll get over that, I suppose. She's been in love before."

"And you don't care for her any more?"

"I don't seem to care for anything that I used to care for. I wouldn't like to be what I used to be."

This sentence was rather obscure, and Barbara still looked at Tom inquiringly and waited for him to explain. But he only went on in the same inconsequential way, as he plucked and rubbed out another poppy-head. "I don't care for anything nowadays, but just to stay with you and mother. When a fellow's been through what I have, I suppose he isn't ever the same that he was; it takes the ambition out of you. Hanging makes an awful change in your feelings, you know"; and he smiled grimly.

"Don't say that; you make me shiver," said Barbara.

"But I say, Barb," and with this Tom sowed broadcast all the poppy-seed in his hand, "yonder comes somebody over the hill that'll get a warmer welcome than Rachel did, I'll guarantee."

How often in the last week had Barbara looked to see if somebody were not coming over the hill! Now she found her vision obstructed by a "laylock" bush, and she came down the path to where her brother stood. As soon as she had made out that the pedestrian was certainly Hiram Mason, she turned and went into the house, to change her apron for a fresher one, and with an instinctive wish to hide from Mason a part of the eagerness she had felt for his coming. But when he had reached the gate and was having his hand cordially shaken by Tom, Barbara came back to the door to greet him; and just because she couldn't help it, she went out on the porch, then down the steps and half-way to the gate to tell him how glad she was to see him.

# XXXI

## HIRAM AND BARBARA

The cordiality of his welcome was a surprise to Mason; he could hardly tell why. The days had dragged heavily since his separation from Barbara, and his mind had been filled with doubts.

The delay imposed upon him by Barbara's circumstances and then by his own was unwholesome; love long restrained from utterance is apt to make the soul sick. During his last week in Moscow he had copied court minutes and other documents into the folio records in an abstracted fashion, while the conscious part of his intellect was debating his chance of securing Barbara's consent. He fancied that she might hold herself more than ever aloof from him now; that her pride had been too deeply wounded to recover, and that she would never bring herself to accept him.

When he had at length finished all there was for him to do in the clerk's office at Moscow, and Magill had contrived to borrow enough money to pay him his fifty cents a day, Mason was too impatient to wait for some wagon bound for the Timber Creek neighborhood. He started on foot, intending to pass the night under the friendly roof of the Graysons, and to push on homeward in the morning; for he would already be a month late in beginning his college year. His mind was revolving the plan of his campaign against Barbara's pride all the way over the great lonely level prairie, the vista of which stretched away to the west until it was interrupted by a column of ominous black smoke, which told of the beginning of the autumnal prairie fires that annually sweep the great grassy plains and keep them free of trees. At length the tantalizing forest, so long in sight, was reached, and he entered the pale fringe of slender poplar-trees—that forlorn hope thrown out by the forest in its perpetual attempt to encroach on a prairie annually fire-swept. But when at last he entered the greater forest itself, now half denuded of its shade, the problem was still before him. He contrived with much travail of mind what seemed to him an ingenious device for overcoming Barbara's fear of his family. He would propose that his mother should write her a letter giving a hearty assent to his proposal of marriage. If that failed, he could not think of any other plan likely to be effective.

Like many conversations planned in absence, this one did not seem so good when he had the chance to test it. The way in which Tom welcomed him at the gate, shaking his hand and taking hold of his arm in an affectionate, informal way, gave him an unexpected pleasure, though nothing could be more natural under the circumstances than Tom's gratitude. And when Tom said, "Barbara'll be awful glad to see you, an' so'll Mother," Mason was again surprised. Not that he knew any good reason why Barbara and her mother should not be glad to see him, but he who broods long over his feelings will hatch forebodings. When Hiram looked up from Tom at the gate, he saw Barbara's half-petite figure and piquant face, full as ever of force and aspiration, waiting half-way down the walk. Barbara paused there, half-way to the gate, but she could not wait even there; she came on down farther and met him, and looked in his eyes frankly and told him—with some reserve in her tone, it is true, but with real cordiality—that she was glad to see him. And by the time he reached the porch, Mother Grayson herself—kindly, old-fashioned soul that she was—stood in the door and greeted Mason with tears in her eyes.

After a little rest and friendly talk in the cool, well-kept, home-like sitting-room, Hiram went out with Tom to look about the familiar place. The fruit trees were pretty well stripped of their foliage by a recent wind and the ground was carpeted with brown and red and yellow leaves, while the rich autumn sunlight, which but half warmed the atmosphere, gave one an impression of transientness and of swift-impending change. It was one of those days on which the seasons are for the instant arrested—a little moment of repose and respite before the inevitable catastrophe. The busiest man can hardly resist the influence of such a day; farmers are prone to bask in the slant sunlight at such times and to talk to one another over line-fences or seated on top-rails. The crows fly hither and thither in the still air, and the swallows, gathered in noisy concourse, seem reluctant to set out upon their southward journey. But Mason soon left Tom and entered the kitchen, where he sat himself down upon a bench over against the loom and watched the swift going to and fro of Barbara's nimble shuttle, and listened to the muffled pounding of the loom-comb, presently finding a way to make himself useful by winding bobbins.

The two were left alone at intervals during the afternoon, but Mason could not summon courage to reopen the question so long closed between them. His awkward reserve reacted on Barbara, and conversation between them became difficult, neither being able to account for the mood of the other.

After a while Janet, tired with following Tom the livelong day, came into the kitchen and besought Barbara to sing "that song about Dick, you know"; and though Mason did not know who Dick might be, he thought he would rather hear Barbara sing than to go on trying to keep up a flagging conversation; so he seconded Janet's request. When Barbara had tied a broken string in the "harness" of the loom, she resumed her seat on the bench and sang while she wove.

### BARBARA'S WEAVING SONG

Fly, shuttle, right merrily, merrily,
Carry the swift-running thread;

Keep time to the fancy that eagerly
Weaveth a web in my head.

For Dick he will come again, come again,
Dick he will come again home from afar
With musket and powder-horn,
Musket and powder-horn, home from the war.

Beat up the threads lustily, lustily,
Weave me a web good and strong;
Heart brimful and flowing with joyousness
Ever is bursting with song.

For Dick he will come again, etc.

Warp, hold the woof lovingly, lovingly,
Taking and holding it fast;
Hearts bound together in unity
Love with a love that will last.

For Dick he will come again, come again, Dick he will come
again home from afar With musket and powder-horn, Musket and
powder-horn, home from the war.

By the time the ditty was ended, Mrs. Grayson was setting the
supper-table by the fire-place, doing her best to honor her guest.
She took down the long-handled waffle-irons and made a plate of
those delicious cakes unknown since kitchen fire-places went out,
and the like of which will perhaps never be known again henceforth.
She got out some of the apple-butter, of which half a barrel had
been made so toilsomely but the week before, and this she flanked
with a dish of her peach preserves, kept sacredly for days of state.
The "chaney" cups and saucers were also set out in honor of Hiram,
and the almost transparent preserved peaches were eaten with
country cream, from saucers thin enough to show an opalescent
translucency, and decorated with a gilt band and delicate little
flowers. This china, which had survived the long wagon-journey
from Maryland, was not often trusted upon the table.

"My! What a nice supper we've got, Aunt Marthy!" said Janet,
clapping her hands, as they took their seats at the table.

"It seems to me you're making company out of me," said
Mason, in a tone of protest.

"We sha'n't have you again soon, Mason," said Tom, "and we
don't often see the like of you."

The words were spontaneous, but Tom ducked his head with a

half-ashamed air when he had spoken them. Barbara liked Tom's little speech: it expressed feelings that she could not venture to utter; and it had, besides, a touch of Tom's old gayety of feeling in it.

When supper was well out of the way Hiram proposed a walk with Barbara, but it did no good. They talked mechanically about what they were not thinking about, and by the time they got back to the house Mason was becoming desperate. He must leave in the morning very early, and he had made no progress; he could not bring himself to approach the subject about which Barbara seemed so loath to speak, and concerning which he dreaded a rebuff as he dreaded death.

They entered the old kitchen and found no one there; the embers were flickering in the spacious fire-place and peopling the room with grotesque shadows and dancing lights.

"Let us sit here awhile, Barbara," he said, with a strange note of entreaty in his tone, as he swung the heavy door shut and put down the wooden latch—relic of the pioneer period.

"Just as you please, Mr. Mason," answered Barbara,

"Oh! say Hiram, won't you?" He said this with a touch of impatience.

"Hiram!" said Barbara, laughing.

He led her to the loom-bench.

"Sit there on high, as you did the night you put me into a state of misery from which I haven't escaped yet. There, put your feet on the chair-rung, as you did that night."

He spoke with peremptoriness, as he placed a chair for her feet, so that she might sit with her back to the loom. Then he drew up another shuck-bottomed chair in such a way as to sit beside and yet half facing her, but lower.

"Now," he said, doggedly, "we can finish the talk we had then."

"That seems ages ago," said Barbara, dreamily; "so much has happened since."

"So long ago that you don't care to renew the subject?"

"I—" But Barbara stopped short. The feeble blaze in the fire-place suddenly went out.

Hiram did not know where to begin. He got up and took some dry chips from a basket and threw them on the slumbering coals, so as to set the flame a-going again. Then he sat down in his chair and looked up at the now silent Barbara, and tried in vain to guess her mood. But she remained silent and waited for him to take the lead.

"Do you remember what you said then?" he asked.

"No! how can I? It seems so long ago."

"You said a pack of nonsense." As he blurted out this charge Mason turned his head round obliquely, still regarding Barbara.

"Did I? That's just like me," Barbara answered, with a little laugh.

"No, it isn't like you," he replied, almost rudely. "You're the most sensible woman I ever knew, except on one subject."

"What's that?" Barbara was startled by the vehemence and abruptness of his speech, and she asked this in a half-frightened voice.

"Your pride. I looked up to you then, as I do now. You're something above me—I just worship you." To a man of maturity this sort of talk seems extravagant enough. But one must let youth paint itself as it will, with all its follies on its head. You've said sillier things than that in your time, sober reader—you know you have!

"I do just worship you, Barbara Grayson," Hiram went on; "but you talked a parcel of fool stuff that night about the superiority of my family, and about your not being able to bear it that my people should look down on you, and—well, a pack of tomfoolery; that's what it was, Barbara, and there's no use of calling it anything else."

Barbara was silent.

"Now, I'm not going to give you a chance to make any more such speeches. But I want to ask you whether, if I should send you a letter from my mother when I get home, and maybe from my sisters too, after I have told them the whole truth, urging you to accept me and become one of our family—I want to know whether, then, you would be willing; whether you'd take pity on a poor fellow who can't get along without you. Would that suit you?"

"No, it wouldn't," said Barbara, looking at the now blazing chips in the fire-place with her head bent forward.

"Well, what on earth would, then?" And Mason tilted back his chair in the nervousness of desperation and brought his eyes to a focus on her face, which was strangely illuminated in the flickering foot-lights from the hearth.

"Did I talk that way last summer?"

"Yes, you did."

"It must have hurt you. I can see it hurt you, from the way you speak about it."

"Yes," said Mason; "I've been in a sort of purgatory ever since."

"And I didn't mean to hurt your feelings. I'd rather do anything than to hurt your feelings." Here she paused, unable to proceed at once, but he waited for her to show the way. Presently she went on:

"Now, Mr. Mason,—Hiram, I mean,—I'm going to punish myself for my foolish pride. I must have felt very differently then to what I do now. The more I have seen of you the more I have—admired you." Barbara stopped and took up the hem of her apron and picked at the stitches as though she would ravel them. Then she proceeded, dropping her head lower, "Somehow I hate to say it,—but I'm going to punish myself,—the more I have seen of you the more I have—liked you. It don't matter much to me now whether your mother likes me or not, and I really don't seem to care what your sisters think about your loving a poor girl from the country."

"Hush! Don't talk that way about yourself," said Hiram. But Barbara was so intent on finishing what she had resolved to say that she did not give any heed to him, but only went on pulling and picking at the hem of her apron.

"I only want to know one thing, Mr. Mason, and that is whether you—whether you really and truly want me?" Her face blushed deeply, she caught her breath, her head bowed lower than before, as though trying in vain to escape from Hiram's steadfast gaze.

"God only knows how I do love you, Barbara," said Hiram, speaking softly now and letting his eyes rest on the floor.

"Well," said Barbara, "as good a man as you deserves to have what he wants, you know"; and here she smiled faintly. "I'll put in the dust all the wicked pride that hurts you so." And Barbara made a little gesture. Then after a moment she began again, stammeringly, "If—if you really want me, Hiram Mason,—why—then—I'll face anything rather than miss of being yours. Now will that do? And will you forgive me for keeping you in purgatory, as you call it, all this time?" There were tears in her eyes as she spoke; partly of penitence, perhaps, but more than half of happiness.

When she had finished, Mason got up and pushed his chair away and came and sat down on the loom-bench beside her, Barbara making room for him, as for the first time she lifted her eyes timidly to his.

"I've been a goose, Barbara, not to understand you before. What a woman you are!"

# XXXII

# THE NEXT MORNING

When Tom waked up the next morning in the gray daybreak, he found that Mason, who should have shared his room, had not come to bed at all. And when Tom came down to uncover the live coals and build up the kitchen fire, he found that the embers had not been covered under the ashes as usual; there were instead smoking sticks of wood that had newly burned in two, the ends having canted over backward outside of the andirons. The table stood in the floor set with plates and cups and saucers for two, and there were the remains of an early breakfast. There was still heat in the coffee-pot when Tom touched it, and from these signs he read the story of Barbara's betrothal to Mason; he conjectured that this interview, which was to precede a separation of many months, had been unintentionally protracted until it was near the time for Mason's departure. The débris of the farewell love-feast, eaten in the silent hour before daybreak, seemed to have associations of sentiment. Tom regarded these things and was touched and pleased, but he was also amused. This sitting the night out seemed an odd freak for a couple so tremendously serious and proper as the little sister and the schoolmaster.

An hour later, when Tom, having finished his chores, came in for his breakfast, Barbara had reappeared below stairs with an expression of countenance so demure—so entirely innocent and unconscious—that Tom could not long keep his gravity; before he had fairly begun to eat he broke into a merry, boyish laugh.

"What are you laughing about?" demanded Barbara, looking a little foolish and manifesting a rising irritation, that showed how well she knew the cause of his amusement.

"Oh! nothing; but why don't you eat your breakfast, Barb? You seem to have lost your appetite."

"Don't tease Barb'ry now," said Mrs. Grayson.

"I'm not teasing," said Tom; "but I declare, Barb, it must have seemed just like going to housekeeping when you two sat down to eat breakfast by yourselves this morning."

"O Tom!" broke in Janet, who couldn't quite catch the drift of the conversation, "Barbara went to bed with her clothes on last night. When I waked up this morning she was lying on the bed by me with her dress on."

Tom now laughed in his old unrestrained fashion.

194

"Say, Barbara," Janet went on, "are you going to marry that Mr. Mason that was here yesterday?"

Knowing that she could not get rid of Janet's inquiries except by answering, Barbara said: "Oh, I suppose so," as she got up to set the pot of coffee back on the trivet and hide a vexation that she knew to be foolish.

"Don't you know whether you're going to marry him or not?" put in Janet. "I sh'd think you'd know. And I sh'd think he'd be a real nice husband." Then after a few moments of silence, Janet turned on Tom. "Tom, who's your sweetheart?"

"Haven't got any," said Tom.

"Isn't that purty girl that was here yesterday your sweetheart?"

"No!"

"Aren't you ever going to get married?"

"Maybe, some day. Not right off, though."

"I wish you would find a good wife, Tom," said Barbara without looking from her plate. "It would cheer you up." Barbara felt a little guilty at the thought of leaving the brother who had always seemed her chief responsibility.

"Say, Tom, won't you wait for me?" said Janet, solemnly.

"Yes, that's just what I'll do," said Tom, looking at her. "I hadn't thought of it before; but that's just exactly what I'll do, Janet. I'll wait for you, now you mention it."

"Will you, indeed, and double deed?"

"Yes, indeed, and deed and double deed, I'll wait for you, Janet."

"That'll be nice," said Janet, continuing her breakfast with meditative seriousness. "Now I'm your sweetheart, ain't I?"

# XXXIII

# POSTSCRIPTUM

It was in the last days of October, a few weeks after the proper close of the story which I have just related, when Henry Miller—the most matter-of-fact and unsensational of young men—threw his family into a state of excitement and supplied the gossip of the neighborhood with a fresh topic by announcing at home and abroad that he was going to leave the country, either for the Iowa country to the west of the Mississippi or for the fertile bottom-lands up north on the "Wisconse" River, as it was called. He was the only son of his father, and had inherited the steady, plodding industry and frugality so characteristic of a "Pennsylvania Dutch" race. Until he was of age he was bound, not only by law, but by the custom of the country, to serve his father much as a bondsman or an apprentice might have served, for an able-bodied son was distinctly recognized as an available and productive possession in that day. When he became of age his close-fisted father made no new arrangement with him, offered him no start, paid him no wages, and gave him no share in the produce of the fields. It was enough, in the father's estimation, that Henry would succeed to a large part of the property at his death. But Henry, on mature reflection, had made up his mind that emigration would be better than a reversionary interest that must be postponed to the death of so robust a man as his father, who was yet in middle-life and who came of a stock remarkable for longevity. Was not his grandfather yet alive in Pennsylvania, while his great-grandfather had not been dead many years? It was after calculating the "expectation of life" in the Miller family that Henry notified his father of his intention to go where land was cheap and open a large farm for himself. In vain the father urged that he could not get on without him, and that there would be no one to look after things if the father should die. Henry persisted that he must do something for himself and that his father would have to hire a man, for he should surely leave as soon as the crops were gathered, so as to get land enough open in some frontier country to afford him a small crop of corn the first year.

Henry's mother and sisters were even more opposed to his going than his father was, and they did not hesitate to blame the senior Miller with great severity for not having "done something" for Henry. Henry's father had never before known how unpleasant a man's home may come to be. He was reminded that Henry had not an acre, nor even a colt, that he could call his own, and that other farmers had done better than that. This state of siege became presently quite intolerable, and the elder Miller resolved not only "to do something" for Henry, but to do it in such a way that his son would begin life very well provided for. He wanted to silence the clamor of the house and the neighborhood once for all, and prove to his critics how much they were mistaken.

It was about a week after Henry's first resolution was taken that he and his father were finishing the corn-gathering. They were throwing the unshucked ears into a great wagon of the Pennsylvania pattern—a wagon painted blue, the "bed" of which rose in a great sweep at each end as though some reminiscence of the antique forms of marine architecture had affected its construction. When all the corn within easy throwing distance had been gathered, Henry, who was on the near side, would slip the reins from the standard over the fore wheel and drive forward the horses, which even in moving bit off the ends of corn ears or nibbled at the greenest-looking blades within their reach.

"Let's put on the sideboards," said the elder, "and we can finish the field this load." Though Miller's ancestors had come to this country with the Palatine immigration, away back in 1710, there was a little bit of German in his accent; he said something like "gorn" for corn. The sideboards were put up, and these were so adjusted that when they were on the wagon the inclosing sides were rendered level at the top and capable of holding nearly double the load contained without the boards.

"Henry," said the father, when the two were picking near together and throwing corn over the tail-gate of the wagon, "if you give up goin' away an' git married right off, an' settle toun here, I'm a-mine to teed you that east eighty an' a forty of timber. Eh?"

"That's purty good," said Henry; "but if your deed waits till I find a wife, it may be a good while coming."

"That eighty lays 'longside of Albaugh's medder an' lower gorn-field," said the father, significantly.

"You mean if I was to marry Rache, Albaugh might give us another slice."

"Of gourse he would; an' I'd help you put up a house, an' maybe I'd let you hav' the roan golt. You'd hav' the red heifer anyhow."

"But I never took a shine to Rache; and if I did, I couldn't noways come in. They's too many knocking at that door."

"But Rachel ain't no vool," said the elder. "She knows a good piece of lant w'en she sees it, an' maybe she's got enough of voolin' rount."

All that afternoon Henry revolved this proposition in his mind, and he even did what he had never done before in his life—he lay awake at night. The next day, after the midday dinner, he said to himself: "I might as well resk it. Albaugh's got an all-fired good place, and all out of debt. And that's a tre-mendous nice eighty father's offered to give me."

So he went up stairs and put on a new suit of blue jeans fresh from his mother's loom. Then he walked over to Albaugh's, to find Rachel sewing on the front porch.

Rachel had been "kindah dauncey like," as her mother

expressed it, ever since her visit to Barbara. She had received as many attentions as usual, but they seemed flat and unrelishable to her now. She began seriously to reflect that a girl past twenty-three was growing old in the estimation of the country, and yet she was further than ever from being able to make a choice between the lovers that paid her court, more or less seriously.

When she looked up and saw Henry Miller coming in at the gate she felt a strange surprise. She had never before seen him in Sunday clothes or visiting on a week-day.

"Hello, Henry! Looking for Ike?" she asked, with neighborly friendliness.

"No, not as I know of. I've come to talk to you, Rache."

"To me? Well, you're the last one I'd look for to come to talk to me; and in day-time, and corn-shucking not begun yet." There was an air of excited curiosity in her manner. It was plain to be seen that she was inwardly asking, "What can Henry Miller be up to, anyhow?" but to him she said, "Come in, Henry, an' take a cheer."

"No, I'll sed down here," he answered, taking a seat on the edge of the porch, like the outdoor man that he was, approaching a house with half reluctance.

The relations between Henry and Rachel were unconstrained. They had played "hide and whoop" together in childhood, and times innumerable they had gone on black-berrying and other excursions together; he had swung her on long grape-vine swings on the hill-side; they had trudged to and from school in each other's company, exchanging sweet-cakes from their lunch-baskets, and yet they had never been lovers.

"Rache," he said, locking his broad, brown hands over his knee, "father says he'll give me that east-eighty whenever I get married, if I won't go off West."

"You'll be a good while getting married, Henry. You never was a hand to go after the girls."

"No, but I might chance to get married shortly, for all that. The boys that do a good deal of sparking and the girls that have a lot of beaux don't always get married first. You'd ought to know that, Rache, by your own experience."

Rachel laughed good-naturedly, and waited with curiosity to discover what all this was leading up to.

"What I 'm thinking," said Henry, with the air of a man approaching a horse-trade cautiously, lest he should make a false step, "is this: that eighty of our'n jines onto your medder and west corn-field."

"Do you want to sell it?" said Rachel. "You might see father; he'd like to have it, I expect."

"Can't you guess what it is that I'm coming at?"

"No, I can't," said Rachel; "not to save my life."

"Looky here, Rache," and Henry gave his shoulders a twitch, "the two farms jine; now, what if you and me was to jine?"

"Well, Henry Miller, if you don't beat the Dutch! I never heard the like of that in all my born days!" Rachel had heard many propositions of marriage, but this sort of love-making, with eighty acres of prairie land for a buffer, was a novelty to her.

"Looky here, Rache," he said, in a tone of protest, "I've knew you ever since you was knee-high to a grasshopper. Now, what's the use of fooling and nonsense betwixt you and me? You know what I am—a good, stiddy-going, hard-working farmer, shore to get my sheer of what's to be had in the world without scrouging anybody else. And I know just exactly what you air. We've always got along mighty well together, and if I haven't ever made a fool of myself about your face, w'y, so much the better for me. Now, whaddy yeh say? Let's make it a bargain."

"W'y, Henry Miller, what a way of talking!"

"Rache, come, go along with me and see where'bouts I'm going to put up a house. Father's promised to help me. It's down by the spring, just beyand your medder fence. Will you go along down?"

"Well, I don't care if I do go down with you, Henry. But it's awful funny to come to such a subject in that way."

Rachel put on her sun-bonnet, and they went through the orchard together.

"We could put up a nice house there. Father's willing to throw in a forty of timber too—the forty that jines onto this eighty over yander. We'd be well fixed up to begin, no matter what your father done or didn't do for us. Whaddy you think of the plan?"

"You—you haven't said you loved me, or anything," said Rachel, piqued at having her charms quite left out of the account. But she could not hide from herself that Henry's proposition had substantial advantages. She only added, "What a curious man you are!"

"Don't you believe I'd make a good husband?"

"Yes, of course you would."

"And a good provider?"

"Yes, I'm shore of that."

"Well, now, I'm not going to pretend I'm soft on you. If you say 'No,' well and good; there's an end. I sha'n't worry myself into consumption. You've got a right to do as you please. I'm not going to have folks say that I'm another of the fools that's broke their hearts over Rache Albaugh. Once you're mine, I'll set my heart on you fast enough. But I never set my heart on anything I mightn't be able to get."

Rachel did not say anything to this bit of philosophy. She had in the last two weeks recognized the advisability of her getting married as soon as she could settle herself. But on taking an inventory of her present stock of beaux, she had mentally rejected them all. They were prospectively an unprosperous lot, and Rachel was too mature to marry adversity for the sake of sentiment. She found herself able to listen to Henry Miller's cool-blooded proposition with rather more tolerance than she felt when hearing the kind of love-talk she had been used to. Why not get her father to do as well by her as the Millers would by Henry, or to do better, seeing he was the richer and had but two children? Then they might begin life with plenty of acres and a good stock of butter cows.

Henry showed her where they could put their house, where the barn would be placed, and where they would have a garden. Rachel felt a certain pleasure in fancying herself the mistress of such a place. But it was contrary to all the precedents laid down in the few romances she had read for a woman to marry a man who was not her "slave"; that was the word the old romancers took delight in. She tried to coquet with Henry, in order to draw from him some sort of professions of love. A flirtation with a lay figure would have been quite as successful. He was plain prose, and she presently saw that if she accepted him it must be done in prose. She couldn't help liking his very prose; she was a little tired of slaves; it seemed, on the whole, better to have a man at least capable of being master of himself.

In much the same tone—the tone of a man buying, or selling, or proposing a co-partnership for business purposes—Henry Miller carried on the conversation all the way back until they reached the corn-crib, where he came to a stand-still.

"Whaddy yeh say, Rachel? Is it a bargain?"

"Well, Henry, it's sudden like. I want to take time to think it over."

"Then I'll take back the offer and put out for the Ioway country. I'm not a-going to have my skelp a-hanging to your belt for days and days, like the rest of them. What's the use of thinking? You don't want to take Magill, do you?"

"He's too old, and his nose is rather red," laughed Rachel.

"Nor Tom Grayson, I suppose?" Henry mentioned Tom as the second because he was the one about whom he had misgivings.

"I give him the sack before the shooting, and I'm not going to go back to him now."

Rachel faltered a little in this reply, but she spoke with that

200

resolute insincerity for which women hold an indulgence in advance when their hearts are being searched.

"Well," said Henry, "if you think you can do better by waiting, I m off. If you think I'm about as good a man as you're likely to pick up, here's your chance. It's going, going, gone with me. Either I marry you and take father's offer, or I put out for the Ioway country. I don't ask you to think I'm perfection, but just to take a sober, common-sense look at things."

Rachel saw that it was of no use to expect Henry to court her, and she could not help liking him the better for his honest straightforwardness. She looked down a minute, in the hope that he would say something that might make it easier for her to answer, but he kept his silence.

"Henry," she said at length, rolling a corn-cob over and over under the toe of her shoe, "I've got a good mind to say 'Yes.' You don't make me sick, like the rest of them. Father'll be struck when he hears of it. He's always said I'd marry some good-for-nothing town-fellow."

"Is it a bargain, good and fast?" said Henry, holding out his hand, as he would have done to clinch the buying of a piece of timber land or a sorrel horse.

"Yes," said Rachel, laughing at the oddness of it and the suddenness of it, "I'm tired of fooling. It's a bargain, Henry."

"Good fer you, Rache! Now I begin to like you better than ever."

www.ingramcontent.com/pod-product-compliance
Lightning Source LLC
Chambersburg PA
CBHW011523240626
47154CB00009B/2935